Rogue
in the
Regency
Ballroom

Helen Dickson

...ted and bound in
...TPM Group (UK) Ltd, Croydon, CR0 4YY

Mills & Boon, an imprint of Harlequin (UK) Limited,
Eton House, 18-24 Paradise Road, Richmond, Surrey TW9 1SR

ROGUE IN THE REGENCY BALLROOM
© Harlequin Enterprises II B.V./S.à.r.l 2013

Rogue's Widow, Gentleman's Wife © Helen Dickson 2007
A Scoundrel of Consequence © Helen Dickson 2007

ISBN: 978 0 263 90620 2

052-0813

Harlequin (UK) policy is to use papers that are natural, renewable and recyclable products and made from wood grown in sustainable forests. The logging and manufacturing processes conform to the legal environmental regulations of the country of origin.

Printed and bound
by CPI Group (UK) Ltd, Croydon, CR0 4YY

Helen Dickson was born and still lives in south Yorkshire, with her husband on a busy arable farm, where she combines writing with keeping a chaotic farmhouse. An incurable romantic, she writes for pleasure, owing much of her inspiration to the beauty of the surrounding countryside. She enjoys reading and music. History has always captivated her and she likes travel and visiting ancient buildings.

In The Regency Ballroom Collection

Scandal in the Regency Ballroom
April 2013

Innocent in the Regency Ballroom
May 2013

Wicked in the Regency Ballroom
June 2013

Cinderella in the Regency Ballroom
July 2013

Rogue in the Regency Ballroom
August 2013

Debutante in the Regency Ballroom
September 2013

Rumours in the Regency Ballroom
October 2013

Scoundrel in the Regency Ballroom
November 2013

Mistress in the Regency Ballroom
December 2013

Courtship in the Regency Ballroom
January 2014

Rake in the Regency Ballroom
February 2014

Secrets in the Regency Ballroom
March 2014

Rogue's Widow, Gentleman's Wife

Chapter One

Charleston, South Carolina—1880

A long column of sullen-looking convicts—black and white—moved slowly and painfully down the sun-baked street. Ragged and barefooted, they were fettered together like beasts of burden, their heavy iron ankle chains rubbing pitilessly against their skin, tearing and making it bleed. The men guarding them walked alongside, thick canes in their hands, urging them along with curses and threats. Others rode in front and behind, the harnesses jingling on their horses.

The traffic was heavy, the pavements swarming with people of all colours, passing through every shade of brown to black. Their clothes were gaily coloured, and the soft blur of the southern speech fell pleasantly on a stranger's ears.

Having become stuck in a mass of horses and traps and fine carriages of the well-to-do to let the convicts shuffle past, Amanda sat beside Nan, her maid. With the sun beating down on them the heat was intense, the humidity making it feel even hotter. Amos, Aunt Lucy's faithful old retainer, was sitting with an air of dignified authority, loosely holding the reins.

He was content to wait it out, but the horses shifted restlessly, eager to be on the move.

Beneath her pretty parasol, which shielded her from the harsh glare, Amanda, too, was restless and impatient to continue, her frustration and temper simmering in the increasing heat. She spared no thought to the wretched prisoners. Her whole focus was on her low spirits. What she did care about was the fact that she was to leave Charleston five days hence for her home in England.

Feeling uncomfortable in the heat, Nan swatted an irritating fly from her cheek. Tipping her bonnet back, she wiped her damp forehead. 'This heat is getting me down. God willing we won't have to endure it much longer and we'll soon be back in England. Never again will you hear me complain about the cold and rain.'

'Trust you to say that, Nan,' Amanda exclaimed impatiently. Coming to America had been a whole new experience for her, and, without her father's domineering presence, she had been enjoying herself far too much to think of leaving just yet. But circumstances had turned against her. 'Oh, why did Aunt Lucy have to die—just when life held such promise. It has all turned out so different from what I had planned. I have failed dismally, Nan.'

Despite her own discomfort, Nan smiled across at her young mistress, thinking how pretty she looked, how cool and elegant in her sky-blue-gingham sprigged gown and a wide-brimmed straw bonnet that hid much of her wealth of burgundy-coloured hair. And yet despite Amanda's sweet and charming look, she was, in reality, stubborn, touchy, intransigent and independent, rebellious of all discipline, truculent when denied her own way, and with passions that were easily stirred, like her father, with nothing of her cousin Charlotte's mild-tempered, forbearing nature. In Nan's opinion, who was ten years her mistress's senior, she called for firm handling. She had been indulged by an adoring father and allowed to go her own way for too long.

'It isn't your fault. You weren't to know your aunt would die and your father order you back home.'

A touch of anger came to add to the bitterness of Amanda's disappointment. She knew, as she had always known, that her father, having made a fortune out of his various business enterprises, had wanted to move in higher circles of society, and that she was the key to help him attain this.

'Since I have failed to find a suitable husband, he will marry me off without delay the minute I get off the ship. He's eager for me to marry and give him an heir, and he's got someone in mind, I know it—some titled old man whose name and position will be Father's entry into the world of blue-blooded aristocrats.'

'Come now. Stop tormenting yourself. If that is so, then I am sure the man he has chosen for you will not give you any cause for reproach. Your father loves you and will take your wishes into account.'

'Father's not like that. Oh, if only I could find someone I wanted to marry, Nan. Aunt Lucy was sympathetic to my plight. I've lost count of the eligible men she's paraded before me—but there wasn't one I wanted to spend the rest of my life with. I'm beginning to think there's something wrong with me.'

Nan sighed. Having had this conversation with Amanda many times over the past weeks, she was beginning to tire of it. 'Then maybe you should marry a man who is senile, who won't last the year. Your father would have to respect a year of mourning and by then you would be twenty-one and independent of him.'

Amanda looked at her sharply, calculating. Now why hadn't she thought of that? Mulling over what Nan had said with sudden interest, she paid no attention to the carriage edging alongside until its occupant spoke.

'Why, my dear Miss O'Connell. I am so happy to see you. I was terribly sorry to hear about dear Lucy—quite a surprise, I must say. I'm only sorry that I couldn't attend the funeral, but my husband and I have been out of town for a while, visiting our daughter in Wilmington. And what of you, dear?'

Amanda turned to look at Mrs Hewitt, an elderly, statuesque, full-bosomed lady. An acquaintance of her Aunt Lucy's, despite being something of a busybody, she was a likeable, well-meaning woman.

'I am well, thank you, Mrs Hewitt. Aunt Lucy's death was all rather sudden. She took a turn for the worst following a chill and sadly never recovered.'

'Well, what a good thing she had you to take care of her. At last she'll be with her beloved Edward. I imagine there is much to do at the house?'

'Cousin Charlotte and her husband stayed on at Magnolia Grove after the funeral to take charge of everything.'

'And you? Are you to remain in Charleston?'

'I'm afraid not. I'm going back to England in a few days' time—although I shall be sorry to leave.' She shifted her eyes to look at the convicts, closer to them now. She was appalled at the pallid, unshaven faces. The heat and moistness of their unwashed bodies released a sickly stench.

Mrs Hewitt followed her gaze, raising her perfumed handkerchief to her nose to blot out the vile odours. 'Look at them—gallows meat, the lot of them. Probably been working at the docks—been some kind of accident as a ship was being unloaded, apparently—some of the cargo tipped into the sea and every available man was needed to retrieve it. I see one of the prisoners is that vile man Claybourne—the one in the middle—the one responsible for that ghastly crime.'

Wishing the prisoners would walk faster so that they could move on, Amanda looked at the man Mrs Hewitt pointed out with scant interest, and then with a growing curiosity. She hardly noticed anyone else—her attention was entirely focused on him. With his mouth set in a thin, hard line, he walked with his head held high, with a kind of arrogance, which, in the midst of so much wretchedness that clung to his fellow prisoners, had its own kind of greatness. She could see that his clothes were of fine quality, but badly stained. The rags of his once-white shirt gave little protection to his broad shoulders and bronzed skin, which showed through in many places, but he did not seem conscious of the hot sun. His overwhelming masculinity stirred some deeply rooted feminine instinct that she acknowledged.

'What did he do?'

Mrs Hewitt turned to look at her, plying her fan with verve. 'Why, don't you remember? He's the man who killed poor Carmen Rider.'

Amanda recalled the scandal that had torn through Charleston. The town had reeled with horrified fascination of the murder. Carmen was a thirty-year-old wealthy widow, a Spanish woman, who had been brutally murdered in her home two months or so ago. It was her maid who had found her. The room had been ransacked and she had died from vicious wounds, having clearly put up a fierce struggle against her attacker.

'I was in Savannah with Aunt Lucy, visiting her sister-in-law at the time, so I do not know the details of the case.' Besides, she thought, she had been enjoying the delightful company of some of the charming bucks belonging to Savannah's elite too much to dwell on a depressing murder case taking place in Charleston. 'What do you know about Mr Claybourne, Mrs Hewitt?'

'Not much, only that he lived out of town—in a wooden

cabin in the cypress swamp—by the river. Bit of a loner, if you ask me. At one time he spent some time in the Smoky Mountains—with the Indians, some say, where he improved his skill with horses. Carmen hired him to break in some of her mounts. Since her husband died she had had a host of admirers but she quite shamelessly threw herself at Mr Claybourne—proclaiming her love for the man to anyone who would care to listen. From what I've heard he was not as enamoured of her as she was of him, but he stayed anyway. Whether or not they had a full-blown affair is open to speculation.'

'He might have fared better had he stayed in the swamp with the alligators,' Amanda murmured. 'I seem to recall there are Claybournes in England—aristocrats, I believe.'

'As to that I wouldn't know, but I shouldn't think there is any connection. I cannot see a peer of the realm coming to America to work with horses.'

'No, I suppose not. Why do you think he killed her?'

'It was known that they quarrelled and he left her the day before she was killed. When she was found, it was believed that he was the murderer—her brother was certain of it, though he's a rogue if ever there was. There are those who know Mr Claybourne that say his behaviour was most out of character, that he is a man of considerable intelligence, and that a man of that stamp does not commit such acts of madness without good reason. But everything seemed to point to him. He was the prime suspect and arrested and taken to gaol.'

'Was there no one else who could have killed her?'

'Opinion was unanimous that he was the only one with a motive strong enough, and in a final quarrel he murdered her. Owing to the seriousness of the case and the social prominence of Carmen—her husband was a well-known and respected attorney in Charleston, you know—the jury found him guilty and he was sentenced to hang.'

'And what did Mr Claybourne have to say for himself?'

'All the time he stuck to his statement that he was nowhere near her home at the time—and there were many who believed him innocent but none who could substantiate his alibi. The servants gave accounts of constant discord between their mistress and Mr Claybourne and testified that a man of his description let himself into the house and went to Carmen's room on the night she was killed.'

As Mr Claybourne passed in front of the carriage, Amanda was aware of the tension and nervousness in herself. He was close enough now for her to see his face more clearly. Beneath his facial growth she could see he was attractive. His jaw was roughly carved, his forehead was high, his eyebrows heavy, his cheeks lean and his hair, though dull and lank, was thick and dark brown.

As if he felt her scrutiny, he turned and met her eyes. She knew instinctively that he was just as aware of her as she was of him. Her heart skipped a beat as she met those eyes steadily, and she saw amber flames ignite within their depths.

His eyes assessed her frankly, taking in her cool, quiet beauty. She was vividly conscious of him, and she felt the unfamiliar rush of blood humming through her veins, which she had never experienced before. Instantly she felt resentful towards him. He had made too much of an impact on her, and she was afraid that if he looked at her much longer he would read her thoughts with those clever eyes of his.

And then he was gone, oblivious to the cane which at that instant the guard thudded on to his back. Amanda watched the convicts become swallowed up by the crowd, her eyes fixed on the tall man until the last.

'When will the sentence be carried out?' she asked Mrs Hewitt.

'In about a week.'

When the congestion began to clear, and after bidding Mrs Hewitt farewell, all the way to Magnolia Grove Amanda turned her thoughts once more to her predicament, trying to find a way to circumvent her father. There must be some way to escape marrying a man of his choosing, there must be something she could do. And then the words of Nan came back to her—that perhaps she should marry a senile old man who wouldn't last the year.

Nan was right—but instead of a man in his dotage, why not a man who was to end his life on the gallows one week hence, a man with the name of Claybourne who could well be a relative of the aristocratic Claybournes in England? Then she could go home and truthfully tell her father she was a widow—whilst keeping the manner of her husband's death to herself—and he would have no choice but to respect a year of mourning. By then she would be twenty-one and independent of him.

But suppose he wouldn't marry her? Suppose, despite all her promises of enough food and comforts to make his last days bearable, he still refused to marry her? Then what would she do?

Amanda clenched her hands, her eyes taking on a determined gleam. I'll make him marry me. I'll make him *want* to marry me, she vowed, with the goad of desperation. Headstrong and tempestuous, she was so accustomed to having her own way that she did not pause to consider that any other way might exist.

She wasn't fool enough to think it would be easy. She would have to evaluate various approaches. Somehow she would have to prevent Mr Quinn from finding out what she was about to do until it was too late for him to do anything about it. He had been in her father's employ for many years, and when she had come to America her father had insisted that Mr Quinn act as her guardian, giving him the authorisation

to vet the suitability of the man she might want to marry—
her father being of the opinion that, as a mere girl, how could
she possibly tell a true gentleman from a rogue? Her only hope
was Amos. Amos was an important man at Magnolia Grove;
he knew everything there was to know about Charleston, and
he could be relied on for his discretion.

Sheltered by massive oaks, palmetto and shimmering
beech trees, Magnolia Grove stood on the outskirts of Charleston, basking in the sun like a jewel. It was a house of considerable proportions. Shaded arches, brightened by cascades of
blood-purple bougainvillea, yellow cassia and the scarlet cry
of frangipani, supported a first-floor gallery that stretched the
full length of the house. It was surrounded by an array of
formal gardens meticulously sculpted, with statues that stood
in their own beds of flowers. The house was spacious and light
inside, the furnishings simple yet tasteful.

Aunt Lucy's husband, Edward Cummings, who had died
shortly after the Civil War, had been a brilliant businessman.
He had made his fortune trading rum, sugar, rice and cotton.
A financier of blockade runners during the Civil War, he was
one of the few people in Charleston who had not gone under
and had kept his grand town house, although following the
devastation of the war and with the emancipation of the
slaves, he had been forced to sell his cotton plantation on the
Cooper River.

Amanda had soon become accustomed to the rhythm of life
at Magnolia Grove and the bustle of servants. Having grown
extremely fond of Aunt Lucy in the twelve months she had
been in Charleston, her sudden death had affected Amanda
profoundly and she missed her terribly. Charlotte, Aunt Lucy's
only child, and her husband, Mark, had taken care of all the
formalities. Unable to bear the thought of selling the old

family home, Charlotte and her husband had decided to leave Atlanta in Georgia and make Magnolia Grove their own.

On entering the house, Amanda found Charlotte arranging fragrant white roses in a glass vase on a circular rosewood table in the centre of the hall. She turned to look at Amanda and smiled.

'Ah, you're back! How was your visit to the shops?'

'Fruitful,' Amanda replied, indicating the packages Nan was carrying, 'though terribly hot. Can I help?' she asked, removing her bonnet and leaving Nan to take her burden up to her room.

'Thank you, but I'm almost done.' Adding the final rose into her arrangement, Charlotte stood back to survey her handiwork, a wistful expression on her face. 'These roses were Mother's favourites. She grew them herself—had them sent out from England.'

'I know,' Amanda said quietly, remembering how Aunt Lucy had patiently shown her how to prune them. 'I'm sorry she's no longer with us. The house isn't the same without her.'

'I take comfort knowing she's with Father now, that she will be content. She always believed in heaven and an eternal life, so I have no doubt that that is where she will be.' Charlotte put out a hand and touched Amanda's arm affectionately. 'Mother grew very fond of you, Amanda. She was so happy when you came to stay with her.'

Charlotte, a quiet, tolerant being, was a petite, rosy-cheeked brunette and eight years older than Amanda. Her grief, Amanda thought, made her look pretty. She had the sort of kind, caring face that didn't need smiles to enhance it.

'I wish you didn't have to go back to England,' Charlotte said, 'but I know you must. Still, you can always come again. I do hope so.'

'If it was anyone else other than Father telling me I must

go home, I wouldn't leave—and I'm so glad you've decided to live here. It wouldn't seem right to part with this lovely old house, for strangers to move in. What about Mark? Will he miss Atlanta?'

'He's looking forward to it, and already seeking premises to set up his law practice. He was born in Charleston. He's always wanted to come back.'

'I can understand why. I've grown terribly fond of Charleston myself.'

'But you miss your father.'

'Of course I do. I love him dearly and I'm so proud of what he's accomplished throughout his life—not many men could have achieved what he has unaided—but how I wish he wouldn't press me so hard to wed. Why is it that men should think that marriage should be every woman's goal in life?'

'When you return to England, perhaps he'll be so happy to have you back in the fold and realise just how much he's missed you that it will no longer seem important to him.'

'Oh, no, Charlotte. In this his mind is made up. In the matter of my marrying he will have his way. He grows impatient. By the time I get home he will have endeavoured to find a husband for me. In fact, I think it's safe to say he will have gone to extraordinary lengths to accomplish that.'

'It could have been different, you know,' Charlotte said gently and without reproach. 'As soon as Mama launched you on to South Carolina's social scene you became an instant success, with offers for your hand made in record numbers.'

This was true; no matter what event Amanda attended, she was always the belle of the ball. Immediately she was surrounded by a crowd of besotted swains and in no time at all had them eating out of her hand. Impulsive, witty and intelligent—and with a zest for life that left Charlotte breathless—Amanda was desired by all and, with her pink cheeks and lush deep-red hair, she glowed like a jewel against white silk. But her popularity wasn't due primarily to her loveliness and wit, or to the fact that she was heiress to a huge fortune; it was because she kept so much of herself hidden that no one really knew the true Amanda. She possessed an aura of pride that warned a man not to come too close. She had become an exciting enigma that intrigued everyone who met her.

'If you had chosen one of them, and the formidable Mr Quinn approved, then he would have been returning to England alone.'

Amanda sighed, bending over the table to smell the roses. 'It's my own fault, I know. Most of the men of marriageable age I found amusing and charming enough, but there hasn't been one that inspired anything stronger than that—and certainly not one I would choose to spend the rest of my life with. Besides, I know the true reason why they seek my company. The contact isn't friendship, so it has to be that they are drawn by the smell of power and money.'

She became despondent. 'I suppose, if I'm honest, I don't want to get married to anyone, because all the pleasures I enjoy so much will be denied me with a husband in tow. Since coming to Charleston I've had a wonderful time. Everyone has been so friendly, hospitable and courteous. I've been invited everywhere—to parties and picnics. I don't want it to end, Charlotte. Where is he, by the way?' she asked, straightening up and doing a quick sweep of the hall, half-expecting her formidable guardian to materialise from one of the rooms leading off.

'Who—Mr Quinn? I have no idea. He comes and goes as he pleases. Of late he's been noticeably quiet—as if something weighs heavy on his mind. In fact, he really is a man of mystery and many secrets. I do wonder what he finds to do half the time. Come, we'll go and sit on the porch. It's the one place that offers a cool and shady place to sit and chat. I'll just go and find one of the servants and have them bring us some lemonade.'

'Let me go—there's something I wish to speak to Amos about.' For a moment Amanda felt regret that she was about to deceive her cousin, but it was gone as soon as she saw Aunt Lucy's old retainer crossing the yard to the stables. Amos had been a part of the Cummings family for years, and with a great sense of pride and full of his own importance, he lorded it over all the other servants and could galvanise the most shiftless into action. Aunt Lucy had come to depend on him a great deal since the death of her husband, and she had always said how he was her mainstay, and that his loyalty was something money couldn't buy.

When Amanda had arrived at Magnolia Grove, Amos had fallen under her spell the first time he had received the full impact of her dimpled smile, and from that moment on had become her most devoted servant.

Amos paused in his stride when Amanda called his name, waiting with proper respect for her to reach him as she ran across the yard, holding her skirts off the ground, her tiny feet moving as though they had wings.

The friendliness Amos had shown Amanda since she had come to Magnolia Grove gave her confidence. 'Amos, I know I can trust you and that you'll do almost anything I ask you to.'

Amos looked at her with ardent curiosity and deep suspicion; despite his devotion, he was under no illusions about her. And when she looked at him as she did now—demure and sweet-talking, knowing such methods always worked with him when she was planning some new escapade—he found himself saying cautiously, 'Yo' can always depend 'pon my complete, unquestioning loyalty, yo' sure know that, Miss Amanda.'

'What I am about to ask of you I don't want to go any further. You do understand that, don't you, Amos?'

'Very well, miss. Ah woan breathe a word,' he said in hushed tones, entering into the conspiracy, unaware of where that conspiracy was to lead him.

Amanda paused to steal a furtive glance about the empty yard; then, moving closer, she looked at him and confided, 'Amos, is it difficult obtaining admittance to the City Goal?'

Stepping back, he stared at her as though her senses had deserted her. There was a gleam of such intense excitement in the young miss's eyes that it aroused sudden distrust in Amos. 'The City Goal? But why'd yo' want to go there? God fo'saken place—sho is, and no respectable young lady should be seen near it.'

'Never mind that. Please, please say you'll help me, Amos,' she pleaded, determined to get her own way in this.

'Not in a 'undred years, I woan,' he stated adamantly, shaking his grizzled head, seeing the scowling expression on her face pass into a smile that would have charmed a fox out of its hole, a smile she knew was difficult for him to resist. 'Ah ain't never been in that place, an don' think yo' can get round me by lookin' like that.'

'Now, Amos, don't be mean,' she wheedled.

'What fo' you want to go there anyhow?' He looked at her piercingly. 'This don' sound right to me—an' are you not tellin' Miss Charlotte?'

'No. Charlotte mustn't know—at least, not just yet. Please, Amos. There's a man I want to see as soon as possible— tomorrow if it can be arranged. I've got to see him. I've simply got to, and I can't do it by myself. If you won't help me, then I will find some other way. It is extremely important to me. Please, please say you will,' she entreated, feigning helplessness.

Amos shifted from one foot to the other like a restive horse. 'What fo' are yo' fixin' to see this man—a gentlemun, I hope?'

'Of course he is, and what I want to see him about is my business,' Amanda replied indignantly, growing impatient. 'Well? Are you going to help me or not?'

'Well…yes, miss—but I don' approve. I want to know what you're up to—so don' you go askin' no one else.'

His capitulation brought a sigh of relief from Amanda. 'Thank goodness. I knew I could rely on you.'

'Only if I go in wid you. Dat prison's full o' dangerous varmints an' 'tis no place for yo' to be alone. What would Miss Charlotte say if she finds out? Flay me alive she would.'

'No, she won't and you know it. You can drive me there but I must go in by myself. I will not have you glowering at me while I converse with the man I want to see. Are the prisoners allowed visitors?'

'Most of 'em.'

'If the person I want to speak to is not, can any of the gaolers be bribed?'

Amos's black brow wrinkled in thoughtful lines. 'One of the turnkeys is a man called Hennesey—though he's a hard, mean character, he's also greedy and gold sings right sweet in his ears. But it shouldn't come to that.'

'Good. That's what I hoped you'd say.' Amanda faced him squarely, the light of decision in her eyes. 'The man I want to see is Mr Claybourne, the horse breaker found guilty of murdering Carmen Rider.' Sensing fresh disapproval, she said quickly, 'I am sure a resourceful man of your position could arrange it for me, Amos. Will you go and see Mr Hennesey and ask him if I can see Mr Claybourne alone? For such considerations he will be well rewarded for his trouble.'

In no way did Amos approve of what she was asking him to do, but he nodded nevertheless, knowing she was capable of going to the prison alone if she took it into her head. 'Ah'll do my best.'

'Thank you. Oh, and, Amos, not a word to Mr Quinn or cousin Charlotte. Remember.'

And so it was arranged. Amos had a word with her before she went in to dinner, quietly informing her that Mr Hennesey would expect her at the City Gaol the following morning at ten o'clock.

The next day there was no sign that Amanda had spent a sleepless night pacing her room with single-mindedness of purpose. Her sights were centred on one goal, her mind bolstering the courage to carry out the wild plan she had conceived with Amos's help. She had everything to gain and nothing to lose— and neither had Mr Claybourne. Her heart and jaw were set with determination, her mind made up. Thank God she wasn't afraid.

However, certain practicalities had to be taken into consideration. She must wear something Mr Claybourne would be unable to ignore, and yet something that would not attract too much attention. Spending several minutes in a frenzy of worry and indecision, she finally decided on a rather modest saffron silk gown and matching bonnet with a veil that would conceal her features until she was in his presence. Hopefully she would succeed in entering and leaving the prison without anyone being any the wiser as to her identity.

Travelling into town, Amanda paid little attention to her surroundings. Her mind was focused one hundred percent on her meeting with Mr Claybourne.

Believing they were going on another shopping expedition, Nan was as absorbed as she always was by this fine city. Despite her aversion to the sultry, tropical heat, she found it a compelling place.

The houses with their shaded porches and galleries, shredding the sunlight through the delicate traceries of their iron balustrades, were tall and narrow and of multicoloured stucco, adorned with wooden shutters that would be opened when darkness came. The streets, ablaze with azalea and wisteria and shaded by tall trees dripping with wispy tendrils of Spanish moss, were a delight.

The old Charlestonians were a proud, close-knit community and strong in their determination to preserve the old way of life as they had known it before the war. Their traditions were a precious inheritance which no one could take from them. This inner circle was for Charlestonians only, and foreigners were kept out.

Nan was drawn out of her reverie when Amos suddenly stopped the carriage in Magazine Street, across from the City Gaol, and Amanda climbed out quickly. Four storeys high and topped with a two-storey octagonal tower, it was an ugly prison, as prisons always are. Casting Amos a meaningful, conspiratorial look before pulling her veil down over her face, she told Nan that she wouldn't be long. Nan was reduced to a state of shock as she watched her mistress enter that frightful building. She was about to get up and follow her, to demand to know what she was playing at and return to the carriage at once, when Amos turned and halted her with a stern look.

'Leave her be, Miss Nan.'

'Leave her be? How can I leave her be? Can you not see where she's going?'

'Miss Amanda knows what she's 'bout and will be quite safe.'

'Safe? In that place? She's up to something. I can always tell. But, in God's name, what is it this time?'

'I'm sho she'll tell yo' all about it later, Miss Nan.'

With that Nan had to be content to wait—not that she wanted to enter that dreadful place anyway—but what wouldn't she say to that wilful, disobedient girl when she returned.

With her heart beating fast, Amanda spoke to the desk sergeant and a moment later Mr Hennesey materialised out of the shadows. He was a distasteful individual, untidy and with sly eyes, which lit up with a greedy light at the sight of the leather purse.

'This is for your silence, Mr Hennesey. No one must know of my visit. Do you understand?'

He nodded, taking the purse from her gruffly and telling her to follow him. The prisoner was expecting her. Under the bombardment of many curious glances and trying to close her ears to an assortment of crude noises made by the dangerous portion of humanity incarcerated within the walls of the City Gaol, she followed Mr Hennesey along corridors between iron-barred doors to the rear of the building.

The prisoner occupied an individual cell, so they could talk privately. It was quite small. Directly opposite the door, high in the wall, was a barred aperture that let in air and daylight. The stench was appalling and Amanda had to resist the temptation to take the scented handkerchief from her pocket and put it to her nose.

She glanced at the turnkey. 'I wish to speak to Mr Claybourne alone.'

Hennesey shrugged. 'Suit yerself. It's not the usual practice, but you've paid for it. But I'll be just outside and will hear if he gets up to any funny business.' Before he went out he threw the prisoner a warning glance. 'Treat the lady with respect now, you hear—or 'twill be the worse for you.'

A voice from the shadows gave a derisive laugh. 'Your threats are useless, Hennesey. Do you forget that I have only one life to lose and that it's already forfeit?'

With a grunt, Hennesey went out, closing the door with a bang. Amanda examined her surroundings and Christopher Claybourne. His feet were shackled together. He was exactly as she remembered him, except that he was fresh shaven and his dark eyes were alert, watching her. His clothes were ragged and soiled, his uncombed hair hanging loose about his face, but even in his wretched state his strength of character shone through.

Kit—the shortened version of Christopher, which was how he had been addressed all his life—had been told to expect a visitor and nothing more. Recognition widened his eyes when the woman lifted her veil back over her bonnet. Miss O'Connell's appearance had taken him unawares—although what she was doing swanning it through this hell hole, like a lure to a pond full of piranhas, he could not conceive. He recalled seeing her the day before, recalled the way she had looked at him, had seen the interest kindle in her eyes, and he was bewildered as to why she had come to see him. He moved forward, watching her, speculative, admiring, alert. She looked magnificent—like a gilded statue.

The rich vibrancy of her hair was neatly coiffed beneath her bonnet, and as she stared up at him he felt himself momentarily fixed on her strong gaze. Her eyes were olive green, incisive and clear, and tilted slightly at the corners. She had a healthy and unblemished beauty that radiated a striking personal confidence. There was about her a kind of warm sensuality, something instantly suggestive to him of pleasurable fulfilment. It was something she could not help, something that was an inherent part of her, but of which she was acutely aware.

To Kit, starved of a woman's beauty—of any kind of beauty—for so long to behold so much loveliness, to find himself alone with her, a woman forbidden, inaccessible to him, to be surrounded by the sweet scent of her, was torture indeed.

Alone with Mr Claybourne at last—alarmingly, nerve-rackingly alone. Amanda stood looking at him by the light slanting through the small window. With his wide shoulders and lean waist, there was no concealing that here was a man alive and virile in every fibre of his being. He had far and beyond the most handsome face she had seen in her life.

However, she felt a moment of unease. It might have been the way his eyes were looking at her, touching her everywhere, an inexplicable lazy smile sweeping over his lean face as he surveyed her from head to foot, that suddenly made her feel as if she had walked into a seduction scene, which momentarily threw her off balance.

She averted her gaze and casually widened the distance between them, stalling for time, steadying her confused senses, while he stood several feet away, towering over her. When she looked at him again his broad shoulders blocked out her view of anything but him. She tried to turn away, but his extraordinary eyes drew her back. She had never met anyone quite like him, and she felt conscious of nothing except the lingering riot in her own body and mind. Despite his deprivations, his manner bore an odd touch of threatening boldness, and she was beginning to regret insisting that she be left alone with him.

Forgetful for the moment of why she was there, with hard-won poise she coldly remarked, 'Do you always look at a woman in that way, sir?'

His broad, impudent smile showed strong white teeth. 'Forgive me, ma'am. I suppose I could find several things to occupy my attention, but nothing that's nearly as enjoyable as looking at you. So much loveliness in my prison cell certainly is a wondrous sight for eyes deprived of feminine beauty for so long that it is not easily borne.'

His smiling eyes were studying her closely and Amanda

was aware of the tension and nervousness in herself. There was a pink flush on her cheekbones, much to her increasing annoyance. His direct, masculine assurance disconcerted her. She was vividly conscious of his close proximity to her. She felt the crazy, unfamiliar rush of blood singing through her veins, which she had never experienced before. Instantly she felt resentful towards him. He had made too much of an impact on her.

'You are conceited, sir. Despite your deprivations, you do not appear to have forgotten how to flatter a woman, and I don't doubt you have used it on a good many.'

'There have been some along the way, but I never lie, and you are unsurpassed. For what reason does a lady come visiting a condemned man in his cell—and looking as grand as a Southern belle going to a ball?'

Forcing herself to ignore the fluttering in her stomach on hearing the rich, deep timbre of his voice, Amanda raised her chin. 'My name is Amanda O'Connell.'

'And I am Christopher Benedict Henry Claybourne,' he replied, bowing his head respectfully, yet without removing his gaze from her face.

'My…' she breathed, impressed '…such a grand array of names for a convict.'

He grinned. 'My father always did have aspirations of grandeur. However, most people call me Kit. And what of you, Miss O'Connell? You are from England?'

'Yes. I've been staying with my aunt, Mrs Lucy Cummings, at Magnolia Grove for the past twelve months.'

'I have heard of Mrs Cummings.' There were few who hadn't, Kit thought. Her husband had been an important, influential man among Charleston's elite, with some rather high connections in the county and beyond.

'She died recently, and as a result I have to return to England.'

Folding his arms across his broad chest, Kit tilted his head on one side and looked at her quizzically. 'Miss O'Connell, forgive me, but I am bewildered as to why you should seek me out. You seem to have gone to a great deal of trouble. I do not believe you would brave the City Gaol merely to pass the time of day.'

'I have a proposition to put to you.'

'Yes?' Kit prompted.

Straightening her back and raising her head imperiously, she met his gaze direct. 'I—I want you to marry me.'

Chapter Two

Kit uncrossed his arms. 'Good Lord!' The words were exhaled slowly, but otherwise he simply stared at her, his eyebrows raised in disbelief, wondering if he had heard correctly. 'You don't mince your words.'

'Before you say anything, I should tell you that my father, Henry O'Connell, is extremely rich and I have a fortune at my disposal.'

He gave a derisive laugh, his easy manner of a moment before forgotten. The absolute arrogance of the woman! 'You are charming, of course, Miss O'Connell, and as a man I cannot help but admire you—want you—but not as a wife. Your oh so delectable backside might be sitting on a gold mine, but what possible good can it be to me in this hell hole?'

Amanda flinched. He was laughing at her, looking her up and down with those casual, derisive eyes. Giving him a speculative look, she was deeply conscious that his easy, mocking exterior hid the inner man. There was a withheld power to command in him that was as impressive as it was irritating, and despite her reason for being there, she was determined he would not get the better of her.

'How dare you mock me?'

'Mock you? Good God, woman, have you taken leave of your senses?'

At any other time Amanda would have snubbed the man for his impertinence, but she remained cautiously alert. 'I understand what you might think, but I am neither dim-witted nor crazy.'

'You do overwhelm a man, Miss O'Connell. Am I supposed to take your proposal seriously?'

Once again his gaze fell on her and narrowed, half-shaded by his lids as he coolly stared at her. Amanda was immediately angry with him. She straightened her back, her chin thrust forward a notch in an effort to break the spell he wove about her with his eyes. 'I assure you, Mr Claybourne, that I am very serious.'

'Tell me your reason for wanting to marry me.'

'That's easy. I need a husband—a temporary husband.'

'Just what, exactly, makes you so desperate for a husband that any man will do?'

'Desperation makes a person do queer things.'

'Why me? The City Gaol is full of rogues. Surely any one of them would suit your purpose.'

'I want your name,' she said quite simply. 'Claybourne— a name that is the same as the aristocratic Claybournes in England—a name that is not uncommon and a coincidence, I am sure—a name that will satisfy my father. I want a rogue I can guarantee won't bother me once the knot has been tied.' Her lips quirked. 'In a manner of speaking, of course.'

He cocked a brow and nodded slightly as he began to understand. 'Guarantee! Now there's a controversial word if ever there was.'

'Not the way I see it.' His eyes never left her, glimmering and changing with his thoughts. Amanda thought, here is a man who reveals nothing of himself, and he rules himself like steel. And yet, she must win him over, she must make him do what she wanted. She must force him to marry her and give her his name.

'And do you mind telling me what's in it for me?'

'I could offer you ease and comfort for the time you have left. I will ensure that, before they hang you, you will want for nothing.'

'Only my freedom—and my new wife.' He raised one thick, well-defined eyebrow, watching her for every shade of thought and emotion in her. 'Would you be prepared to spend a night with me in my prison cell, Miss O'Connell, and perform the duties of a wife?'

Startlingly aware of the wifely duties to which he referred, Amanda stared at him aghast, unable to stem her expression of repugnance as she cast a swift glance at her surroundings and then at the man himself. 'Of course not. I couldn't possibly.'

Kit's face was inscrutable as he watched her pert nose wrinkle as her gaze swept over his shabby garb. Briefly anger flickered behind his eyes, but then it was gone. 'Then, under the circumstances, I must respectfully decline your offer.'

'You cannot possibly ask that of me. You are, after all, a common criminal and far below my own social level,' Amanda burst out before she could stop herself. Shaken to the core by the bewildering array of sensations racing through her body that his question had aroused, she tried to fight the power of his charm. For a second the intensity of his dark eyes seemed to explode and an expression she could not comprehend flashed through them, then it was gone. His eyes met hers in fearless, half-challenging amusement, saying things she dared not think about.

Kit smiled sardonically. 'We are not all as fortunate as you, Miss O'Connell. However, it is not for the want of trying on my part.' His deep voice was thickly edged with irony. 'How pathetic I must seem to you if you could believe I would agree to your outrageous request. Marriage is the last thing I need right now.'

Automatically Amanda took a step closer to him. 'Please—I ask you to reconsider.'

'Give me one good reason why I should sacrifice myself on the altar of matrimony for your sake—a woman unknown to me until now?'

'Have you no dependants I could take care of—?'

Kit's eyes turned positively glacial. 'Now you really do insult me, Miss O'Connell,' he retorted, his voice scoffingly incredulous. 'What family members I have are not charity cases and are more than capable of taking care of themselves. As for myself, I have everything I need. Why should I want more? You could have saved yourself the embarrassment of this unnecessary visit—but, since you are here, perhaps you should tell me why you are so intent on marrying me, a murderer sentenced to hang any day.'

'I came to America to find a husband, Mr Claybourne,' she told him coolly, 'a husband of my own choosing. My father gave me eighteen months to do so, informing me that if I didn't find a man he would be proud to receive in the allotted time, a man worthy of his only child, he would find one for me. Since titles are paramount to my father, he will choose the man of the highest rank who offers for me—and he will have a choice to make,' she said, unable to suppress the bitterness that crept into her voice, 'since his bottomless income will be like a beacon to every impoverished aristocrat in England. Unfortunately, my aunt's demise means that I have to return to England sooner than expected, and marry a man my father has chosen for me.'

'And isn't that how most marriages in upper-class families

in England come about? Although I always did find it distasteful the way British aristocrats see marriage as a cold-blooded business arrangement.'

'So do I. Such a marriage is not for me.'

'So, you do not run with the pack, Miss O'Connell?'

'I have a mind of my own, if that is what you mean,' she replied.

'So you have. And how will marrying me solve your dilemma, should I agree to your offer? As I see it, when you return to England you will still be minus a husband.'

'If I return a widow, then Father must respect the customary year of mourning. By the end of it I shall be twenty-one and able to do as I please.'

Kit looked at her hard. Despite her delicate features and feminine beauty, Amanda O'Connell was apparently a woman made of steel, a woman who put her own interests first. If nothing else, Kit decided as he appraised her, they certainly had that in common. And he had to give her credit. At least she was honest about what mattered to her. In retrospect, he rather admired her courage, if not her standards.

'And how would you explain the demise of your unfortunate husband to your father, Miss O'Connell?'

Amanda lowered her head, feeling that her courage and control were beginning to slip. 'I would tell him that you became ill on the voyage and died. After all, it's not uncommon for people to die of fevers and all manner of things on board ships.'

Kit contemplated her bowed head. 'Look at me,' he said. His voice was very quiet. Unwillingly she met his eyes. 'You must want to marry extremely badly—have you not had the good fortune to entrap the wealthy bucks of South Carolina's society? Wasn't there one who could cause your maidenly heart to beat to the strains of love?'

Amanda's green eyes snapped with disdain, and for one brief instant Kit glimpsed the proud, spirited young woman behind the carefully controlled façade. 'Love—what has love got to do with anything? The answer to your question is no, I am desperate, Mr Claybourne—had I been given any other choice I would not be here.'

'It is kind of you to consider me the lesser of two evils,' Kit remarked with smiling sarcasm. 'But my answer is no.'

A deadly calm came over Amanda, banishing everything but her regret that she had been foolish to come to the gaol and humiliate herself before this common horse breaker. She knew with rising dread that no one could push Mr Claybourne into any decision not of his own making. For the first time since she had devised this wild scheme, she knew the real meaning of failure. Her small chin lifted primly, her spine stiffened, and before his eyes Kit saw her put up a valiant struggle for control—a struggle she won.

'It's the best I can do at this time. However, since you refuse to marry me, then I shall have to reconsider my options. Good day to you, sir. I am sorry to have wasted your time.'

Kit watched her move towards the door with her head raised haughtily. His stomach quivered and he felt the blood run warm in his veins as he observed her trim waist, the gentle sway of her hips and the train of her skirts stirring up the filth on the floor of the cell. He was a man well used to the charms of women—hadn't he burned his fingers with Carmen? Preferring more honest, uncomplicated relationships, he regretted ever becoming entangled with her. He should have refused her request to break her horses, for hadn't he been warned that Carmen Rider represented the worst kind of danger to a freedom-loving single male like himself?

Continuing to watch Miss O'Connell, he suspected her of being a quick-tempered, calculating vixen, but at that moment he perceived an air of seriousness about her. She must be pretty desperate for him to marry her to go to all this trouble, and somehow she had let herself hope that he would comply with her wishes. The thought that she wanted to marry him to secure her position and the use of his name was acutely distasteful to him. In truth he didn't want to think of her, of her actions and desire, at all. She was not for him and never would be. He'd left her world long since. And yet she had created a situation that could prove useful to him.

'Miss O'Connell, wait.'

She looked back. His tall, broad-shouldered figure seemed to fill the whole cell. Despite his shabby garb, never had any man looked so attractive or so distant, and never had her heart called out so strongly to anyone. His eyes were unfathomable, and at once she knew she must fight her attraction for him. Christopher Claybourne was out of her class, a social inferior. His standards were not hers, and the smell of scandal clung strongly about him.

Slowly she came back to him. Her senses felt dazed, snared by dark eyes that roamed leisurely over her features, pausing at length on her lips and then moving back to capture her gaze. They glowed with a warmth that brought colour to her cheeks, making her want to forget what his crime might be. Compared to the numerous suitors who had come her way, despite his deprivations, Christopher Claybourne was as near to perfect as she had ever met.

Mentally chiding herself for lacking the poise and behaviour of the lady she had been brought up to be, she reminded herself harshly that he was a condemned murderer and stepped back a pace, preferring to keep a secure distance between them.

'Maybe I have been a trifle hasty in dismissing your offer,' he said. 'It could work out to be beneficial for us both.

However, I do believe this to be the most outrageous proposal of marriage I have ever heard of. You really are the most unprincipled young woman, Amanda O'Connell, and you do seem to be in something of a fix,' he said with a wayward smile.

'Which you obviously find amusing.'

'You have to admit it's a little unusual.'

'At the very least,' she agreed.

'Do you not think that by solving one problem you might be creating another?'

'I hope not, but it's a risk I'm prepared to take. The truth is that I don't want to marry anyone, Mr Claybourne, just yet. I value my freedom and independence too much to let it go.'

'So, your goal in life is self-indulgence—to fill your head with nothing except gowns, parties and beaux, to break gentlemen's hearts, gentlemen who will swear their undying love for you and promise you the earth and jewels and the like.'

'If you want to think so.'

'Well, Miss O'Connell, I'm afraid that at this time I'm unable to profess my undying love for you and I appear to be fresh out of expensive jewels right now.'

'That's not what I want from you. Your name will suffice.'

'Then you can have it—but not for prison comforts or fine clothes in which to meet my maker.'

'Then what do you want?'

Taking a step back, he gave her a hard look, his jaw tightening as he stared into her bewitching eyes. She might look fragile, but he was beginning to suspect she was as strong as steel inside, and that he could trust her with the one thing that mattered to him most in life. She was also so stunningly beautiful he could feel himself responding to her with a fierceness that took his breath away. And she was offering herself to him, knowing, if he married her, that he could never take her as a husband should.

With eyes intense with purpose, he moved closer to her. 'If your cause is really so desperate, then a bargain we will make. You could be useful to me after all.'

Amanda stared at him, already feeling the trap that was closing about her. Had her cause been less dire, she would have turned away in disgust at the thought of bargaining with the likes of a criminal, but there was too much at stake and so no limit to her patience. She tilted her head to one side and looked at him quizzically. 'A bargain? I hardly think you are in a position to make bargains, Mr Claybourne.'

'I'm not dead yet.'

'You very soon will be.'

He stared at her, the lean, hard planes of his cheeks looking forbidding in the dull light. 'A bargain we will have or there will be no marriage. However, it will be a bargain that will have a high price for you.'

'I am listening. What is it you want?'

'The first part of our bargain is that our marriage will be legal and binding for the time I have left to live, with papers to prove you are my lawful wife. If I manage to secure my freedom, you will acknowledge me as your husband and become my wife in truth.'

Alarm sprang to her eyes. 'Why, is there some doubt that you will hang? Is there any chance of a reprieve?'

'Don't look so worried, my dear,' he drawled. 'Already I feel my neck straining at the noose. The second part of our bargain is another matter entirely. There is something you can do for me in return for my name—something that will make my mind easier when they hang me.'

Amanda wouldn't like what he was going to say, she could see it on his face. 'What is it?' she asked quietly.

He turned from her, raking a hand through his hair in agitation, and when he turned back she had difficulty reading his expression, but she could see his features were taut with some kind of emotional struggle.

'If it's so bad, perhaps you should tell me outright,' she said.

'I was not being truthful when I said that what relatives I have are capable of taking care of themselves. There is one member of my family who is too young and vulnerable to care for herself.'

Somehow Amanda knew from the look of pain and despair that slashed across his taut features that the person he spoke of meant a great deal to him. 'Who is it?' she asked softly. The pain vanished and his features were already perfectly composed when he looked at her and quietly answered.

'I have a child, Miss O'Connell, a three-year-old daughter. Will you take her with you to England, when you go?'

Amanda stared at him, feeling as if the breath had been knocked out of her. A child! Mrs Hewitt had said nothing about a child—and if there was a child, then surely there must be a mother. A wife? Suddenly she was confronted by a stumbling block the size of an unconquerable mountain.

'A—a child? But—I know nothing about looking after children.'

He grinned. 'Take it from me, it's easy. There's nothing to it—and you have a maid to help, don't you? You seem to be a sensible young woman. Look after her. Take her to my cousin in London. Is that too much to ask?'

He was looking at her hard, studying her features for her reaction. 'But—what would happen to her if I didn't? Where is she now? What about her mother? Who is caring for her?'

'Her mother—my wife, who was a Cherokee—is dead. She died in childbirth. My daughter is called Sky and she is being cared for by a good family. The mother, Agatha, has a loving heart, but life is a struggle, with five children of her own to raise and precious little money.'

'But I could give her money,' Amanda was quick to offer, anything to avoid admitting a strange child into her life, a child she would have difficulty explaining.

'No,' he said sharply. 'That—is not what I want.' His voice became strangely hesitant and Amanda thought he wouldn't go on, and when he did it was almost as if he was testing his ability to talk about it. 'I have nightmares when I think what might happen to Sky when I am no longer here to take care of her. And now you appear as an answer to my prayers. Can I give my daughter into your keeping, for you to take her to my cousin?'

Amanda heard the appeal behind his words, sensed the desperation he must feel for his daughter's well-being, and how much he must miss not being with her. 'H-h-have you not seen her since you were arrested?' she asked, not yet ready to give him her answer.

He shook his head. Even now he marvelled at how profoundly he could be affected by one dimpled smile from a raven-haired child, how it felt to hold her, feeling the bond between them growing stronger and deeper than anything he had ever known. 'I love her, and she knows it. She is the child of my heart, and I would not have her see me like this.'

All the sympathy Amanda felt was mirrored in her eyes. 'I'm sorry,' she whispered, feeling a lump of constricting sorrow in her chest. 'I realise how hard this must be for you.'

'Best that she remembers me when we were together— happier times. I wish there had been some way to spare her this. What happens to me cannot be kept from her. She will not always be a child, and will hear the rumours sooner or later. So—what do you say? Do we have a bargain—or does marriage to me not seem such a good idea after all?'

'A bargain is a bargain, I suppose.'

'And do you pledge yourself to honour this one? Do you promise to look after my daughter until you have placed her in my cousin's care?'

Amanda hesitated as she thought of the enormity of what she was committing herself to. Dazed by confusing messages racing through her brain, driven by the need to help his child and by something less sensible and completely inexplicable, she conceded. Whether he agreed to marry her or not, this request was made from the heart and she could not—would not—refuse him.

'I will make your daughter my responsibility and I will not fail you.'

'Thank you. It means a great deal to me. You have no idea just how much.'

Amanda would have to deal with the consequences. And yet what did it matter? she thought. Mr Claybourne's crime was proved and he would hang for sure. This time next week she would be on the ship homeward bound, and her husband nothing to her but a name. And yet there would be his child to remind her.

'When the ceremony has been performed, you can tell me where I can find her. Do you wish to see her before...?'

'No.' His word was final.

'Very well. I will leave you now. Mr Hennesey will let you know about the arrangements. Are you a Catholic, by the way?'

'Why?'

'It could complicate matters.'

He grinned. 'With a good Irish name as you have, Miss O'Connell, are you not of that persuasion?'

'No. My father was an Ulsterman.'

'And I adhere to any form of Protestant denomination, so that should not be a problem.'

Amanda turned to go. At the door she paused and looked back at him. 'There is one thing I will ask you before I go—and I would appreciate the truth.'

'And that is?'

'Did you really murder Mrs Rider?' With a mixture of dread and helpless anticipation, Amanda met his steady, dark gaze.

'No, I did not. I'd like you at least to believe there is a possibility I'm telling you the truth.'

'Then if you are indeed innocent, surely there are ways to help you—someone with influence and means.'

'If you are suggesting there is someone out there to redress the wrongs done to me, then sadly the source is exhausted. However, your concern touches me deeply, Miss O'Connell.'

His voice was casual and his face was serious, but Amanda distrusted the gleaming, mocking humour lurking in his gaze. He did not believe for one minute that she or anyone else cared one iota what happened to those in his position.

'Then if you did not kill her—where were you?'

'Fishing.'

Amanda stared at him and then slowly her lips curved in a smile. 'You were fishing? Oh, I see. Well, good day, Mr Claybourne.'

Kit watched her go. For the time they had been together her beauty had fed his gaze, creating inside him an ache that could neither be set aside nor sated. When the door had shut, at that moment the prison walls closed round him with a ferocious pressure. His filthy and torn clothing, the roughness of his unwashed skin, the stink of himself, his absolute hopelessness, stirred a rage in him that was almost overpowering.

As Amanda followed Mr Hennesey, a treacherous seed of doubt about Mr Claybourne's guilt planted itself in her mind, and before she had left the prison that seed was taking root, nourished by her horror at the possibility that an innocent man would hang. Her mind argued that she was being a fool to think like this, but every instinct she possessed shouted that he was innocent. She knew it. She could feel it. And if he was, then she could hardly bear the thought of what he was to go through.

Of course the worst thing that could happen for her would be for Mr Claybourne to be released; yet, though she bore no feelings for him one way or the other, she could only admire his courage as he faced imminent death. He had impressed her, and the idea of such a fine-looking man, in his prime and full of life, dying in such a cruel manner, depriving a child of its father, was repugnant to her. Surprised to find her eyes were wet with tears, she raised her hand and wiped them away.

'Mr Hennesey, if you please, may I have a quiet word?'

Hennesey stopped and turned to look at her. His pace had quickened and he was studying her with a keen eye. 'Aye, a quiet word is it? And would I be right in thinkin' it concerns Claybourne?'

His tone gave Amanda confidence—although she did wonder if he had had his ear to the door of the cell. In a low voice, not wishing what she had to say to be overheard, she said, 'Yes, it does. Mr Claybourne and I wish to be married—before…'

'He hangs.'

'Yes.'

Hennesey gave a low whistle. 'That's a serious matter.'

'I agree, but it is what we want—and I would like it carried out with the utmost secrecy. Time is of the essence. Can you help me?'

Hennesey rubbed his chin as he thought about her request. 'Well, now—the governor has to know about such things happenin' in his prison.'

'Is that necessary, Mr Hennesey? Can't we keep this between ourselves?' Amanda knew that if she confronted the governor of the prison all kinds of embarrassing questions would be asked—and he might even be acquainted with Charlotte and inform her, which would dash all her hopes.

Mr Hennesey rubbed his stubbled chin thoughtfully. 'Well, now, we could—but it will cost you.'

'Money is not a problem, Mr Hennesey.' Amanda's relief was so great she almost sank to her knees. 'Do you know of a minister who will agree to perform the ceremony?'

'There is one I know of, although the gaol has its own chaplain, and ministers come and go all the time to visit prisoners, especially the condemned—hoping to save their souls,' he said scathingly.

A sudden instinctive caution made Amanda add, 'I will give you half the money before and half afterwards. I ask for the utmost secrecy for the present. No one must get wind of it—no one. Do you understand me, Mr Hennesey? And we must act quickly. I will leave you to make the arrangements—to appoint the time. Oh, and one more thing. See to it that Mr Claybourne is made decent—a wash and a change of clothes wouldn't go amiss.'

On reaching the carriage, she lost no time in telling a shocked Nan of what she intended and that she would appreciate it if she agreed to be one of the witnesses at her marriage, along with Amos. Nan was so appalled she was momentarily rendered speechless, but when she recovered herself she lost no time in telling Amanda what she thought of the whole dreadful affair. As usual, however, the words of reproach went in one ear and out the other.

'It's unfair of you to make me a part of this,' Nan persisted, 'to ask this of me. What you're doing is wrong and your father will probably disown you.' But Nan could see from the stubborn set of Amanda's jaw and the determined gleam in her eyes that nothing would change her mind. No one could stop Amanda O'Connell doing what she wanted once she'd got the bit between her teeth—and she'd had the bit between her teeth from the moment her father had summoned her back to England to marry the man he had chosen for her.

And so, when the prison governor was away from the prison and there was no danger of him walking in on them, with Nan and Amos standing like statues behind her to bear witness to her bizarre wedding, Amanda moved to stand beside Kit, impatient for the affair to be done.

She had told herself that when they next met he would seem less attractive, and that the image she held of him would vanish, but it was scored into her mind and there it would remain. And as she waited for the moment when she would become his wife, she felt the delight of secrecy and a dizzying madness at what she was about to do.

She was relieved to see Mr Hennesey had done what she had paid him to do and found Kit some decent clothes—a white shirt and dark blue trousers—and that he was clean. And now, as she stood beside him, he was more attractive than ever, more desirable. He turned to look at her, and she saw his deep, black eyes, and the long, silken lashes and well-defined brows. She felt an urgency to reach out and touch him, to be even closer to him, and suddenly, standing there beside him, she felt that when she walked out of that prison cell there would be an emptiness in her life that she didn't want to admit to, a solace that would not be appeased no matter where she was, and her arms would be achingly empty.

As the ceremony was conducted, Amanda replied to the droning questions the minister presented to her, and Kit's voice rang out in the stillness of the cell as he, too, gave his troth towards the marriage, looking deep into her eyes as he promised to love and cherish her. The minister presented a

ring, a ring Amanda had bought and given to him when she
had arrived. Taking her hand in his own, a hand that was
warm and alive, Kit placed it on her finger.

In that brief time Amanda had become the wife of Christopher Claybourne.

The day was hot and sunny, but in the prison it was cool,
and when, still holding her hand, Kit bent his head and gently
kissed her mouth, his lips warmly touched hers. A part of
Amanda's mind warned that to return his kiss was insane. It
would complicate everything, and she didn't need any more
complications, but the need to taste his lips was too strong for
her to resist.

The moment she yielded her lips to his, Kit sensed her capitulation. Unaware of the others present or Nan's gasp of
shocked disgust, Amanda let him part her lips and of their own
volition her fingers curled around his. She felt his swift,
indrawn breath when she tentatively returned his kiss, and
suddenly everything began to change when his kiss deepened.

Somewhere in the back of her mind Amanda knew this was
only a formality, she knew that as clearly as she knew she had
no choice but to participate, but if this was true, then why did
her heart beat faster, and why couldn't she open her eyes?

Kit's head lifted just enough to break contact with her
mouth, and when he spoke his voice was husky and soft. 'You
will belong to me until I die, but for now I guess I'll have to
be content with that.'

It took an unnatural effort for Amanda to move, but she
pulled her hand from his grip. Panicked by her inexplicable
lethargy she stepped back.

Stunned by the hint of tears in her eyes, Kit stared down
at her creamy skin and soft mouth with a hunger that he was
finding almost impossible to control. The exquisite sweetness
of her lips, the way it felt to have her close, to feel the gen-

tleness of her fingers holding his, almost made the notion of making love to her in his prison cell seem plausible—a notion she demolished when he automatically reached out to take her hand once more and she snatched it back.

'Don't think you can repeat kissing me just because of our altered circumstances,' she warned him indignantly, angry with herself for having actually enjoyed his kiss. No matter how hard he protested his innocence, he was still a convicted murderer and she must not, dared not, ever forget that.

Kit was too preoccupied with the results of their kiss to rise to her anger—anger she had bidden to conceal her sudden vulnerability. Her cheeks were tinted an adorable pink, and her dark-lashed eyes were lustrous.

The documents that made their union legal were signed and handed to her, and the minister, being unable to wish the couple a long and happy life as was usually the case, quickly departed.

The closing of the door reverberated around the cell.

'For goodness' sake, hurry up and say your goodbyes,' Nan whispered, shrinking towards Amos and the door. 'I hate this place and want to be out of it. No good will come of this. What will Mr Quinn say—and your cousin Charlotte?'

Taking her arm, Kit drew Amanda aside. Rousing to awareness, she looked at her husband. Despite her angry words of a moment before, she felt an aching dread as to his fate. Her despair must have shown, for he said, 'Take heart. In no time at all you will leave Charleston and you can put all this behind you. You will be a free woman, Amanda, and able to do what you want with your life.'

Amanda struggled impotently for the last vestiges of control, feeling it beginning to crack under the strain as his eyes looked down into hers. She had a strange sensation of falling. 'I don't think I shall ever be able to do that,' she whispered, swallowing down the hard lump that had risen in her throat.

Seeing the distress in her eyes, Kit placed his fingers beneath her chin and tilted her face to his. 'Do not look so sorrowful, Amanda. Congratulate yourself. Your plans have gone according to your wishes. When you return to Magnolia Grove you must raise a toast to your success.'

'When I think of what is to happen to you I can summon no feelings of satisfaction.'

'Nothing can be done to save me now. All I ask is that you take care of my daughter.'

From his pocket Kit withdrew two sealed envelopes. Amanda watched him, noting the authority, the strength held in check as he handed them to her. So many conflicting emotions swirled inside her, fighting for ascendancy.

'When you reach England go to my cousin in London and give her this letter,' Kit said, indicating the letter addressed to Mrs Victoria Hardy with her address in Chelsea written on the envelope. 'I have explained everything. Victoria has children of her own and will take good care of Sky.'

'Where is your daughter? Where can I find her?'

'Take a boat up river—the steamer, if you prefer. Tell the boatman who you want—Samuel Blake, and his wife is called Agatha. Sam is a fisherman and well known on the river. Their home is close to the water—the boatman will point it out. Give this letter to Agatha and you'll have no problem obtaining custody of Sky.'

'Have you no message for your daughter?' Amanda asked, wondering how the child would feel, dispossessed of her father's love and protection, and cast adrift in an alien world.

'Tell her—tell her that I'm thinking of her,' he said tremulously, a great and tender pain bursting within his heart when he thought of his beautiful daughter, 'that I love her, and to remember me in her prayers. After that go home and have a good life, Amanda Claybourne, and I thank you for this.'

Amanda walked towards the door, feeling the words of farewell sticking in her throat. The remorse that gripped her was powerful and sudden, the injustice of Kit's fate filled her. On the threshold she turned back. She saw his eyes fixed upon her with an expression of such sadness in them that it wrenched her heart.

'Farewell, Kit,' she whispered, with tears in her eyes.

'Farewell, Amanda.'

As she followed Nan and Amos out of the gaol, a gust of chill air broke into her solitary world, bringing cold reality with it. She was appalled to think Kit's end was so close, that he was going to be hanged by the neck until he was dead. It all seemed so monstrously unjust. She genuinely forgot that only a short while before she had given no thought to his fate, only what he could do for her.

Dashing away a tear, she quickened her pace. The sooner she was gone from this place, the better she would feel. She tried telling herself that Christopher Claybourne's misfortune was of his own making, but there was a voice in her head telling her that none of this was right and that they would hang an innocent man.

Never again, she vowed as she emerged into the light of day and felt the sun on her face, would she put herself in such a fraught situation. She had succeeded in her plan, but she had the suspicion that she was only storing up trouble for later.

As the carriage carried her back to Magnolia Grove, she rested her head against the soft upholstery, closed her eyes and allowed the memory of the kiss to invade her mind—the kiss, vibrant and alive, soft, insistent and sensual—the kiss she'd been forced to participate in. When Kit had bowed his head to place his lips on hers, she'd understood instinctively that it was a common practice between a newly wedded couple, but her reaction to it terrified her. She'd wanted more—much more. She'd wanted it to go on and on and to kiss him back with soul-destroying passion, to feel his hands on her bare flesh and his body driving into hers.

Dear, sweet Lord! How could she have felt like that? she thought with bitter self-revulsion. Was it not bad enough that she had allowed him to kiss her—and, worse, to revel in it? The truth was that she'd believed Kit's assertions because she'd wanted to, and because the nauseating reality was that she was disgustingly attracted to Christopher Claybourne, who'd fascinated her from the moment she had seen him in the street.

Amanda realised that any attempt to keep what she had done secret was useless. She was in deep trouble and knew it. First she sought out Mr Quinn. He was in the study, pacing the floor as he read through some correspondence from her father that had just arrived.

Mr Quinn was a quiet, private man—secretive, even. Where he went and what he did Amanda had no idea and nor did she care, providing he left her alone to do as she pleased. As her father's employee of two decades or more—more than she could remember—she had respect for the man, but she could not like him. His past was a mystery to Amanda, and she had not enquired into it. He had served her father well, which was why he had entrusted the care of his daughter to him for the time she was in Charleston.

Now his features were set in a stern, unsmiling expression. With the width of the desk between them, Amanda raised her chin with a touch of defiance, steeling herself for Mr Quinn's wrath that would descend on her like an axe when she told what she had done.

As quickly as she could, she told him everything there was

to tell about her marriage to Mr Claybourne. All the while her eyes never left his furious face. Such a transformation came over him as he listened to what she had to say that she recoiled before the change. All that had been calm and controlled had given way to fury and positive revulsion. They stood facing each other, but before Amanda could utter one more word, Mr Quinn erupted with fury.

'By all the saints, have you taken leave of your senses? You foolish, stupid, reckless girl. You have brought shame on your good name and will break your father's heart because of it.'

Amanda stood her ground, her face as stubborn and angry as his. 'Do calm yourself, Mr Quinn. I know how greatly disappointed you must be—'

'And what did you expect? For me to raise a toast and congratulate you and that—that horse breaker—that murderer—on your new-found happiness? I can only think your youth and thoughtlessness prompted such irresponsible conduct. And what of your cousin? Was Charlotte in on this—this escapade?'

'No.'

'I thought not. She has more sense. And this is how you repay her kindness—and your Aunt Lucy's.' He gave her a withering look. 'Your father placed you in my care. What do you think he will say when he hears of this—this farce of a marriage? This is one time you won't be able to wheedle and sweet-talk him. His punishment will be severe—on both of us. One thing is certain—my dismissal from his service will be immediate. He does not deserve to be deceived, and there will be hell to pay when he finds out.'

Amanda flinched at the harsh words. She had no doubt that the shock on his face was genuine, and yet she sensed another emotion there too, as if a distant fear that had nothing to do with her father's finding out were suddenly shimmering in the older man's eyes. There was a fierce, almost frightening anger about him, but there was not a thing Mr Quinn could do about her marriage now. She was Mrs Christopher Claybourne and she had the papers to prove it.

'Then all the more reason not to tell him. We can spare him the details. It can be our secret.'

He stared at her in appalled amazement. 'You are asking me to become your co-conspirator? You were not brought up to be devious,' he snapped.

'It's too late for recriminations, Mr Quinn. It's done. I am Mrs Claybourne now. There is no need for my father to know my husband was a murderer hanged for his crime. He will be told Mr Claybourne died on board ship.'

'I do not like conspiracies.'

'To bring this matter to his ears will hurt him, Mr Quinn, you must see that, and nothing will induce me to wound him.'

'It's a little late for that. My congratulations on your deceit. Your visits to the shops had me completely fooled. You must be the cleverest young woman this side of the Atlantic. I demand to know why you did not see fit to tell me.'

'You know why. You would have prevented me.'

'Damn right I would.' His expression was set and hard. 'To plan this—to enter the City Gaol and to tie yourself to a murderer—is nothing less than outrageous…scandalous. And to try to use his name… Has it not entered your head that your father will question you about the family you have married into, that he will want to know to which branch of Claybournes your husband belonged to, and that he may well communicate with them to offer his condolences for their relative's loss?' When Amanda blanched, a coldness closed on his face. 'No, I thought not.'

'I confess that I haven't given it a deal of thought and I shall face it if it happens. However, because I shall be a widow, Father will have to respect one year of mourning, by which time I shall be independent of his authority and able to choose myself a husband in my own good time. At this particular moment I am impatient to leave for England. I have no wish to be in Charleston when they hang Mr Claybourne.'

Cursing Amanda to hell and back, Mr Quinn seethed as he paced the carpet. He had reasons of his own to quit Charleston at the earliest opportunity, and when Henry O'Connell had ordered their return he had looked on it as a Godsend. However, if he valued his position, he had no choice but to take part in Amanda's subterfuge.

'Mark my words, this spells trouble. If it is ever known what you have done, it will bring disrepute on your family— and all because of a moment of intense madness. May God help you—and me—should your father ever find out the truth. It was badly done, Amanda—badly done indeed.'

Amanda looked at the letter he was holding. 'Is there a message for me in Father's letter?'

'Only that he's arranged what he considers to be a suitable match for you—but I suppose he will have to explain to the gentleman that you are no longer available.'

'What gentleman?'

'It is Lord Prendergast he has in mind.'

Amanda's mouth dropped open and her face lost all vestige of colour. 'Lord Prendergast!' she gasped. 'That man is nothing but an old bag of bones. To marry him would be a fate worse than death.'

'You might wish you had when your father gets wind of what you've done. You haven't a care in the world beyond getting whatever you want out of life, have you?'

'Which certainly isn't Lord Prendergast.'

Faced with Mr Quinn's wrath, for once Amanda felt afraid. She did not feel reckless or defiant now. She felt young and guilty and conscious of the seriousness of what she had done—and fear, should her father ever learn of his daughter's deceit and scandalous marriage. But she took heart that England was an ocean away and he would never find out the true nature of her husband. Because Mr Quinn would face instant dismissal, he wouldn't tell. Besides, it would put him in such a bad light as a chaperon.

'There's—something else you should know,' he said hesitantly, 'something that will affect you. You father's getting married—to a Lady Caroline Brocket. She comes from a Coventry family who were loosely connected to the aristocracy. She married a baronet who died after fifteen years of marriage. There was no issue.'

Amanda froze and stared at him. 'Married? I don't believe it.' She had never entertained the idea that her father would marry again, and she'd never even heard of Lady Caroline Brocket.

'It's true. He is also selling the house in Rochdale and moving to the country, where he has purchased a large property—Eden Park. He fancies his hand at breeding horses. Lady Brocket is in favour of this and has given him a good deal of encouragement. By the time we arrive in England the move will be complete.' Meeting her eyes, which were dark with worry, he frowned. 'Your reaction tells me that you disapprove of your father's actions.'

'That I am surprised is putting it mildly. Business has always come first with Father. He's never listened to me when I've told him he works too hard. This—Lady Brocket must be quite exceptional to have succeeded in finding the chink in his armour when everyone else has failed,' Amanda said, feeling a stab of resentment towards this unknown woman. 'While he plays the country squire, who will be running his business empire?'

'He is employing others to do it for him.'

'I suppose it will take some getting used to.'

'Change always does. Be happy for him—and perhaps then, if he discovers the disgraceful facts of your own marriage, he will not be so hard on you.'

Chapter Three

Mr Quinn's chilling expression was bad enough, but the worst part of it all was that Charlotte was disappointed in her and shaken and stricken by her deceit. Her painful attempt to reprimand her formed more of a punishment than any violent demonstration of anger, and in an agony of mortification Amanda begged her forgiveness. On this edifying note of repentance she hoped the conversation would be concluded, but Charlotte had to have her say.

'When Mr Quinn told me what you had done I could not believe it of you, Amanda. What can I say? I knew how much you wanted to avoid an arranged marriage, but—well, I never thought you would go to such lengths—and to go inside that dreadful place... Oh, I shudder when I think about it. Still, it is done now, so it's no use getting all emotional about it and indulging in petty displays of hysterics. But I have to say that I'm disappointed in you, and what your father will have to say I dread to think.'

Amanda could see the expression of shock on Charlotte's face, and yet she was confident that soon she would understand the desperation that had made her do it. 'Charlotte, I am so sorry if I've upset you.'

Charlotte looked at her sharply. 'But you're not sorry you married Mr Claybourne, are you?'

'No.'

'At least it will stop your father marrying you off in a hurry.'

Amanda brightened. 'Yes, it will all be changed—especially now he is to wed himself—and a lady, too. So at least there is one good result from today's events.'

'I'm glad you think so,' Charlotte said drily. 'Well, in no time at all you'll be a widow. No doubt your father will hold me responsible for all this. What you do in England is, of course, entirely your own concern, Amanda, but here Mother had her standards—and so have I, and I wish you had observed the proprieties.' Since her mother had died, Charlotte felt responsible—certainly morally accountable—for Amanda's brazen behaviour and her restless, dissatisfied state. 'I suppose I had better write to your father and explain everything.'

'Please don't,' Amanda said quickly. 'I'll tell him, Charlotte, I promise I will.'

'He has a right to know. You cannot conceal the fact that you married a convicted murderer.'

'He is innocent, Charlotte, I know it.'

'The judge who sentenced him does not think so.'

'There are many who do not believe it and never will accept his guilt.'

'And if he is innocent, will you devote your life to saving him from the undeserved penalty awaiting him? Because, if so, imagine what it will mean to you.' She put her hands to her flushed cheeks. 'Oh my goodness, what a muddle all this is. I'll talk it over with Mr Quinn. Perhaps by now he will have calmed down and will be in a more logical frame of mind.'

'There—there is more, Charlotte.' Charlotte looked at her, waiting for her to continue with absolute dread as to what might be coming next. 'Mr Claybourne has a child. I have promised him I will take her to England—to her cousin.'

Shaken by this latest piece of news, Charlotte listened in an appalled silence as Amanda told her of the promise she had made to Kit. 'I am his wife, even if only in name. I promised I would take care of his child, and I will honour that promise.'

Charlotte took a moment to assess the situation. At length she sighed with resignation and said, 'Very well. You and I will see to it in the morning. I can only hope that none of this gets out. A scandal is the last thing we want. Perhaps it's a good thing you're to return to England.'

The scene was one of tranquillity and sparkling water snaking inland. The surface of the river tumbled and tossed its white foam on either side of the river steamer as it ploughed its way through. Gulls screeched overhead and an assortment of waterfowl swam in the shaded reaches. They passed several plantation houses, some lived in, some still nothing but empty shells—the scars of the Civil War. It was a beautiful day. Nature was at its grandest, with the landscape wrapped in a warm, golden haze as Amanda and Charlotte sat in the boat beneath their parasols.

When the steamer neared a small landing the whistle bellowed. A flock of alarmed egrets exploded into flight, their plumage snowy white against the black water and sombre trees. The boatman pointed to them the house where Samuel Blake lived. Tall shrubs allowed only a glimpse of the roof of the timber-framed house, and several others. Walking up a dusty lane, they stopped outside the house as a motherly woman, robust and with a kindly face, came out, wiping her flour-coated hands on her wide pinafore. There was a warm light in her eyes as she introduced herself as Agatha Blake. A small child of three came up behind her, peering round her skirts at them curiously.

'I do hope we are not putting you to too much trouble, Mrs Blake, descending on you at such short notice. I am Amanda O'Connell,' she said, having decided not to tell anyone about her marriage to Christopher Claybourne, 'and this is my cousin Charlotte. It was Mr Claybourne who told us where you lived. We—we've come to see you about the child—Sky. He gave me a letter for you.'

Agatha looked at them both, assessing them carefully, and then a large smile broadened her lips as she took the letter. 'Of course you are no trouble. Come inside and have some tea. It's rare enough I have visitors—and please call me Agatha. A friend of Kit's is a friend of ours. You are fortunate to find Sky and me the only ones at home just now. I have a large brood and usually there are children all over the place, but my husband has taken them fishing to give me some peace.'

Amanda smiled at the little girl, realising for the first time that this child was her stepdaughter. She was a startlingly attractive child, her Cherokee ancestry evident in her features. Her mane of jet black hair was loosely caught by a thin ribbon so that its length hung down between her shoulder blades. What entrapped Amanda was the compelling blackness of her eyes. They were large and widely spaced, set above prominent cheekbones and heavily fringed by glossy lashes. The incredible black eyes regarded her with interest.

Having heard her father's name mentioned, she tugged on Agatha's skirts to gain her attention and said, 'Is Papa coming home, Agi?'

'No, child, but he has sent these ladies with a message.'

Charlotte held back when Agatha turned to go inside. Holding out her hand to the child, she smiled. 'Would you like to come with me and show me the pretty flowers in the garden, Sky? I'd love to see them.' Sky nodded and took her hand trustingly.

Amanda looked at her cousin gratefully. It would be easier talking to Agatha without the child. She watched the two of them go into the small garden, feeling her throat tighten. Poor little mite, she thought. Wasn't it bad enough being without her father, without being taken away from those she loved by strangers? She followed Agatha inside the house. It smelled lovely—of baking and polish and all the other smells that mingle together to smell of comfort and home.

'Have you known Mr Claybourne long?' Amanda asked as Agatha busied herself making tea.

'Sam and me have known Kit for five years. I know all about what they say he's done, but don't you believe it. He's a good man. We like him—and I would trust him with my life if I had to—and our five children adore him. Kit never killed that woman. I'd swear it on my life.'

'And what of Sky? What shall I tell her?'

Agatha glanced at her sharply, alert. 'Tell her? What do you mean?'

'Mr Claybourne has asked me to take her back to England with me—to be looked after by his cousin. She will be well looked after, you can depend on that. Read the letter, Agatha,' she said, handing it over. 'He explains everything in that.'

Agatha read what Christopher had to say, then she nodded, her eyes moist and her face set in sombre lines. 'It will sadden my heart to part with her, but I can see it's for the best that she goes. She's a bright child who learns quickly. When she begins to hear the rumours about her pa, she's bound to find out what happened. It cannot be kept from her and the stigma will always be with her. When do you go to England?'

'The day after tomorrow.'

Pain slashed across Agatha's features. 'So soon. And you want to take her with you today?'

'Yes,' Amanda said softly.

Agatha nodded, resigned to letting Sky go. 'I'll get her things together. She never knew her mother—a lovely little thing she was, Cherokee. Sky has come to accept me in that role and we all love her dearly. But I always knew the day would come when she would have to go, that Kit would take her to his own people in England. How is he?'

'Bearing up, I'd say.'

'And will they really hang him?'

'I don't see how it can be avoided. He continues to reiterate his denials of guilt—even though there does not seem to be anyone else who could have done it.'

'What kind of justice is it that will hang a man like him?' There was anger in Agatha's voice as she wiped away a tear with the corner of her apron.

'What kind of man is he?' Amanda asked gently.

'Kit? Why, he's a man of the open, an active man, and I know how much he must hate being confined. He's his own man is Kit. Often he would disappear into the woods following trails made by the Indians with nothing but his rifle. He would be gone for days and return to lead Sam back to a freshly killed and skinned deer. The mountains became his mentor. He learned to read the signs of the sky and forest like an Indian. He became a hunter and a trapper—shooting a deer or trapping possum.'

Amanda could imagine Kit, striding towering and unafraid through the Smoky Mountains, as controlled and silent as a great cat. 'Then I can imagine how difficult his imprisonment must be for him.'

'I will never believe he's guilty. The attorney who conducted the legal proceedings against Kit was a friend of the Riders. The jury listened to him and Kit didn't stand a chance. He swayed them with his clever talk and worked on them with his sympathies, portraying Mrs Rider as some kind of poor, defenceless widow, when in truth she was anything but. The jury was out less than ten minutes when they filed back with the verdict of guilty.'

'He told me he was fishing at the time Mrs Rider was killed.'

Agatha nodded. 'And so he was—with Judd Freeman. They often went off for days and weeks at a time. Kit would always leave Sky with me. On that last trip, as soon as they reached Charleston Judd went off again and he's not been back since. He could be anywhere between here and Boston. He won't know anything about this, otherwise he'd be back to save his friend.'

'Hasn't anyone tried to contact him?'

'Sam has—and others—but no one's seen hide nor hair of him. The trouble is that he lives on his boat. Our only hope is that he puts into port somewhere and hears about it.'

At that moment Charlotte appeared with Sky. The child was clutching a little bunch of flowers in her hands, which she handed to Agatha.

'What does Papa say, Agi?'

Placing the flowers on the table, Agatha gently touched her dark head. 'I know this is a big surprise for you, sweetheart, but your papa wants you to be very brave and grown up. He says you are to go with this lady on a journey across the sea.'

The look of happiness on Sky's face fled and a kind of bewildered worry took its place. 'Are you coming, too, Agi?'

Tears sparkled in Agatha's eyes. 'No, love. I have to stay and look after Sam and the children. You know what they're like. Just think what they might get up to if I wasn't here to keep them straight.' Agatha saw Sky's constricted throat swallow with difficulty.

'I don't want to be sent away,' she whispered.

'No one is sending you away. It's just that your papa has to go away for a while—and thinks it best that you go to England.'

'Will Papa find me there? He will, won't he, Agi?' she said, her face full of hope.

Dragging their eyes away from the forlorn little face, wet with silent tears, Agatha and Amanda looked at each other, each knowing what the other was thinking. How hard it would be when the time came telling this three-year-old child that her papa was in heaven.

Knowing how much Sky was going to need her in the weeks ahead, for her sake as well as her own, Amanda had to be strong and clear-headed. But how small she was. It seemed ridiculous to be sending such a tiny thing away to the remote unknown. On impulse she knelt beside her and took her hand.

'I know this will be hard for you to get used to, Sky, but your papa really has asked me to take care of you. He told me he loves you very much, and that you are to remember him in your prayers every night.'

'I'll always pray for Papa.'

'We'll have lots of time to get to know each other and perhaps I can show you Charleston and the shops before we leave on the enormous ship. Is there anything you would like to take with you?'

'Only Papa, but I know he can't be with me just now,' she said in a quaintly philosophical way for one so young. 'I like ponies, too—like Papa. He said he would get me a fine pony of my very own when he got back.'

'When we get to England—which is where I am taking you—lots of young ladies have ponies of their own, and so will you. But since we can't very well take a pony on the ship, is there anything else you would like?'

Suddenly her eyes brightened. 'I would like a doll of my very own, one I can dress in nice clothes.'

'Then I shall see to it that you have the prettiest doll in the whole of Charleston,' Amanda told her soothingly, relieved to see the stiffness ease from Sky's small body. 'Now that is settled, would you like to help Agatha put your things together? My name is Amanda, and I am sure we are going to be good friends, Sky.'

'You have a way with children,' Agatha said as she straightened up.

'I haven't had any experience, so I have a lot to learn.'

This was true. Many times over the next two days Amanda had to fight back an impulse to take her back to Agatha. Sky cried all the way back to Charleston. Her parting from Agatha and all that was familiar upset her, but, arriving at Magnolia Grove and with all the attention showered on her, and doting on the doll and other toys Amanda bought for her, she soon brightened up. It was when she went to bed that she suffered moments of homesickness and cried for Agatha and her papa. Finding herself drawn to the child in a way that surprised her, Amanda would hold her tenderly and soothe her with words of comfort until she fell to sleep.

The ship bound for England via New York sailed out of Charleston's harbour with playful dolphins swimming alongside. At the same time a small fishing boat, with its sun-bleached sail bellied out and curls of white foam on each side of the bow, sailed in, with Judd Freeman at the tiller. It was after he'd put into Wilmington to take on fresh water that he had heard what Kit had been accused of and that he was to pay the ultimate penalty for his crime. Immediately he had set sail for Charleston, praying he would not be too late to save his friend.

Back in England, as the train sped northwards, carrying Amanda to her new home, she had time to dwell on her parting from Sky. It had been difficult to say goodbye, more difficult than she had imagined. During the two weeks' voyage from America she had become extremely fond of the child and found pleasure in her company. When the ship had docked at Southampton, they had taken the train for London. Victoria Hardy lived in Chelsea with her husband and two children. Leaving Mr Quinn and Nan at the hotel—where they were to spend the night before taking the train north the following morning—Amanda went to see her with Sky.

Kit's cousin was a tall, attractive, dark-haired woman who welcomed Amanda warmly. The minute she laid eyes on Sky she knew who she was. The moment was an emotional one for her; scooping the wide-eyed child up into her arms, she hugged her tightly. 'So you are Kit's little girl,' she said when she had composed herself, setting Sky on her feet once more and tracing her cheek with her finger. 'I have waited a long time to meet you. I have heard all about you in the letters your dear papa sent to me from America.'

Sky's dark eyes did not flinch from the older woman's touch. She was gazing up at her with interest, for, like Amanda, she, too, noted the similarities in Victoria's features that likened her to her dear papa. Becoming distracted when a fair-haired little girl entered the room, no bigger than herself, she went to her to introduce her to her doll, the one Amanda had bought for her in Charleston and from which she refused to be parted.

'She's a delightful child—quite adorable,' Victoria said. 'So like Kit in her mannerisms, but her Indian ancestry is evident in her features.'

'She's been so good and brave, poor lamb. Everything has been so confusing for her of late.' Taking Kit's letter from her reticule, she handed it to Victoria. Amanda had no knowledge of what the letter contained, but she knew it would bring

Victoria pain. 'Kit asked me to give you this. He explains everything. Although—I must tell you that the news will be upsetting for you.'

Victoria looked hard at this lovely, rather solemn young woman she didn't know, and then turned and moved away to read her cousin's letter. Amanda went to the nurse who had accompanied the little girl into the room. Telling her that Mrs Hardy had just received some distressing news, she asked her to take the children to play in the nursery for a while.

After Victoria had read the letter, wiping the tears of grief from her eyes, she slowly folded it and turned to Amanda, shaking her head in disbelief. 'How could this happen? Kit never hurt anyone in his life—and to accuse him of murder... I will never believe it.' Her voice was raw with pain. Suddenly a thought occurred to her. 'Does Sky know that her papa will not be coming back?'

'No. When we left Charleston the—the execution had not been carried out, and I have heard nothing since. I—asked some friends of his—Agatha and her husband—to write to you, to let you know when...'

Victoria swallowed hard, trying to contain her grief. 'Thank you. Do—do you think he did it?'

'No, I don't—and I'm not alone in that. Unfortunately, proving his innocence is another matter. There isn't a whisper of proof to support his side of things. The one man able to bear him witness has disappeared.'

'How can I tell Sky that she'll never see her papa again, that he's dead? I won't say anything to her—until I know more. Poor Kit. He didn't deserve this. If he is dead, then may he rest in peace, and, wherever he is, let him be assured that I shall do my best in raising his daughter, that she will be like one of my own.'

Amanda hadn't stayed long after that. She had been deeply

anxious about her meeting with Victoria Hardy and how Sky would react when the time came for them to part, but now she had met Kit's cousin she realised that there had been no need. Sky had taken to her at once, and the fact that her new cousin had two children would help her settle in. In fact, when Amanda had left, the two little girls had been playing happily together in the nursery.

And now, on the train heading north, thinking of Kit—about how angry and unhappy he must have been, worrying about how his daughter would be taken care of—she asked herself if there was anything more she could have done, and finally decided that there was not. She had done everything he had asked of her and now she must put it behind her. It was over and she must look to the future. A year of widowhood would soon pass and then she could do exactly as she pleased. She looked out of the window, watching the landscape fly past, and wondered why her heart felt so heavy and why she should feel so despondent when she had finally got what she wanted.

It was because now she could see that what she had done had been no more than a spoiled desire to thwart and outwit her father. What a fool I've been, she thought bitterly. And now I've got to pay for it. She'd wanted a temporary husband; now that he was dead, she was filled with remorse over the manner of it, and to add to that she missed Sky more than she could have imagined.

She looked at Nan dozing across from her. She, too, was sad to be parted from Sky. The little girl's constant chatter and laughter had lightened the voyage. As for Mr Quinn, who also had his eyes closed, he had hardly uttered a word since leaving London, and no amount of casual banter seemed to be able to break his grim mood, so Amanda had given up.

* * *

At last they reached their destination—Sheffield. Amanda saw that her father had sent his coach to meet them. She climbed in with Nan while Mr Quinn and the driver saw to the luggage. It was a brilliant summer's day, when the hedgerows were full. Travelling the six miles to Eden Park, after leaving the industrial city behind, Amanda watched the countryside unfold in a rich patchwork of field and meadow and undulating moor land.

Her thoughts turned to her father, to how much she had missed him and how impatient she was to be reunited. Henry O'Connell was the son of an Irish navvy who had come from Ireland to work on the Liverpool and Manchester railway. When Henry had been old enough to join him, he had soon seen that navvying wasn't for him and he'd struck out on his own, starting at the bottom. After that all directions led upwards. Driven to succeed, money became everything to him—it made everything possible and his driving energies and ambitions had made him one of the richest men in England.

Amanda was proud of all he had achieved. They had always been close, and the only stumbling block in their relationship was the issue of her marriage. He had planned great things for his only child. Wealth, power and social prestige would be hers. But, as he had soon discovered, it took more than money to gain entry to the exclusive inner world of Victorian respectability. He was not a boastful man and rarely offended anybody, but the fact remained that he was a parvenu. In his early days he had not been accepted in established society, but his burgeoning wealth gradually became so prodigious that it overwhelmed class.

After leaving the village of Thurlow behind and skirting the edge of a lake, the coach approached a long drive of limes.

Eden Park loomed ever closer. Seeing the house, Amanda blinked her eyes, staring. On that first encounter she was touched by the opulent splendour.

Eden Park was an architectural gem on the edge of the Derbyshire moors. It stood in four hundred acres, thirty of which were given over to gently undulating parkland and beautiful terraced gardens—with short, velvety green lawns, clipped yew hedges, statues and fountains—the rest to the home farm. To the west the land rose steeply to the Derbyshire peaks, and eastward was Sherwood Forest and all its legendary tales of Robin Hood. Over the Derbyshire hills lay the sprawling metropolis of Manchester, which was where Amanda had lived all her life.

Her father must have been watching out for her because, the moment the carriage came to a halt, he came hurrying down the steps with a restless vitality, beaming broadly and as fast as his short, barrel-chested frame allowed. Despite having a brilliant head for business there was something coarse and earthy about Henry O'Connell that most people found appealing, especially Amanda—although she did not realise that this was because she possessed some of those same qualities, despite twenty years of effort on the part of her nanny and governess to eradicate them.

With a happy smile and carrying her veiled black bonnet, Amanda hurried to meet him, throwing her arms about his neck and hugging him, the smell of brandy and cigars on his warm breath fanning her cheeks.

'Here, now, let me look at you,' he said, holding her at arm's length and examining her face with his piercing grey eyes. 'Aye, you've grown lovelier than ever. You get more like your mother every day. You've enjoyed your year in Charleston—Quinn kept me informed. Though you made a spectacle of yourself on occasion, you've done nothing to bring shame on us. But why did you go all the way to Southampton? Why not Liverpool?'

Amanda laughed awkwardly, unable to look him in the eyes as she avoided mentioning the real reason that had taken her to London. 'I—I wanted to spend a few days in London, do some quality shopping—you know how it is with us females, Father.'

'Aye, I do that. Spent more of my money, I don't doubt,' he said, tweaking her cheek with mock reproach, 'but to my mind there's nothing wrong with the shops in Manchester.'

Amanda laughed lightly. 'Since you know absolutely nothing about ladies' fashions, Father, that is exactly the sort of remark I would expect from you.'

'And where were all the letters you promised to write? No doubt your head was too full of nonsensical matters and you were too occupied to read letters from your old da that you considered to be monstrously dull, eh?' he reproached her good humouredly, his eyes all of a twinkle.

Amanda laughed, looking fondly at his round face with its ruddy features and his mutton-chop whiskers, which, like his hair, were vividly white. 'You're not old and I did read them— I just never got round to writing back as often as I should, that's all.'

''Tis sorry I am to hear about Lucy, and 'tis sad I am that I never got to see her before she died,' he said on a more sombre note, the brogue of his native Ireland still heavy on his tongue despite his thirty years in England. 'But what's this?' Detecting an air of dejection about his daughter, he tipped her chin and peered sharply into her face. 'Where's the sparkle I remember in those bonny green eyes, eh—and when did you take to wearing black?' he remarked, eyeing her sombre garb with distaste.

'When Aunt Lucy died,' Amanda replied, feeling that now

was not the time to tell him of her widowed state. Uncomfortable under his scrutiny, she smiled to reassure him. 'Don't worry, Father, I'm perfectly fine. It's been a long journey and I swear I can still feel the wretched motion of the ship. I never was a good sailor. There—is something I have to tell you, but it can wait until later.'

'So it will—and cheer up. What with all the parties and such we've got planned to be having here at the house, you'll be forgetting all about Charleston in a month.'

Amanda looked up at the towering edifice. Built in golden yellow stone enriched by splendid carving, with its long front and central Ionic portico, and three storeys high, Eden Park was quite remarkable. 'You've been busy while I've been away. I never dreamed you'd be so extravagant as to buy a house of such grand proportions. I swear there must be enough rooms to house an army.'

'So there is—so there is,' he agreed, puffing out his chest and looking at his new domain with pride. 'I told Quinn what you could expect. Did I exaggerate?'

'Not at all. I am impressed, although I can't help feeling a certain sadness at not returning to Rochdale. It has always been my home.'

'Aye, lass, I know, but you'll find this place is like a tonic. You'll soon forget about Rochdale and agree that Eden Park is a desirable retreat from the engine and factory fumes and noise of Manchester.'

Amanda's brows lifted over knowing green eyes. 'Maybe so, but not too far away so you can't keep your finger on the pulse, eh, Father?'

Henry's lips quirked and, reaching out, he brushed his fingers against her cheek. 'You know me too well.'

'Will you be able to stand being a gentleman of leisure, Father?'

'The company is as vigorous and healthy as it always has been so I've no worries there.'

Amanda smiled at him. 'Which is a striking endorsement to your skill in selecting the people who work for you.'

'Aye, well, I pay them well enough for it. I only wish I'd bought something like this years back. You wait until you see the stables. Splendid, they are, splendid, and I intend filling every box with only the finest horseflesh. I'll have the best in the district, you see if I don't. What I need is someone who knows a good horse when he sees one. But come and meet your new stepmother—and don't be saying anything untoward now,' he warned, seeing her eyes cloud over, 'because it's been a long time since your mother died and you won't be with me for ever.'

'So you thought it was time to consolidate your gains and get married,' Amanda remarked, unable to hide the anxiety this had caused her.

'Caroline married me for myself, not my money, if that's what you are thinking—she has plenty of her own without mine. She's good for me—a true lady she is, too—none finer.'

Amanda stiffened when a woman came to stand by his side and linked an arm through his. It was a casual gesture, as if it were the most natural thing to do. Her father beamed down at her, patting her hand.

'This is Caroline. Caroline, my dear, this is my daughter, Amanda.'

'I know.' She laughed. 'Your father has told me so much about you that I feel I already know you. Welcome home, Amanda—to your new home, that is. I'm so pleased to meet you at last. I do so hope you will be happy living at Eden Park.'

There was such an air of kindliness about her that Amanda felt herself begin to relax. 'Well, it's certainly a change from where we lived before.'

'I've been urging your father for months to move to the country. To get him away from the office,' she said, looking meaningfully at her husband.

Henry patted her hand affectionately. 'Aye—you'll find Caroline gets her own way in most things.'

'I am also selfish, self-centred and inclined to say and do things without thinking and Henry gets furious with me, but it does no good,' she told Amanda with a twinkle in her eye for her husband. 'But come, let's go inside. I'll show you around later. I'm sure you're in need of refreshment after your long journey. I hope you don't mind, but I've arranged what rooms you shall have. I'll take you there now and we can have a quiet gossip as we go.'

Warming to the older woman, Amanda decided there and then that Caroline would be good for her father. In her late forties, she was still attractive. Independent and tough-minded, too, Amanda supposed. Undoubtedly someone who could persuade her father to pay less attention to his work that had been his life, and move away from Manchester, which had been the hub of his empire, had to have those qualities to be successful. It was not going to be as hard accepting her as she had thought.

Upon entering the house, Amanda looked dazedly about her, wondering if she had come to a royal palace by mistake. Everything about this eighteenth-century house was light, graceful and elegant. It was filled with paintings, delicate, gilded scrollwork and thick carpets, softer than the smoothest lawns. Her own rooms were furnished with an eye to luxurious comfort and fashionable elegance. The ivory and white, pale green and gold theme was reflected in the heavy curtains screening long windows, and the bed and its hangings. Clearly Caroline had excellent taste and her father had spared no expense.

* * *

It was after dinner that same evening when Henry brought Lord Prendergast into the conversation. He was seated in the elegant drawing room beside his wife, swirling his brandy around the bowl of his glass and smiling a trifle fatuously upon his only child, glad to have her home again. However, there was an air of certainty about him that Amanda found disquieting and reminded her that now was the time to tell him about her marriage and put that particular subject to rest once and for all. Taking a deep breath, she plunged in.

'Mr Quinn told me you have aspirations for me to marry that gentleman, Father. Unfortunately, it's quite out of the question. Besides, he's an old fool and a dead bore. I cannot believe you could imagine him to be an eligible suitor for anyone, let alone your only daughter. I have something to tell you that may come as something of a shock. If so, I apologise, but it is done and there is no going back.'

'And what is that, may I ask?' Henry's face lost its relaxed amiability and became cold, hard and wary; he sensed she was about to divulge something that would not be to his liking.

Amanda's eyes met his, suddenly sharp, questioning, and she quailed inside as she began to explain calmly and reasonably about her marriage to Christopher Claybourne. 'Before I left Charleston, I—I met someone and married him.'

Henry's face took on the look of a bright red apple and his eyes almost protruded from their sockets. 'Married! Did I hear you aright? Like hell you did. What is the meaning of this?' he bellowed, a vast disapproval in his tone, which asked what the devil she had been playing at.

'The meaning? Why—I got married, that is all,' Amanda said in defiance of his thunderous glower, his quick-to-anger attitude reminding her of why she had taken the reckless step of marrying

Christopher Claybourne. 'You agreed that I could do so—should the right man come along,' she reminded him pointedly.

'Aye, I did that, but I also remember insisting that I must be informed before you entered into any marriage contract. Married? And you did not consider it important enough to inform me—your father—first?'

Sensing that her husband's temper was straining at the leash and knowing she was the only one who could soothe it to manageable proportions, Caroline put a soothing hand on his arm, taking his glass and placing it on a side table. 'Listen to what Amanda has to say, Henry,' she voiced mildly, for there was something about her stepdaughter's manner that alerted her to a state of affairs unknown to either of them. She smiled reassuringly at the young woman opposite, who returned her smile, grateful for her support.

'Who is he?' Henry demanded, hoisting himself to his feet and glaring at his daughter.

'Christopher Claybourne.'

'Do I know him?'

'No, you couldn't possibly.'

'What sort of man is he—a gold-digger?' he bellowed, holding on to his anger until he knew what the devil was going on. Amanda's impulsiveness was not something he cared for.

Amanda sprang to her feet, anger flashing from her eyes, her voice harsh with tension. 'No—far from it. That is a vile, horrible accusation and you have no right to speak that way of a man you have never met. Christopher has no use for your money, Father, and if you are to be offensive before you've listened to what I have to say, then there is no more to be said.'

Amanda looked ready to stride from the room, but Henry put a restraining hand on her arm, giving her a narrow, quizzical look. 'Did you plan to outwit me by marrying this man? Is that it?'

The two faced each other in timeless attitudes of belligerence until Amanda capitulated and lowered her gaze. 'Yes,' she replied truthfully, knowing her father would be sure to detect a lie, 'but I never meant to hurt you and I'm sorry if I've made you unhappy, but had you ever listened to me you would know that when it came to choosing a husband I would do it. When I went to Charleston, you hoped I would find a man to marry—a man you would consider suitable to be your son-in-law. Christopher was eminently suitable. Our marriage was sudden—just before I left Charleston. There was no time to write and let you know.'

She went on to explain her marriage to Christopher as best she could—the crime he had been accused of, and the sentence duly passed, she omitted. Her father looked at her, listening to what she had to say incredulously, reluctant to let go of his anger. 'Christopher was a fine man, Father—handsome, too. You would have liked him. He also had an active interest in horses—he was a wonder with them—broke them in and trained them himself in a way you would have envied.'

Caroline stood up and went to her husband. His face was still angry. He wanted to curse, to explode with resentment, but, because he knew his wife in her own quiet way wanted him to listen to Amanda, he clamped his mouth shut.

In the space of seconds Caroline considered Amanda's shuttered face and correctly assumed it was a façade to conceal some sort of deep hurt. 'You speak of your husband in the past tense, Amanda,' she remarked softly. 'What did you mean when you said your father would have liked him? And why did he not come with you to England?'

Amanda turned her gaze on her stepmother, her eyes having taken on a pained, haunted look. 'Christopher—he— he died.' Her voice was soft and sad, no more than a whisper, and Caroline felt her heart go out to her.

'Oh, my dear—I see. I'm so sorry. So your mourning is not only for your Aunt Lucy.'

'No.'

Henry shook his head slowly as he tried to come to terms with his daughter's situation and her loss. As suddenly as it had come, the dreadful fury vanished. 'So—no sooner do you find a husband than he makes a widow of you. I'm sorry, lass.' He became thoughtful. 'He was a Claybourne, you say? One of the southern Claybournes? Not that I'm familiar with any of them.'

'I—I believe so—although the family is large and I am uncertain as to which branch he belonged.'

'Aye, well, he had the right pedigree and that's what's important. And he died, you say.'

She nodded. 'A week after we left Charleston,' she said, wording it to imply that Christopher had died on board ship while not actually telling an untruth. She imagined telling him the truth, and immediately cancelled the vision. Generous and loving he might be, but understanding he was not.

'And has he left you well taken care of—financially?'

Amanda sighed. Trust her father to think of the money aspect. He might bluster his way through his social life, but when it came to business he was deadly earnest. 'We—we were married for such a short time. Now he is dead I want to put it behind me. I don't expect or want anything from his family.'

Henry frowned, thinking this highly irregular, but, seeing how despondent she seemed and not wishing to distress her unduly, he decided to let the matter rest for the time being. No doubt Quinn would provide him with the details.

'Aye, well, I am sorry for your loss.'

Amanda nodded slightly, as if accepting his comfort. Inside she was full of self-disgust at deceiving her father.

'So, you are a Claybourne now. I suppose it will take

some getting used to. You're also a widow and will be of age soon. You're your own mistress and I can't stop you doing what you will.'

Amanda put her arms about his rotund middle and placed her head on his shoulder. 'I won't disappoint you, Father, I promise.'

Peering down at her, suddenly anxious, he said, 'It would be well for you to consider marrying again—and soon. I'm not getting any younger and I want to see you taken care of.'

'Never fear.' She laughed. 'You'll outlive us all—long enough to bounce your grandchildren on your knee.'

And so began a time of frenetic activity. Little was said of Amanda's marriage and her dead husband—the subject was for the curious to speculate about and for her to try to forget. Casting off her mourning clothes in favour of grey and any dark colour other than black—following the precedent set by Queen Victoria after the death of her beloved Albert— Amanda relaxed and prepared to enjoy herself, trying steadfastly to keep her thoughts from wandering back to Christopher Claybourne.

She wasn't always successful, for there were times when she recalled how his unfathomable eyes had locked on to hers as they had spoken their marriage vows, how, when he bent to kiss her lips, her own had parted and he stole her breath, taking it and more from her. She had never met anyone like him. There had been something in his eyes of another world to the one she knew—and she longed passionately to see it again, if only for a brief while.

Kit was the reason why she felt so restless and dissatisfied. All the young men she knew now seemed to her intolerably dull, contemptible, even, beside him.

Every time she found herself dwelling on Christopher Claybourne, in some peculiar way it felt as if he were trying to seduce her from beyond the grave. Angry with herself, at her own weakness, she would try to close her mind to him. It was incredibly stupid to think of her dead husband in this way, stupid and dangerous, too, for it only brought her torment and heartache.

Life was never dull at Eden Park. The house was used for entertaining on a vast scale, and whole sections had been set aside to accommodate staff, including the servants of weekend guests. Caroline had an enormous circle of friends and Amanda soon discovered that her stepmother's energy was boundless as she concentrated on providing entertainment guaranteed to attract both friends and neighbours.

Weather permitting, there were luncheons served at a long table under the trees on the lawn and picnics on the moors, with hampers filled with every kind of delicacy to tempt the appetite, from pâté and lobster to the finest claret. There was croquet on the smooth grass, the increasingly popular game of lawn tennis, swimming for the men in the lake; then there were village fêtes to attend, and, in the evenings, dinner parties, with a string quartet playing lilting music in the background.

Amanda embraced the countryside and the countryside embraced her. Heads turned wherever she went and she was creditably besieged by young men who flocked to her side. Courted and sought after, she enjoyed herself to such an extent that her life began to resemble an obstacle course, but she allowed none of the pressing young men to come too close. Her father was right. She was her own mistress and could do as she liked. She was in no hurry to wed again.

Chapter Four

Autumn passed into winter and a jolly Christmas came and went. Henry liked things to run smoothly at Eden Park and kept a busy schedule. He always allowed himself enough time to indulge his passion for horses, travelling to horse sales near and far in his desire to buy only the finest horse-flesh—hunters and Thoroughbreds alike. His search for a decent trainer wasn't so simple. There were plenty of clever, knowledgeable men he could take on for the task, but he was determined to hold out for the best.

Amanda, an accomplished rider, shared her father's love for the hunt, feeling there was no other thrill to compare with riding a courageous horse across fences and grass at speed, trying to keep up as close as possible to the pack of hounds hunting their fox. The challenge was manifest, the demands on her nerve clear, the test of her skill less easy to define, but the pleasure and thrill of the hunt were compounded of many other elements.

It was after one such day when they held the meet at Eden Park that Amanda went to her bed exhausted but content. A buffet had been provided for the hungry hunters of hot, spicy soup; roast beef; saddle of mutton, venison and pork and all the appropriate trimmings; cheese; jellies; tarts and pies for after. It had been a hectic day, with much hustle and bustle both above and below stairs as the servants worked feverishly to make sure everyone was replete with both food and drink.

The house was dark and totally silent when Amanda left her room. Surprised that she was unable to sleep following the day's excitement, she padded down to the kitchens as the grandfather clock in the hall struck midnight, thinking a cup of hot milk might solve the problem. Sitting before the fire that Cook had banked down before going to bed, in an astonishingly tidy kitchen with no sign of the earlier chaos, she sipped her milk, feeling the hot liquid relaxing her. She took a quicker route back to her room, going quietly up the back stairs and along a narrow landing that passed through the servants' quarters—not that many of the servants lived in at Eden Park. Most of them came from nearby Thurlow and went home after their day's work.

Listening carefully for any small sound that might indicate that someone else was awake, she squinted in the darkness, having to be careful where she trod. She was just coming to the end of the landing when she heard a sudden cry coming from a room on her right. It was softly uttered, as if someone were in pain, but trying to stifle it. Greatly concerned, she moved towards the door, turning the knob and opening it to investigate.

She halted abruptly at the sight that confronted her. At first she could see little, the only light coming from the dying embers in the hearth and a single lamp at the side of the bed. But then she saw two figures so entwined they could easily have been one. Totally immersed in each other they were unaware of her presence. Her eyes saw the voluptuous nakedness of a young woman lying on the softness of the sheets. Her head was flung back, her eyes closed, her face contorted with pleasure as the man moved rhythmically between her legs.

'My goodness, it's Sadie Jenkins,' Amanda gasped softly, unable to believe such wanton behaviour from a seventeen-year-old parlourmaid. The girl turned her head and half-opened her eyes. Amanda realised she must have heard her gasp. Sadie cried out in horror and began shoving at the man's shoulders to try to push him away.

Her face flaming with embarrassment, Amanda was about to leave, but at that moment, recognising the man as none other than Mr Quinn, anger took hold of her and all she could do was stare. She knew she had no business being here, that what the servants got up to when they were off duty was their own affair, but the nausea welling inside her kept her rooted to the spot.

Only slowly did the naked man become aware that there was someone standing in the open doorway. Turning his head, he saw Amanda, his face registering neither surprise nor shame. As if he had all the time in the world he rolled away from the girl, leaving her shapely young body defenceless and exposed. Not in the least discomposed, he pulled on a long robe that fastened with a belt around the middle, covering his nakedness. Amanda could see the smugness in his eyes; he was full of conviction, not remorse, for his actions.

Wrapping a sheet around her to cover her own nakedness, Sadie slipped off the bed and stood looking at Amanda with a light of defiance gleaming in her large dark eyes.

'Is this your room, Sadie?' Amanda demanded, struggling to sound calm and in control.

Sadie shook her head. 'No, mum. It's farther down the landing.'

'Then go to it. I will speak to Mr Quinn alone.'

Casting an indecisive glance at Mr Quinn, who indicated

with a slight nod that she should do as Mrs Claybourne bade, Sadie crossed to the door, the sheet trailing behind her.

'Just a minute, Sadie,' Amanda said. Sadie turned and looked at her. 'I thought you went home after work.'

'I do as a rule, Mrs Claybourne, but today being so busy and with so much to do, I promised Cook I'd stay on and help. Besides, Ma doesn't like me having to pass through the woods and by the lake, you see. She says there are too many scallywags roamin' about for a decent girl to be walking home alone after dark. Why, she says anything might happen.'

'I see. You may go.'

'How long have you been here?' Mr Quinn asked calmly when Sadie had closed the door behind her. 'And by what right do you spy on me in my private rooms?'

Undaunted, Amanda lifted her head with a small but stubborn toss. 'I have been here long enough to see the shameful thing you have done. Sadie is young enough to be your daughter. What were you thinking?'

Mr Quinn threw up his hands. 'Amazing! A proper little prude! And you a married woman,' he mocked. 'Sadie is seventeen going on thirty. Did she look ashamed to you?'

Recalling the way Sadie had thrown back her shoulders and lifted her head, her action had told Amanda quite clearly that she was neither ashamed nor regretful.

Mr Quinn smiled, a smug, self-satisfied smile that infuriated Amanda. 'She wanted it as much as I did. It was not the first time and it will not be the last. But if you must prowl around after dark, to save any embarrassment on your part, I would advise you to confine yourself to your own part of the house—unless, of course, you were looking for something that might be of more interest to your habits.'

Amanda seethed. How dare the man take the offensive by

accusing her of creeping about the house and spying on the servants? 'You forget yourself, Mr Quinn. My father will have harsh words to say to you about this.'

'Really?' He lowered his head, becoming thoughtful. Henry O'Connell was the only man Quinn had any regard for, and he had never told anyone the role that his employer had played in his life, or the gratitude Quinn felt for him. However, over the years since he had begun working for Henry, he had acquired a good, strong foothold both in the business and with Henry. Yes, it was a good, strong foothold and it was not a position he was prepared to relinquish because this girl could not keep her mouth shut.

'Now listen to me,' he said, moving closer until he towered over her. 'Your father must never hear of this. You must never tell him what you have seen.'

'But I have a duty to tell him what goes on beneath his roof, especially something as sordid as this. He does not condone this kind of behaviour among the servants and you, more than anyone, should know that. You hold a position of trust in this house, and you have just breached it.'

'Have I? We shall see. Who do you think will benefit from the confession? Certainly not Sadie or her poor, misbegotten family that depends on what she earns here. If she is thrown out, there'll be no work for her in any other house. Would you want that on your conscience—to see her family go to the workhouse? Think what it will mean. The story will become common gossip. Oh, no, Amanda, for her sake—and your own—you must say nothing.'

Amanda looked at him steadily. His words sounded like a threat. 'What do you mean—for my sake?'

He gave a small, corrosive laugh. 'I mean, I wonder how your father will react when he learns of your own guilty little secret—you know…about what you got up to in Charleston.'

Watching her face with idle malice, he saw it change, grow pale, then freeze.

'You would not tell him about that?'

'Not if you keep your mouth shut about Sadie and me. You have much to be grateful to me for on that matter; when Henry questioned me, I told him Mr Claybourne was an English gentleman, well connected, and with sufficient means to keep his daughter in the manner in which she had been raised. Since he has done nothing about that, I can only assume he has decided to let the matter of your marriage rest. So, you see, you owe me. For your silence we both stand to gain something, and you will have nothing to fear from me.'

Amanda saw a viciousness in Mr Quinn's expression she had never seen before. She had known this man nearly all her life. She couldn't credit what he was saying and the coldness in his eyes. She knew she was trapped. Caution alone trimmed her anger. If this was to be the price of her silence, then so be it.

Mr Quinn read her thoughts correctly. 'I see we understand each other.'

'Oh, yes. I understand perfectly, Mr Quinn,' she replied tersely.

'Good. Then if you don't mind, my time has been disturbed quite enough for one night. But one thing before you go. I need no instructions from you on how to conduct myself in public or in private. Remember that.'

'Oh, I will. I can see you are quite besotted with Sadie, but you're a little long in the tooth, don't you think, to turn lovesick over a seventeen-year-old girl with a well-rounded bosom.'

'I assure you I am not in my dotage yet. Sadie will attest to that.'

'I'm sure she can, but I have no intention of asking her. Goodnight.'

With an artificially subservient sweep of his arm as she left, Mr Quinn bade her goodnight.

Making her way through the house to her room, Amanda now realised that she had never given much thought to Mr Quinn as being anything other than her father's most trusted employee who always kept himself aloof and apart from the lowlier servants, but beneath his austere mien he was nothing but a brute.

By the time she reached her room she had come to accept that the bringing of the incident to her father's attention would do her no good. What mattered was that her marriage to Kit must not be brought into the open. She realised that she must never divulge what she had seen and must subdue her own feeling of outrage, wiping the sordid incident from her mind; but she would never forget and never, ever, forgive Mr Quinn for daring to think he could threaten her with exposure to cover his own sordid misdeed.

On a cold day in February, tired of being cooped up in the house, buttoning herself into a warm coat and heading for the stables, Amanda went in search of her father. There had been a rainstorm earlier, but now the land glinted and shone beneath the sun's glow. Yesterday two horses he had bought at the Doncaster horse sales had arrived, and along with the animals a man to look after them. A man, her father had proclaimed excitedly, who knew more about training horses than anybody he knew.

Standing beneath the foggy green shadow of massive ancient oaks, she paused, her eyes drawn to her father. Wearing a chequered cape and hat, he was leaning on his walking stick, looking over the fence into the paddock. Amanda shifted her gaze to see what held his attention.

Two splendid horses caught her eye, one a rich chestnut and the other a glistening black stallion with a man astride its back.

It was a fine, spirited beast, tossing its noble head and twitching its tail. Fighting the bit, the animal bucked and pranced sideways and then reared up. Amanda was spellbound as she watched the rider, with spontaneous talent, master that huge, half-wild horse with superb skill. Riding with the easy grace of a man in perfect harmony with his own body, he was obviously a genius. Eventually he brought the animal under control so that it became almost docile. Sliding off, he dug into his pocket and produced a tasty titbit. The horse looked at him suspiciously before curling his top lip and eating it.

When the man strode over to her father, Amanda was about to turn away, not wishing to interrupt, when something about the man, something familiar, caught her attention, causing her eyes to open wide in overwhelming disbelief.

Immobilised in the cataclysmic silence that seemed to descend on her world, her right hand pressed to her throat, she was rendered incapable of thought, speech or action. As her mind raced in wild circles, her thoughts tumbling over themselves, she thought she must be seeing things, that she must be suffering from some kind of delusion. But that rich dark brown hair, rough and tousled, his harshly angular face, the hardness that was an integral part of him, the arrogant way he held his head—surely there could be no other man like that anywhere. Suddenly and quite inexplicably, Amanda's heart gave a joyful leap, but as quickly as a cry sprang to her lips, so it was silenced. Shock waves tingled up and down her spine and she wondered at this cruel trick of fate.

Christopher Claybourne—Kit, her husband—was alive and well. But how could this be? The shock that he was made her forgetful of the soft meanderings of her mind whenever she thought of him. Now his very name scalded her being with hot indignation, and she wanted to scream in utter rage. Of all the people her father could have hired to train his horses, why did it have to be him? She looked this way and that for a means of escape, but her father had seen her and was beckoning.

Reluctantly, her tension mounting, she walked towards them. Christopher climbed over the fence and stood beside her father, watching her approach, so sleek, so confident, so devilishly attractive in his riding jacket and breeches and tan leather boots. In fact, with his wicked smile and hair tumbling darkly about his face, all he needed was a ring in his ear to make him a handsome buccaneer. The man she had seen in prison in his shabby garb was gone for ever—metamorphosed into this taut and fine-drawn man of steel and iron.

Please, God, Amanda thought with a feeling of terror of what his appearance could mean for her, don't let him have told Father who he is. What did he want? What was he doing here—with her father?

Wide awake to the implications of his reappearance into her life, she stopped in front of them. Her heart set up a wild beating as she looked up into her husband's face. Something in his bold look challenged her spirit and increased her ire.

Taking her arm, her father drew her closer. 'Amanda, it pleases me greatly to introduce to you Kit Benedict. He's the man I told you about who's to train my horses. Many of them are novices and need bringing on, so he's going to have his work cut out.'

Yes, Amanda thought, he had told her how he had met someone at the sales who was more than willing to work for him, but she had only listened with half an ear. Now she looked at Kit directly, into his dark eyes set beneath sweeping brows. His look was in no way threatening, yet there was a sense of force distilled and harnessed in his stance. His lips curved as he bowed his head, his eyes never leaving hers.

To Kit at that moment, this woman, his wife, was the most ravishing beauty he had ever seen, and despite her delicate features and soft olive green eyes and the rosy softness of her full lips, there was a boldness and confidence about her look he well remembered from his prison cell. Her long hair hanging down her back was as straight as a horse's tail and quite astonishing—a hundred different shades and dazzling lights, ever changing in the sun's glow. He could not decide if it was wine red, claret or the deepest colour of burgundy.

'I am honoured to meet you, Miss O'Connell.'

There was no denying the reality of that familiar deep voice. Her face expressionless, Amanda merely inclined her head slightly in acknowledgment.

'Nay, not O'Connell, Kit. My daughter's Mrs Claybourne—sadly a widow, but 'tis not a permanent state, is it, daughter? Though you seem to be in no hurry to be acquiring another husband.'

Amanda looked at her father and her eyes flared. 'It will be as permanent as I want it to be, Father. It is not that I oppose the institution, but I am in no hurry to relinquish my single state just yet.'

'Aye, well—' Henry chuckled in good humour, his nose red from the cold as he winked at Kit '—it becomes apparent to me that you've an error in your way of thinking. What say you, Kit?'

Kit seemed to digest his words with a certain amount of knowing amusement. The quirk in his lips deepened as he peered at Amanda enquiringly. 'Perhaps your daughter's experience of marriage was not to her liking and she is reluctant to repeat it.'

Amanda responded with a feigned smile. 'My marriage did not last long enough for me to form an opinion of it one way or another, Mr—Benedict.'

Consulting the huge turnip-size watch he carried in his waistcoat, Henry frowned. 'I must be getting back to the house. I've my lawyer coming from Manchester to talk over some affairs. He should be here any time so I'll be off.' He glanced at the two of them. 'Stay and let Kit show you my latest acquisitions, Amanda,' he said, beginning to walk off, 'and you can give me your verdict over dinner.'

Watching her father's retreating figure, Amanda was alone with her husband for the first time in seven months, alarmingly, nerve-rackingly alone. 'Please tell me I'm not dreaming. I truly thought I would never see you again,' she said, determined to speak to him with a calm maturity and not to let her anger and confused emotions get the better of her. It was important that she made it absolutely clear to him that she wanted no part of him, that she was not his responsibility. 'I thought you were dead.'

'As you see, my dear wife, I am very much alive.' He cocked a handsome brow as he gave her a lengthy inspection, his teeth gleaming behind a lopsided grin. 'Even the best-laid plans go astray. My reprieve came when Judd Freeman sailed into Charleston Harbour.' His expression became serious. 'I want to thank you for taking care of Sky. You did an excellent job and she speaks of you with affection.'

Mention of the little girl Amanda had missed after their parting caused her heart to stir. 'I'm surprised she remembers me after all these months. How is she? Better now she has her father, I know.'

'She is well—and happy with Victoria. Sky is a resilient child; apart from missing me, the removal from everything and everyone familiar to her has left her with no apparent ill effects.'

'I'm happy to hear that. So what now? What are your plans?'

'I've returned to England to reclaim the life I was raised to live—and to become reacquainted with my wife. I do not expect you to fling yourself into my arms and weep tears of joy on my return, but to hear you say that you are pleased to see me would have a nice ring to it.'

Amanda stiffened. 'You speak as if you have already decided the course of our future.'

Christopher passed his hazel, dancing eyes over her face, heedful of the wrath gathering pace in her expression. 'I have. You are my wife, after all.' His voice was soft, though knowingly chiding.

As dearly as Amanda wished to fling an angry denial in his face, she could not. The truth of it stung, but she was determined she would have it otherwise. 'In name only. You did me a great service in exchanging marriage vows and so making it possible for me to escape an intolerable situation at the time. I am grateful to you for that, but that is where it must end. I did as you asked and brought your child safely to England. Be content with that and let us put an end to the charade—the pretence that there can ever be anything between us.'

Kit's hazel eyes were suddenly cold under the dark flare of his brows. 'Believe me, Amanda, it is no pretence. We made a pact. Part of our bargain was that our marriage would be legal and binding for the time I have left to live—and I fully intend to be around until I'm ninety. On my reprieve I hoped I wasn't mistaken in you, and that you were the type who would keep a bargain, who wouldn't forget important promises, whose word when given meant something, which to me was as binding as the marriage vow itself. When I came back to England and thought of you and Sky waiting, I thought I had something to come home to. You promised me that if I succeeded in securing my freedom, you would acknowledge me as your husband and become my wife in truth. All this was in return for my name—my family name, a name I honour.'

'Then do you set so little worth on your family's honour that you will hold me to an arrangement made in desperation?'

'My family's honour!' He gave a humourless laugh. 'If you

knew anything about my family's honour, you would close your mouth rather than ask such a damning question.'

Amanda was momentarily taken aback by the ferocity of his statement. She was curious as to where the remark had come from, but quickly thrust it from her mind. 'I know nothing of your family and care not at all. I am only interested in putting an end to the arrangement we made.'

'So you do not deny that we made a pact?'

'No, that I cannot do,' she lashed out in anger, with a thrust to her chin that told him she was ready to fight. 'I know I am bound by my word, but it is hard for me.'

'You belong to me, Amanda.'

'That is a matter of opinion. Yes, we had an arrangement, an arrangement that profited us both. I cannot yield to a man who, at best, is a stranger to me.'

Christopher peered at her closely and took note of her sudden uneasiness. 'I will not always be a stranger. I delivered on our bargain, only to find you reneging on your vow. Do not imagine that you can rescript the rules to suit yourself. How do you feel now you find I am alive?'

'Cheated,' she spat. 'Cheated—and I want no part of you.'

'Come now, Amanda, why so hostile? We have a lot to discuss, you and I.'

Mutinously she glared at him. 'I have nothing to discuss with you. Nothing at all. You were supposed to hang, leaving me a widow. This was not part of my plan. I did not want this.'

The hazel eyes sparked. 'You mean you want me dead?'

'Yes—I mean, no— Oh, I am so confused I don't know what I mean. I just want you to go away—to leave me alone. I don't want a husband.'

'Be that as it may, Amanda,' he said lazily, 'but you have a husband—and he is not going to go away.'

'He will if I have my way. I don't want you. You will not

have me. What are you doing here anyway? How have you managed to wheedle your way into my father's favour?'

'Our mutual interest in horses.'

'I advise you to have a care. Father will treat you with the same courtesy he shows to anyone in his employ—as long as he has no inkling that there is anything except casual friendship between the two of us. If he so much as suspects there is anything between us, he will treat you with freezing contempt.'

'I'll risk it.' Beneath a raised quizzical brow his gaze travelled over her beautifully cut coat of dark blue-coloured tweed that flared out from the waist over her high-necked grey dress. 'I was under the impression that a period of one year's mourning is customary after the death of one's immediate family,' he remarked with underlying sarcasm.

'I am in half-mourning. I do try to observe the rules even though I can see no point in doing so. After all, I am no grieving widow. How dare you come here? You cannot stay. You must leave at once.'

'Your father has hired me to train his horses. I aim to do just that.'

Amanda didn't believe him. His meeting with her father had been by design rather than chance, this she was sure of— so what did he want? Could he be bribed to go away?

His face hardened, as if he had read her thoughts. 'Do not think you can buy me off, Amanda. No amount of money you offer will tempt me to disappear now that I have found you.'

'Why not? Your promise to stay out of my life in exchange for a few thousand pounds seems fair enough trade to me.'

'I am not going to go away, so you'd save yourself a great deal of trouble and heartache if you got used to having me around. I will make it impossible for you to ignore me. Everywhere you go you will be aware of me, of my presence, watching you.'

'Like a rat nibbling away at a floorboard, you mean.'

He laughed softly. 'Aye—with flawless success.'

The olive green eyes narrowed in a glare. 'You're pig-headed, arrogant and impossibly conceited, Kit Benedict. I will not be your wife.'

'There I must contradict you. Pigheaded I may be, but you are my wife.'

'And you seem to take a special delight in reminding me,' she remarked drily. 'I am your wife in name only.'

'Which I intend to rectify as soon as can be.' His lips curled into a rakish smile as his eyes captured hers. 'I'm already looking forward to it. I find the mere thought of marriage to you most entertaining. I think we shall do very well together. You're looking beautiful, Amanda. Just as I remembered.'

'And you're looking disgustingly smug and self-righteous.'

Leaning back against the fence, he folded his arms across his broad chest, grinning leisurely as his perusal swept her. 'I have plenty to be smug about. I am a man, Amanda,' he assured her softly, the laughter gone from his voice, 'with all the desires, all the needs of a man. When you came to my prison cell, when I first saw you, you were so beautiful it tortured me. You captured my thoughts, my dreams, my fancy, and when you left me I became hopelessly entangled in my desires for you. You made me want, made me yearn for things I could not have. Now I can. I want you.'

Amanda was taken aback by his blunt honesty. 'I am surprised. I never imagined I had made so deep an impression.'

'The very knowledge that you are here with me now makes me even more determined to find a way of breaching that barrier of thorns you have wound about yourself.' As her husband, he could insist she kept her side of the bargain, but some inbuilt sense of chivalry prevented him from doing so, dictating that if she came to him under duress it would only increase her resentment. 'Yet I must accept the fact that your shock of finding me alive has been great and that you are confused. I have no wish to cause you any embarrassment. I even gave your father an assumed name.'

'How thoughtful of you, but it isn't assumed, is it? You've merely omitted your surname.'

'Which I share with you.'

'I have no wish for my father to find out who you are. He has no idea. It would distress him terribly.'

Kit's eyes grew warm as he gave her a lazy smile. 'I am no black-hearted villain, and I accept there are times when it is expedient to hold back the truth—for the present. However, you, my dear Amanda—'

Her expression was mutinous. 'I am not your dear anything.'

'As I was saying, you, my dear Amanda, seem to have a penchant for self-destruction. Better to have told your father the truth in the first place. He will find out one day, that I promise you. We are man and wife and must live as man and wife.' He shrugged. 'That equation seems perfectly logical to me, though not apparently to you. You are going to be difficult?'

'I am going to be impossible.'

He smiled at that, not in the least discouraged. 'Then it should be interesting getting to know one another. In time I shall insist on you becoming my wife in truth.'

'And if I don't comply?'

'If you don't, then I will confront your father.'

There was a wealth of warning in the words the deep voice uttered and no drawl to soften them. Swirling round in a flurry of skirts, Amanda tossed him a cool glance askance. 'Then for the time being don't get any high-minded ideas that you're any better than any other hired help.' She was about to walk away, but whirled round when Kit's hand suddenly shot out and gripped her arm like a vice.

'I am trying to be patient with you, Amanda,' he said quietly, 'but you're trying me sorely. Now listen to me and don't anger me. For the present I am happy to work for your father. I shall train his horses and train them well, but I will not be treated like an underling. Rest assured that, despite my time spent in the Smoky Mountains with the Cherokee, I am quite civilised. I will not be dictated to by anybody—especially not by my own wife, whose schooling in manners appears to be somewhat lacking. I trust I've made myself abundantly clear?'

Amanda yanked her arm from his grasp, her eyes spitting fire. 'Perfectly. Good day to you, Mr Benedict.'

'And good day to you, my loving wife. A pleasure meeting you again.' He chuckled aloud as he watched and admired the indignant sway of her hips as she left him, which, to his sceptical mind, was the most piquant of provocations. It was clear that a submissive, compliant wife Amanda was not. She was like a vixen, fierce and ready to fight, and he thanked God for it; he wanted her to match him strength for strength, as an equal, and in that, he was not going to be disappointed. But first he must show her that no matter how hard and furiously she fought against him, she was his wife.

He grinned broadly, totally assured in his arrogant masculinity that he would have his way, no matter what.

Kit's low, mocking laughter followed Amanda all the way back to the house and for a long time after. Cursing beneath her breath, she fed her wrath as she stalked homeward with her fists clenched by her sides. Be damned if she'd discuss their marriage any further, not until she'd had time to face the rest of her emotions and consider the best way forward. The matter was complicated, but it must be resolved somehow.

The trouble was that since her marriage, which had

brought her independence, she had become herself again and valued her freedom, and she was regretful and resentful that she would now have to set it all aside. She realised she wasn't being fair to Kit—but then life wasn't always fair, and her father had been right when he had said that to succeed in life you had to be ruthless. He might have been referring to the world of business, but Amanda would apply it to her personal life.

Still fuming silently to herself and a mass of conflicting emotions, she found her father in the hall still waiting for his lawyer to arrive. Amanda appeared before him looking for all the world like she'd like to commit murder and proceeded to speak without thinking, to act without considering the consequences.

'I'm sorry, Father,' she flared when he enquired why she was looking as cross as a bucket full of crabs, 'but I think Mr Benedict is overbearing. He is also insufferably arrogant and I cannot see why you like him. You must dismiss him at once and find someone else.'

Henry looked at her as though she'd taken leave of her senses. His daughter seemed to be in the grip of a fury and to have lost all reasonableness. Her anger was out of all proportion to what appeared to be a perfectly normal and innocent situation.

'Don't be absurd, Amanda. Kit hasn't been on the place two minutes and already you find fault with the man. What the devil has happened between the two of you? Has he offended you—made untoward suggestions?'

Amanda could feel the pull of her explosive fury dragging her into further turmoil, but somehow she must control it and be careful. 'No, no, nothing like that,' she hastened to assure him, softening her tone, not wishing to give away anything about her relationship with Kit and hoping she sounded convincing. 'In fact, his manners are in order. But surely you don't need him. You know enough about horses to train them yourself. You were doing splendidly before he arrived.'

'Nay, lass,' he said, his tone reproachful. 'Kit is a man of good and able character. He also has a good mind and a deeper understanding of horses than I ever will. He'll prove his worth to me in no time—even suggested we get one of them trained up in time for next year's Gold Cup at Ascot,' he said, rubbing his hands and puffing his chest out with glee at the mere thought. 'Think about it, Amanda—me—with a runner in the Gold Cup. Aye, it'll be a proud moment—so it will.'

'I agree, Father, but—where is Mr Benedict to live?'

'I've thought of that. I've put at his disposal a nice little furnished cottage in the park—close to the stables. He'll be comfortable enough there.'

Yes, Amanda thought crossly, he would be—right on her doorstep. 'I still think you could manage to get your horses to the standard required without Mr Benedict's help.'

Henry looked at his daughter for a moment, his eyes piercing her through. 'Impossible. Kit is an expert in buying, selling and management and has all the expertise to be a racehorse trainer in his own right. I want only top-class horses in my stable and to do that I need him. He also has a young daughter who is being taken care of by a cousin of his—his wife died some time ago, so he's going to need time off occasionally to see her. Have you such a strong aversion to the man?'

Simmering in her breast, tightening with pressure, was the urge to blurt out the truth into his innocent face, that he was being deceived, but she bit her tongue and damned the truth inside her. 'Well—no—not really, only—'

'Then he stays—and as my daughter you will be as gracious towards him as you are to any other guest I invite to the house. Which reminds me—he will be dining with us tonight, so ask Caroline to have an extra place set at the table.

It seems senseless for him to dine alone when we have food going spare.'

Having delivered that diatribe, he went to the door to greet his lawyer, who was just arriving.

Amanda received the news that Kit was to dine with them with less enthusiasm than she would a public flogging. Seeking some outlet for her indignation, she headed towards Caroline and her father's suite of rooms, and found Caroline in her sitting room of gold leaf and pink-and-white furnishings, décor that suited her stepmother's lavishly feminine temperament exactly. Sifting through some correspondence, she looked up and smiled, but the smile faded when she saw Amanda looking down in the mouth and her dark eyes sparking with ire.

Having become well used to and tolerant of father and daughter's altercations, which always ended up in laughter, she said, 'Oh, dear. What's Henry done to upset you this time?'

'He's invited his new horse trainer to dinner tonight, Caroline, and has asked me to tell you to have another place set at the table. Doesn't he realise that it's highly irregular for an employee to join the gentleman of the house and his family for meals?'

The vehemence in Amanda's tone quite startled Caroline. 'Why, Amanda, you sound quite heated. I had no idea you would mind so much. I suppose it is rather unconventional; nevertheless, Henry has a high opinion of Mr Benedict, so you must be prepared to endure him without complaint as best you can—for your father's sake.'

Seeing she wasn't going to acquire an ally in Caroline, Amanda sighed. 'I suppose I must, but I do hope he isn't going to make a habit of inviting the servants to dine with us,' she retorted ungraciously.

* * *

When Amanda entered the drawing room at seven o'clock she was disappointed to find Kit alone and was immediately put out, although she could feel his presence in her home with every fibre of her being. It was difficult to believe that this extremely handsome, fashionably dressed man was the convict Christopher Claybourne.

The rustle of her taffeta gown caught Kit's attention. Glancing up he immediately put his drink down, for the apparition in the doorway in an amethyst gown, cut low to reveal her white shoulders, was like a jewel set against a background of unashamed opulence, wiping his mind clear of anything but sheer appreciation. His lips curving in a slow, appreciative smile, he came across to meet her while his eyes plumbed the depths of her beauty, touching her all over, giving her the sensation of being naked.

'It's a pleasure to meet you again, Amanda. The servant who let me in informed me that your father and his wife have been detained by a domestic matter and will join us presently. May I say how lovely you look.'

Amanda gritted her teeth and forced a smile to her lips. Never had a man looked so attractive and never had her heart called out so strongly to anyone. As she looked into his eyes, all at once she knew she must fight her attraction for him.

'You can say what you like just so long as you stop ogling me like that.'

'I'd be a fool to ignore the way you look,' he answered smoothly, his grin mockingly congenial as he affectionately reached out and chucked her under the chin, which made Amanda step back, torn between giving him a kick in the shin or slapping his face.

'You really are the most unmannerly of men,' she hissed, thankful that her father and Caroline were not present. 'Kindly keep your hands to yourself. Did you have to accept my father's invitation to dine?'

'My dear wife,' Kit murmured. 'It is not for inferiors like me to refuse the powers that be. That is not a right expected of underlings such as myself.'

His voice was soft, casual, but his face was serious, and Amanda mistrusted the gleam of mocking humour lurking in his gaze. 'I'm sure you could have found an excuse if you'd wanted to. I have no doubt that you accepted just to annoy me.'

'Not at all. I was delighted to join such gracious and delightful company.'

'Do you have to look so pleased with yourself?' she snapped irately. 'You must forgive me, Mr Benedict. I don't often find myself entertaining my father's employees.'

'I will not argue the point, but I scarcely suspect that my mere presence at your dinner table can disrupt the smooth running of things, however much you may wish to claim it will. But worry not, my pet. I shall not expose your most intimate secrets to the scrutiny of your father just yet. You have my word that I shall comport myself with such dignity and propriety that you need have no fear that I shall make a fool of either of us.'

'As long as you realise this is just dinner and certainly no high affair—and as long as you don't smell of the barn, I suppose I can tolerate you. I find it difficult coming to terms with your presence at Eden Park—or the fact that they didn't hang you,' she uttered scathingly. 'Your guardian angel has a lot to answer for.'

'She did work overtime to get me acquitted,' Kit replied in undaunted spirits, his eyes gleaming devilishly. 'Come, my love, stop scowling at me and try smiling. Your father will arrive at any minute and he has sharp eyes.'

Amanda obliged—albeit reluctantly. 'I suppose there is nothing like a bright smile to confuse an adversary.'

'Or charm a friend,' he countered.

'You are not my friend.'

'No, I am much more than that, so don't fight me, Amanda,' he said softly, his voice a caress.

'But I *will*,' she said vehemently. 'I will fight you with every ounce I possess.'

He smiled. 'Then do so, my love. Torment me all you like—I may even come to enjoy it—but in the end you will be mine. It is your destiny.'

His statement was said with such certainty that Amanda chose to let him have the last word on the subject—for now. This was neither the time nor the place to become embroiled in an argument about their marriage. 'I trust you find your accommodation to your liking. You are comfortable in your cottage?'

The sweetness of her tone did not conceal the sneer she intended. Kit smiled in the face of it. 'Perfectly, thank you. I'm looking forward to showing you around.'

Amanda met his eyes unwillingly and saw they were as teasing as a small boy's. 'I don't think so. You really are conceited, Mr Benedict. I cannot think of anyone who has gained my father's interest as you have done.'

'Amanda!' Overhearing his daughter's remark as he came in with Caroline on his arm, Henry was reproachful. 'You will watch your tongue and be gracious to Mr Benedict. Employee he might be, but he is also my guest.'

'Of course. I apologise if I seemed rude, Mr Benedict. I did not mean to cause offence.'

As before, the sweetness of her tone did not conceal the sneer she intended. Kit smiled again. 'None taken, Mrs Claybourne.'

Dinner was announced and they proceeded to the dining room, Caroline escorted by Kit and Amanda by her father. Once seated, Amanda demurely arranged her skirts, and when she looked up she met Kit's amused regard across the table as he took his seat. Henry was seated at one end of the dining table and Caroline at the other, from where she nodded at the servants to pour the wine and begin serving.

Content to let Caroline carry on an animated conversation, playing the perfect hostess with a natural flare and elegance she admired, Amanda treated Kit with polite reserve. For most of the time she was distant and ignored him as best she could, but it was no easy matter, for he sat with the infuriatingly natural relaxed elegance of a gentleman born and bred.

As he conversed with her father, somewhere in the past he had obviously acquired a social polish and smooth urbanity that amazed her. He was perfectly able to converse on everything as well as equestrian matters. In fact, he was the perfect guest, with a natural manner that Amanda reluctantly admired.

'You are certainly well informed on most subjects, Mr Benedict,' she couldn't help commenting when he had just finished discussing the present government and what he thought about the Prime Minister, Mr Gladstone's, second ministry.

Kit smiled at her with bland amusement. 'I know how to read as well as the next man—and educated woman,' he added as an afterthought. 'However, the fact remains that no matter how well educated a woman is she will some day have to submit to the authority of her husband.'

Amanda's face snapped into a familiar expression of rebelliousness—familiar to her father at least. 'Some may well do that, but I never will,' she quipped haughtily.

'Really?' Kit mocked, meeting her gaze as he spooned the last of his soup into his mouth, his eyes holding a subtle challenge. 'You may find that your husband has something to say about that.'

'Amanda means it,' Henry chuckled. 'Self-willed, she is, and defiant and argumentative. Goes her own way, she does, and the devil take the rest. There are times when I wonder how

I bred such a daughter. I sent her to Charleston to stay with her aunt, hoping she would meet some personable young man, marry him and settle down and present me with grandchildren. She completed the first part, but unfortunately the young man expired shortly after the wedding without my meeting him—which I regret.'

Amanda toyed with her food, not looking at the man opposite, who was watching her like a cat watching a mouse. How she wished he was back in Charleston Gaol where he belonged.

'Your husband has been dead long, Mrs Claybourne?' Kit enquired, placing his spoon down and lounging back in his chair.

'Seven months,' she answered tightly, without looking at him.

'A tragedy it was,' Henry remarked. 'She's far too young to be a widow.'

'I'm sure Mr Benedict doesn't want to hear about that, Father. Besides, I still find any discussion concerning my dear departed husband quite upsetting.' Consciously feigning a sigh, smiling wistfully and dropping her eyes, she said, 'I'm sure you understand, don't you, Mr Benedict?'

Kit's eyes waited on her words, cynical amusement in them, and when she fell silent he said, 'Oh, absolutely, Mrs Claybourne. Absolutely. It is no easy matter losing someone you care for—and of course you must have loved your husband dearly,' he said with elaborate gravity.

Seeing his mouth pulled down in mock-sympathy, Amanda felt a furious surge of indignation that he should think her such a fool as to have fallen in love with him. 'What my feelings were for my husband are my own affair, Mr Benedict. But it would be disrespectful of me to say I wasn't.'

Having been manoeuvred away from this particular discussion by a meaningful look from Caroline, Henry immediately launched into the subject closest to his heart and talked animatedly about his horses, so Amanda kept herself excluded, despite Kit's frequent attempts to draw her into the conversation. Her father didn't appear to notice how quiet she was, and if he did he would probably take it for ladylike reserve.

The meal was delicious and would have done credit to the finest chefs in the land—it must seem like a veritable feast, Amanda thought crossly, to the likes of Kit Benedict. As soon as she had spooned her last mouthful of raspberry meringue into her mouth she broke her self-imposed silence and stood up. Calmly excusing herself, she said she had letters to write that couldn't wait.

The moment she rose, her gaze met Kit's own—and Caroline almost saw the lightning flash that passed between them, causing a tension that held and held, teetering on the brink of—what? Catastrophe, or gathering strength for an assault on their emotions, their baser instincts?

Amanda spent the night tossing and turning in her bed, finding it impossible to dispel thoughts of Kit from her mind and unable to understand the turbulent, consuming emotions he was able to arouse in her. Just when everything was running smoothly, this arrogant man with mocking dark eyes and breezy, determined manner—and far too handsome for his own good—had forced his way back into her life.

She recalled the moment when she had risen from the table, the moment her frigid gaze had settled on his features. He had leaned back in his chair, fingering his wine glass. His gaze had raked over her with the leisure of a well-fed wolf, with an irritating smile flirting on his lips. The assured gleam in his eyes had told her he was not going to go away.

Chapter Five

During the days that followed Kit's arrival at Eden Park, Amanda scrupulously resolved that any future contact between them would be brief and impersonal. It was a decision made calmly and without emotion. But emotion set in whenever she set eyes on him. The effect he had on her, the emotional turmoil he evoked, was nothing short of frightening. In fact her thoughts were so preoccupied with him that she could not sleep.

Kit seemed to be everywhere and perfectly gauged, appearing when she least expected him, lolling on a tree or a fence somewhere, casually striding about the place as if he owned it in search of her father, not once stepping over the line, but for ever battering at her defences.

She was beginning to feel like a fox being run to earth by a pack of hounds, for she knew he was after total submission and Kit, in his supreme arrogance, knew he would succeed. She could see the sensuality behind every look and could no longer pretend that desire did not burn just beneath the surface in them both, waiting to flare into passion. There was nothing she could do to prevent it, to deny the hold he already had over her senses. Just when she had been enjoying her freedom he had arrived to disrupt her present contentment. Suddenly her future was precarious, her life beset with tension and apprehension, like a threatening storm on a hot and humid summer's day.

And Nan didn't make things any easier when she learned that Christopher Claybourne had returned from the dead. Shocked and shaken, Nan had no sympathy for her whatsoever, saying she had no one to blame for her predicament but herself, and that no good would come of it.

'The point is, Nan, what am I going to do?'

'As to that, no one can tell you. You will do what you want in the end.'

'Father is not going to know, Nan—at least, not yet,' Amanda said curtly. 'Unless you tell him.'

'I won't say anything,' Nan answered with an air of injured dignity. 'I am just warning you to have a care. I know your father has always allowed you to do much as you please, but that doesn't mean he's soft.'

'Neither am I,' Amanda said grimly.

Nan didn't reply, although she privately thought Amanda was storing up a world of trouble for herself.

Amanda was relieved that Nan promised not to tell a soul, and in particular Mr Quinn. Amanda sincerely hoped Mr Quinn had not met Kit in Charleston; if he had, he would recognise him immediately and her secret would be out.

Kit's feelings where Amanda was concerned, now he had seen her again, made him more determined than ever to make her fulfil her side of the bargain. Beautiful, intelligent, with a natural-born wit and as elusive as a shadow, she was a prize, a prize to be won. He tried telling himself that his growing fascination with his wife—a fascination that was becoming an obsession—was merely the result of the lust she had stirred in him in Charleston Gaol, but he knew it was more than lust that held him enthralled.

As he considered Amanda indisputably his, the days spent watching her were the ultimate in frustration. His expectations grew more definite by the day, increasingly becoming more difficult to subdue. He wanted her to be his completely, recognised as his, to openly establish the link between them as an accepted fact, but he must be patient since, contrary to what Amanda might think, she was not the only reason that had brought him to Eden Park.

However, he could not ignore the irritation and abrasion at watching other men dance attendance on her—a primitive reaction against any man casting covetous eyes on her.

Kit didn't dine at the house again. Amanda told herself that as an employee this was as it should be, but she was unable to quell her disappointment and he was conspicuous by his absence. She avoided him for days, although she could not stop thinking about him and allowed her imagination to torment her. Unbidden, his image would enter her mind—the hazel eyes flecked with gold, his rich dark brown hair and slanting grin. Her body responded to the image with a treacherous melting, while her emotions drifted through guilt and longing to self-exasperation.

Whenever she closed her eyes, flitting between conscious moments and her dreams, he haunted her. Maybe thoughts such as these were causing her irritating preoccupation with him. Perhaps if she could just see him she would be cured of it. And so, for the first time in a week, she went to the stables, hoping to catch a glimpse of him, intending to ride over the moors anyway.

With the addition of more and more horses, which meant

employment of more grooms and stable lads to look after them, the stables were a constant hive of industry. Amanda's gaze did a quick sweep of the yard and paddocks, hoping to see Kit's tall figure, but he wasn't there. When she casually enquired of a groom as to his whereabouts, he told her Mr Benedict had taken one of horses out on to the moors for some exercise. She was unprepared for the feeling of disappointment that swept through her.

In no time at all one of the lads had saddled her horse and she was cantering out of the yard. The landscape changed as she headed for the moors, scanning the unfolding hills for a horse and rider, but there was nothing, only sheep and the occasional farm with smoke curling from its chimney into a windless sky. She sighed, pointing her horse in the direction of the high peaks, still capped with winter snow. Kit could be miles away in any direction.

The sun had lifted and the day was crystal clear as Kit rode up the steep valley, the mount's hooves striking sharp against the rocks, and crackling bracken. He felt completely at home riding among the craggy hills that lay all about him and almost touched the clouds which raced above. The Derbyshire peaks were high and cold and breathtakingly beautiful. It was a wild, spacious terrain, with patches of woodland and open lakes. Here he felt completely at peace.

Why this should be so was no mystery to him since his incarceration. Crushed by the unsupportable distress his time in Charleston Gaol had caused him, he often came to the tranquil and everlasting peaceful valleys and hills to gain relief from the empty stillness, which was quite profound. The very power and strength of the rocky peaks, their durability, gave him hope for the future.

There were times when he was exercising one or another of

the mounts on the moors when he would see Amanda riding out, supple and trim in her tweed habit, and he would pause out of sight and drink in the sight of her. As she galloped over the rocky terrain, she rode like the wind, with the blind bravado of a rider who has never fallen off—and if she ever had fallen, it had been into the straw. The clash of his emotions as he watched her would leave him irritated and he had to struggle to stop himself breaking cover and riding out to meet her.

He was trying to do the right and honourable thing by keeping his distance, to give her time to get used to having him around. A lifetime of obeying the strictures of society, an exacting schooling, authoritarian grandparents and his mother, who imposed an upbringing of firm discipline, all served him well now, but fate and the adorable creature he was married to were conspiring to tease him. How much longer could he play the role of a civilised male while she tweaked and teased his baser instincts at every turn? Now, seeing her riding along the high ridge, tired of keeping out of her way until she deigned to seek him out, he rode towards her.

Having slowed her horse to a walk, the reins held loosely in her gloved hands, allowing the animal to choose the route among the raised boulders, Amanda heard the jingle of bridle and the snort of a horse before she saw him. She stopped abruptly, completely still, like a young deer aware of danger, knowing instinctively that it was Kit. Turning, she saw she was not mistaken.

He was riding a big mean hunter, a chestnut, with a rippling black mane and tail. The horse's sleek coat gleamed. She knew the animal because it was in the box next to the horse she always chose to ride. The chestnut was always much in evidence because it was highly strung. It was known as a notorious kicker and a bucker and the stable lads refused to ride it. Now, as she saw it striding along the ridge towards her, it was plain the man on its back today didn't mind because he could certainly ride.

She saw how Kit looked at one with the environment, as if he had been born to this untamed savagery, the rugged wildness matching his own. Attired in beige kid breeches, polished knee-length boots of brown leather and a riding jacket of green-and-brown tweed, he looked lean and hard and utterly desirable, exuding virility and a casual, lazy confidence. Sunlight burnished his thick dark brown hair flecked with gold.

Meeting his calm gaze, she felt an unfamiliar twist of her heart, an addictive mix of pleasure and discomfort. His warm, dark eyes looked at her in undisguised admiration as he drew alongside, a smile curving on his firm lips. Thinking how nice it would be to run her fingers through his wind-tousled hair and to feel those lips cover her own, Amanda could feel the colour tinting her cheeks despite all her efforts to prevent it. She did not want to feel that way—not about him.

Unaware of the thoughts his companion harboured, Kit kept his wicked stallion away from Amanda's more sedate mare.

'Good heavens, Kit,' she said, seeking refuge in anger to hide her discomfort, 'how you do love to take a person by surprise. Are you stalking me, by any chance?' The fact that he might be yielded a glare and a pert recommendation to mind his own business. He raised a dark brow and considered her flushed cheeks and soft, trembling mouth beneath the net of her black bowler. Damn the man, Amanda thought indignantly beneath his steady regard. She was certain he could read her mind.

'Since your mare was in the stable when I left, I could say the same of you. We do seem to be destined to meet in the most unusual places, do we not? I apologise if I startled you.'

'You are a long way from the gallops,' she remarked. 'Do you frequently ride so far from the stables?'

He nodded. 'I bring the horses on to the moors for exercise—and today I have the added bonus of meeting you. It is a pleasure to see you, Amanda—and all the better since we are quite alone and miles from anywhere.'

His tone of voice made her look more closely at him, at his dark gaze that gleamed beneath the well-defined brows. He looked back at her, a smile beginning to curve his lips. There was a withheld power to command in him that was as impressive as it was irritating. What kind of man are you, Kit Claybourne? Amanda asked herself, and realised she had no idea at all.

'Time has a habit of passing, Amanda,' he said, thinking how lovely she looked dressed in sapphire blue—a jacket bodice, a neat white cravat and a full-length skirt. 'We have been man and wife these seven months past. We have to talk, so stop being evasive. You cannot go on avoiding me or the issue. It will not go away, no matter how much you might wish it.'

Amanda's eyes narrowed and little pinpoints of fire gathered in their pupils. 'Not now,' she said, haughtily turning her head away from him and looking into the distance. 'You are ruining my ride and I would like to move on.'

Kit scowled darkly at her stubbornness. 'Then far be it from me to detain you—although on that particular matter I feel I must give you some advice and urge you to be more careful,' he admonished firmly, showing not the slightest inclination to move out or her way and let her ride on. 'Do not ride with such speed—especially up here on the ridge. Should you go over, 'tis a long way down. And nor should you ride alone. It's foolish at the best of times for a young woman to be seen riding without a groom in attendance, but up here among the crags it is highly dangerous. I'm surprised your father hasn't raised the matter. Should you take a tumble and injure yourself, there is no one to help. You could be up here for days before anyone found you—and even then it might be too late.'

Kit knew as he spoke that it would make no difference. What he had learned about his wife, having watched her and listened to Henry's constant appraisals of his lovely, wild young daughter, was that she railed against restrictions, that she was not pliant or submissive and was unwilling to be moulded to the whims of others, and that her actions often went well beyond the bounds of propriety.

Amanda's eyes flared angrily at his audacity, that he thought he had the right to chastise her. 'I find your concern rather touching, but I can do well without your advice. I am perfectly able to ride a few miles without mishap and without a man to protect me'—especially you, her expression seemed to say. It dared him to attempt to take control.

'I'm sure you can. Indeed, I would say you are of the nature to go looking for danger among the peaks, that you thrive on the danger that exists up here. But I still say you should not be roaming about up here alone.'

'Kit,' she exclaimed indignantly, ignoring the judicious set of his jaw, 'I would be obliged if you would mind your own business and stick to training my father's horses.'

'But you are my business, Amanda. As my wife, what you do concerns me, and when I see you doing things that are reckless and foolhardy I have every right and a responsibility to speak out. Come, I'll ride with you back to the house.'

'I'd rather you didn't. I came here to seek solitude, and if you were any sort of a gentleman you would leave me in peace. Besides, I'm not ready to go back yet.'

'Very well, but I insist on accompanying you—and I suggest we go to lower ground.' He looked sideways at her. 'You don't mind, I trust?'

She shrugged, urging her mount on. 'It would seem I have little choice.'

'No, you haven't.'

They followed a path that meandered down into a valley through which a river tumbled over its rocky bed. Kit paused to let his horse take a drink of the icy water. Amanda's horse did likewise. Kit swung lightly down from the saddle and left his mount to quench his thirst.

'What a lovely place this is,' he said, going to Amanda and holding up his arms to help her dismount. 'Come, let's walk a while.'

'Only if you are prepared to be civil and not chastise me.'

'I shall endeavour to be as charming as my nature will allow.'

Amanda looked at him with doubt. She slid from her horse into his arms and quickly sidestepped out of them. Removing her hat and hooking it over the pommel on the saddle, she walked towards the river and sat on an accommodating boulder, gazing out across the hills surrounding the valley. The view was beautiful, wild and verdant, and the only sound to disturb the peace was the sound of the river as it hurried on its way. Kit stood with one shoulder negligently propped against a tree, close to her rock, his arms folded across his chest, watching her, wanting more than anything to go to her and snatch her into his arms and kiss her senseless.

'Are you still angry with me for trying to assert my authority over you up on the ridge?' he asked.

There was a moment of silence. Amanda gazed at him. His voice was deep, throaty and seductive, a voice that made you think of dark, cosy places and highly improper things, and Amanda knew there weren't many women who could resist a voice like that, and not if the man speaking looked like Kit Benedict. Not if he had warm hazel eyes flecked with green, not if he was over six feet tall and built like a Greek athlete of old. He was dazzling, and Amanda knew she was not as immune to that potent masculine allure as she would like to believe.

'I am,' she replied in answer to his question, her animosity fading as warmth seeped through her system. 'But I realise you only said what you did out of concern. Tell me, do you like working for my father?'

'Of course. Henry is a fine man, easy to get on with, and he has a love of horses to equal my own.'

'Chosen by you, mostly. You have a way with them, I am told. Father says you can have the most spirited mount eating out of your hand in no time at all.'

'How I wish it was as easy to gentle my wife,' he murmured. 'I think you have the loveliest eyes I have ever seen and I like the way they sparkle when you laugh, and darken with desire—as they did on the day we were wed and we were close. I remember an unbelievable softness when I kissed your lips, and a warmth the likes of which set my heart afire.'

A wicked grin highlighted his lips as he glanced at her. 'I also like the way you look in your riding habit, and if you do not stop looking at me as you are doing at this moment, I am going to come and sit with you on that rock. Since meeting you again, I frequently see your eyes flashing with defiance and anger—now they are dark with some emotion I know I have caused.'

Amanda felt the soft caress of his gaze. Visions of him coming to sit beside her rose to alarming prominence in her mind. Hoping that by speaking in a calm, reasonable voice, rather than crossly protesting his statement, she could take the heat, the seduction out of his words, she said, 'You are very eloquent, Kit, but please don't go on.'

His voice took on a lighter note and his eyes twinkled with golden flecks of mischief. 'I am a wilful, determined man, Amanda—you should know that by now. We will take our relationship a step at a time, but my feelings will neither yield nor change.' Before she could voice another objection, he quickly switched tactics.

'I enjoy my work with the horses. They have always been a part of my life—often a necessary part. Henry spends a good deal of time at the stables, watching them exercise and often riding out himself. I can only assume he has an understanding wife.'

'She is—very understanding. In fact, she encourages him. Caroline doesn't share his love of horses and doesn't care to ride.'

'Nevertheless, they seem happy—although most newlyweds usually are.'

Glancing at him, Amanda noted his narrowed, reproachful gaze fixed on her face and detected the underlying meaning of his words. He was silently saying something to her, in the curl of his lips and the lounging insolence of his long body. After all, they were newlyweds themselves, but their relationship was far removed from that of her father's and Caroline's. 'I wouldn't know,' she murmured, averting her gaze, determined not to be drawn into a discussion on their marriage.

'One only has to look at them when they are together to see that.'

'I suppose so.' Amanda looked at him and he smiled then. It was such a wonderful smile that curled beautifully on those chiselled lips, the kind of smile that would melt any woman's heart if she didn't know him for the arrogant, superior being he was. Suddenly she was very much aware that they were alone and far from other civilised beings. She felt nervous, exactly like a goat must feel, tethered to a stake to lure hungry wolves. Unfortunately she couldn't run away, so, while he continued to gaze at her with that wonderful half smile curling on his lips, she must stay where she was and keep all her wits about her.

'Father has always immersed himself in his work,' she said, glad that she was able to speak without her voice shaking. 'I never thought he would marry again, after Mother, but they seem well matched. Caroline is good for him.'

'What happened to your mother?'

'She died when I was a child.'

'I'm sorry. That must have been hard for you.'

'Yes, it was—and for my father,' she admitted, unsure whether she wanted his sympathy, but comforted by it nevertheless.

'Your father has only recently purchased Eden Park, I believe.'

'Yes, while I was in America.'

'And do you like living here?'

'It's an improvement on the last house we lived in— although living in the country, after living in Rochdale in a large house with extensive grounds, takes some getting used to.'

'Yes, I can imagine it would. It must be a change for your father, too.'

'Caroline is determined to make him take it easy and enjoy himself, but I can assure you that he still has his finger firmly on the pulse.' Amanda looked at him, suddenly curious about his own background. 'What about you? Is your mother still alive, Kit?'

He turned to look at her. 'No. She died when I was a youth. It was a riding accident—nasty business.'

'I'm sorry,' she said, glad that the handsome, enigmatic man she had married was beginning to open up to her at last.

'No need to be. You know what it's like growing up without a mother.'

'Nevertheless, it must have been hard for you and your father.'

He nodded, his features becoming tense. 'He took it badly— never really got over it. I was not enough to ease his pain.'

His tone held a hint of bitterness that did not go unnoticed by Amanda, and she wondered at its cause. 'Do you have any siblings?'

'No.'

'And your father? Is he still alive?'

Kit's eyes darkened with remembrance. 'No.'

His reply was brusque, warning Amanda to pry no further, but she pressed on. 'Will you not tell me about him, Kit?'

'If you don't mind, Amanda, I do not wish to discuss it. Ever.'

'But why?' Recalling the bitterness she had evoked when she had touched on his family's honour on the day he had arrived at Eden Park, she was curious to know more.

'I am not going to give you a blow-by-blow description of what my life was like before I went to America. It was my hatred of gossip and my need for privacy that drove me there. I told you. I will not discuss it.' Striding to the water's edge, he stood looking down, as if trying to rid himself of unpleasant thoughts. After a moment he came back to her, the harshness of a moment earlier having gone from his expression.

Amanda gazed at him. 'It makes you uncomfortable, doesn't it? Talking about your family, I mean—especially your father.'

'Nothing makes me uncomfortable,' he murmured. 'I'm sorry, Amanda. Your questions were perfectly natural, only I would appreciate it if you would not mention my father again.'

'I won't,' she replied quietly. 'Not if you don't want me to. It's your own affair after all.' She wondered what could have happened between Kit and his father that had made him go all the way to America in search of peace. Kit clearly prided himself on his control of his emotions. A man's grief and pain should be a private matter, but if, as Kit insisted, they were to have any sort of life together, she would have to know some time.

Resuming his lounging stance with his shoulder propped

against the tree and looking down at her, he said, 'Tell me about Mr Quinn. How do you get on with him?'

Amanda looked at him, surprised by his question that seemed to come out of nowhere, and having a rather peculiar suspicion that this was what the conversation had been working up to. His features were closed, giving nothing away. 'Mr Quinn? What makes you ask about him?'

'Because he was with you in America.'

'Yes, that's right, he was. Why?'

'What do you know of him?'

'Not very much, really. He's been with us for years, but I have no idea what he did before that.' She looked at Kit sharply. 'Why do you ask?'

He shrugged nonchalantly. 'No particular reason. I am merely curious. Do you like him?'

'No, not really. He's a man of cold pride and duty—a quiet man, hard to get along with, although Father seems to manage well enough—and he likes to keep himself to himself. Father sets him various tasks, mainly in Manchester; sometimes he sends him to London. You must have come into contact with him?'

'No. He's been away from Eden Park on your father's business, I believe, and since he doesn't appear to have any interest in horses and my work is away from the house, it's hardly surprising that we haven't met.'

'Well, I am surprised. No doubt Father will introduce the two of you eventually.'

'Yes, no doubt.'

Feeling strangely uncomfortable about Kit's interest in Mr Quinn and not wishing to discuss him—in fact, she'd prefer to forget all about him since that sordid incident between him and Sadie—Amanda stood and smoothed down her riding skirt. 'I think I'd better be getting back. I've promised

Caroline to help her write invitation cards for some of her forthcoming entertainments. She'll think I've forgotten.'

Kit relinquished his stance against the tree and followed her to her horse, reluctant to end their time together in this secluded place and wanting to savour the delight of her company a little longer. He could not let her go. Not yet.

'Amanda, wait. We must meet again. There are things that must be said—soon. On your ride tomorrow I shall accompany you. We will talk then.'

She turned away. 'I do not think that would be appropriate. I would rather not—not yet.'

He moved closer, temptation getting the better of him, and the last thing he wanted was resistance. He knew he needed to entice her if he was to make her face up to the reality of their marriage. Reaching out, he gripped her upper arm and drew her back against him.

Amanda moved as if to push his hand away, but it stilled in the air, hesitant. The unbelievable pleasure of his touch took her by surprise. The intimacy of his grip on her arm reached out to some unknown part of her, which she had not been aware she possessed. It touched and lightened some dark place she had not before now been aware of, but it was elusive and was soon gone when he removed his hand. But she did not move away from him or turn round.

Kit stood quite still, his body only inches from hers, studying the exposed flesh at the back of her neck and watching the dappled sunlight that filtered between the bare branches of a large beech tree bring out a multitude of glorious lights in her hair. Fashioned in intricate twists and curls, it was held in place by tiny, decorative tortoiseshell combs. He wanted to remove them so that her hair could fall free, so that he could run his fingers through the heavy mass. Placing his hands on both her arms, he pulled her against him.

To Amanda they were like tender manacles, drawing her back so that she could feel his body, his thighs, rock hard against her spine. His warm breath caressed the back of her neck, and then his lips trailed over her sensitive flesh to her ear, while she turned liquid inside.

'Don't,' she breathed, shakily. 'Kit, please don't do this.'

Sliding his arms around her waist, he held her tighter, glad it was just her voice that resisted and not her body. 'Are you certain you want me to stop?' he murmured, blowing warm breath into her ear and flicking his tongue against her lobe.

Her body came alive with pleasure, unfolding like the petals of an exotic flower. Never in her imagination had she experienced anything so erotic as this. All her senses became heightened and focused on him and what he was doing until nothing else mattered. But she dare not turn round in his embrace—she dare not, otherwise, feeling as she did at that moment, she would submit to anything. She half-turned her face to his and he placed his lips on her cheek.

'Yes, I want you to stop—please, you must not go on,' she gasped, shaking her head lamely in a denial, wanting him to stop before she was consumed.

'There will be many times in the future when I shall hold you this close—and for longer; each time you will welcome me, my sweet, I promise you.' He smiled, content in his belief that he had measured the weakness of her character in the strength of her awakened passion.

With a soft chuckle he released her, and Amanda's mind went spinning as he stepped back. Shaken to the core of her being, she could not turn round and meet his eyes. This sensual web he wove was insubstantial yet unbreakable. He moved to stand in front of her, his eyes roaming over her ex- quisite features and provocative figure, a mocking, knowing gleam in their dark depths. She could only stare at him, helplessly caught up in the web of her own desires. Nothing she could say could erase the look of wonder from her face, nor still the chaotic pounding of her heart.

Reaching out, he cupped her chin, tilting her head back to look deep into her eyes. 'Be satisfied with your self-imposed chastity, Amanda, if you can. Or face the truth of what you really want. You will never be fulfilled, not until you become mine completely. You belong to me. From the first you have been mine. I shall try to restrain myself until you come to me of your own free will—and you will come. That I promise you also.'

Confused by her own emotions and feeling a terrible ache of vulnerability that was something quite new to her, Amanda, almost in a daze, watched him as he turned and strode towards the horses. She stared at his back, still feeling the tingle of his fingers on her chin. Slowly she followed him. After securing her hat, she placed her foot into his cupped hands and he raised her into the saddle. Arranging her skirts, she looked down at him. It was impossible not to respond to Kit as his masculine magnetism seemed to take precedence over the rugged landscape and dominate everything around him. The attraction between them was almost palpable. He stood watching her, his eyes alert, holding a challenging gleam, above the faintly smiling mouth.

'You really are quite impossible, aren't you, Kit? Conceited, too.'

'Indeed I am, and you'll see just how impossible I can be if you continue evading the issue that is important to us both.'

Uncomfortably aware of the man riding alongside her, Amanda kept her eyes directly in front of her, sitting stiff and erect. The memory of what had just happened between them made her plight more unbearable and she couldn't wait to be rid of him. When she was with him she didn't know herself. Dear Lord, what kind of sorcery did the man employ so that he could have this effect on her—on her of all people, who had always prided herself on being in control? She would like to believe she had not enjoyed what he had done to her, but that was not the case, and she feared that she was destined to remember his ardent embrace and would want for more.

Henry, in fine fettle as usual, beamed when the two of them rode into the stableyard together. 'I see you've been taking care of my daughter, Kit.'

'Merely looking after her welfare, Henry,' Kit replied, swinging down from his horse and going to assist Amanda, who gracelessly shoved away his hand and slid off herself, which brought an exasperated frown to his handsome face. 'She should not be riding about the moors alone. There are dangers aplenty, without going looking for it. Should she take a tumble, she could come to grief.'

Listening to the sense of what Kit was saying, Henry gave his daughter a reproachful glance. All her life she had been given free rein to do as she pleased, but there were times when she went too far and in this instance Kit was right. 'I confess I haven't given much thought to it, but I have to agree with Kit. See you take a groom with you next time—unless Kit's exercising one of the mounts, then you can go with him.'

Amanda merely looked from one to the other, her eyes hurling daggers at Kit, the determined gleam in their olive-green depths telling him she would as soon ride with the devil as repeat today's episode. Bidding him a haughty but polite good day, she turned on her heel.

A half smile quirked Kit's mouth as he watched the tantalising twitch of her skirts as she stalked off. There was something so richly provocatively pagan about her—her vivid colouring, and the swift animal grace with which she tossed her head. 'And a good day to you too, Mrs Claybourne.' He chuckled softly. 'You've bred a firebrand there, Henry. Lord, what a handful.'

Henry gave him a long-suffering look. 'More than a handful. You'll have to excuse my daughter, Kit. Volatile and high spirited, she has an aversion to being told what to do. Excuse me. I'll walk with her back to the house. Maybe a few well-chosen words of tact will placate her.'

'So, Amanda, it's happy I am to see the two of you getting on,' Henry said when he caught up with his daughter. 'I knew you'd get to liking Kit when you became better acquainted.'

'We met on the moor, Father, and he rode back with me, that's all. It doesn't mean to say I've changed my opinion of Mr Benedict in the slightest.'

'Ah, but you will. Mark my words, you will. He's an excellent man,' he said, casting his daughter a twinkling look, 'good looking, too—and don't be telling me you haven't noticed.'

'It's only because he has a knack with horses that you are biased in his favour,' she retorted sourly.

Henry glanced at her sharply. 'You've not been having a difference of opinion with him now, have you?'

'No, of course not. What makes you say that?'

'It was just a thought. I sense an unease whenever you are together—a constraint, as if you had quarrelled.'

'Not at all,' she said. 'I do admire his skill with horses, but you are right. There is some constraint between us which I can only put down to our being too much alike. We grind together like a couple of rusty old cogs.'

'Aye, well, there's no denying that he's a catch all right and any young woman would be proud to be seen walking out with Kit Benedict. Mark my words, Amanda, he'll not be a widower ere the year is out.' He levelled a meaningful gaze at his offspring, reminding her of her single state, seeming to have forgotten her widowhood.

'Don't despair, Father. You will see me wed again, I promise you—though whether you will consider it a suitable match remains to be seen. But for the time being I shall strive to behave as a widow should—properly.' She glanced at him as he strode beside her. His shifts of opinions were so unpredictable that Amanda had wearied of ever trying to understand him. 'Tell me, Father, are you saying that you have changed your mind and would approve of me marrying someone of Mr Benedict's station in life, after all your blusterings about suitability, titles and how important it is for the man to have the right connections?'

'Aye, lass, I am that—though 'tis not easy for a man like me to make a climb down. These past months married to Caroline have taught me what marriage is all about, and it's about being happy with the right one. You are my darling girl and I want only the best for you, you know that. When you meet the right man you will know it, and, no matter what his station in life, accept him as a man, if not your peer.'

Amanda's heart warmed to him and with a laugh and a lightening of her spirits, she linked her arm through his and hugged it close. 'Now why would I be wanting a husband when I have you, Father? Have I not told you time and time again that you are the only man in my life and I want no other—besides, there is no other who could measure up to you.'

With an acute sense of pride, Henry beamed at her and patted her hand. She was the light of his life—a bonny lass, wonderful to listen to, wonderful in her laughter that made people want to look at her and to smile and want to know her better. She was alive with hope and a fervent belief that life was for living, for love, marriage and children. One day he knew all that would be hers.

* * *

Amanda kept out of Kit's way as best she could after that incident on the moors, but, try as she might, she could not get him out of her mind. She wanted him more than she had ever wanted a man before, a feeling so unexpected given the way she strove to avoid all contact between them.

At a weekend house party in March, when Amanda joined her father and Caroline and the thirty assembled guests in the long library for drinks before dinner, where a string quartet was playing Bach, she was surprised to find another visitor, one who immediately set her emotions tumbling.

When she first saw Kit standing alone by the hearth, looking at the gathering with amused indolence—tall, slender hipped and broad shouldered and so sickeningly attractive and sure of himself, he looked so much a part of some of the landed gentry present that he could be mistaken for one of them.

His manner bore an odd sense of boldness. He appeared to set himself apart from everyone in the room, and yet by his mere presence dominated the scene around him. Anger and resentment welled inside her at his audacity to appear among her father's friends. Even though she knew her father would have invited him, he could have refused.

In an attempt to regain some of her composure that had dropped a notch on seeing Kit, exhaling a slow, steadying breath and taking a glass of wine from a salver being carried by a servant, she moved farther into the room, greeting people on her way. Resplendent in a beaded deep-rose satin gown and every inch the competent hostess, Caroline found her way to her side. Her eyes were alight with pleasure at the way the party was progressing.

'Everything seems to be going well, don't you think?' she remarked quietly.

'You've surpassed yourself, Caroline.'

'With your help.'

'I made a few suggestions, that is all.' Amanda smiled. 'And you look lovely, Caroline—the perfect hostess. Father must be feeling immensely proud of you tonight.'

Caroline returned her smile fondly. 'Thank you, dear, and I must compliment you on your gown. That colour is so becoming on you,' she said, looking with admiration at her stepdaughter's cream watered-silk gown, its sheath-like style so in vogue. The front fitted perfectly into the waist and over the bodice, the back drawn back over a crinolette in a series of short flounces cascading down to the hem. The gown shimmered in the light and brought out the rich, deep tones in Amanda's hair.

'I am so glad you've decided to come out of mourning at last—and I know Henry is relieved. You're far too young to be wearing such drab colours. Now come and circulate.' Caroline took Amanda by the arm as her eyes did a quick scan of the room, coming to rest on Kit. 'Although I think Kit could do with some company. He isn't acquainted with many of the guests. Why don't you go and have a word with him?'

Amanda held back, regarding Kit with a sceptical frown. 'Must I? I really don't know why he was invited.'

'Why on earth shouldn't he be? Everyone is intrigued by Henry's new horse trainer, so your father thought it only right that he attend tonight. He is much talked about in the area— far more than anyone else. The way he keeps himself to himself, never joining the hunt or partaking of any of the social events in the neighbourhood. Yes, he is a man of great mystery is our Mr Benedict.'

'Considering he spends all his waking hours training Father's horses, I don't suppose he has time for anything else. I still say he should not have been invited.'

Wide eyed, Caroline looked at her for a moment. What on

earth could have prompted Amanda to speak in such a fashion? It was most unlike her. Kit had truly gotten under her skin and she wondered how this unexpected animosity had come about. Amanda had developed an unfair impression. It puzzled Caroline and one way or another she was determined to get to the bottom of it. Where she was concerned she could see nothing wrong with him. When Henry had first introduced them, she had been immediately struck by his immense personal attraction. There was a warmth about him and humour in his smile, and yet his mouth was hard and firm with a twist to his lips that said he was not a man to be trifled with.

'Kit comports himself with as much dignity and propriety as anyone present.' Caroline placed her head close to Amanda, speaking softly. 'I must say that he cuts a dashing figure and is by far the most handsome man here. There is more than one unattached young lady just dying to make his acquaintance.'

'Then perhaps you should introduce them and spare me the trouble of having to converse with him,' Amanda suggested ungraciously, looking around and seeing the reaction of several young girls practically melting into the floor as they gazed at him. No doubt he was accustomed to this kind of feminine reaction, she thought crossly.

Caroline glanced at Amanda, puzzled as to her apparent dislike of Kit when Henry thought the sun rose and set with him, and she was utterly charmed by him. 'I know you don't have a very high opinion of Kit, Amanda—and heaven knows why—but I do wish you would try to get on with him—for Henry's sake, if nothing else.'

'I have no opinion of him one way or another, Caroline. It's just that I hardly know him and he failed to make a favourable impression on me when we first met.' When Caroline shot her a pleading look, she smiled and nodded in acquiescence. 'Oh, very well. To please you I'll go and talk to him.'

Kit was eyeing the company with a great deal of disdain. It was peculiar indeed that here, after all these years of being apart from it, surrounded by the society into which he had been born, the society he now eschewed, it was one of the few places he least wanted to be.

He had seen Amanda the instant she entered the room. Sparkling and gleaming beneath the crystal chandelier, she looked like a shimmering butterfly, bright and beguiling, the exposed flesh of her arms and shoulders soft and inviting. The effect of seeing her, the visceral tug and the sense of possessiveness surprised him. He watched her pause in the doorway, her large green eyes scanning the room before moving farther in, dispensing smiles and laughter upon the guests, her laughter reaching him with a sweet seduction. After conversing with Caroline, when she looked his way and began walking towards him, his cynically amused mask was in place.

'Thank you for taking pity on me,' he said when she stood in front of him.

'Caroline told me to. I could hardly refuse now, could I? What are you doing here?'

He grinned infuriatingly. 'Trying damned hard to seduce my wife.' Laughing softly when she shot him a look of ire, he said, 'Set aside your fears, my love. I would not be here if it were not to please your father and to see you. I would rather not attend these occasions, but seeing you amid so many people is better than not seeing you at all.'

'Why? So you can remind me of our bargain?' she snapped.

'There is that—and stop glowering, my dear wife. Your stepmother is watching us.'

Immediately Amanda pinned a smile on her face while her eyes glared at him. 'I am not your dear wife,' she whispered. 'And please keep your voice down. Someone might hear. Had

I known Father had invited you, I would have pleaded a headache and stayed in my room.'

'You mean you haven't fallen madly in love with me yet?' he asked with a broad grin.

'You conceited ass. I will never do that. We are incompatible. In fact, I think you exist only to antagonise me. Why don't you go away?' Her rebuke only seemed to amuse him further, for his grin deepened, making her doubt if she would ever be effective in making him disappear.

'What, and leave you to the wolves I see devouring you at every turn?' he retorted, his eyes doing a quick sweep of the unattached males hovering on the sidelines like the aforesaid animals ready to pounce the instant they parted.

Amanda stared at him, searching his handsome visage, taken aback by his nerve. 'What are you now? My protector—as you tried to be out on the moor?'

'No. Your husband. You belong to me and I choose to safeguard against those who try to get too close to you.'

Irate sparks flashed in her eyes. 'Your persistence astounds me.'

'I simply know what I want. You are a married woman. Please behave as such.'

'How dare you?' she gritted.

'And such a proud one,' he chuckled. 'A lovely one at that. I am happy to see you out of those dreadful mourning clothes. They were most unbecoming on you, my love.'

'Please be quiet.'

'I will be happy to—for the price of a kiss from your soft lips, my sweet.'

'Never,' she retorted. 'I would rather kiss a rattlesnake.'

'Guard yourself well, for no amount of armour will protect you from me—and I know just how vulnerable you can be, don't forget.' He raised a dark brow and considered her soft features. His gaze moved even lower to her swelling breasts and then back to her eyes, a light gleaming in his own. 'I will have a full marriage and nothing less. You have my name and all you desired. Your part of the agreement has yet to be fulfilled. It is not going to go away—no matter how much you want it to. Don't forget that you were the one who sought me out in my prison cell and the situation we now find ourselves in was of your making—and in part mine for agreeing to your request. You will have to face the reality of it some time.'

Amanda glanced uncertainly at him. He was watching her intently. Suddenly she felt foolish and bad tempered. What he said was perfectly true. A rueful smile lit her eyes and she regarded him with a new respect. 'You are right. I have felt guilt about what I did, and I hoped that a moment like this would never come about. However, I accept that I must deal with it—but—I don't know how to, and that's the crux of the matter. I apologise for the way I've behaved towards you— and apologies don't come easy for me—but—I've been so confused of late.'

Kit's eyes smiled his approval at her sudden and welcome change of attitude. He perceived her disappointments and was fully aware of the reasons behind them. 'It's understandable. It's not often a woman has her husband return from the dead. Do you resent me for that?'

'I do resent you, but not for the reason you state.'

'Then I assume your resentment stems from the disruption I have brought to your well-ordered life. You are making this very difficult for us, Amanda.'

'Am I?'

'You know you are.' His gaze caressed her upturned face, and then his eyes caught and held her own. 'I am single-minded in my pursuits—you may have noticed. I have played out my hand with patience, and I will not be satisfied until I have you.' Raising his hand, he boldly touched her cheek, caressing it with the backs of his fingers. 'All of you.'

The warmth of his tone caused Amanda's heart to do strange things, and his touch brought a pink hue creeping over her face. On the edge of the crowded room, she was overwhelmingly conscious of the man facing her. Everyone else seemed to fade away. However, she was irritated by the way in which he always managed to skilfully cut through her superior attitude, and she knew she asked for it, but the magnetic attraction still remained beneath the surface.

Recollecting herself, she took a step back, glancing about her to see if anyone had noticed his caress. 'Kit, will you mind your manners and please behave yourself.'

A low chuckle preceded his reply. 'Behave? How would you have me behave, my love—as a gentleman? And how can I do that when I am only a hired hand unschooled in the postures of a gentleman?'

'If you would cease currying favour with my father and stick to the stables and your cottage, it would ease matters.'

His eyes seemed to glow from deep within. 'Ah—my cottage. Perhaps you would care to drop in some time. I will show you around if you like. The bed I can recommend—all feathers and down and large enough for two.'

Amanda flushed scarlet at what he was implying. 'I am not the sort who goes easily, without thought or affection, to a man's bed,' she hissed.

'Come now, can I not persuade you to risk your heart's defences in one night of love? Perhaps you will find it agreeable and want more.'

'How conceited of you to think you can make me want you. Do you really believe you can do that?'

His smile was feral as he moved closer. 'Judge for yourself. You will come to me. I have no doubt about that.' The light in his eyes, the subtle undertone in his voice, was a challenge—a warning.

'And what do you think people would make of it if they saw me entering your home?'

'It is no crime, Amanda.'

'No—but it would be dangerous.'

'A little danger adds spice to the excitement.'

'I have enough excitement in my life without indulging in an illicit interlude with my father's horse trainer.' As Amanda was about to turn and walk away, his hand shot out and gripped her wrist.

''Tis not an interlude I seek with you, my love. I want something deeper, more profound, more lasting than that. We have to talk, but not here. You will find me at home later. Will you come?'

Amanda took another step away from him, suddenly afraid of being alone with him in his cottage and what he could do if he set his mind to it. But they must talk if they were to resolve matters between them and in doing so move on with their lives. She nodded. 'If I can.'

Amanda moved away from him at the same moment as Mr Quinn made his appearance. Pausing in the doorway, he looked at the chattering throng with little interest.

If Amanda had turned to look at Kit, she would have noted a hardness that infused his face as his eyes settled on her father's most trusted employee, and would have detected a grimness in his dark eyes that boded ill for Mr Quinn.

Chapter Six

Dinner was a splendid affair—which was all down to Caroline. When she had married Henry she had brought with her that well-bred way of life she had known and been trained to from birth.

The long mahogany table had been polished to a mirror shine. Small bowls of attractive and colourful flowers marched down the centre, adding a light and graceful effect, and the white crockery with a narrow margin of gold was of the best and most expensive English china. Places were set with silver cutlery on white damask place mats edged with the finest Honiton lace, and to the right of the setting, four differently sized, cut-crystal wine glasses. The food was the best of its kind—plain and simple and cooked to perfection.

Throughout the meal, Amanda was aware of Kit seated on her father's right hand on the opposite side to her. He was constantly within her sights. Their eyes would meet, his full of meaning and seduction. Heat would suffuse her cheeks and she would look away, trying, often without success, to appear serene and composed.

* * *

When dinner was over the ladies rose and followed Caroline to the drawing room. Fluttering and cackling like hens that have seen a fox in their coop, they plumped themselves down on cushioned sofas and chairs and began to discuss frivolous matters as freely as they would in their own homes. When the gentlemen joined them, they began drifting back into the library, where the musicians were playing a waltz. Couples began taking to the floor.

Of their own volition Amanda's eyes sought out Kit. When she couldn't find him, disappointment washed over her, but then he was there, standing only an inch behind her. She instantly felt his presence as if it were a tangible force. She even recognised the elusive sharp scent of his cologne. Her heart gave a leap and missed a beat. His breath, when he spoke, was warm on the back of her neck.

'Dance with me, Amanda.'

Before she could raise a protest, he slid his hand about her slender waist, and, capturing her hand and drawing her close, swung her into the dance. The unbelievable pleasure of his touch, of being in his arms, took her completely by surprise, but, as light as his grip was, she felt the steel beneath and she knew he wasn't going to let her go.

Caroline's face, showing pleasant surprise on seeing her dancing with Kit, flashed by in a haze, and Amanda's concerns were for the speculation of being seen dancing with her father's horse trainer. After a moment everything was forgotten as she found herself being whirled around in time to the music by a man who danced with the elegance and the easy grace of a man well trained. Beginning to relax, she sank into the dance with an enjoyment that Kit couldn't help appreciating.

'Look at me,' he murmured. She did as he bade, and, when

he looked into her eyes, he felt his chest tighten. 'Has anyone told you that you dance divinely, Mrs Claybourne?'

'Yes, frequently. Thank you for the compliment. So do you, Mr Benedict. I am surprised.'

He lifted an eyebrow. 'Why? Do you find it such a strange phenomenon for a horse trainer to be able to dance?'

'No, and I meant no offence. Are you having a pleasant evening?' she asked in an attempt at polite conversation, while trying to ignore her pounding heart.

'Not really. I'm only here because of you and you know it.'

'Then perhaps you shouldn't be so selective,' she remarked flippantly. 'There are lots of attractive ladies who are dying for you to ask them to dance. I know most of them. They are the very souls of amiability. In fact, I would even go so far as to say that their hunting instincts are at fever pitch with such prime prey in sight.'

Kit's gaze shifted over the brunettes and blondes about the room, registering heightened colour and eager gazes as they looked his way. Considering them of no consequence, he gazed down through half-closed eyes at the woman in his arms.

'Then I am sorry to disappoint them. I am already committed to an exquisite redhead who I hope will develop a *tendre* for me in a very short time. What I want is to be alone with you, my love.'

'And do you always get what you want?'

'I got you,' he pointed out, as if that ended the argument.

In the hazel depths of his eyes, which rested upon her as boldly as ever, Amanda saw something relentless and challenging. She looked away, trying to clear her mind of the warm, intoxicating haze his nearness inspired.

Kit's smile was one of satisfaction when he saw the soft flush to her cheeks that his words had invoked. 'Relax,' he murmured.

'I am relaxed.'

'Your body tells me otherwise. Give yourself over to the music and enjoy yourself. I am sure you will survive to the end of the dance.'

'It's difficult to do that when there are people to observe and gossip.'

'And that bothers you?'

'No, I suppose not.'

'I observe several males drooling for your attention. I can imagine their disappointment when they learn you are no longer available.'

Amanda bristled at his words, wishing he would stop reminding her at every opportunity that she was his wife. 'Since I have no wish to argue about that particular issue on a crowded dance floor, I shall ignore that remark. I am acquainted with all of them and most of them are extremely charming.'

Kit glanced past her, eyeing the would-be competition with withering scorn. 'I wouldn't bother with them,' he said drily.

For a surprised moment Amanda wondered if it was jealousy she heard in his voice, and then she dismissed it as preposterous. 'Why, what do you see when you look at them?'

'Envy,' he answered, scowling suddenly when he glanced around at the hungry, expectant, hopeful male faces looking at her as they would a banquet about to be served up to a tribe of cannibals. 'For what those scoundrels are thinking about when they look at you they ought to be horse whipped.'

'Why, I do believe you are beginning to sound like a jealous suitor,' Amanda remarked, slanting him an amused look from the corner of her eye. 'And doesn't what you're thinking about when you look at me also merit a whipping?'

'No. A man has a right to look at his wife any way he chooses.'

'In the hope of attracting a husband, my father wants me to be nice to them. So unless you want to draw attention to yourself, I would advise you not to object when I dance with them.'

'Just so long as you remember that you belong to me—and for that you can thank yourself.' He smiled infuriatingly. 'I blame you entirely, my love. However, you will soon come to realise that when I set my mind on having something—be it of material value or a woman—I am not easily dissuaded from that end.'

'I am beginning to realise that you can be a mite persistent.'

'Steadfastly so. I never waver far from my purpose.'

'And do you always win the object of your attention?'

'Through relentless pursuit—always,' he said, whirling her round in the final movements of the waltz.

'Then since I find myself the thing you propose to have, it would seem there is to be a struggle of wills ahead—mine pitted against yours.'

'I am glad you get the picture.'

The dance ended and there was no time to say more because Henry chose that moment to claim Kit's attention.

Deeply uneasy about the conversation she had had with Kit, and rather than dance with anyone else, Amanda had escaped to her room to sort out her thoughts and to freshen up, spending longer than she intended. When she returned to the festivities, reluctant to join the gathering, she went out on to the moonlit terrace. She stood there, near the stone balustrade, staring out over the dark shapes of the trees. She didn't know how long she stood there, not thinking, not moving, just letting the peace wash over her, when something—not a sound, just a feeling, heightened her consciousness and caused her to turn—and she saw the end of his cigar, glowing like a firefly in the shadow of the house.

Kit came forward to meet her, out of the dark into the light of the moon.

'Is the company not to your liking?' he asked calmly.

'Yes, I just wanted some air, that's all. And you?'

'The same—and something else.'

'And what is this something else?'

Tossing his cigar into the flowerbed, he studied her for a long time before he spoke. 'Do you really want me to tell you the truth—or make polite noises?'

'The truth, naturally.'

He moved closer, capturing her eyes with his own. 'When you came to my prison cell you took me off my guard—it's not often anyone succeeds in doing that. To see my visitor—particularly a woman as young and attractive as you, Amanda—was, frankly, disturbing. It wasn't the first time a woman had insinuated herself into my company, but the object was usually more of a passionate nature. But with you it was more than that.'

'More?' she echoed.

He nodded slowly. 'Much more. I am a man of scruples, and I'd never met a woman as self-assured or as presumptuous as you. Until then I'd lived on the assumption that all women are sisters under the skin. You are different to any woman I have ever met. You are no fool and I believe will forgive yourself for things you condemn in others. Your father has placed you on a pedestal—you know that and I have seen it—which is why you have an air of reserve about you, which would explain your difficulty and reluctance to enter into any kind of close relationship with any of the adoring males who attempt to get too close. Maybe it would pain you to discover that you have blood in your veins and passion in your heart.'

Slightly offended by his remarks, Amanda stared at him coldly. 'I'm flattered that you've taken the time to try and analyse me, Mr Benedict. In fact, I hardly know how to answer you. Perhaps I am like I am because I haven't had the advantages of a mother's love and rearing. You are right when you say that my father has placed me on a pedestal, but I never sought it. Indeed, I've shocked him no end at times, and he will be outraged if he should learn of this latest escapade of mine. It's by far the most daring, scandalous thing I've ever done, but there's little I can do about it now. However, for the time being, discretion is required.'

'And honesty.'

'Yes, that too. No doubt Father will lock me up with nothing to eat or drink but bread and water for a week for my shameful behaviour.'

Kit grinned. 'As your husband, he would have to ask my permission first.'

'Nevertheless, he will be furious with me. There are times when I don't behave or express myself as a lady is supposed to.'

'Feel free to express yourself in any way you like when you are with me,' Kit said, his sensuous lips curving in a slow smile.

'I can be frightfully blunt,' she uttered softly, looking up into his dark face, which was relaxed into a noble, masculine beauty that drew her gaze like a magnet.

'So can I,' he replied, his eyes the eyes of a hunter, instantly clear in the moonlight. 'In fact, if you weren't my wife, I'd—'

'What? Attempt to make me your mistress?' she interrupted, feeling the heat and vibrancy of him reaching out to her. For her own safety, and her own sanity, she knew she had to try and stay one step ahead of him.

'Exactly. Out here alone with a beautiful woman in the moonlight, what man in his right mind wouldn't have seduction on his mind?'

'Then please don't. If you tried, I'd resist you with all my strength—only I'm afraid I don't know how my strength would hold out with you.'

He tilted his head at her. 'Afraid?' he said. 'Are you afraid of me, Amanda?'

'Yes,' she whispered. 'I'm afraid of both of us.'

Kit looked down at her a long time. Then he sighed. 'All right, Amanda. You win—this time. But don't look on it as a victory, because it's anything but.'

'You don't give up easily, do you, Kit?'

An eyebrow lifted. 'No—and remember that I hold all your secrets.'

'Only some,' Amanda countered. 'Before I left Charleston I met Agatha, and she told me how you became a hunter and a trapper, that you followed forest trails like an Indian and learned to read the signs of nature, so you will realise that there is no pleasure to be had in shooting tame and tethered creatures. Do you understand what I'm saying, Kit?'

He nodded. 'Yes,' he said, and he stepped back and opened his arms to let her pass, as one would free a captured bird.

'Thank you.'

'But do not forget that the night is not yet over. You began this game. I've just altered the rules—and we will play to the end. I hope I will see you later.'

'Maybe.' Then, with enormous dignity, she turned and walked back into the house.

Later, Amanda stood in the shadows of the hall and watched Kit leave. Her father bade him goodnight and her gaze followed him to the door. Mr Quinn stood nearby, also alone—as he preferred. He nodded in greeting as Kit walked by him. Kit coolly returned the nod and left.

On a sigh Amanda returned to the party, strangely dejected now Kit had left—although she was relieved that Mr Quinn had not recognised him and had no suspicion as to his true identity, which would complicate matters more than they already were. Until she had sorted out the mess, no one must know that Kit Benedict was her husband and was hell-bent on making her his wife in every sense.

For Amanda the remainder of the evening passed in a blur. The music and polite discourse could not distract her from her present predicament. Before the party she would have been ready to blame Kit for her troubles, but seeing and speaking to him had done much to change that. She thought of him a great deal—not as disparagingly as she had at first. The hurt and shock of his reappearance into her life was healing. Nevertheless, her dilemma continued, and its solution hid itself in the chaotic frenzy of her thoughts.

It was a moment of reckoning, the moment when she had to decide whether or not to go to Kit's cottage. Suddenly the noise of thirty people altogether was like the noise of a race crowd. The party began to chafe on her to such a degree that she could stand it no longer. Pleading a headache she bade her father and Caroline goodnight and went to her room. Donning her coat and telling Nan not to wait up, that she would put herself to bed, ignoring the suspicious look her maid cast her way, she slipped out of the house by a back way.

The night was cold, and the wind whipping about her in an ever-deepening chill made her shiver. Clouds borne from the north gathered overhead in a heavy, threatening mass. She raised the deep collar of her coat and gripped it under her chin, her feet crunching on the gravel as she hurried past the stables, her eyes focused on the cottage in the distance set back against the trees and standing in its own small garden. Smoke spiralled upwards from the chimney and a light shone out of the diamond-paned windows, indicating that the occupant was at home.

Apprehension and a sense of panic settled in as Amanda pushed open the garden gate, grimacing when it squeaked loudly on its hinges, heralding her arrival to the man within. She walked towards the door as the first large, splashing droplets of rain began to fall, but it opened before she could knock. She hesitated.

Kit noticed. Taking her hand, he drew her inside and closed the door. His face was impassive, his thoughts impossible to guess. He was still wearing his evening clothes, having removed his jacket and cravat, his shirt open at the throat.

Glancing around the room, with its low-beamed ceiling, and which glowed with soft golden light glimmering on brass fittings and casting deep shadows on the walls, she could smell old wood and beeswax polish, and underlying this the tangy, alluring scent of the house's occupant.

Inside Kit's domain Amanda sensed that a subtle shift of power had taken place. Until now she had thought herself confident and in control, but now she felt confused and strangely vulnerable, while Kit seemed decisive and self-assured. After building up the fire with logs stacked tidily in the wide hearth, he turned and looked at her, the firelight behind him gilding his hair.

His softly spoken words were part-invitation, part-order. 'Come here, Amanda.'

Hypnotised by his voice and those mesmerising dark eyes, she did as he bade, moving cautiously, as if in a trance, a quiver tingling up her spine.

'Take off your coat.'

'I—I'd rather not.'

Ignoring her resistance, he unfastened the top buttons. 'I insist. You'll not feel the benefit of it when you go back outside.' Helping her out of it and tossing it carelessly over the back of a chair, he looked down at her. 'I'm glad you came.'

'I very nearly didn't.'

'Afraid?'

She nodded. 'Of you—of myself…' She looked away.

'And of what might happen,' he uttered quietly.

'Yes, I suppose so. But you are right. I have come to take the thunder out of the storm. We must talk.'

'And we have much to discuss.'

Finding his nearness disconcerting, Amanda moved away from him. There was an aloof strength, a powerful charisma about Kit that had nothing to do with his good looks, his perfect physique and lazy white smile. 'You—are comfortable in the cottage?'

'Your father has gone to considerable lengths to ensure I am. There is a female servant who comes from the house daily to see to my needs and to take care of things.'

'A servant?' Amanda enquired, her curiosity piqued. 'Which one?'

'Sadie Jenkins.'

She stiffened suddenly, as prickly as a porcupine. 'Sadie? But Sadie is—'

With a teasing twinkle in his eye, Kit cocked a brow at Amanda. 'Good at what she does, lovely to look at, with the face of an angel, unattached—and she could talk the hind leg off a donkey.'

'I know perfectly well what she looks like,' Amanda retorted more sharply that she intended. 'Sadie is also a dreadful gossip, extremely brazen, spreads her favours about like Lady Bountiful, and she has every male at Eden Park eating out of her hand.'

'I know that, too.' He grinned, seeing the workings of her mind. 'But worry not. I always make myself scarce when she's around.' His grin deepened. 'Jealous are you, my love?'

The olive-green eyes narrowed in a glare. 'Jealous? Of a servant? Certainly not. Anyway, I did not come here to discuss domestic matters.'

'No, you came to talk about us—which I find far more interesting.'

'Surely you must realise there can be no us. Can't you see that it's useless hoping for things when in your rational mind you must see it can never happen?'

'Why? Because you are the daughter of a fabulously wealthy business magnate, and I am a mere horse trainer—' he cocked a dubious brow '—a hired hand, I recall you saying?'

Having her own words quoted back to her was a bit disconcerting. Kit might not have a title or any claim to being a gentleman in society's interpretation of the term, but she knew instinctively that he was an honourable and proud man, and that pride was stamped on the way he comported himself and his handsome features.

'I did say that, and I apologise for it. Think what you will, but none of that matters to me—though it might to my father.'

His eyes met hers in half-challenging amusement. 'Despite my own lowly station, his reaction to our marriage may surprise you. Think how happy he might be when he learns you are wed and finally going to provide him with the grandchildren he's been plaguing you to give him.'

'I'm not ready for that. You can't honestly say you wanted any of this.'

He smiled. 'I've always held myself adaptable to the circumstances.'

'But I'm the one responsible for this entire nightmare. I cannot deny that.'

'Nightmare?' He frowned, offended by her choice of word. 'I'm sorry if that's the way you see our relationship. It needn't be a nightmare if you don't let it.'

'No? I think you are right.' Pausing to draw a fortifying breath, she said, 'Which is why I want a divorce. It's the only way out that I can see.'

Kit looked at her hard for a moment and then shook his head with infuriating calm, as if he'd half expected this. 'A divorce,' he repeated. 'And would you care to tell me how you intend to accomplish that and keep it from your father at the same time?'

'I don't know. I haven't thought about the legalities of it yet, but I will. I suppose it will involve solicitors and people like that. Together I'm sure we can come up with something.'

'No, Amanda. You will be wasting your time. To go through that will be an embarrassing and completely futile ordeal for you.'

'Futile? But why?'

'Because I refuse to consider a divorce,' he stated firmly.

'Then—the marriage can be annulled and declared void on the grounds of non-consummation.'

His eyes narrowed. 'Ah—I wondered how long it would take you to mention that. Since we are talking of legalities, I believe I have legal rights of my own I have yet to claim from you.'

Panic stirred within Amanda. This wasn't going the way she had planned it. 'Please, Kit, don't do this. An annulment should not be difficult to obtain—under the circumstances.'

'Why—because you are still a virgin? And do you think you will be believed when it is made known that you spent a night here with me—that the two of us were completely alone?'

'But nothing has happened between us,' she cried. 'We both know that. You must see that this is for the best—for both of us.'

Kit stared down at the tempestuous young woman. Her eyes were stormy, her face both delicate and vivid in the soft light. He wondered why, even now when she was almost begging him to release her, he should feel this consuming, unquenchable need to possess her.

'It is a dilemma for you, Amanda, I do realise that, but I will not release you from our bargain. Absolutely not. We are bound together by ties that can never be broken. You see,' he said, slowly moving closer to her, 'one day a convincingly wayward young woman with an unforgettable face and form came to visit me in my prison cell. When she left she had seared her brand upon my mind and my heart and stirred my imagination to proportions I had never known before. Such an impression did she make that when I was set free I was determined to seek her out. And now I have found her I will not let her go.'

Kit's words caused the internal war going on between Amanda's mind and heart to escalate to tumultuous proportions. Trying to avoid both his searching gaze and the entire discussion, she moved farther away from him, no longer feeling entirely the injured and innocent party.

'Have you always been so persistent?'

'It is one of my unattractive qualities,' he replied smoothly. 'Now, no more talk of divorce tonight—or any other night, come to that. It will get you nowhere. But come, I forget my manners. I've never entertained a guest in my cottage before. I'm most happy to have you here. Please,' he said, indicating the sofa set at right angles to the fire, 'make yourself comfortable and I'll pour us a drink—madeira, I think.'

Amanda sank into the sofa's deep upholstery. Surprisingly she did not feel too disappointed that he refused to consider her suggestion of a divorce—deep down she had expected it. He would be like a dog with a bone until she had fulfilled her side of the bargain. Kit uncorked the wine and handed her a glass, before seating himself in a wooden chair with a high carved back across from her. She sipped the wine. It was rich and full bodied and brought sunlight to mind. After a few moments of companionable silence she felt that familiar twist of her heart, that addictive blend of pleasure and discomfort whenever she was with Kit.

She was young and had never experienced love. Kit was strong and virile and his eyes glittered with a restless passion. Her own restless spirit wanted to savour it, to touch it and feel it, and with Kit she was at liberty to do just that if she wanted to. But she held back—afraid, afraid of what further disruption he would bring to her life and her emotions if she got too close. And yet, if he had his way and refused to release her, how long could she hold out against this forceful man?

The wine, the soft light, the sound of the heavy rain pelting against the windows and the warmth of the fire were beginning to have an effect. The cottage was a warm and cosy place to be. Gazing across at Kit, Amanda felt very peaceful and at ease with him. He was watching her with those warm brown eyes that were really the most attractive eyes she had ever seen. She smiled.

'If you intend to seduce me, I'll fight you,' she said.

He chuckled softly, highly amused. 'Like you did the last time I held you close? As I recall, there was no fight in you.' Where Amanda was concerned he knew exactly what he was doing, and he had decided that tactics would be much smoother than force. 'Relax, Amanda, nothing is going to happen to you that you don't want to happen.' Resting his foot on his knee, he settled himself more comfortably. 'Tell me what you think about marriage in general—what do you want out of that?'

Amanda thought seriously about his question before replying. 'In a proper relationship I suppose I want what most women want: to love and to be loved, for it to be deep and true and lasting, and to be made happy by it. Of course—' she sighed '—I would prefer not to be married at all so that I could travel and sketch and paint and do all the things that are forbidden a young woman to do alone.'

'You paint?'

'Occasionally—although I'm a novice and do it rather badly. I should love to go on the grand tour, to go in pursuit of intellectual, artistic and philanthropic interests—to see all the fascinating places I have read about—Italy, France, Egypt.' Even saying the names lit up her eyes and stirred something inside her, a longing she had often felt but never acknowledged.

'You widened your horizons by going to America. Was that not enough?'

'No. It only made me long to see more. What an adventurous life it would be—to travel. Men are so fortunate to be able to do that I always think. How I envy you your sex, Kit. Women have little control over their lives.'

Kit stared at her, surprised by her admission. 'But you have money. If one has that, it makes everything possible.'

She gave him a level gaze. 'That's how I planned it to be when I married you—enabling me to be independent of my father. But things don't always turn out the way one wants. Since you came back into my life, and won't divorce me, I no longer have the opportunity to do as I please.'

Kit considered her thoughtfully. Her voice was low and serious, but he was relieved to note it was without regret. It was as if she had carefully considered all the alternatives and had come to realise she could no longer escape the bargain they had made—that she could no longer escape him.

'Marriage to me may not turn out to be such a bad thing, Amanda. There will come a time for gaiety and laughter, I promise you.' Averting his eyes, he looked into the fire's glowing embers. Something in the soft romanticism of her words about love and marriage brought memories to the surface, memories that had lain buried for six long years. Kit ruthlessly shoved these memories back down, giving no indication to Amanda of his momentary lapse.

'I can tell you are a romantic at heart,' he murmured.

'Perhaps that's because my parents were blessed to have loved each other passionately. I want what they had and will settle for nothing less.'

While his own parents had been cursed, Kit thought bitterly, placing his empty glass in the hearth. 'Love is all very well,' he said, getting up and standing with his back to the fire, 'but in most cases it has nothing to do with marriage. Look among the couples you know, the ones who attend the same social functions as you. Most of them are in love, I grant you—but not with their spouses.'

She smiled softly. 'I suppose you think all my high-blown sentimentality is ridiculous.'

'Quite the opposite, although some think that love and marriage are two separate things, that one need not have anything to do with the other. What do you think of that?'

'That the person who has opinions such as these must be sadly cynical. To spend a lifetime with someone you only have a passing liking for must be a miserable existence. Tell me, Kit, are you of the opinion that love is not a necessary part of matrimony?'

He smiled. 'Perhaps not—who am I to say—but it would be an added bonus—provided, of course, that it didn't conquer all reason.'

'You know, as it turned out there was no need for me to marry you at all.'

'Why do you say that?' he asked, joining her on the sofa and sitting sideways the better to look at her.

'Perhaps now you have met my father you will understand why I did what I did in Charleston. You see, as the son of an Irish navvy he's had little to do with society. In the early days, work always came first.'

'And hardship breeds determination, which is why he's managed to get where he is now.'

'Yes, something like that. Mind you, he has always loved hunting—following the hounds and all that. He has friends who partake, but the lords and ladies who also partake are very different from the ordinary hoi polloi.'

'Are you saying they snub him?'

'In the beginning he was cut all the time. They can be quite vindictive. Anyone who starts with nothing and becomes very rich expects that.'

'Your father is a fine man. Those who cut him are not even worthy of his contempt.'

'Maybe you're right. Personally I don't care a fig for it all, but Father does—although half the time he doesn't see it. Rubbing shoulders with the gentry on the hunting field merely fosters his illusion. He doesn't realise that his membership in that exclusive set is conceded by himself alone. He might have the money, and the panache to carry it off, but he is grudgingly tolerated by the gentry. In the long run society can be implacable and invincible. It's always been his sense of self that's sustained him through every social encounter— although, before he met Caroline, deep down he felt that only my marriage to one of them would grant him complete social acceptability.'

'And in desperation you married me to escape all that.'

'Precisely. Father had an impoverished lord way past his prime waiting for me on my return from Charleston. Everything changed while I was away and I didn't know about it. You see, Father went and married Caroline, whose closets are stuffed with aristocrats, giving him easy access to all he desires—a true place in society without any help from me.'

'Rendering you redundant.'

Amanda nodded and half-laughed. 'And in four days' time, as he will have told you, he's off to London to test the waters. His dream has finally come true. They are to stay with Lord and Lady Seagrove at Seagrove House in Mayfair—Lady Seagrove being Caroline's sister. She's to give a ball in honour of her husband's fiftieth birthday and many people of note are to attend. It will be Father's introduction into London society. Anyone else would find the prospect daunting, but Father's been like a dog with two tails for days now and doesn't know which one to wag first. It's all so ironic really, don't you think?'

'Quite,' Kit said, thinking what a truly adorable creature she was when she laughed and letting his eyes dwell on her. At that moment, bathed in soft light, with loose tendrils of her remarkable burgundy-coloured hair around her face, and those large eyes looking across at him, she seemed softer than she ever had before. 'However, I'm glad you didn't know about his marriage to Caroline before you came looking for me, otherwise I would never have met you.'

Amanda met his gaze, hearing the warmth in his voice that implied he was glad he had met her, and there was something deep in his eyes that warned her not to delve any deeper and ask him to explain what he meant. Instead, keeping to safer territory, she said, 'It would have avoided the mess we now find ourselves in.'

'You can't expect everything to be sorted out overnight, but it will be, in time.'

Part of Amanda listened to him while the other part centred on Kit himself. In thoughtful silence she contemplated the tall man reclining beside her, completely at ease. She found herself wondering where he came from, about his family and the woman who had nurtured him—and the woman he had married.

'Tell me about your wife,' she asked.

Kit delayed answering her. His countenance grew serious.

'I can see I shouldn't have asked. I don't mean to pry. It's just that I know absolutely nothing about you—where you come from and what you were doing in America—whereas you know a great deal about me. Caroline was saying earlier that you really are a man of mystery, secretive, and it's strange that you seem reluctant to mix in company. People are beginning to comment about you.'

'My time is usually taken up training your father's horses. I like solitude and guard my privacy well. To be my own person, to shake off the rigours of life as I had known it in England, was the reason why I went to America.'

Amanda smiled softly. 'You put me in mind of a rolling stone, Mr Benedict,' she teased.

He returned her smile. 'I suppose I must seem like that to you. However, as my second wife you have every right to know about my first, so I will tell you. Her name was Fern. She was a Cherokee who had lived in the Smoky Mountains all her life. When Georgia state officials evicted the Cherokee during the eighteen thirties, countless Cherokee families, including Fern's own, refused to comply with orders to move to the West, and, at great risk to themselves, escaped to the forests and mountains to live.'

'How did the two of you meet?'

'I was travelling alone when I came into contact with a wild bunch of unsavoury characters out for what they could get. I was attacked and badly wounded. Tsali, Fern's father, found me, took me in and saved my life. I stayed with them in the mountains for several months.' He smiled as he remembered. 'Tsali was also a horse trader—he worshipped them and taught me much. Unfortunately he suffered from an old war wound he'd acquired during the Civil War, when he'd fought for the South. When he died, Fern was alone and needed my help.'

'So you married her.' He nodded. 'Was it necessary to go to such lengths?'

He shrugged. 'I owed a great deal to her father. When my life was threatened he was the only person who came to my assistance. I owed him a debt of gratitude—and it was a debt I was happy to settle. Fern was young—no more than eighteen—simple and good, gentle and pretty—'

'Biddable?'

'Naturally.'

'Unlike me.'

'Never were two people less alike.' He looked past her as he remembered. 'Fern wanted nothing more than to be my wife—and she was a good wife. For the short time we were together she was content. She died giving birth to Sky.'

There was a husky rasp to his voice, and an edge of sadness. Amanda longed to ask him if he had been in love with his Cherokee wife, but thought that would be prying too deeply. 'I'm sorry,' she said quietly.

'There's no need for you to be. It happened. I did love her in a way, but I wasn't in love with her,' he said, answering Amanda's unspoken question. 'It was a long time ago. She is but a memory to me now.'

'Kept alive by Sky.'

He nodded. 'Which reminds me. I must take time off to go to see her.'

'I'm sure Father will grant it—indeed, he is so glad to have you here that he will grant you anything. Please remember me to her, won't you?'

'It would be better still if you were to come with me.'

Amanda stiffened. 'No, Kit. You know I can't. It—it's out of the question.' Afraid that he would begin trying to persuade her, abruptly she stood up. 'I must go. I've been here long enough.'

Kit frowned and sighed, shaking off the mood. 'There is still a great deal for us to discuss—things that should be understood between us.'

'Another time,' she said, unable to look at him as she tried to clear her mind of the warm, intoxicating haze his presence inspired. 'It's late. I must get back.'

'You can't go anywhere in this. You'll be soaked to the skin in no time. Unless you want to drown yourself, you will have to stay here until the rain abates.'

'If you have an umbrella I could borrow, I would be most grateful. There must be one somewhere.'

'Unfortunately there isn't.'

Not to be deterred from leaving, Amanda reached for her coat, but did not get that far. Suddenly, with the stealth of a panther, Kit was behind her.

Determined to prolong her stay and see that she understood the full weight of what she had started when she had sought him out in his prison cell, Kit's arms snaked round her waist and drew her back against his hard chest. 'You intend to leave, and I intend to do all I can to persuade you to stay. 'Tis no simple passion that torments me, Amanda, but an ever-increasing desire to have you with me every moment and to claim you as my own.'

His breath was warm and close to her ear. Amanda could not remain unmoved by the husky, caressing voice that was like a seductive whisper. Slowly, she turned within his arms. Placing his hands on her bare shoulders, he felt his fingers burn her flesh. Gently he squeezed, and when she tried to pull away his fingers tightened.

Looking into his eyes, warm and liquid with desire, she saw what was in them and felt afraid and excited at the same time. Day after day she had kept herself aloof from him, but now as he stood close to her, he was more attractive, more desirable than ever, and the urgency to be even closer to him was more vivid than it had ever been. She swallowed, feeling her body grow warm.

'Please, Kit—don't do this,' she whispered, her gaze focused on his lips.

'There's nothing wrong in what I do, Amanda. Do you forget that I have some claim to you? I want you,' he told her, shifting his hands to her waist and bringing her full against his hardened frame. His voice was a soft murmur, a gentle caress, his mouth close to her own. 'I know you want me, too.'

'Oh…' she breathed, unable to look at anything other than those finely sculpted lips just inches from her own '…I may scream if you kiss me.'

He laughed softly. 'Pride and foolishness,' he mocked, while his eyes seared into hers. 'I understand perfectly. Sometimes I have that effect.'

Never had Amanda been as aware of another human being as she was of Kit at that moment. Each of them was aware of a new intensity of feeling between them, a new excitement. They stared at each other for a second of suspended time, which could as well have been an hour or two, and Amanda had a strange sensation of falling. She saw the deepening light in his eyes and the dark, silken lashes. She saw the defined brows and wanted to touch his face, to know him. Then slowly, almost haltingly, Kit lowered his mouth to hers in a kiss that warmed her to the core of her being. Parted lips, tender and insistent, caressed hers, moulding and shaping them to his own while his arms wrapped round her.

The moment he raised his head she panicked and abruptly pulled away from him. Quickly she went to the door, where she stopped, breathing hard, her heart hammering in her chest.

'Amanda?' he said, not moving, just watching her, knowing that she, too, was a victim of the overwhelming forces at work between them.

She had intended flinging open the door and running out into the rain, anything to escape these new, alien feelings Kit had brought to life inside her. She knew he was trying to snare her—it was like a clarion warning in her mind—and she knew it would be wise to flee, but she simply couldn't. It was as if her feet were made of clay. Standing there, she suddenly realised that she didn't want to leave, that without Kit there was an emptiness in her life that she did not want to admit.

When she made no move to open the door, Kit walked quietly towards her. Raising his arms, he placed them on the door, one either side of her, caging her. Slowly she turned within his arms and settled her gaze on his face. His eyes held hers. Then he raised a hand, and, with fingers curved he brushed the backs, featherlight, down her cheek.

'Why didn't you leave?'

'I—I couldn't.' Her own lack of discipline and restraint frustrated her, but she wasn't entirely certain whether to blame it on him or herself. She liked to touch him and welcomed his attentions, and the heat and craving he awakened in her.

'Will you stay?' When she didn't reply, he went on, 'I told you, Amanda, you don't have to do anything you don't want to. If you're nervous, then you shouldn't be. I'm not an animal. In fact, I think you'd find me a remarkably patient man.'

His voice had deepened. His strength and heat were palpable, touching her. When he lowered his head she lost sight of his eyes and fixed her own on his lips. They brushed hers, gently, testing their resilience, then, with the confidence that there would be a welcome, he covered her lips assuredly. That kiss almost sent her to her knees. Sensations she had never imagined overwhelmed her. The feel of him, the smell of him, sank into her bones. In response she slid her fingers to his nape.

Kit deepened his kiss, savouring, teasing, and he soon realised that although she'd been kissed before, she had never yielded her lips to any man. She tasted sweet, vulnerable and innocent, and he gloried in her softness. He wanted more of her, to appease his need. The kiss ended and he drew back slightly, sliding his hands down her bare arms. His eyes searched hers, seeing desire in their depths, and hearing it in the rapid whisper of her breath.

'You will stay?'

'Yes,' she murmured.

Taking her hand, he drew her towards the fire, seizing her lips once more, drawing her senses again into the heated depths of a kiss, as his hands deftly slipped the straps of her dress off her shoulders, revealing the cleft between the round fullness of her breasts. Her cheeks flushed scarlet at his boldness; raising his head, he laughed softly. There was still so much of the girl in her at war with the assertive young woman, and Kit had the knack of bringing it quickly to the surface. He knew that in this particular arena he had absolute control.

Bending his head to pay homage to the soft flesh glowing like creamy pearls in the soft light, he placed his lips in the hollow of her throat where a pulse throbbed. The contact was a shock to Amanda, a delicious one. Heat blossomed and spread. But the heat building inside Kit, fed and steadily stoked, was escalating into urgency. He needed to touch more, to explore without the encumbrance of fabric.

As he broke from their kiss, his long fingers fumbled with hooks, laces and buttons, cursing the constricting layers of clothing it was fashionable for women to wear in order to achieve the perfect outline, when Amanda had a faultless figure, making such clothes pointless.

'There ought to be a law against women wearing these infernal things. In fact, my love—' he breathed as his eyes lowered in appreciation of her body '—there ought to be a law against you wearing anything at all.'

Surrendering to the call of her blood, Amanda was as impatient as he to resume contact between them. Eventually, between them, they managed to slip gown, chemise and other undergarments down over the curves of her hips and thighs and toss them on to the sofa, after dragging the cushions on to the floor to create a fitting bed. Finally, holding her gaze, Kit pulled the pins from her hair and shook the thick tresses free to tumble down to her shoulders.

Her glorious body was a lustrous shade of pale gold in the wavering blur of the flickering gaslight and the flames of the fire. Chest tight, eager to seize, to devour, to slake the lust that drove him, every nerve Kit possessed stilled as slowly his gaze traced up the curves of her long legs, the gentle swell of her thighs, over her taut stomach and miniscule waist to her breasts, full and tipped with rosy peaks.

Amanda's throat dried. His gaze focused upon her figure and the ardour in his dark gaze was like a flame to her senses. She was unable to free her rational mind from the overwhelming tide of desire that claimed her, fuelled by a whirlpool of emotions she didn't recognise, much less understand.

'When you've finished ogling me, Kit, kindly remember you're supposed to be a gentleman and take off your clothes, too—unless you intend to make love to me with them on.'

Kit continued to drink his fill, noting her shallow breathing, sensing anticipation rising like scent around them. Nimble-fingered and driven by a sense of racing urgency, Amanda began fumbling with the studs securing his shirtfront. Desire having become a physical torment, he disposed of his clothes and pulled her down on to the cushions beside him, feeling the warmth from the fire fan over them. As he held her tight against him, his kisses consumed her in the violent storm of his passion. His mouth moved to circle her breasts, kissing each in turn; his lips then travelled down to her stomach, caressing, teasing, until Amanda moaned with pleasure and soared with every long sweep of his hands on her skin.

Operating wholly on instinct since her wits had flown long

since, her neck craned back and her fingers laced through his thick hair as she abandoned herself to his lips, his hands—intimate and evocative, exploring the secrets of her body like a knowledgeable lover, savouring what he found—and the pleasure that burned through her, expanding, mounting, until her body shuddered with the force of her passion.

Kit was hungry to take possession, longing to end his celibacy—forced on him in prison and self-imposed when he was released, for no other woman but his lovely young wife would do—yet he prolonged and savoured the exquisite tension, initiating new delights. When he shifted position to take control, the warmth of his body pressing full against her own, wrapping her arms about him Amanda opened up to him, her kisses driving him on, inciting his passion until he could no longer control the force that had claimed him, and she gasped as the bold, fiery brand intruded into her delicate softness, penetrating deep within her.

She cried out, but he appeared not to notice as his lips touched her brow and she could feel the beat of his heart against her naked breast. And then something new, something incredible occurred as the pain turned to pleasure. Amanda knew nothing beyond, and she began to move as he moved. He revelled in her eagerness, in her unfettered sensuality, a sensuality that spoke to his as she responded to his passion, his desire. Kit felt her body soften under his, felt her resistance melt away in total surrender.

No moment had ever felt like this. He was filled with a sense of rightness, of it being his due, as if to possess her had been his goal ever since she had come to his prison cell, an ambition at long last realised. They strained together in one all-consuming need, no longer two separate entities but one being, swept away, hurtling and twisting, onwards and upwards in a frenzied wildness, striving to reach the same goal.

At last a blissful aura broke over them. Spent and exhausted, slowly they drifted back to earth, drained and incapable of any movement other than holding each other close. Amanda sighed, the physicality of their lovemaking, her vulnerability and her implicit surrender sweeping over her as her hand caressed Kit's furred chest. He eased away from her, and, drifting on a tide of glory, in the aftermath of their passion she curled against him, her body aglow, her limbs weighted with contentment, firm in the belief that her husband was a man of extraordinary skill and prowess. Finding his lips, she kissed him softly, then, lost in the wonder of completeness, naked limbs entwined, with a soft sigh she sank into the cushions and let exhaustion claim her.

Looking down at her flushed features and knowing she slept, Kit disentangled her arms and legs and rose. Going into the bedroom, he turned down the covers. Returning to Amanda, he gathered her up into his arms and carried her to the bed. Placing her on the sheets, he stretched out beside her, and it wasn't long before she stirred and she reached for him once more.

Chapter Seven

Much later, Kit leaned on his elbow and gazed down at the young woman with the silky mass of her hair draped about her, his mind still reeling when he thought of the flagrant sensuality of the creature lying next to him. He was engulfed in a swirling mass of emotions, emotions that were new to him, emotions he could not recognise and could not put a name to. His every instinct reacted to the fact that he had this woman in thrall, that he'd finally breached the walls and captured the elusive creature at its core. He gloried in the fact that she was his, here, now, without reserve. Gently he touched her hair, brushing her flesh with his arm, feeling the warm reality of her.

Conscious of the languor that weighted his limbs, of the satiation that was bone deep, he realised that this state had been reached not by mere self-gratification, but by a deep contentment more profound than at any other time in his life. Amanda had succeeded in tapping the source of his wellbeing where every other woman he had known had failed.

And yet what did it mean? What was the next step? No matter how hard he had worked to lure her into his bed, to force her to accept once and for all that she was his wife in every sense, he could not openly acknowledge her as such, not until he had fulfilled his mission—that other reason that had brought him to Eden Park.

Amanda sensed the presence of a warm, naked, masculine form pressed against her as she floated in a comforting grey mist, drifting in and out of sleep. Lying soft and acquiescent beside him, she could smell his skin, his hair, and he was drawing her to him like a magnet.

'Good morning,' Kit murmured huskily. 'I trust you slept well.'

Opening her sleepy eyes, she gazed up at him. His tousled hair, with an errant wave falling over his brow, was dark against the snowy whiteness of the pillows, and sleep had softened the rugged contours of his handsome face. He was a magnificent male, and utterly irresistible in his naked state. She thought of the times he'd made love to her throughout the night. The first time he had loved her with a wild abandon, but thereafter he had exercised more control, lingering over her, holding himself back while he guided her to peak after peak of quivering ecstasy, caressing and kissing her with the skill and expertise of a virtuoso playing a violin.

With these memories shifting in her mind, she felt her lips, swollen from his kisses, part in a smile. 'I seem to recall you gave me little time for such luxury, Mr Benedict,' she answered, her voice low, throaty and warm. 'How long have you been lying there watching me?'

His smouldering gaze passed over her naked shoulders, lingering on the twin peaks straining beneath the sheet. 'Long enough to come to the conclusion that you are too much temptation for a man not long out of prison and starved of a woman's company. In fact, my love, if you were not already married, after our night making passionate love, I would have to marry you,' he teased, kissing the tip of her nose.

'Then it's a good thing I'm a married woman,' she purred, trailing her fingers lightly across his chest, 'although I shudder to think what my husband will have to say about it. Why, he might even insist on divorcing me.'

'You may strive at times to drive him to it, being the stubborn and temperamental wench that you are, but I can promise you that he will never divorce you,' Kit stated. His voice still held a hint of teasing, but his eyes were dark and deadly serious.

'What time is it?' she asked, stretching like a sated cat, her gaze going towards the window. Seeing a weak shade of grey, which told her dawn was about to break, she was jolted awake as a mild panic set in. 'Heavens, it will soon be daylight. I must get back before anyone sees me.' Sliding from the bed, she quickly sped into the other room and pulled on her clothes as best she could, making Kit—now properly clad in breeches and shirt—do up the laces and hooks on her undergarments and button her into her dress.

'I'll walk with you to the house.'

Shoving her arms into the sleeves of her coat, which he was holding up for her, she flicked him a glance. 'You most certainly will not. Should anyone see you with me at this hour, sneaking me into the house by the back door, they'll put two and two together and make four.'

'Surely the doors will be locked and bolted at this time.'

'It's past five o'clock; with so many guests in residence, the servants will be about their business earlier than they normally would be. Some of the doors at the back of the house will have been unlocked so they can have access to the yard where the coal is kept.' Before leaving she turned to him, her face grave. 'Kit, I really don't want our relationship to be known just yet. Let this be our secret a while longer. Last night was wonderful but it has confused things. The truth will have to come out, I know, but I have to figure out a way to tell my father. You do understand, don't you?'

His expression became grave and he felt defensive. 'When the time comes for him to know we will tell him together. There is bound to be gossip—and I regret that, but it cannot be helped. But fear not, my love. I, too, have reasons for our marriage to remain secret for the time being.'

Amanda frowned in puzzlement. 'Why is that?'

'You say people are beginning to comment on my presence here at Eden Park. I do not welcome that. They do not know me, and the mystery Caroline says surrounds me will allow the gossips to build my life into some sort of fantasy. For both our sakes I sincerely hope that does not happen. I don't like gossip, Amanda. I don't like my life and everything I do to be the topic of discussion. I take a great deal of trouble to avoid it. I cannot afford to give anything away. Should our marriage be made known, my identity would be exposed.'

Amanda was puzzled and quietly alarmed. 'Kit, is there something I should know about? Why would that matter?'

'I have my reasons,' he said, placing a kiss lightly on her lips, 'which I will tell you soon enough. Until then, you know the path to my door.'

Standing by the window, Kit watched her go. His face was quite still, his eyes drawn compulsively to the woman who was now his wife in every sense hurrying away. A deep and satisfying contentment engulfed him as he gloried in the sweet, wild essence of her. The instant he had taken her in his arms she had ceased to be an impudent, recalcitrant female and had been transformed into a sighing, pliable, sensual creature, as placid as a mill pond. She was womanly, beautiful and tantalising, her body a hidden treasure. And she belonged to him. He watched her until she had disappeared past the stables, and he stood there long after, deep in thought.

Amanda was unaware as she slipped through a back door that she was being watched. Mr Quinn's rooms were in the part that overlooked the stables, well away from the family quarters. Always an early riser, he had watched Amanda hurry past the stables and was puzzled as to what she could be doing out and about at such an early hour, her hair tumbling in disarray about her shoulders.

His gaze shifted to the park and the cottage in the distance. He frowned as he considered this, and a suspicion that there might be something going on of an intimate nature between her and her father's horse trainer took root. Quinn cursed the man—Sadie, with a spring in her step and a warm glcam in her eyes for Mr Benedict, continued to clean for him despite Quinn's interference in domestic matters to have someone else do Benedict's daily chores.

But thinking of Amanda, considering her behaviour in Charleston and her marriage to a convicted murderer, staying overnight alone in a house with a man should neither surprise nor shock him. He would not put anything past her. However, it had certainly given him something to think about and he would be more watchful of her from now on.

After leaving Kit's cottage an uneasy disquiet had begun to settle in before Amanda reached the house. In an attempt to try to snatch a few hours' sleep before Nan came in, she undressed and climbed into bed, but the unease would not go away. Now she was away from Kit and the delicious afterglow of their coupling had diminished, she told herself she would have to take a grip on herself and try to think about this new turn in their relationship and what it would mean for both their futures.

Deep inside she was afraid—afraid of the power he was capable of wielding over her emotions, and afraid of what her father's reaction would be to her marriage to Kit and the manner of it. Would he be angry, heartbroken? She would have to leave Eden Park in exchange for the sort of home Kit could offer her, she knew that. But how would she fit in when she had always had so much? She had always had the best of everything, absolutely everything: a fine house to live in, expensive clothes and no financial worries.

These thoughts caused her to think about her life and her eyes darkened with despair as she contemplated the future in which she would be just as she was now. Surely there had to be more to life than this. And what would she do if Kit walked away—when she wanted him more than she had ever wanted anyone? How would she feel if he told her he didn't want her after all? Dear Lord, she thought, she couldn't bear it.

'Oh, Kit,' she whispered to herself as she drew the covers over her head, 'what have you done to me? What might you do to me if I let you?'

He roused such wanton emotions in her she could scarcely believe it of herself. Closing her eyes, she tried to close her mind, and suddenly she could almost feel Kit's hands on her body, his mouth covering hers, his warm lips moving, gently coaxing, then deepening in a kiss that was wildly erotic and she was joyously surrendering to him as she had earlier. She felt as if she were slowly suffocating. At the height of their lovemaking he had told her they belonged together, and she had felt it just like he had, she had known it—as surely as she knew how difficult it would be.

His parting words—that it was imperative they kept their relationship secret for the time being—caused her some unease. Who was this man she had married and what did she really know about him? Where did he come from and why this need for secrecy? She no longer believed his reason for coming to Eden Park as Kit Benedict and not Christopher Claybourne was solely because of her, and, if not, then what other reason could there be? Had it anything to do with what had happened to him in Charleston? But if the charges of murder against him had been dropped, then why the subterfuge and the need for secrecy?

The weekend house party came to an end. All the guests had enjoyed themselves to such a degree that they lingered, eating and drinking and enthusing over the magnificence of Eden Park, the entertainment and their hosts' generous hospitality. And then they were gone, and after a brief interlude of quiet to enable everyone to catch their breath, servants began scurrying all over the place in a frenzy of activity as preparations were made for Henry and Caroline's visit to London. The visit was for two weeks, but anyone seeing the enormous heap of baggage would think they were about to embark on a grand tour of Europe.

Henry hugged his daughter and went to get into the carriage, telling Caroline not to linger lest they missed the train.

Looking extremely fetching in an elegant magenta-coloured travelling suit and hat with an elaborate feather curling round the brim, Caroline told him they had ample time and then turned her smiling face to Amanda.

'You really should have been coming with us, Amanda—after all, you were invited. You would have enjoyed yourself so much.'

'I'll be all right here, truly. I hope you and Father enjoy yourselves—but there is one thing I will ask of you.'

'And what is that?'

'That you promise to introduce Father to every aristocrat at the ball—I would suggest in the whole of London, but two weeks doesn't give you time for that.'

Caroline laughed and kissed her cheek. 'I promise I shall do my absolute best. By the end of our stay, Henry will be so tired of crowns and coronets that he will be glad to come home to his horses.'

Amanda waved as the carriage pulled away. She stood for a moment, watching it disappear down the drive, her thoughts turning to Kit, as they always did when she was alone.

She hadn't seen him since she had left his cottage four days ago, when she had been swept away on a great rush of emotion and longing and desire. Their night together had been special and wonderful and the thought that it might never be repeated was unbearable and hurt so deeply that it settled on her heart like a stone. Kit was the reason why she couldn't sleep, why she tossed and turned, restless and unsatisfied. Closing her eyes, she wrapped her arms around her waist tightly, letting her mind drift to the prospect of repeating what she had experienced.

When the carriage had disappeared from sight, on a sigh she turned to go back into the house, only to find Mr Quinn behind her. She stiffened. After finding him coupling with Sadie Jenkins, she found each encounter extremely distasteful. Dressed all in black and with a face as inscrutable as the Derbyshire crags, he looked like the harbinger of woe. Suppressing a shudder, she looked at him, keeping her face clear of thoughts. It was best to do so with Mr Quinn.

'You startled me, Mr Quinn. I didn't know you were behind me.'

'I apologise, I did not mean to. I am surprised you did not accompany your father to London—knowing of your liking for enjoyment—though perhaps the enjoyment you seek is not to be found in London but here, at Eden Park.'

His voice was as cold as his eyes were accusing. Amanda stared at him. In the brief, heavy silence that fell between them, her heart almost ceased to beat. 'I really have no idea what you mean, Mr Quinn.'

'I think you do. No doubt their absence will enable you to continue your affair with Mr Benedict.' His words were hard edged and meaningful.

Animosity combined with resentment surged through Amanda. She was appalled that he should know, let alone mention that there was anything going on between her and Kit. She would neither confirm nor deny anything to Mr Quinn.

'I happened to see you leaving his cottage several days ago— it was dawn to be precise.' Quinn hadn't actually seen her come out but the look she gave him confirmed his suspicion.

Having paused to gather her wits before she could speak, Amanda's eyes narrowed furiously. 'Did you indeed,' she uttered between clenched teeth. 'Mr Quinn, I think you forget yourself. I deeply resent your interference in what I do, particularly about something that does not concern you.'

'And whom does it concern? Your father? I doubt he is aware that your relationship with his horse trainer is rather more than that of a mere acquaintance.'

'No, Mr Quinn, he is not, and if Mr Benedict and I are involved in any kind of relationship, I shall be the one to inform my father, not you.'

'Ah, but will you? After all, we both know you are a connoisseur in the art of deceit.'

'And so are you, Mr Quinn. So are you.'

'Are you saying my observation of you coming from Mr Benedict's cottage at dawn might have been misconstrued?'

She gave him a hard stare. 'Yes, Mr Quinn, I am. Interpret it as you will, but it is none of your business.'

He smiled thinly. 'Come now, Amanda, such harsh words are hardly justified. I know too much about you for you to make me your enemy.'

'Enemy? Are you threatening me again, Mr Quinn?'

His eyes narrowed ever so slightly. 'I never threaten, Amanda, I always act. However, in this instance I am merely trying to point out the embarrassment it may cause should it be made known that you are carrying on an illicit relationship with your father's horse trainer. If ever I should take a notion to tell your father to what lengths you went to acquire yourself a husband in America in order to gain your independence from him, the scandal it would create would be vicious indeed without the added awkwardness of an illicit affair while still in mourning for your dear departed husband,' he finished with biting sarcasm.

Amanda paled, unable to believe what he was saying. 'How dare you? There is a cordial understanding between us, lest you have forgotten—your own words, Mr Quinn,' she reminded him drily. 'I kept my silence regarding you and Sadie Jenkins, and I fully expect you to do the same.'

'Not a word has passed my lips.'

'And never will, if you value your position. Have you got your feet so firmly fixed under my father's table that you forget you are an employee just like Mr Benedict?'

'Who, as it turns out, is nothing but a social-climbing parasite,' Quinn retorted coldly.

Appalled by his uncalled-for remark about Kit, Amanda stepped away from him. 'I will not stay to listen to any more of this, and I would appreciate it if you didn't spy on me in future. I need no instruction from you on how to conduct myself in public or in private—again, I recall you saying those very words to me, Mr Quinn,' she said, her voice heavily laced with sarcasm. 'My father may have made you my guardian for the time I was in Charleston, but your duty ended when we reached England.' Abruptly she turned on her heel and walked into the house.

* * *

It was later in the day when Nan came to tell Amanda that Kit had been called away urgently. 'Something about Sky being taken sick,' Nan told her, concern written all over her face, for she, too, had become extremely fond of the little girl on the crossing from America and had not forgotten her.

Amanda stared at Nan, her face drained of colour as she thought of Sky. 'Is it serious?'

'You'll have to ask your Mr Benedict.'

'Is he still here?'

'He was ten minutes ago when he ordered the carriage to take him to the station in Sheffield.'

Amanda's response was immediate and, with the strength that comes from somewhere when it is needed, abruptly she left the house and began running towards Kit's cottage. How could he leave without telling her? Without knocking she burst in to find Kit dressed for travelling and packing his clothes into a large leather bag. His shoulders stiffened when she entered, and when he turned and looked at her, she could almost feel the effort he was exerting to keep himself calm. His handsome face seemed carved in stone, and the look he gave her was sufficiently cold to send a chill through her heart.

Suddenly Amanda's attention was taken when a young woman emerged from the tiny kitchen carrying a basket of cleaning equipment. She was wearing a white apron over her flouncy skirts, and her strawberry-blonde curls were pulled up in a loose knot, a few corkscrew curls bouncing free.

It was Sadie Jenkins—voluptuous, voracious, alluring Sadie. She drew men to her as moths to a flame—almost without benefit of conscious effort. According to Nan, who seemed to know everything that went on on the domestic front, Sadie did not allow the lowlier male servants to fondle and grope her, and they soon learned that the wickedly flirtatious

Sadie had her heart set upon a loftier destiny. And, Amanda thought drily, who was loftier at Eden Park than Mr Quinn, until some other came along to take her fancy? Now Amanda realised from the way her big, calf-like eyes were devouring an unsuspecting Kit, that that particular fancy had fallen on Eden Park's new horse trainer, the handsome Mr Benedict.

'Thank you, Sadie,' Amanda said sharply, deeply resentful. 'You can go now. I wish to speak to Mr Benedict alone and I am sure you have duties at the house to attend to.'

Sadie glared a little at being so summarily dismissed, but any indignation she might be feeling she stifled. She glanced warily at Mrs Claybourne, surprised that after she had caught her and Mr Quinn in bed together she hadn't been dismissed, and wondered what Mr Quinn could have said that had persuaded her to let her stay on. Still, it wasn't for such as her to question the decisions of Mrs Claybourne. She was just glad she was still in employment. And it was nice having the handsome Mr Benedict to do for. Perhaps when he got back from wherever it was he was going she might succeed in tempting him. There could be many cosy evenings to be had in his snug cottage.

Bestowing on the aforesaid gentleman her most provocative smile, with a flutter of her long lashes and a toss of her curly head, she swept out of the cottage with an exaggerated sway of her rounded hips.

'Amanda! To what do I owe the pleasure?' Kit mocked harshly when the door had closed on Sadie. 'Just when I thought you'd forgotten the way to my door—here you are, when I am about to go away.' He glowered at her from beneath heavy brows. For one endless, timeless night she had belonged to him, body and soul, but then she had snatched away that brief glimpse of heaven by purposely avoiding him, leaving him to exist in a state of seething frustration.

'Kit, I've just heard about Sky,' she said breathlessly, tucking a heavy lock of hair that had escaped its pins behind her ear. 'I'm so sorry she's ill and do hope it isn't serious.'

'Really. Children become sick all the time. Victoria has written to tell me Sky has a fever—nothing to get unduly worried about—and is fretting for me, that she is quite inconsolable, so I am sure you will understand why I have to leave immediately.'

'Did you intend leaving without telling me?'

'No. I would have come to the house when I'd packed, but since you're here you've saved me the trouble. Where have you been, by the way?'

Amanda was taken aback by his harsh tone, and put his ill temper down to his anxiety over Sky. 'You seem to forget I have duties…'

He looked at her sharply. 'I would have said it was you who forgets, Amanda. Might I enquire why—after that night—you chose to avoid me, why you have abandoned your daily ride?' He arched his brows mockingly. 'Afraid of coming into contact with me, were you, my love?'

She noted there was nothing lover-like in his endearment and was sorry for it. 'I didn't—not purposely. Caroline has kept me so busy—we had calls to make…' Amanda said lamely, knowing he didn't believe her, and in truth she had been so confused since that night that she didn't even know herself why she had kept away from him.

'Forget it. I am not in the least bit interested in your social engagements. I am more interested in catching my train.'

His remark stung like salt in an open wound and at any other time Amanda would have hit back with some cutting remark, but this was not the time for acrimony. At that moment she wanted him so much, wanted to feel his arms about her, to give him the warmth and love he deserved. But she could only stand and watch him pack his bag, distanced by his cold manner.

'It's a pity you didn't know about Sky earlier. You could have travelled down to London with Father and Caroline.'

'Yes, isn't it,' he ground out, having put everything in his bag he would need and fastening the buckles on the leather straps. 'I've left instructions to make sure the horses are well looked after.'

Amanda moved closer to him as an awful thought suddenly occurred to her. 'Oh—damn the horses. Kit, you will be coming back, won't you? You cannot leave Eden Park. Father depends on you, you know that.'

'Your father?' he repeated, astounded. 'What is more important to me, Amanda, is do *you* want me to come back?'

'Yes,' she said in a small voice. 'Of course I do.'

He paused in what he was doing and stared down at her. As he searched for the truth behind her words, there was anger and sickness within his heart. 'Damn you, Amanda!' he exclaimed furiously. 'You have placed me in an intolerable position. I am tempted to give you your divorce and end this chaos you have brought to my life.'

She bristled. 'Then why don't you?'

'Never!' His eyes flashed their dark fires. 'I will never do that, so do not torment me,' he warned. 'Has it not occurred to you that you might be carrying my child? Have you not thought of that?'

'No, I must confess I haven't.' Her hand instinctively went to her abdomen with a mixture of emotions—a wistful sort of excitement, hope and fear.

'Well perhaps you should. I'll not be made party to any kind of games you fancy playing, when you know as assuredly as I that we will be together. It will be so.' When he turned back to his task, there was no softening to his features. 'I have come to have a true liking and respect for Henry and would not just up and leave him. I also have unfinished business to attend to here at Eden Park—and I am not talking about the horses. When I return, I promise you things will be different between us. You belong to me, as I belong to you, whatever you may suppose. I will speak to your father, and after that we will leave for my home.'

Amanda stared at him. 'Home? And where is that?'

'Cambridgeshire—and I can promise you you will be comfortable living there.'

'But what about this matter you have to resolve? I am extremely puzzled and concerned, Kit—what could there possibly be at Eden Park that, apart from coming to see me, brought you here?'

'I shall resolve that, too—which will be a damn sight more unpleasant than telling your father about us. I may also bring Sky back with me—I'll hire a nursemaid to look after her during the day while I'm working.'

'There will be no need for that. She will find it strange enough without a stranger looking after her. I know Nan would love to have charge of her and Sky will remember her, I'm sure. They spent a great deal of time together on the voyage from America and became close—in fact, your daughter left a lasting impression on us both.'

Kit's features softened. 'Thank you, but I do not wish to deprive you of your maid.'

'The house is full of maids and my needs are small. Nan will regard looking after Sky as a pleasure.'

'I have to say it will solve the problem. When I came back to England I thought it was in her best interests to leave Sky with Victoria while I became reacquainted with my wife, but as things have turned out I should not have left her—we have been apart too long my daughter and I.'

'Kit, you cannot blame yourself.'

'I don't. I blame the bastard who set me up for a murder I did not commit and was prepared to let me swing for it,' he said savagely. The muscles flexed in his cheek, giving evidence of his constrained anger. 'I swore I would not rest until I found him.

'Because the man who killed Carmen was never caught, there are many people who doubted I was nowhere near at the time and thought that Judd's evidence was fixed. Mud sticks, and I had plenty thrown at me to drown in. The only way, the surest way, I can claim social acceptability—not just for myself, but for you and Sky—is to prove beyond doubt that someone else committed the murder.'

'So the reason for your subterfuge, for the concealment of your true name, is because of this man?'

He nodded. 'I could not have come to Eden Park and claimed you as my wife otherwise, nor could I think of a better ploy to outwit Carmen's real killer than to alter my name.' Hearing the jingle of harness outside, he went to the window and looked out. 'The carriage is here,' he said, seizing his bag. 'I have to go.'

Amanda's throat swelled with pain and she felt tears prick the backs of her eyes. She looked at him with eager tenderness. He could not go like this, not with anger in his heart. 'Yes—yes, you must,' she heard herself saying. 'I hope you have a safe journey—and please give Sky my love, won't you. Tell her—I—look forward to seeing her.' He turned and walked to the door. Amanda's eyes followed his tall figure helplessly.

On the point of going outside, Kit stopped and slowly his dark eyes came back to her. She looked so piteous, so defenceless, and her eyes begged him to go back to her. With the irrationality of the emotions only she had the power to stir in him, the memories of that shared night were reinforced and compassion moved his heart.

Dropping his bag, he took four long strides back to her and fiercely caught her to him. Her arms crept around his neck and she clung to him with all her strength. They stood locked together in an embrace, which contained longing, peace and a calm acceptance that eventually they would be together. After placing his lips against her sweet-smelling hair and drawing a long breath, Kit released her.

'I'll be back just as soon as I can. In the meantime, take care of yourself. If my true identity becomes known, the situation will turn dangerous—not just for me, but for you also.'

'Why—what do you mean? Kit,' she cried in earnest, grasping his arm lest he disappear, 'you have to tell me. You can't leave me like this—not knowing.'

After a moment, Kit spoke, his eyes on hers. 'The man who killed Carmen believes I was hanged for the crime, that the matter is closed and he is safe. If my identity is made public, the murderer will find himself under threat. Do you understand what I am saying, Amanda?'

She nodded, her eyes locked on his as she juggled the facts. 'And do you think he will strike back in some way?'

'I'm certain of it. If he can kill once, he will think nothing of doing so again, which is why I want you to take care and be alert at all times.'

'But who from? Who is this man you suspect…?' Suddenly, as the final piece to her mental jigsaw was slotted into place, Amanda knew, and everything seemed plunged into confusion. Her face became drained of colour at the dreadful thought and what it could mean for them all.

'You think it's Mr Quinn, don't you, Kit?' she whispered, as if afraid to say it out loud lest it be true. 'But it can't possibly be him.'

'Why not? You said yourself that you know nothing about him.'

'Because he was in Charleston at the time doesn't make him a murderer. I have known him for a long time—he may be many things but he is not a murderer. He is my father's most trusted employee. He has always considered his position and my father's good name and acts with complete discretion. I could never believe that Mr Quinn—so private, so reserved with his extraordinary self-possession—might end another's life.'

'Who can claim to know what motivates a man when he is obsessed by a woman as beautiful as Carmen was? I do not lie to you, Amanda,' Kit stated firmly. 'He killed her in a fit of rage when she rejected him.'

Amanda stared at him in disbelief. This really was shocking if it were true. 'And do you have evidence to link him with Carmen's death?'

He raised his brows fractionally. 'Enough to prove it was him. Only one servant, an old gardener, gave testimony that didn't incriminate me, but because he was old and often given to fantasising when in drink, his evidence was thrown out.'

'And you questioned him after you were released?'

'Yes—and he was completely sober. Three days before her murder, the gardener had seen Carmen go into a greenhouse and he had started after her, intending to ask her about digging over some flower beds. He had not approached her, however, because he saw her with a man, a man not unlike me in stature and colouring—but he was adamant that it wasn't me. The man had his back to the gardener and they were arguing. He again saw the man approach the house and let himself in on the night Carmen was murdered—this time he saw his face, but the man was a stranger to him.'

'Then how did he know it was Mr Quinn?'

'He saw him once more—at the harbour, on the day Mr Quinn left Charleston—and enquired as to his name.'

'I see. And you believed him.'

'Yes, absolutely. So you see, Amanda, your father's most trusted employee is not what he seems.'

'When do you intend confronting him?'

'Until I decide what steps to take next, I have no wish to see him just yet. It is fortunate that Mr Quinn and I never met, which was why I deemed it safe to come here. Amanda, I didn't want you to know about Quinn until I returned, but now you know, you can be on your guard.' Looking at his watch, he drew her to him and took her lips in a brief kiss. 'I must go.'

'Yes—go then. Go quickly—and please come back soon.'

'When I return I will tell you everything. I promise. And remember, Quinn mustn't suspect a thing.' Turning resolutely, he picked up his bag and went out.

Amanda watched him climb aboard. The driver, aware of Kit's need for haste, whipped up the horses into a gallop. Watching the carriage disappear down the drive through a blur of tears, she felt strangely bereft, and not for the first time wondered at her feelings for Kit. It was foolish, she knew, to know she would miss a man she had married for no other reason than to thwart her father in order to be independent of him. The sense of satisfaction she had felt at outwitting him had long since departed.

From the moment she had known Kit was alive she had been telling herself that she was drawn to him because of his handsome looks and his aura of powerful magnetism. She had almost convinced herself that this was the reason, that the strange hold he had over her was nothing more than his ability to awaken the sexual hunger within her. Now she realised that this was just a small portion of the truth, and that what she shared with Kit went far beyond either physical or romantic love. It was deeper, something primitive and dangerously enduring, weaving its spell about them both and pulling them inexorably together.

As she walked slowly back to the house her mind dwelt on all Kit had told her about Mr Quinn, which she found so hard to believe. It was as if he had suddenly thrown off his human shape and become some kind of monster. Until now she had thought of him as calm, stoic, dutiful and completely loyal to her father, but Kit's revelation had presented a picture of an unscrupulous and cold-hearted man of unpredictable violence. But whether he had it in him to kill was difficult for her to judge.

She dreaded the moment when they would next meet. Fortunately she was given a temporary reprieve when he went off to Manchester early the following morning about her father's business.

Henry and Caroline arrived back at Eden Park in good spirits after their time in London, and with twice the amount of luggage they had taken.

With quiet amusement, Amanda looked knowingly at her stepmother. 'I see you've been shopping, Caroline.'

'Oh, my dear,' Caroline enthused, taking the pin out of her elaborately adorned hat and handing both to the maid, 'how can anyone resist Bond Street or Oxford Street? I bought you a present—the most exquisite silk fan from the Far East, which I shall give to you just as soon as my maid has unpacked it.' Ordering tea to be brought into the drawing room, she proceeded to tell Amanda all about their visit.

'Things turned out very well. It was a wonderful visit. It was lovely to see my sister and catch up on everything that's been happening. Henry enjoyed every aspect of it, didn't you, Henry?'

Caroline cast her husband a fond look that didn't go unnoticed by Amanda. It gladdened her heart to see how close they were, and that they were a fulfilled and happy couple.

'He was in his element,' Caroline went on. 'I have a feeling he will insist on a return visit and will be inviting my sister and her husband to Eden Park before too long. He was introduced to simply everyone of note and capable of such eloquence that he had everyone enthralled.'

Amanda smiled at her father. 'There is nothing new in that. He's never had any difficulty conversing with people.'

'We're not home for long, Amanda. We've been invited to stay with Lord and Lady Covington in Cambridgeshire for a few days in three weeks' time. Lord Covington has a racehorse to sell that Henry's interested in taking a look at—and of course Kit will have to be there. The invitation extends to you, too. Do say you'll come. You will be company for me and a change of scene will do you good.'

'I might. I'll think about it.'

'Please do. You may also be interested to know that we have a guest arriving in two days' time,' Caroline went on. 'He's to stay with us for while. He was introduced to us in London. His name is Señor Rafael Ortega—quite a mouthful—and would you believe he is from Charleston, so the two of you will have plenty to talk about. He's also extremely interested in horses.'

'I think you'll find his interest is limited to the race track,' Henry remarked, setting his cup down with a rattle and standing up. 'Didn't know what to make of him myself, though Caroline was quite taken with him—and about a hundred other ladies too, I might add. I'll leave you girls to catch up,' he said, crossing to the door, 'while I go about my business.'

'And where would that be?' Amanda asked, knowing perfectly well that he intended going to the stables.

'To see Kit. I have some catching up of my own to do.'

'Father, Kit isn't here.' Henry stopped and looked back at her enquiringly. 'He had to go to London—the same day as you, as a matter of fact. His daughter had been taken ill and he was most anxious when he left. He might even bring her back here when she is well enough.'

Henry harrumphed and nodded. 'Aye, well, that's as it should be. As long as the little mite gets better, that's what matters. Child without a mother needs its father—big responsibility—and I should know. Well, I'll go to the stables anyway—see if everything's running as it should. Hopefully Kit should be back before we have to leave for Cambridgeshire.'

Two days later the gentleman from Charleston arrived at Eden Park. Impeccably dressed in a black suit, which emphasised the stark whiteness of his cravat, he was about thirty-five, neatly handsome in the Spanish style. His skin was tanned, his hair shiny black and wavy, his eyes dark and extraordinarily penetrating. He had the erect bearing and outward steeliness of a man who knew what he wanted and got it.

'How do you do,' Amanda said when Caroline drew her forward to be introduced and then drifted off to speak to Henry. The Spaniard's keen eyes fastened on Amanda as though to sound her very depths. An involuntary shiver ran down her spine, which she suppressed. 'I am very pleased to meet you.' She extended a hand and he responded by taking her fingers and gallantly brushing a kiss upon them.

'Enchanted, Mrs Claybourne. The pleasure is all mine, I assure you,' he said with the well-remembered drawl of the American south and no hint of a Spanish accent. He frowned, studying her thoughtfully. 'Claybourne—Claybourne,' he repeated. 'I've heard that name before but I am plagued if I can remember where.'

Amanda met his deliberate stare. 'It is not an uncommon

name. There are a great many Claybournes in England. I do hope your stay at Eden Park will be pleasant.'

'How can it fail to be anything else, with such charming company. I've come to see how you enjoy yourselves in the north.'

'My father tells me you are from Charleston, Señor Ortega.'

'Please call me Rafael. We Americans do tend to be informal.'

'I do remember.' She smiled. 'That was one of the things I liked about Charleston.'

'I was born in Mexico, but I have lived all my life in Charleston. I regret not meeting you when you were there. You enjoyed your visit, I hope?'

'Very much—although it was saddened by my aunt's death. What is your occupation—or are you a gentleman of leisure?'

'Oh, I dabble in this and that—as long as I can afford a few creature comforts I am content.'

'And you are interested in horses.'

'Purely from a racing man's point of view.'

'So you are a gambling man.'

'I certainly am—and I am eager to see Henry's stable. He has told me how splendid his horses are and how he hopes to start a stud.'

'Yes, but it's early days yet.'

'Nevertheless, I'm looking forward to seeing them, and to meeting his trainer—Mr Benedict, I believe he said his name was.'

Amanda perused him speculatively. Was she imagining it or did a hint of the predatory reach her, and was there a trace of disguised intent in his dark eyes? 'Yes. Kit's highly experienced with horses and recognises good bloodstock when he sees it. He's become extremely valuable to my father—in fact, he relies on his judgement entirely. I don't know what he'd do without him.'

'No one is indispensable, Mrs Claybourne—not even your Mr Benedict.'

He was looking at Amanda closely, but she couldn't read the expression on his face. It was too complicated, too masked, and it gave her a deep-rooted feeling of unease. Nor did she like his slight emphasis on the word *your*. She was relieved when Caroline came back to join in the conversation.

Throughout the exchange between Amanda and Rafael, Caroline had been studying her stepdaughter intently. It was evident that Amanda was making a valiant effort to seem casual, but there was a tension about her stance that told Caroline she needed rescuing. 'Do you ride, Rafael?' Caroline asked of their guest.

'I most certainly do.'

'Amanda is an excellent rider. I don't ride myself—never have—never wanted to. In fact, I have an aversion to getting too close to a horse, which Henry will never be able to understand.' She looked at Amanda. 'Perhaps you will take Rafael out with you tomorrow, Amanda. Make sure he has a decent mount. I am sure we can accommodate him.'

'Yes, of course,' Amanda instantly replied, giving Rafael a polite smile.

'And, in the meantime, I am sure Henry will look up the next race meeting for you,' Caroline said.

'I would be grateful if he would. Maybe your trainer can give me a few tips on the runners,' Rafael said, idly picking up a dainty figurine and making a play of examining it closely. 'Local man, is he?'

'Why, I've really no idea where he comes from,' Caroline replied.

'I believe he comes from Cambridgeshire,' Amanda offered without thinking, and regretted it the moment she'd said it.

Caroline looked at her in surprise. 'Does he? Well, now we know. Sadly Kit has been called away for a while—some illness in the family. Henry received a letter from him this morning, Amanda. Did you know?' Caroline saw something quicken in Amanda's eyes and she smiled quietly to herself, satisfied that her announcement had had its desired effect.

'No—no, I didn't,' she answered, trying to sound calm and look composed, when all the time she wanted to run from the room and read the letter. 'Is everything all right—did he say?'

'Yes, I believe so. His daughter is recovering nicely and he is to travel back in the next few days.'

'Then that's a relief,' Rafael said, his gaze settling on Amanda. 'I was sorry indeed to hear about your husband's demise, Mrs Claybourne—so soon after you were married. You were married in Charleston, weren't you?'

His question took Amanda by complete surprise and chilled something within her. 'Yes, we were.' His keen eyes fastened on hers intently.

Caroline's sharp eyes saw the colour drain from Amanda's face. Sensing her discomfort, she steered Rafael off the subject of her stepdaughter's marriage. There was something strange about that that had yet to be explained. 'I recall you telling me in London that you spent some considerable time in New York before coming to England, Rafael.'

'I did—busy, bustling place it was too.'

'Then I shall look forward to hearing all about it over dinner.' She looked at Amanda. 'Don't you think you should go and change, Amanda? Dinner will be announced soon and you know how impatient Henry always is for his meals. He so hates to be kept waiting.'

Amanda gave her a grateful smile and excused herself. As she left the room she asked herself what a man from Charleston could be doing at Eden Park. Was it just coincidence, or could it spell trouble for Kit? She had no way of knowing, but, whatever the reason, she must not utter one word that would jeopardise him.

Chapter Eight

Later, Caroline came to Amanda's room to accompany her to dinner.

'Amanda, are you all right?'

'Yes, why shouldn't I be?' she asked, studying her appearance with a critical eye in the cheval mirror, unsure that the green dress she was wearing went with her hair. 'Do you think this colour green suits me, Caroline?'

'Of course it does. You look as lovely as you always do. You don't mind Rafael staying with us, do you?'

'No, of course not. He's your guest, after all. He seems quite charming—although I think your Spanish gentleman is not all he seems, and that his smooth tongue is his finest asset. Why do you ask?'

'I saw the way he was looking at you. You noticed it, too. It made you nervous—especially when he enquired about your husband.'

'He touched on a raw nerve, that's all, Caroline.'

Lowering her gaze, Caroline smiled, not entirely convinced by Amanda's reply. 'Well, if that's all it was. You know, Amanda, men like Señor Ortega generate enough sexual energy to drive a train. It's a power they have and they use it on any attractive woman they meet. Take care, won't you?'

'He has a lot of charm and a lot of polish and is handsome, I suppose. I can quite see why some women must be dazzled by all that, but after a year in Charleston, Caroline, I've developed an understanding of his type,' Amanda said firmly, 'and therefore an immunity to it.'

Caroline tilted her head to one side and met her eyes in the mirror. 'And Kit? Have you developed an immunity to him?'

Amanda turned away and began fiddling with her hair, which had been arranged by Nan perfectly and needed nothing else doing to it. 'Kit? Why do you ask?'

'Oh, no particular reason. I was just surprised that you seemed to know more about him than I realised.'

'You mean when I told Señor Ortega that he comes from Cambridgeshire? I can't see anything strange in that. Kit just happened to mention it—I don't recall when.'

'Of course. I was surprised you volunteered the information, that's all.'

Amanda sighed. 'I didn't mean to. It just came out.'

'Kit's—a different "type" to Rafael, wouldn't you say?'

'I—I wouldn't know,' Amanda answered with an embarrassed laugh, feeling her cheeks grow hot.

'Oh, but he is—tall and extremely good looking, a solitary, brooding individual with a smile—when he condescends to use it—that would light up a house. He is also a study in contrasts, is our Mr Benedict, too untamed for a nobleman, yet he looks as appealing and at home in a room full of gentleman as he does when he is messing about with the horses. In fact—' she smiled, linking her arm through Amanda's and accompanying her out of the room '—I would say Kit Benedict is Mr Perfect in the flesh.'

Amanda lifted her eyebrows and glanced askance at her

stepmother, highly amused by the description she gave of her supposedly departed husband. 'Good heavens, Caroline! If you weren't married to my father and so obviously besotted with each other, I would say you were enamoured of Mr Benedict yourself.'

'Oh, no,' Caroline countered. 'But I think you might be.'

'Me? Now you are being ridiculous. How could I be? I hardly know him.'

'Then heaven help you when you do. Ah—here is Henry.'

Seeing her father on the stairs, Amanda had no time to reply to her remark, which was a relief. Caroline was far too perceptive and wily for comfort and she would have to be on her guard in future.

Rafael talked ceaselessly and enthusiastically throughout the meal—as Henry commented afterwards—the way all Americans did. He told them about his early childhood in Mexico and later in Charleston, his travels to the West and New York. Her mind on Kit, Amanda listened without hearing for most of the time and was glad when she was able to escape to her room.

For the following week Rafael became her escort to the various local social events they attended—when he wasn't attending a race meeting with her father, which they did on one occasion in Liverpool, staying overnight. He accompanied her daily on her rides, and, much to her relief, so did her father. Thankfully he made no further reference to her marriage. She sensed his attraction to her, but the attraction was not reciprocated.

To avoid any unpleasantness while he was a guest at Eden Park, she was always polite and courteous, but kept him at arm's length. It was a delicate juggling act that took all the skills she had developed on the social scene, but he followed her about with his eyes, and his watchfulness made her feel decidedly uneasy.

But no matter how she smiled and laughed, her thoughts were constantly on Kit. Each night she fell into bed thinking about him and got up thinking about him, and when her father received his letter informing him that Kit was to return two days hence, she was elated.

Kit had written to Henry to inform him of the time he would be arriving at the station with his daughter, so a carriage was there to meet them at that late hour. With the motion of the vehicle Sky was soon asleep curled up on Kit's lap. Frank, the coachman, was well known to Kit and was soon regaling him with what had been happening in his absence—both concerning the stables and the goings-on at the house.

Gazing down with tenderness and pride at the warm bundle cradled within his arms, Kit listened with only half an ear, interested in the horses, though not about the functions at the house—not until Amanda's name was mentioned and the visitor who had arrived after his own departure. Suddenly the tranquillity of his mood was shattered.

'Spanish gentleman called Señor Ortega,' Frank provided, 'though no one would guess. Speaks like a native American, so he does, though he looks Spanish enough, I suppose. Talk of the neighbourhood, he is, too, with invitations to visit being sent from every house round about.'

Kit's initial feeling was one of astonishment, but it was succeeded by a burst of rage so pure, so blinding, that it burned inside him. He listened to Frank, watching him, but he wasn't really seeing the man at all. Something black and formless came alive within his heart, wrapping its tiny tentacles around his chest.

In a low, deadly voice, he said, 'What did you say the man's name was?'

'Rafael Ortega—a gentleman from Charleston in South Carolina.'

The name dropped on Kit's heart like a rock. Rafael Ortega was Carmen's brother. He was also both cunning and dangerous. How had the man known where to find him, and, more importantly, what did he want? When Carmen's body had been found, Ortega had been the first to point the finger at him, and he had not believed him to be innocent of the crime despite Judd's testimony.

Kit had come back to Eden Park with the hard resolve to confront Quinn, and reveal all to Henry, regardless of the consequences. But things had changed with Ortega's arrival, which he knew was by design and no coincidence. Suddenly Kit found himself between the devil and the deep blue sea, his fate held in the palm of Rafael Ortega's hand.

'Polite, charming enough bloke,' Frank went on chattily, unaware of the murderous fury glaring out of his passenger's eyes, 'at least Miss Amanda seems to think so. Appears to be taken with him, she does, quite bowled over, in fact—and he so attentive. Go everywhere together, they do—wouldn't be surprised if an announcement were to be made—when Miss Amanda's year of mourning ends, that is.'

After listening to Frank's tales as the carriage traversed the dark country lanes, Kit endured the rest of the journey in alternate states of boiling rage and barely held calm, and by the time he reached Eden Park the full flood of his rage had reduced to a dull anger. What the hell did Amanda think she was playing at? Did she take him for a fool? While he had been worried sick about his daughter and trying to console her, his wife had been flaunting herself at every event—smiling and flirting—on the arm of the man he most despised.

* * *

The following morning found Nan on the doorstep waiting to see Sky. The child, her eyes as big as two bright saucers, beamed at her excitedly, remembering her straight away, and immediately the two disappeared into Sky's bedroom to unpack her things and decide what she was to wear that day. It left Kit free to go to the stables and take one of the mounts for exercise over the moors.

Amanda had remained uppermost in his mind all night—as the memory of her had ever since the night she had stayed with him—visual, tactile, soft and tender, with odour and texture, and she had been perfect, beautifully so, and to even think of her looking at another man as she had looked at him when he had held her within his arms was not to be borne. He told himself that when he next saw his wife he was going to wring her neck, but the image that filled his mind as he rode out of the stableyard on a half-wild stallion was not of his hands round her throat, but around her body, and all his energy expended in kissing her deceitful, soft mouth.

Shortly after Kit had left the yard, Amanda found herself riding over the moors with Rafael. It was the first time they had ridden alone together. The day was cold and sparkling, with just a few clouds skimming the lofty peaks. Riding along a path that skirted a dense wood—an area that she was unfamiliar with and farther than she had ridden before—it was then Amanda spotted the lone rider in the distance. At one with his mount, he moved fast and furiously, as if both horse and rider were trying their utmost to expend their energies.

Suddenly her heart gave a sickening lurch as she recognised the rider. It was Kit. She knew he had arrived back late last night, but she hadn't thought to see him out so early. She could feel his seductive power reach out to her across the distance.

He had appeared too suddenly for her to prepare herself, so the heady surge of pleasure she experienced on seeing him was evident, stamped like an unbidden confession on her lovely face. With a jolt of disappointment she realised that he had seen them and was deliberately avoiding them when he swung his horse around and headed back the way he had come.

Rafael had seen him also—and also the sublime expression that had burst like a sunbeam on his companion's face. When his gaze locked on Kit in the distance, his eyes narrowed to two black points of hatred, but he made no comment.

Kit wasn't around when they got back. After handing their mounts over to a stable boy, they returned to the house to change. Rafael was unusually quiet and preoccupied when they parted in the hall, and Amanda, unable to do anything until she had spoken to Kit, hurried back to the stables.

She found him by the paddocks, which were filled with prancing horses. He was in conversation with her father, who was wearing an old tweed jacket and muddy boots. It occurred to Amanda that he might have spent all morning cleaning out the stables in his desire to get closer to his horses. Sitting obediently by him was his dog Bracken, the latest in a line of golden Labradors, who turned and looked at her with big, solemn brown eyes and a thump of his solid tail on the ground.

Kit's head jerked towards her as she approached, and Amanda stiffened at the hard anger flaring in his eyes. Looking away, he continued speaking to her father. She sighed, wishing he was as pleased to see her as Bracken.

Dressed in tight breeches that outlined long, muscular legs and an open-necked white shirt under a jerkin of supple leather, there was an undeniable aura of forcefulness, of power, waiting to be unleashed. It was so hard pretending to the world that Kit meant nothing to her when that one night had altered the balance of her life for ever. During his absence she had tried to concentrate on everyday matters; outwardly she had succeeded. Only she knew of the chaos within. If only Kit knew the craving he had awakened—or perhaps he did and he felt the same.

For what seemed an eternity she stood perfectly still, in a state of jarring tension, as she waited for her father to finish speaking to him. When they ceased discussing a sorrel stallion, one of Henry's prize horses, they went on to talk about something else without bothering to look in her direction. Her patience turned to annoyance and she decided she'd had enough. Obviously Kit considered her of less importance than the horses. She was about to walk away when her father turned and saw her.

'Amanda, wait. I'll walk back with you.'

She looked at Kit, who was just straightening from his lounging posture on the fence, watching her. 'No, you go on. I would like to speak to Kit about his daughter.'

Giving her a queer look, Henry made no comment and walked off. Not until he was out of earshot did Amanda move towards Kit.

'I am glad you are back.'

'Are you?'

Amanda thrilled to the sound of his voice, yet the tone of his words sent a chill coursing along her spine. 'Yes. Is Sky quite recovered?' He nodded. 'And is she with you?'

'Of course.'

'I sent Nan to the cottage earlier. I hope she was of help.'

'Thank you, she was. I appreciate that.'

His tone was brusque and she frowned. 'Then—why are you being like this, Kit?'

Without bothering to answer he moved closer, looming over her like a black thundercloud. Since encountering her riding alone over the moors with Ortega, he had been unable to find an innocent cause for her behaviour except that of guilt. 'Do you expect me to react reasonably when I learn that during my absence my wife has been carrying on with another man?'

'Carrying on?' she burst out, stung by his scathing remark. 'How can you say such a thing? I have not—and you have no right—no reason—to act like a self-righteous, outraged husband.'

'I have every right,' he ground out.

Sparks of anger darted from her narrowed eyes. 'Husband you may be, but there isn't a man born who will tell me what I will and will not do.'

'No? Well, my darling wife, things are about to change. Do you want this other man?'

'Might I ask to whom do you refer?'

'I am referring to Ortega and you know it,' Kit said in an icy, authoritative tone that Amanda resented.

Anger and confusion were warring in Amanda's mind. 'How dare you? Your accusations are unjust.'

'Are they? I think not.' Looking around and seeing the surreptitious glances of the lads working with the horses, all avidly curious as to what could be the cause of the heated confrontation between the master's daughter and his trainer, he took her elbow. 'Let's take a walk. We're attracting too much attention. I'm eager to know what you have to say for yourself.'

Amanda was prompted to protest about the hand that gripped her elbow with a bruising hold as she walked quickly to keep up with his long strides. 'Kit, you can release me. I am not about to disappear.'

'No? Forgive me if I appear cautious. I am just beginning to understand the follies of marriage. My past experiences where you are concerned have made me somewhat wary as to what you will do next.'

Following a path that disappeared into a large thicket at the back of a hay barn, Kit did not stop until they were out of sight. So absorbed were they with each other and the burning issue on both their minds that they failed to hear the song of birds overhead, and to see that all around them spring was running riot with bursting buds and the scent of sap.

With his hands resting on his hips, Kit stood glowering down at his wife. 'Ever since I came to Eden Park I have always treated you the way you deserve to be treated—that's how it will always be between us—but I have no intention of letting you walk all over me by flaunting yourself with Ortega. From what I've heard, the Spaniard is panting after you like a bloodhound and you encourage him.'

'My relationship with Señor Ortega is relatively harmless, but when you say it like that you make it sound like an indictment.'

The dark eyes narrowed and the rugged features took on a brittle firmness that was almost cruel. 'Don't even think of denying it. It would seem that he shows more than a mannerly interest in you and receives much more than courtesy in return. I saw you, don't forget, riding out with him across the moor, alone and farther than you would normally ride.'

'I know. I saw you, too,' she flared in a burst of frustrated anger, infuriated by his unreasonable reprimand. 'Were you spying on me? If not, you must possess startlingly good instincts to have tracked us there. It was extremely rude of you to ride off like that.'

'I beg your pardon?'

'You heard me.'

Kit stared at her, unable to believe the alluring temptress he remembered had become this fiery termagant. 'If you must know, it was because I had no wish to come face-to-face with Ortega. Are you trying to persuade me that your affair is innocent?'

'Well, of course it is. Kit—where has all this distrust come from? You didn't arrive back until last night—hardly time to have gathered so much gossip. Who have you been talking to?'

'Frank.'

'Frank?' Her eyes opened wide in astonishment. 'Frank Hoyle, who does numerous menial tasks in the stables and drives the carriage? And Frank knows all about it, does he? Ha—then it is damning and shocking indeed if it comes from Frank,' she uttered sarcastically, planting her hands on her hips. 'I thought you would have had more sense than to listen to him.'

'Apparently the whole damned neighbourhood is abuzz with gossip about you and Ortega. Since coming to Eden Park, I have been forced to watch countless males drooling after you, but I draw the line at Ortega. No matter the reason that brought him here, undoubtedly he's been much attracted to you from the beginning.' His eyes raked over her. 'But I do not intend to share you with him—or any other man, come to that. The vows we exchanged were permanent enough for me, but you seem to be having trouble coming to terms with them. A little further help from me will not go amiss.'

Amanda tossed her head and glared at him, her eyes sparking ire, her chin set firm. 'I remember them well enough. Leave me alone. I need no help from you.'

Her words brought a feral gleam to his eyes. 'Have a care, lady,' Kit muttered. 'Don't fight me. I *know* you too well. I know how you feel.' And before she could walk away, with a vicious jerk he pulled her into his arms, his mouth capturing hers in a brutal kiss that was meant to hurt, to retaliate—and to appease his hunger for her, which had increased the longer they were apart.

But Amanda didn't care for his reasons as his kiss set spark to tinder, unlocking all the hidden passions she had held in check since he had gone away. It was just what she wanted, what she needed, and her reaction was to wrap her arms around his neck and kiss him back with a hunger of her own.

As he crushed her pliant body to his, spearing his fingers through her hair falling like a silken sheen about her shoulders, his head filled with the fragrance of her, Kit felt the passion flare in her, felt her heart race, and he felt a burgeoning pleasure and astonished joy that was almost beyond bearing. He deepened the kiss and she shivered. He felt it bone deep. A moment later he finally forced himself to lift his head, and he gazed down into her eyes, his anger unappeased despite her surrender to his kiss.

'Tell me he means nothing to you.'

'How can you believe that of me?' she protested.

'I cannot ignore what stares me in the face. Must I remind you that I did you a great service in Charleston, Amanda—unfortunately, it did not bring you the independence you so desired.'

Pulling away from him, she drew herself up, tears of rage brimming in her eyes. 'I owe you nothing. My life is my own, to make of it what I will, and neither you nor anyone else will tell me how to live it.'

The choking fury melted from Kit's face, leaving remorse in its wake. Dragging her back into his arms once more, he held her tightly against his hard frame. 'Don't weep,' he implored. 'I cannot bear to see a woman's tears.'

'Then why behave like this? Why say the things you do?'

He gave a wry smile. 'Because I was angry. Because I thought you were beginning to care for Ortega and I could not bear it.'

'And would it matter to you?'

'Yes, it would.'

Suddenly Amanda glimpsed in his eyes the pain of a man deeply wounded by what he saw as her betrayal of the trust that had been steadily building between them before his departure for London.

'I had no idea I had such an impact on you,' she murmured with a wobbly smile, 'but if you are to suspect every man who speaks to me and behave like this, then what hope is there?'

Without releasing her, Kit stared down into her upturned face, tracing with his gaze the beautiful lines, the soft round-ness of her cheeks and the delicate hollow of her throat where a strand of her deep red hair had come to rest against her creamy flesh. She was extraordinarily lovely, with an untamed quality and a wild freedom of spirit that found its counterpart in his own restless nature.

'Señor Ortega means nothing to me, Kit, you have to believe that—in fact, if you really want to know, I don't even like him, but you seem to forget he is a guest at Eden Park. It is out of courtesy that I make him feel welcome. Besides,' she murmured with a teasing smile, 'it's rather pleasant being courted by a gentleman; despite what you think, he is ex-tremely charming.'

Kit's eyes hardened. 'By the very definition of the word gentleman, I assure you Ortega is not. And would he continue being such a welcome guest if I were to tell you he was Carmen's brother? He's a dishonourable, black-hearted villain who is not to be trusted—a riverboat gambler who stood in the witness box prepared to swear my life away. He has somehow discovered where I am and is here for no other reason than to cause trouble.'

Amanda leaned back in his arms and stared at him, stunned. 'Her brother? Good heavens! I had no idea—although I had my doubts about him from the start. Something didn't seem quite right. When Caroline told me he came from Charleston, I did wonder if there might be a connection between the two of you, but when nothing was said I thought I was mistaken.'

Kit released her and combed his hair back from his forehead with his long fingers. 'Has he met Quinn?'

'No. Mr Quinn went to Manchester the day after you left for London. Why, are they acquainted with each other?'

Kit shook his head, his expression grim. 'No—at least I don't think so. For the past two years Ortega has spent most of his time haunting the riverboats on the Savannah and Mississippi rivers. But they are two of a kind, both gamblers, though Quinn has more control. Ortega is notorious in the gambling hells stretching from New Orleans to New York, where he is better known by his sobriquet as Mexican Jack. He is one of the most ruthless and skilful cheats and sharps ever to exist.'

The shock that had been gripping Amanda's heart began to relax its hold, and in its place was fear as a dreadful thought suddenly struck her. 'Kit—do you think he knows about us?'

'How were you introduced?'

'As Mrs Claybourne.'

'Then, my pet, I have to say that he will know all there is to know.'

'What do you think he means to do?'

'Time will tell. He's been biding his time—calmly assessing the situation here at Eden Park while waiting for me to show up. Now I am back, I doubt we will have long to wait.'

'Kit, do you think he will try to harm you?'

He shook his head, his expression grim. 'I think he has something else in mind.'

'But you will be careful, won't you? If he still believes you killed his sister, I hate to think of the direction his revenge might take.'

Kit did not kiss her again, nor did they attempt to shape their futures by plans and promises. This could only be done when this business with Ortega and Mr Quinn was resolved.

It was late afternoon and Kit was in the stable, rubbing down the horse he had just been exercising when a shadow darkened the stall. Without pausing in his task, he looked up to find Ortega standing in the doorway. He eyed him with distaste. Ortega was handsome enough at first sight and rather prepossessing in his immaculate, fashionably cut suit. The dark eyes were cold and unemotional, and the soul that animated Carmen's brother was a chilling quagmire of selfishness, deceit and wickedness. It was a soul its owner would willingly have sold to the devil for a handful of gold.

There was menace in his manner and his voice. Kit looked at him with cool, level eyes, refusing to be intimidated. He scorned Ortega's attempt at blackmail when he threatened to tell Henry the truth about Kit's past and marriage, and called his bluff by informing Ortega that he would tell Henry himself.

Ortega went out, thinking he could make things more than awkward for Claybourne if he so chose. But if he exposed him to his host at this time, he would gain nothing for himself— without funds to settle his debts, it would be suicidal for him to return to America. The thought caused sweat to break out on his neck.

Something about Claybourne didn't ring true, so perhaps a little delving into his background might rake up something unpleasant. He knew that going out on a limb to obtain what he wanted had its dangers. While he was prepared to accept them, his confidence had been shaken by Claybourne's arrogance. He had treated Ortega as being of no significance whatsoever.

When Amanda entered the morning room for breakfast the following day, she found Caroline alone. The sun shining through the tall windows facing south was clear and bright, polishing the mahogany table to a deep glow.

'Am I late?' she asked, helping herself to bacon and toast and seating herself across from her stepmother.

'Not at all. Your father was up and away early to accompany Rafael to the station.'

Amanda paused in spreading her napkin on her lap and stared at her in surprise. 'Away? Why, where's he gone?'

'He has some matters to take care of in London and friends to visit, apparently.'

'It's all rather sudden, isn't it?' Amanda remarked, smiling at the butler as he filled her cup with coffee. 'And why leave so early? He made no mention of it yesterday.'

'No, but I did notice a change in him when he returned from the stables yesterday afternoon. At first I imagined he was going riding—although, as I recall, he wasn't dressed for riding—but he returned after half an hour and was quiet and preoccupied for the rest of the day. You must have noticed.'

'No, I can't say that I did,' Amanda answered truthfully. All her thoughts had been centred on Kit and what he had told her concerning Rafael.

'I wonder if Kit had anything to do with it.'

Amanda glanced up sharply to find Caroline watching her with an uncomfortable steadiness, which lent considerably to her unease. Not for the first time did she sense that her stepmother knew more about her and Kit than she had ever offered and her question sounded a warning note in Amanda's mind. 'Kit? Why on earth should he have anything to do with Rafael's leaving?'

'No reason. It's all so curious, that's all.'

'Well, I can't say that I shall miss your house guest, Caroline.'

'No, neither shall I. On better acquaintance I found there was something disquieting about him, and the longer he stayed only increased my mistrust. No matter how polite I tried to be, I detected a slight mockery in his manner which was not to my liking.'

'Father seemed to get on with him well enough—at least when they were discussing equine matters.'

'Mmm, but even Henry had his doubts about him. His devil-may-care attitude—your father, to whom life is all about drive and taking risks, did not appreciate it. Henry is generous and tolerant of most things, but those traits do not extend as far as his business dealings. As you well know, Amanda, he can be utterly ruthless.'

Amanda smiled across at her. 'You know, Caroline, I can't help recalling the time I asked him if he would ever marry again.'

'And what did he say?'

'Oh, he huffed and he puffed a bit and said he was not one to fall for female charms, no matter how temptingly wrapped, and that business arrangements were by far the best. So what did you do to ensnare him? Wave a magic wand and sprinkle him with pixie dust?'

Caroline laughed lightly, her eyes sparkling as she spread a thin layer of marmalade on her toast. 'We were attracted to each other from the moment we were introduced. I did play it cool and kept a distance between us at first—which turned out to be the sensible thing to do because it wasn't long before orchids and invitations to dine started coming to the house on a daily basis.'

'Gracious! I never took my father for the romantic kind.'

'Oh, he is, believe me.' Caroline swallowed a bite of toast, then her expression became serious. 'There is one thing I should tell you. Henry did feel compelled to invite Rafael back before he goes on to Liverpool to take the steamer for New York.'

'And no doubt Señor Ortega accepted.'

'Oh, yes. He said he would be delighted.'

Amanda was extremely relieved Rafael had gone and only sorry they had not seen the last of him—her instinct told her that his leaving had everything to do with Kit.

With a lifting of her spirits brought about by Rafael's departure and the whole day stretching ahead of her and nothing much to do, Amanda asked Cook to pack a small picnic hamper, intending to reacquaint herself with Sky—and the thought that she might see the child's father was a powerful stimulant.

Caroline walked with her as far as the stables and, instead of going back to the house to write her letters, stood breathing in the sharp spring air, watching Amanda walking with a definite spring in her step towards Kit's cottage. With a wistful smile on her face she was about to turn away when the most curious thing happened. The cottage door opened and Nan appeared with a small, dark-haired girl by her side.

Caroline was quite unprepared for what happened next. On seeing Amanda the child waved and, leaving Nan behind, ran down the garden path and out of the gate as fast as her little legs would go. Laughing delightedly, Amanda stopped, dropping the hamper on the ground. Bending from the waist, she opened her arms wide, and with a squeal of absolute joy the child ran into them. Amanda hugged her tight, lifting her off the ground and spinning her round. Setting her back on her feet, she took Sky's hand and headed for the cottage, the happy child skipping along beside her.

Caroline was dumbfounded. There was something going on concerning Kit and Amanda that was beyond her understanding, but only because she did not have sufficient knowledge about what it was. 'Well, who would have thought it?' she murmured as she turned to go back to the house. 'There's more to this than either Henry or myself know about.'

Chapter Nine

Sky gazed up at Amanda with her big dark eyes, a smile stretching from ear to ear. 'Nan told me you'd come and see me.' She pointed to the hamper on the table. 'What's in there? Is it a present?'

'Well, sort of. I've come to take you on a picnic. Do you know what a picnic is, Sky?'

Sky shook her head, her eyes alight with excitement.

'Well, the hamper is filled with all sorts of nice things to eat. I thought we might take a walk to the lake.'

Nan gaped at Amanda, thinking she'd taken leave of her senses. 'A picnic? In April?'

'Oh, come now, Nan, where's your sense of adventure? It's a perfect day and it will be lovely down by the lake.'

Suddenly a shadow fell across the doorway. Amanda turned and saw Kit. His eyes held hers in an enquiring glance. 'Am I missing something?'

'I've come to take Sky on a picnic. Nan's coming too, aren't you, Nan?'

'I think a picnic is a splendid idea,' Kit said before Nan could reply, 'and so as not to disappoint Sky, Nan, since you are party to our deception, would you mind if I went on the picnic instead?'

Nan thought it highly inappropriate for the two of them with Sky in tow to be seen going off together to picnic by the lake. What on earth would people make of it? Still, it was one thing to criticise Amanda's actions when she was alone, but an entirely different thing to do so in front of her husband.

'I'm not really one for eating outside,' Nan said, wiping her hands down her apron. 'And I'm sure Sky would rather her father went with her than me.'

Kit looked at Amanda. 'We'll ride over the moors—Sky would like that, wouldn't you, Sky?'

Sky nodded, jumping up and down and clapping her hands.

'But are you sure, Kit?' Amanda said. 'Do you have the time?'

'I doubt Henry would object to my taking time off to spend with my two favourite ladies.' His gaze encompassed them both, his expression holding a rare look of softness and pleasure.

'I'm glad Sky still remembers me,' Amanda murmured as Nan began buttoning the little girl into her coat. 'I was more than a little apprehensive that she might not.'

'I made sure she would,' Kit told her.

Amanda looked at him and smiled her gratitude. 'Thank you. You have a beautiful daughter, Kit,' she said with undisguised admiration.

All the sweetness of spring was in the air as they rode over the moors. The sun was warm and the grass sparkling with dew. Amanda had the picnic hamper strapped to her horse, and Kit rode with a beaming Sky in front of his saddle. They stopped for their picnic near a stream tumbling busily over rocks. Discarding her bonnet to reveal the glorious, luxuriant hair upswept in glossy curls that almost took Kit's breath away, unaware of the effect she had created with such a simple act, Amanda spread a large blanket on the ground. Sky helped her take the food out of the hamper and place it on a separate cloth, thinking it great fun.

'This is what I do when I give a tea party for my dolls,' she told them, happily kneeling on the edge of the cloth and helping herself to an egg sandwich.

As they talked and ate, Amanda was vaguely aware of Kit's appreciative gaze on her animated face as she handed Sky a cup of lemonade. When the child had eaten and drunk her fill, Amanda picked some thin reeds growing by the side of the stream. Sitting beside Sky on a large flat rock, she proceeded to show the child how to plait them together. When Sky had become completely absorbed in her task, Amanda left her to it and returned to Kit, who was sitting on the blanket with his back resting against a boulder, one knee drawn up against his chest and his arm draped across it.

Kit was watching them closely, thinking how demure and yet bold Amanda looked in a swathe of brilliant sapphire blue. He could see the outline of her legs and thighs beneath her skirts as she came towards him; when he remembered how they had looked and felt wrapped around him, his blood ran hot.

'You have a way with her,' he said, giving no evidence of his feelings. 'It's good to see her so happy.'

'Sky's easy to get along with. I discovered that on the crossing from America.' Sitting beside him and tucking her feet in their brown leather boots beneath her, she looked at him. 'You know Señor Ortega has left, don't you, Kit?'

He nodded, his eyes turning hard and cold. 'Don't worry, he hasn't gone for good. He'll be back as soon as he's worked out how to extort money out of me.'

'Money? Good heavens! What happened between the two of you, Kit, that made him decide to leave like that?'

As Kit gave her a run-down on all that had been said between them, Amanda listened, horrified that a man her father had invited into their home could be so cunning, so despicable. 'So he is trying to blackmail you. He wants you to use your position as my husband to obtain money through me. The man is a criminal, Kit, and must be exposed.'

'Not yet. Not until I have confronted Quinn.'

'Then let me give you the money and be done with him.'

'No,' he said succinctly.

'But—'

'I said no, Amanda,' Kit said sharply. 'If I wanted to pay him off I would do it myself.'

He meant that to end the discussion, but Amanda refused to let it drop. 'But twenty thousand pounds is an awful lot of money. Where will you get it?'

There was an imperceptible hesitation before he answered. 'I could lay my hands on it if I wanted to. I am not destitute— and even if I were, I would not accept your money.'

Amanda was astonished that he could raise such a large sum. It deepened the mystery that clung to him like a fog. She raised a questioning eyebrow, but he did not elaborate. 'Kit, you don't understand. I wouldn't miss the money. Father established an account at the bank for me years ago, and it has a huge balance.'

'No,' he said implacably. His jaw hardened into an uncompromising line. With cool finality he said, 'As a man, it is my responsibility to provide for you, not the other way round. I mean that, Amanda.'

Kit's authoritative tone silenced her. He sighed, a harsh sound that was filled with anger that Amanda sensed was directed more at himself than her. He was carrying the issue of pride too far, but since he felt so deeply about the matter of her money, she decided to let it rest for now.

'If you imagine paying Ortega off would be the answer then forget it,' Kit went on. 'He would soon be back for more. Besides, I have no intention of being driven into a corner by him or anyone else.'

'I hope Señor Ortega doesn't come back, and that he leaves you in peace.' Gazing up at the high peaks, she was determined to put the Spaniard from her mind. The day was perfect, and like Kit she didn't want anything to cloud the day. 'This is such a wonderful place. Surrounded by the high peaks and all these huge rocks one feels quite small and vulnerable—rather humble, in fact.'

Kit's expression gentled and a glint of amusement came into his eyes as he slanted her a wicked look. 'You couldn't be humble, Amanda Claybourne, if you tried. You're unpredictable and quite outrageous and you never cease to amaze me.'

She looked at him and laughed—like everything else about her, her laughter was golden. 'And isn't that how you want your wife to be? Predictability can be so dull—much more exciting for her to have many interesting and diverting contradictions to her character.'

'Not so many that she would take some keeping up with.'

'Then what is your idea of an ideal wife? A woman who should lose her individuality completely, and live only for her husband—to always be at his beck and call and spend her days carrying out her part of the marriage contract?'

Kit stretched out on his back and closed his eyes, and the mobile line of his mouth quirked in a half smile. 'Carry on, my love—it gets better all the time. I'm certainly in favour of a married woman knowing her duty is to take care of her husband, to cook his meals and to clean the house. And do not forget that the husband always likes his wife to be gentle and sympathetic to himself—to place him on a pedestal and be humorous, witty and cheerful at all times.'

Amanda was momentarily dumbstruck by his speech, then she burst out laughing at his teasing. 'While he doesn't always concern himself very particularly about the means to make and keep her so. And what are your opinions concerning an intelligent wife? Would that be acceptable to you, or would you be afraid that if she were too intelligent she would be capable of perceiving the mind of her husband—should he be of lesser intelligence than herself, of course?'

Kit grinned at her. Her beauty and mischievousness delighted him, and he saw the impudence shining from her olive-green eyes. 'Which he never is,' he uttered conceitedly.

'Is that right?' she retorted with mock indignation. 'If women were more forthright and didn't appear to be dim-witted half the time, convincing their men folk that they are smarter and wiser than we are, their egos would be well and truly shattered.'

'Then if that should prove to be the case, men would use their brute strength to gain supremacy over them in the time-honoured way.' A seductive languor in his eyes when he turned his head and looked at his wife made her heart start to hammer. 'However, I'd consider it necessary that my wife should be intelligent if she is to conduct my concerns through life, but not too intelligent—just enough to appreciate my own intellectual mind.'

'But you would allow her to have some freedom of her own.'

'The truth of it is that I would not have to permit my wife to do anything. In law you are my wife, so whatever is yours is mine also. I can, if I choose, treat you harshly and without consideration, and confine you to the kitchen—and the bedroom.'

Amanda almost choked on her laughter. 'You would not. You wouldn't dare. I would kill you first.'

Kit linked his hands behind his head, staring up at the blue sky dotted with white clouds. Her soft laughter entwined him as he closed his eyes once more. 'You have a beautiful laugh, Amanda. You should laugh more often.'

Wriggling into a more comfortable position, Amanda looked down at him. 'You're only saying that to change the subject. Please don't tell me you really meant all that rubbish about wives being completely subservient to their husbands?'

Kit half-raised his eyelids and looked into her eyes, shining softly so close above him. 'I was just making a point—and a valid one at that. Many a husband would not allow you so free a rein as you have, my sweet.'

Amanda sighed, stretching out on the blanket and rolling on to her stomach. Cupping her chin in her hands, she feigned despondency. 'I am beginning to regret I am not a widow after all.' That said, she very quickly changed her mind as she let her gaze travel down the long, superbly fit and muscled body stretched out on the blanket beside her.

'If we were to live together as man and wife, would you expect me to do all those things, because, if so, then you are going to be sadly disappointed. I've had no practice in the ways of a wife. I can't cook and I don't know the first thing about keeping house—apart from the managerial side, which is something all young ladies are taught. I do have other interests and accomplishments, but I doubt they would be of much use to you. Will you always be a horse trainer, Kit? Don't you ever want to do anything else with your life?'

'Horses are what I know about, Amanda.' Sitting up, he looped his arms around his knees. Turning his head, he looked at her directly. The hazel eyes tensed slightly and the good humour was suddenly overlaid with caution. 'Does it matter to you what I do?'

'No, not if you are happy doing it,' she said, also sitting up.

'I would expect my wife to be happy with what I could give her. I would promise her that she will always have clothes to wear and food to eat and a roof over her head that does not leak, and if she loves me she will accept that.'

Amanda's brow puckered in a thoughtful frown and she turned her face away. 'Love? In truth, Kit, I don't know what I feel. I don't even know what love is. What I do know is that ever since you came here I have been so confused, with my emotions all over the place. I—I have also come to have a strong attraction to you—which you already know.'

Reaching out, Kit gently cupped her cheek to turn her face towards him. 'And I have an extremely strong and passionate desire for you, Amanda, and if we were alone I would show you.'

She met his gaze steadily, strangely disappointed that he couldn't think of a stronger emotion to describe what was between them other than desire. 'Desire, as wonderful as it is, is not enough to base a marriage on, Kit. It is only a temporary emotion, and I have no wish to become trapped in a loveless marriage.'

'It won't be, that I promise you. Don't forget that it was a mutual decision for us to take our marriage vows, Amanda. Honour and duty must run side by side with our emotions. In a short time we will face the world together. On that I am determined.'

In his expression Amanda saw a resolute determination that he would have his way. It was an expression she was coming to know quite well. 'I will not be your duty, Kit. I want more from you than that.'

Sky chose that moment to come and show them her plait. 'That's perfect, Sky,' Amanda praised, as the little girl, pleased with her first attempt, went off to begin another. Amanda began packing things away in the hamper. Reaching out to pick up a napkin, she suddenly found her wrist taken in a hard grasp and looked up. Her eyes became locked on Kit's.

'That was not the most romantic thing I have ever said,

Amanda; if I have hurt you by discussing our marriage in such a blunt fashion, then I apologise. Our marriage was not an ideal affair, and the fault lies with both of us, so there is no point apportioning blame. We have to continue the charade a while longer—at least until Quinn returns from wherever it is he's gone. I cannot claim you openly just yet for reasons that I have made known to you and until we can set aside your father's wrath. He is not an unreasonable man, but our marriage, and the manner in which it was entered into, will take some understanding. I wish it could be different.'

'So do I,' she murmured.

'If you want the truth, I will tell you that in my eyes you are as alluring and desirable as any woman I have ever known. I want you, and I shall go on wanting you. You are beautiful and vibrant, and you were made for love. In my prison cell when I was awaiting the worst, it was my dreams of you and Sky that made life more bearable, and when you spent the night in my arms, I found something that bound me to another human being more assuredly than anything else in my life. There was a sense of rightness to it, as if that was where you were meant to be. You have become a passion to me, and I cannot bear the thought of losing you. If I could, I would lay the whole world at your feet—and I have never been so serious in my whole life.'

Perhaps it was the way his head was slightly tilted to one side, perhaps it was a trick of the light, perhaps it was the yearning softness of his voice, but whatever the reason, Amanda had the impression that his face had changed. His features were relaxed, making him look younger, less hard and cynical. She had a momentary glimpse of the young man he must have been before he had gone to America.

'I don't want the world, Kit. I will be satisfied for a very small and humble part of it, if it is somewhere we can call home.'

They sat for a moment in silence. Amanda looked towards the stream where Sky was still plaiting her reeds, feeling that nothing existed but the feelings of her body as she lusted for her husband with increasing desire. Then she turned back to him, seeing how the sunlight caught his head in a halo of light. She gazed at his face and caught her breath at something she saw there. No man had ever looked at her quite like that before. She cursed herself for being unable to free herself from the sensual trap he had set for her.

She would fall in love with him. She knew she would.

Leaving the station behind and travelling in the Covington family coach that had been waiting for the train, they travelled down narrow winding lanes and through pretty villages.

Seated beside Caroline and across from her father, Amanda was missing Kit and was curious as to why he had decided to travel to Cambridgeshire the day before. He had said he wanted to go to Newmarket to look at more horses, but Amanda wasn't entirely convinced. Ever since her father had told him of his intended visit to Covington Hall he had been quiet and preoccupied, as if something plagued his mind.

At first she had thought it was because he would have to leave Sky behind. The child was reluctant to be parted from him, but when Nan told her she could stay at the big house with her, she became so excited she said she didn't mind Daddy going away for a little while. Amanda still thought Kit's behaviour was a little odd, since Newmarket wasn't far from Covington Hall and there would be plenty of time for him to go there if he travelled with them.

Fixing her gaze on the passing scenery, she gave up trying to analyse the workings of Kit's mind—what Amanda didn't know was that the carpets in the cottage had been receiving some significant wear as Kit had paced back and forth ever since Henry had told him they were to go to Cambridgeshire.

In the distance, about half a mile away, her gaze picked out a house set against a backdrop of trees and gently rolling green hills. The grounds were on a large and far grander scale than Eden Park, and the huge three-storey stone and glass house reigned in stately splendour. It was beautiful beyond any other house she had ever seen and, believing it to be Covington Hall and looking forward to seeing more of it, she was disappointed when the coach passed by and continued for a farther five miles before turning in through the gates of a smaller, more sedate manor house, with none of the awe-inspiring grandeur of the house she had just seen.

They were shown into the drawing room where Lord Covington and his wife Alyce were waiting to receive them. Lord Covington, noted for his charm and good manners, was tall and elegant, his wife dark haired, with a warm smile and friendly blue eyes. They were received warmly and Amanda was surprised and curious at the attention her presence seemed to attract. Lord Covington bowed politely over her hand and observed her in a way she found difficult to interpret.

Alyce Covington said, looking her over carefully, 'What a pleasure it is to meet you. We have heard nothing but praise about you from your father when we met in London recently—but he failed to tell us how lovely you are.'

'You are too kind, Lady Covington,' Amanda said, smiling softly. 'Thank you for inviting me.'

'May I call you Amanda? My name is Alyce and my husband is Paul. You will find that neither of us are dragons of social etiquette and when we have a small party of friends staying we do like to relax the rules. It will be lovely having you with us—if you'll excuse the constant talk about horses.

I'm afraid Paul is as enthusiastic as your father—in fact, his whole life seems to revolve around them.'

Amanda laughed with mock-sympathy. 'Don't worry. I've grown quite used to it.'

'Has Mr Benedict arrived?' Henry asked, taking a welcome glass of brandy from Paul.

'He arrived yesterday,' Paul replied. 'He set off for New-market in the early hours—something about visiting some stables—and he wasn't sure what time he would be back—depends if anything with four legs takes his fancy, I suppose.' He chuckled softly.

'And what about this horse you want to sell me—when can I see it?'

'Whenever you like, Henry. Finish your drink and I'll take you to have a look. We'll get him into the paddock in the morning. Kit's seen him and he's impressed. Top-class horse you'll find.'

Henry laughed. 'I don't doubt that for one moment, Paul, but if you don't mind, I'll let Kit be the judge of that.'

At that moment Paul and Alyce's sixteen-year-old daughter Jane came in. With her pale skin, large brown eyes and dark, glossy hair, she was stylish and neat in a jade-green dress. After being introduced, Jane took Amanda to one side as the four older people discussed the horse they hoped Henry would purchase.

The friendliness in Jane's eyes had given way to a frank stare when Amanda had been introduced as Mrs Claybourne. 'I'm afraid that name will attract too much attention in these parts. If word gets out we are entertaining a Claybourne, we will be inundated with callers. May I call you Amanda, by the way?'

Amanda looked at Jane in astonishment, not quite sure she had heard correctly. 'Of course you may. But what do you mean? Are there Claybournes in Cambridgeshire?'

'Oh, yes—at least there used to be. Was your husband connected?'

Amanda thought of Kit in his prison cell, of Kit training horses to provide for himself and his motherless daughter, their home a wooden cabin near the river. Shaking her head, she said, 'I don't think so. I am sure the name is purely a coincidence.'

'In which case you don't have anything to worry about.'

Amanda gave her a puzzled look. 'Why do you say that?'

Jane shrugged. 'The whole family's a bit of a mystery if you ask me. You must have seen Woodthorpe Hall on the way here. You can't miss it—it's so grand and dominates the landscape for miles.'

'I believe we did pass a house like that.'

'I've been there often on my rides out,' Jane told her in a conspiratorial whisper. 'Papa tells me I'm not to go there, but I do sometimes, just to look at it.'

'Why, is there some kind of mystery about the house?' Amanda asked, her curiosity piqued.

Jane smiled a sad little smile. 'The house is empty—has been for years. I don't really know what happened, but the family was plagued with disasters. I think they live abroad somewhere, although I do believe a woman comes with her children now and then to make sure everything's as it should be.'

'If the house has been empty for a long time, what about the tenants? Does anyone take care of the estate, because, with a house as big and grand as the one I saw, it must be large?'

'Oh, yes, it's a worthy estate with hundreds of acres. As far as I know the family has not relinquished the lands and the taxes are still being paid. There is an agent who collects the rents for Lord Claybourne and sees to the running of things.'

'Then it sounds to me that Lord Claybourne has every intention of returning.'

Suddenly Alyce entered the conversation. 'What is my daughter telling you, Amanda?'

'I was just asking her about the house we passed on the way here. Jane was telling me it belongs to a family by the name of Claybourne. Because it is the same name as my own, naturally I was curious.'

'What have I told you about gossiping, Jane?' Alyce said sharply.

'It wasn't gossip—I mean—I didn't say anything that people in these parts don't know. Besides, this is a close-knit community where very little happens, so everyone watches what everyone else does, and they gossip about it.'

'Nevertheless, what goes on at Woodthorpe should not be talked about. You know that.'

There was reproof behind that cool, soft voice, and it seemed to put Amanda on the defensive. 'I did ask Jane to tell me. After all, the house I saw was so imposing it is difficult not to comment on such a splendid building.'

'True,' Alyce agreed, 'and Lord Claybourne may not be in residence but it is his own affair,' she said, looking pointedly at her daughter.

Jane was undeterred. 'But Papa takes an interest in local affairs—hunting parties and the like—which is what the lord of every manor should do if he wants to keep the harmony of his estate.'

'I am sure his obligation weighs heavy on Lord Claybourne, Jane,' Alyce remonstrated, 'and, wherever he is, he obviously prefers solitude and privacy to gadding about the countryside. Now, enough of this. Perhaps you could make yourself useful. I am sure Amanda would like to refresh herself and rest before dinner. Why don't you show her to her room?'

'Yes, all right.'

'Jane will make certain you are comfortably settled,

Amanda. I hope your room is to your liking. Make yourself at home, won't you? We'll see you at dinner.'

Kit came to the ornate iron gates of the house and stood there looking at it. He had the feeling that he was seeing it for the first time, which was madness. He'd been born here, grown up here, and for the past six years since he had left he'd been back here in his mind. As he began walking towards it, it came to him that he'd never really looked at the house before, never seen it with eyes stripped of all illusion and emotion. At a glance it looked the same, but it was far from it. Kit attributed this sense of strangeness, of darkly brooding sadness, which hung over the house, to what had happened in the past.

Standing alone with its eye-catching façade, a serene harmony of mellowed silvery pink, ivory and blue and a gentle dusting of gold, it seemed suspended in time—waiting— waiting for its owner, before it could be brought to life again. It was a house that still meant something in these parts. Surrounded by a riot of flowers, the lawns had been freshly mown, and beyond the surrounding trees, well-tilled fields stretched time out of mind into the distance.

He went up the steps to the big double doors and turned the highly polished brass knob, not surprised to find it unlocked. Pushing the door open, he stepped inside the hall, breathtaking in its combination of architectural grandeur and subtle coolness of colouring. Standing quite still, he fought against the pain and sickness inside his chest as memories flooded his mind, of music and light and dancing in this very hall. His eyes were drawn to the wide, curving staircase that soared to the upper floors. It was the glory of the house, like the magnificent glittering chandelier suspended from the ceiling.

Woodthorpe was dead, it had lost its soul. Could he get it

back? Could he rid the house of all its ghosts, of old sins, old injustices—grief? Could Amanda and Sky help him do that? What was important now was to begin the long climb back to a place that was rightfully his. Taking hold of himself and squaring his shoulders, Kit closed the door and walked forward to further inspect his domain. Hearing children's laughter coming from somewhere above, he glanced up. He felt the tension ease, his face relaxed and he smiled.

Amanda's longing to see Kit was so strong that she stood looking out of the window of her room that overlooked the drive, hoping to catch a glimpse of him when he returned from Newmarket, but he failed to show up. Thinking he would be sure to join them for dinner, she took particular care with her toilet, but he didn't appear and her disappointment was profound when she finally excused herself and went to bed.

The following morning she went down to breakfast early, hoping to see him, only to discover he'd risen early and left the house. Later, she donned her coat and accompanied Caroline to the paddock, knowing Kit was sure to be there with her father and Paul.

The day was warm and shreds of clouds scudded across the sky, dappling the paddock with moving shadows. A grey stallion, a beautiful, restless beast, clattered across the stable yard. A young man was leading it on a short rein, and he was having difficulty keeping the high-stepping animal under control as it zigzagged towards the paddock. Amanda observed the scene beside Caroline, and, with Jane hanging over the paddock fence next to her father on the opposite side, her attention was caught by the horse's tossing head and flowing mane, and the hint of restrained power in every movement of its muscular body. Here was a Thoroughbred of high spirits that would present a challenge to even the most accomplished rider.

Suddenly Kit appeared. Amanda watched him saunter across the yard then vault over the fence into the paddock. Taking off his coat, he handed it to a groom. The young man leading the horse stopped in front of where Kit stood in the middle of the paddock.

Together the young man and one other managed to steady the horse as Kit, as cool as ice and ignoring its rolling eyes, ran practised hands over it, picking up a hoof, looking at its teeth, walking round the horse and examining it. And then he seized the reins and soared in a beautifully timed, perfect motion, like a great and masterful bird of prey, on to the horse's back. He walked the horse round the paddock before pushing him to a canter and then a gallop, clearing one of the barred jumps and reaching upwards in an arc as clean and sure as though it had been imprinted on the air by a giant compass. The sight of Kit mastering the huge stallion and displaying such a spontaneous talent filled Amanda with a combination of admiration and anxiety.

'I do hope he's careful,' she murmured to Caroline, unable to conceal her concern.

Caroline glanced at her, placing a gentle hand on her forearm. She had noted that Amanda only had eyes for Kit as she watched him test the horse, which was a marvel of speed and took the fences as though he were half-bird. Beginning to understand the situation, she said kindly, 'Don't worry. I don't think the horse has been born yet that can unseat Kit. Not only does he know everything there is to know about horses, Amanda, but he is also an expert rider—one of the best—so put your mind at ease.'

Amanda looked at her stepmother. She had grown so used to hiding what she felt, to appearing calm and outwardly happy, but Caroline seemed to know everything and now, seeing a knowing glint in the older woman's eyes, she realised she had let the façade slip a little.

'I know how you feel, Amanda—one would have to be blind not to. I also understand your dilemma. Kit is a fine man and I know there is something between the two of you. I do approve of your choice. He is so right for you. But…oh, dear, how snobbish and inflexible is the society to which we belong—which is a great pity, I always think.' She spoke so quietly that it seemed as if she was talking to herself.

Amanda swallowed down a hard lump in her throat and looked at Kit. The pain of what Caroline said filled her. What she said was right. Kit's background, his station, everything, was all wrong for her. But he was so very special—without equal. If only she could confide in Caroline and tell her everything, but Kit had said they must keep up the charade a while longer. She kept her mouth closed, overcoming the momentary weakness.

Kit trotted the horse back to Paul and her father, standing in the centre of the paddock, and pulled him up. Sliding off, Kit reached for his coat and shrugged it on. When the horse was being led back to the stable, Amanda found herself waiting feverishly for Kit to come and speak to her. She was burning with eagerness to see him close to her, to seek in his eyes for such a look as he had given her on the day of the picnic, but, absorbed as he was in serious discussion with her father and Paul, his eyes barely rested on her as they turned and left the paddock.

The rest of the day was uneventful and throughout dinner Amanda tried to convince herself she was merely imagining Kit's complete change of attitude, thinking he must be feeling ill at ease dining with the Covingtons, speaking only when he was spoken to and when it was absolutely necessary.

Afterwards, when the men had finally joined the ladies in the drawing room, he was different somehow, distracted, and she wanted to understand why. He sat with his long legs crossed in front of him, his face turned in the direction of Paul as they spoke quietly together across the room. After a while Paul went to join Henry, leaving Kit alone. He sat staring into the fire burning in the wide stone hearth, as if to find there the answer to the problem that made his fine-drawn face look stern, and brought a dark, brooding look into his eyes.

Amanda observed him from a distance, wanting to go to him while wishing he would come to her instead. What was wrong? He had been like this ever since he knew of this visit to Covington Hall. He had withdrawn from her. It was as if the closeness, the tenderness and laughter they had shared on the day of the picnic had never existed.

Tossing and turning in her bed, sleep eluded her. She could not bear another minute, let alone another hour, of this awful suspense. Getting out of bed she donned her robe, and with her long tresses falling in a rippling, luxuriant mane over her shoulders, she left her room.

The house was deathly quiet. She knew which was Kit's room, having seen him come out of it earlier, and she was soon at his door. With her heart hammering in her chest, before anyone should see her she opened it and stepped inside, closing it and leaning against the hard wood. A low fire burned in the hearth. Kit was seated before it. The light fell on his face, his hard profile taking on a curiously softer look. He had discarded his coat, waistcoat and neck cloth; above his trousers he was wearing a white cotton shirt, open at the neck to reveal a firm, strongly muscled throat. Forgetful for the moment of the reason that had brought her there, she was conscious of a feeling of tenderness at the sight of a lock of dark hair that fell over his forehead.

She might have stood there for hours, content just to look at him, had Kit not looked up and seen her standing there. He smiled slowly, holding out his hand, and Amanda could not retreat if she tried. With a captivating boldness she moved forward until she stood beside him, looking down into his eyes.

'You seemed deep in thought,' she murmured.

'I must have been if I failed to hear you come in.'

'Kit, is there something troubling you?'

'As a matter of fact, I'm in dire need of a little feminine companionship.' Tilting his head to one side, he slanted her a smile. 'You have become quite forward of late, Mrs Claybourne—seeking me out in my chamber like this.'

Her eyes sparkled above a puckish smile. 'I need more practice at being a wife.'

He gave a barely perceptible nod. 'What is it, my love? Do you strain beneath the bridle of restraint?'

'You could say that,' she said, taking his hand and pulling him to his feet. 'You've been like a shadow eluding me for days. I am not made of stone and I cannot stop wanting you. So please don't torture me any more and take me to bed.'

Kit raised a brow at her. 'Brazen hussy! I did not think you had come to make idle chit-chat.' He chuckled.

Quickly she shed her robe, letting it fall to the carpet. Kit's hungry gaze settled on her flimsy nightgown outlining the shape of her body beneath. He cocked an eyebrow in mock-surprise. 'What—no stays?'

'No,' she said breathily, her nimble fingers unfastening his shirt and pulling it away from his shoulders. 'They take up far too much time getting them off.'

Tossing his shirt aside, Amanda tilted her face and drew his lips to hers, fusing them together, moving farther towards the bed until their senses knew nothing but each other. Hunger grew and expanded, racing through their veins, so intense, so intimate. The heat of their bodies dissipated in the cool night air as, effortlessly, Kit possessed her so deeply, so thoroughly, letting his power flow through her, that never again would there be any sense of separateness.

When Amanda stirred from the passion-induced slumber into which Kit had sent her, reaching out her hand to feel for him, she found the bed next to her was cold and empty. Clothed in just his trousers, his hands shoved deep into the pockets, he was leaning on the wall by the window, looking out over the dark landscape, his jaw as hard as granite. Reaching for her robe, Amanda sighed. Any hope that Kit would bounce back from his sombre mood had proved a little too optimistic. Slipping out of bed, she padded across the carpet towards him and wrapped her arms around his waist. He felt as rigid as a statue.

'What is it that's troubling you, Kit? You've been like this ever since you came here. You seem to get on well with Paul and Alyce, so what is it that you don't like about Covington Hall? Why don't you talk to me?'

'Nothing's wrong, Amanda. You're imagining things, that's all.'

'I don't think I am.' She saw his face was tense, his eyes hard as he stared into the distance. 'You know,' she said softly, removing her arms from his waist, 'I am willing to be open about myself—indeed, you know things about me that I would never dream of revealing to anyone,' she said, the shameless manner in which she had arranged their marriage uppermost in her mind. 'In fact, you know almost all there is to know about me, yet you refuse to tell me anything about yourself. Clearly you find it hard to talk about your deepest feelings, but perhaps if you did they would not seem so bad.' She smiled, taking his hand in her own and twining her fingers with his in an attempt to get closer to him. 'I may be a wilful, obstinate, extremely disobedient female, Kit, but I am a good listener.'

Kit continued looking ahead, not moving. He did not reply, but Amanda sensed it was not through coldness but out of fear, and that for some unknown reason he was hurting. She wondered what he must be feeling, what was going through his mind, what his relationship could have been like with his father that had made him like this.

'I know you are a private person,' she went on, 'and that keeping your own counsel has become second nature to you, but, aside from all else, if we are to have any kind of future together, how can we have any chance of happiness if you keep everything bottled up inside you? You know, sometimes you look as though you're riding the devil, that your hurt is eating away inside you. You can't keep running from it for ever, Kit. The only way to face it is to start at the beginning and face it down. Won't you share it with me?'

'Not now, Amanda,' he said, pulling his fingers from her own. 'I left England six years ago and went to America to make a new life, although I did intend coming back at some point. I have never told anyone about my past—what it was like—and now is not the time, so please don't ask me again.'

His voice had a dangerous edge, but Amanda refused to back down. 'Then when will it be the time, Kit? Don't you agree that I'm entitled to answers?' She watched his expression turn guarded.

'Possibly. It depends on the questions.'

A little unnerved by his unencouraging response, she nevertheless forged ahead. 'Tell me about your father.'

'Ask another question,' he said flatly.

His unnecessary sharpness grated on her, not only because she still felt warm and sated from his love-making and extremely sensitive to his attitude, but because she honestly felt she was entitled to answers about his life. Keeping her voice sincere and soft, she said, 'Please don't try to brush me off, Kit.'

'Then ask me something else.'

His stubborn refusal to open up annoyed her. 'No, Kit, I won't. Don't you understand that I need to know about you?'

'No, Amanda. Not now.' He turned towards her, placing his hands on her upper arms and drawing her towards him. 'Let's go back to bed.'

Something stirred in the depths of his eyes, something hot and inviting and Amanda had to use all her willpower to resist. She shrugged his hands off, hurt and insulted by the injustice of his attitude. 'No, I will not. I have a right to know.'

The declaration somehow put her instantly beyond all limits of tolerance, and Kit's voice took on a chilling, deadly tone. 'You have no right to anything.'

Amanda flinched at the bite in his voice, alarmed by this new side of him, the streak of ruthless finality that enabled him to push people to one side without a backward glance. It wasn't so much that he refused to tell her about his life and family, it was the way he said it and the look on his face. It was with great effort that she managed to keep her fury and humiliation out of her voice.

'I see.' And she did. He wanted her to share his bed and that was it. Shaking with anger at her own gullibility, she jerked away from him and walked quickly to the door.

'Amanda, wait.'

'No. I'm going to bed—to my own bed. I realise now, more than at any other time, that although we have been intimate together you are still a virtual stranger to me, so until you can bring yourself to rectify that I shall sleep alone.' Amanda opened the door, only to find it slammed shut in her face as Kit issued a warning, his breath warm on the side of her face.

'This is an extremely unwise decision on your part, Amanda. I suggest you reconsider.'

'I will not. Your tone just now was callous and needlessly harsh. I don't know you. Was your life so terrible that you cannot bring yourself to talk about it—to me—your wife?' There was a pause before he answered, and Amanda could almost feel the pain inside him.

'I can't. Not yet.'

'Then there's nothing more to be said. Goodnight, Kit.' Opening the door she slipped out on to the landing, walking quickly to her own room and disappearing inside.

Chapter Ten

Keeping away from Kit was a hard thing for Amanda to do. How do you avoid a man you want? How do you make him keep his distance when what you most want is him up close, holding him to you and never letting go? She half expected him to come to her, but he didn't. Was he furious with her for leaving him like that? She had no way of knowing.

Two days after the night she had left his room, she returned to Eden Park with her father and Caroline. Kit had postponed his departure until the following day in order to accompany the horse Henry had decided to buy from Paul.

When Amanda entered the house she was about to follow Caroline into the drawing room, but halted when she caught sight of Ortega coming down the stairs. Dressed in black as if he disdained the light of day, he had about him an aura of a figure of the night.

'Why, Señor Ortega, I'm surprised to see you back here so soon.' Knowing what she did about their Spanish guest, she was unable to inject any warmth into her voice or to appear civil. As she looked into his face, what she saw sickened her.

'I've only just arrived myself,' he said, moving towards

her. 'My business was completed sooner than I expected. I'm on my way to Liverpool and with a few days to spare I thought I'd take advantage of Henry's generous invitation to spend a few more days at Eden Park before my ship sails for New York.'

'To see my father, or Mr Benedict?' Amanda remarked pointedly. 'I know why you have come back, so let's not pretend, Señor Ortega.'

Their eyes met. A grim smile creased the corners of Ortega's eyes, but did not light the eyes themselves.

'So, your husband told you.'

'Everything, and if I knew it would not upset my father I would order you from this house. Mr Benedict did not take kindly to being threatened by you. Do you think he will ever yield to a man who is a crook, a scoundrel and a blackmailer?'

His shoulders lifted in a dismissive shrug. 'A man must survive. Call it payment for my sister's life.'

'He did not kill your sister.'

'And you're sure of that?'

'Yes, because I believe in him. You are a despicable man, Señor Ortega. It makes me ill to look at you.'

'At least I'm not a murderer.'

They were interrupted by the sound of approaching footsteps. Mr Quinn, as sombre and grim faced as ever, came towards them. Amanda realised the two men had yet to be introduced and she was interested to see how they would react to each other—one the brother of Carmen and the other her murderer.

'Oh, Mr Quinn. I don't believe you have met Señor Ortega. You were in Manchester when he stayed with us recently.'

Both men's eyes were arrested by the sight of each other. To Amanda's observant eye Mr Quinn was deliberately casual, almost cool as she introduced them. He held himself extremely upright, giving the impression of superiority to the

Spaniard. However, Mr Quinn was not in the best of moods. He had heard rumours about Ortega's fondness for the pretty maids of the house, especially Sadie, and his patience had been well tested of late. He trod very near to the edge of losing his temper entirely.

Stifling his pride, his resentment and what he knew, Quinn merely nodded a greeting.

'Mr Quinn,' Rafael said thoughtfully. 'I've heard that name before.'

'That's hardly surprising, since he works for my father. Unless, of course, you encountered each other in Charleston,' Amanda remarked, looking from one to the other as she tried and failed to detect any hint of recognition.

'Charleston?' Ortega enquired, with a lift to his brows.

Quinn met his deliberate stare. 'I accompanied Mrs Claybourne to Charleston when she went to visit her aunt. I do not believe we met, Señor Ortega. I am certain I would have remembered.'

At that moment Sadie appeared from the kitchens, carrying a tray of tea things. She was taking them to the mistress in the drawing room, but on seeing Amanda and the two men she slowed her pace. Quinn seethed when her gaze swept from one to the other before coming to rest on Ortega. Her high, firm breasts beneath her bodice and the curve of her hips would tempt any man, and her lips were parted in a self-assured smile of invitation.

Quinn watched the small-minded, greedy and immoral, though highly desirable, young maid, barely able to control his fury as he caught the glitter of feminine allure in her eyes. Not only was it Sadie's attraction for the Spaniard he saw in their depths, but cold-hearted calculation. Her betrayal scorched his soul. Quinn would not be spurned by any woman.

Not until Sadie had disappeared into the drawing room did

Quinn excuse himself. 'Please excuse me. I have urgent matters to attend to.'

A smile crossed Ortega's face as he watched a hard-faced Mr Quinn disappear into Henry's office and close the door. 'What an odd fellow is your Mr Quinn. Is he always so sombre?'

'I'm afraid he is. You get used to it after a while.' Amanda gave him a scalding glare that could have melted the largest ice floe. 'Please remember that you are wearing out your welcome, Señor Ortega. However, I suppose I shall have to endure your presence as best I can while you are my father's guest—albeit a singularly ill-fitting one. Do not delay your departure.'

'Come down off your high horse, little lady.' He smirked. 'I'll be gone as soon as my business with your husband is finished.'

He followed Amanda into the drawing room, prepared to be bored and make polite chit-chat until he could confront Claybourne.

Unable to stay in the same room as Ortega with his high-minded arrogance and breathe the same air, Amanda excused herself and went out on to the terrace. Concerned about her step-daughter, Caroline followed, leaving Henry to entertain their guest. There was something wrong—had been for days. At first she had assumed Amanda's air of tension was due to what she felt for Kit and the stress of the situation in which she found herself. She had no way of reading Amanda's thoughts. She had a trick of hiding strong feeling behind a mask of calmness.

Amanda was standing quite still, looking out over the gardens, her arms hugging her body. 'Amanda, are you all right?' Caroline asked in concern. 'You haven't been yourself for days.'

Amanda turned her head and looked at her. Caroline's gaze was shrewd and perceptive, and it was too late for discretion. 'No, Caroline,' she replied with a travesty of a smile. 'I'm not.'

'Is it Kit?' she said then, without preliminary.

Amanda glanced at her, a flash of startlement visible in her eyes, and then Caroline saw the tense line of her shoulders ease.

'Yes. You must have read my mind—and I confess that I hoped you would. I desperately need to talk to someone, Caroline.'

Caroline listened in complete absorption, interrupting only for clarification, widening her eyes in disbelief when Amanda told her how she had gone to Charleston Gaol, frowning with disapproval but more often with sympathy, especially over Kit's plight and his belief that he would never see his daughter again. When Amanda had finished speaking and confided everything, including the bargain she had made with Kit in the gaol, Caroline met her eyes.

'What a tale. Had it been anyone else I would never have believed a word. Thank you for telling me. I can see now why you have been so troubled—and I would never believe Kit capable of killing anyone. I am sure that things will right themselves, but this deception cannot go on. Henry must be told. There are no secrets between Henry and me and it isn't right to keep something as important as this from him. But I sense there is much more you haven't told me. Am I right?'

'Yes. I know you hold strong opinions regarding honesty and truth between husband and wife, and I am sorry that I must ask you not to speak to Father just yet—to be patient a while longer, Caroline. You see, the man who killed Mrs Rider believes Kit was executed and that he is safe. It's imperative that Kit's true identity isn't revealed just yet, otherwise the real murderer might take desperate measures to silence him.'

Caroline paled. 'And is this man in England?'

'Yes.'

'And is he close?' Amanda nodded. 'Is it Señor Ortega?'

'No.'

'Then I will say nothing for the time being.'

The hour was late and the house quiet when Sadie slipped out of Ortega's room in a dreamy, half-awake state. Hidden from sight, Quinn's tall, still figure waited. He watched Sadie walk away with mounting fury, her hair loose and foaming like a curling cascade around her shoulders. He stepped back, the pictures in his mind hideously clear—Sadie in the arms of Ortega, her body soft, warm and inviting as he, Quinn, knew how it could be, her fingers moving caressingly over his flesh. Ortega would be gone soon, and what then? Would the whore turn back to him to ease her lust? Be damned she would. He was not sunk so low that he would take another man's leavings. When she descended the stairs he followed.

Sadie stopped in the passage, taking time to don her hat and coat before letting herself out of the house. Unbeknown to her, the figure had slipped out before her. As she hurried away from the house down the lane that led to the lake and Thurlow village beyond, Sadie's feet sped over the ground as though they had wings. Not until she came to the trees bordering the lake did she pause.

Something moved in the undergrowth and she blinked herself to attention until she caught the sound again. The depth of darkness was impenetrable. Fear gripped her. It might be a poacher or the Devil himself. Then a breeze stirred and the clouds broke, allowing a shaft of moonlight to sweep across the lake, casting a silver sheen on the surface of the black water.

A shriek of pure terror caught in her mouth, for there, standing in the silvered light, was a man she recognised, and she realised that it might just as well have been the Devil, for she sensed the evil in him. 'Mr Quinn,' she whispered. 'You scared me half to death. What are you doing here? Are you following me?'

'Whore,' he hissed. Half-crazed with fury, he hit her across the mouth. 'You greedy, grubby little whore. You didn't think to see me, did you? Thought you could make a fool of me with Ortega, you slut.'

Sadie saw murder in his eyes. Her legs suddenly felt weighted down and she couldn't run. She could do nothing but stand and stare in terror as he reached for her. A scream tore itself from her throat, but it was silenced when hands were placed around her neck and squeezed. Scratching and kicking, she struggled and fought with a strength surprising for one so slight, dragging her attacker to the water's edge and tumbling him into the lake with her.

Common sense and humanity had long since left Quinn. What he felt now was his lust to punish, to avenge himself. He had wanted Sadie the moment he had laid eyes on her, so intently that it had become a bitter, twisted thing. This feeling glowed within the dark, secret places of his mind. He could stand it no longer.

As he watched Sadie struggling for her life an image of Carmen invaded his mind. Carmen had got inside him, like fire, like poison, until he had no mind for anything but her, and he had almost died of wanting her. But, like Sadie, she had spurned him for another man, and she had paid with her life.

The unrelenting hands still around Sadie's throat squeezed tighter, pushing her head beneath the water until she couldn't breathe. In no time at all darkness engulfed her and death claimed her.

Dragging himself to his feet, Quinn staggered back from Sadie's corpse and looked down at her without remorse. Using his foot, he shoved her contemptuously farther into the lake, before turning and walking back up the lane.

* * *

Nan encountered Mr Quinn on his way to his room. Normally she would have thought little of it, but as she was taking hot milk to her small charge in the hope of sending her back to sleep after a bad dream, they came face to face. His face was stern, his eyes cold and penetrating, and she hurried away, quite terrified by the look on his face.

Sadie's body was found floating in the lake by one of the servants on her way to work the following morning. At the house everybody was astounded and could not believe what had happened. It seemed that Sadie had been viciously attacked after she left the house the previous night. Her mother hadn't raised the alarm when she had failed to come home because Sadie often spent the night at the big house rather than walk home alone in the dark.

The marks around her neck proved she had been strangled and that she had not fallen into the lake and drowned. Two members of the police arrived to speak to everyone. Caroline lost no time in going to comfort Sadie's mother and to see if there was anything she might need. Sadie's death was so tragic and felt by everyone. Amanda thought of her—lovely, seductive, mischievous Sadie, who had roused a fierce jealousy in her when she thought she was showing too much interest in Kit. Her death and the manner of it had thrown a shadow over the house.

Kit didn't arrive until the following day. Amanda couldn't stand being apart from him a minute longer. It was early evening and, as soon as she heard he'd arrived back at Eden Park, she hurried to his cottage. Drawing a long, deep breath, she restrained herself from flinging back the door. Composing her features into formal lines, she knocked. It opened, and in the mellow glow of the gaslight Kit was framed in the doorway. He looked devastatingly handsome, the power and virility stamped in every line of his body, but his profile was so bitter and desolate that Amanda's chest filled with remorse. His face changed when he saw her. His eyes pierced through her, his expression unreadable, neither friendly nor hostile.

'Come in.' There was no emotion in his voice.

Stepping inside, he closed the door behind her. The atmosphere was tense. Amanda tightly controlled a small shiver of irritation and hurt pride. She managed a faint smile, but she was so nervous she couldn't think of what to say and was glad when he took the initiative.

'Are you staying?'

She pushed away a strand of hair as she tried to hide the pain in her heart, to forget how miserable the last few days had been. 'If I may.'

'Then take off your coat.'

Amanda complied and handed it to him. Tossing it carelessly on to a chair, he said, 'Can I get you anything—a drink?'

'Not just now,' she replied. He stood before the hearth, his hands in his pockets, and she saw the deeply etched lines of strain and fatigue on his face and in his eyes. Anxiously she scanned his features. 'Kit, you look exhausted.'

One black brow rose sardonically. 'I don't think you've come here to discuss the state of my health,' he said brusquely.

'No, only I don't like seeing you like this.' He was cold, remote, his granite features an impenetrable mask. She sighed. 'You aren't going to make this easy for me, are you, Kit?'

His eyes were impassive, his voice coldly unemotional. 'That depends what you have to say to me.'

She stood there, feeling lost. His complete indifference tore at her heart, and her throat constricted with tears. 'I'm sorry.'

'Really?' he said in a low voice.

'I don't want things to be this way between us, truly, but I can't bear all these secrets—knowing you're keeping things hidden from me. You are furious with me, I know, only—I'm not sure why.'

Kit closed the distance between them and pulled her into his arms with stunning force. 'Because you have avoided me,' he said tersely. 'When you left me I waited for you to come back, I waited all the next night and the one after that, and each time you didn't come the sun went down and I died a little bit more.' His voice sounded rough, as if it were gouged out of his chest.

As she felt again the thrill of being in his arms, unable to stem the tears that had built up in her eyes, Amanda bent her head back and gazed up at him. 'Then why didn't you come to me? Was it your insufferable pride that prevented you from doing so?'

'Perhaps, and because I didn't know what kind of reception I would get from you,' he replied—and also because, despite being proud and self-assured, where she was concerned he seemed strangely vulnerable. 'I don't want to spar with you, Amanda,' he said with quiet sincerity. 'That's the last thing I want to do. But please try to understand that I do not want to discuss my past or my future until this mess with Quinn and Ortega is cleared up.'

'I do understand, Kit, and I promise I won't put any pressure on you.' Looping her arms around his neck, she raised her lips to his and pressed against him, fitting her pliant body to the hardening contours of his. 'I didn't want to avoid your bed.'

His lips curved as he gazed hungrily at her proffered lips. 'I hope not, otherwise that wouldn't bode well for the next fifty years.' His eyes held hers in one long, compelling look, holding all his frustrated longings, his unfulfilled desires, everything that was between them.

'Kiss me, Kit,' she whispered, her warm, sweet breath fanning his lips.

Kit's mouth descended hungrily on hers, and he kissed her with an ardour and passion so intense that Amanda could think of nothing but the exciting urgency of his mouth and the warmth of his breath. With a low moan of joy she returned his kiss, glorying in the familiar feel of his lips locked fiercely on hers and the strong, muscled legs pressed against her own. The force between them had grown powerful and impatient in its captivity, and the longing could no longer be denied. Kit's iron-thewed arms tightened possessively on her back and hips, moulding her closer to him. Lost in that wild and beautiful madness, Amanda knew she loved Kit as she had never loved any man before.

The exquisite feel of her, the taste of her lips responding to his with a fervour that betrayed her own longing, was almost more than Kit could take. Drawing back slightly, he looked down into the languid pools of her eyes.

'My God, how I've missed you,' he murmured softly. His gaze probed with flaming warmth into hers. 'I've wanted to do that ever since you walked out on me, and you do not know how hard you make it for me to resist you. I want you now, Amanda. Come to bed.'

'In a moment, Kit. Something has happened that I think you should know about.'

Kit listened intently while Amanda told him about the terrible thing that had happened to Sadie.

'Someone killed her?' he said, astounded and saddened that the life of the bright young woman who had cleaned his cottage had been snuffed out like a light.

'It appears so. Police are questioning all the servants in the hope that one of them can throw some light on why someone would want to kill her, and who was the last person to see her alive.'

'Who would want to?'

'I don't know. But someone did.'

'Was she seeing anyone—a young man?'

'I couldn't say. She—did share Mr Quinn's bed for a while.'

Kit glanced at her sharply. 'Quinn? You're certain of that?'

'Yes. I saw them together. It was most embarrassing.'

Kit was looking at her intently. 'Tell me everything.'

So Amanda told him how she had found Sadie and Mr Quinn in bed together and how he had sworn Amanda to secrecy in return for his silence that she was Kit's wife.

'And the affair finished?' Kit asked.

'I believe so. By all accounts she transferred her affections to Señor Ortega. Kit, do you think Mr Quinn might have had something to do with her death?'

His lips twisted wryly. 'Why not? He's killed once.'

'Nan said she passed him on the stairs that night and he looked ferocious. She was quite scared of him.'

Becoming thoughtful, Kit turned away.

'Kit, what are you thinking?'

'I know what Quinn is capable of when a woman rejects him. It is possible that he killed Sadie, and if so he will have to pay very highly for his sins. But enough of Quinn for one night,' he murmured, his eyes warm with desire. 'Come to bed.'

Taking her hand, he led the way into the bedroom. The bed looked soft and inviting, but before they could proceed a low knocking sounded on the door. Kit cursed softly.

'Go and see who it is,' Amanda whispered, placing tantalising little kisses on his lips. 'And get rid of them quickly.'

'Never fear, my love. It will take nothing short of an earthquake to keep me from you.'

Kit went out, leaving the door slightly ajar. He opened the outer door to find Ortega standing there.

'Can I come in?'

Without saying a word, Kit opened the door farther, his expression far more ominous than amiable. However dangerous Ortega might be, Kit had reached a degree of indifference. It was therefore without the slightest trace of feeling that he closed the door behind him and accorded his unwelcome visitor no more than a chilling glance.

'What do you want, Ortega?'

'A few moments of your time. I've been in Cambridgeshire for the past few days—a county you are familiar with, I know.'

'And did your visit prove fruitful?'

'Absolutely. I even visited Covington Hall—I was invited by Lord and Lady Covington when I was in London recently, which was where I met Henry and Caroline. I often dined with them.'

'I trust you found London entertaining. There are enough gambling halls to satisfy even you, Ortega. No doubt you lost a bundle,' Kit retorted with contempt. The deliberate flow of talk was beginning to irritate him.

Ortega shrugged, unabashed. 'It happens. London is a gambler's paradise. The first night I kept on winning, but then my luck changed. The last night I was down to my last coin. I put it on a black and a red came up.'

Ortega pretended not to care, but Kit knew how difficult it must be for him to meet his losses without having Carmen to bail him out. 'If you want to squander your money, it is no concern of mine, Ortega. Just don't expect me to fund your next gambling session.'

'I have impatient creditors to pay off in America and they are baying for my blood. Your money will enable me to settle my debts. I enjoyed my stay in Cambridgeshire, by the way,' he went on lightly. 'Delightful place, Covington Hall, and I might even say that dear Alyce has a great affection for me.' He sauntered round the room, looking at the rather crude furnishings with distaste. 'I'm surprised you choose to live in such a primitive abode when you own one of the finest houses in Cambridgeshire.'

Kit swung round to face Ortega. So, his snooping had indeed yielded results. 'Enough, Ortega. You did not come here for idle gossip. Say what you have to say and then get out. What is it? Money?'

'What else? I know you have plenty without having to go cap in hand to your wife. So you see, rather than force me to divulge to Henry what I have discovered about you—about which I am impressed, although I can see it might be highly embarrassing for you—it would be infinitely preferable for us to reach an understanding.'

'And what kind of understanding have you in mind?'

'Mr Claybourne—oh, I do beg your pardon. I forget to give you your due as the Earl of Rossington. Tell me, how does one address an earl?'

'My lord,' Kit ground out sarcastically, making no attempt to deny Ortega's implications, 'but stick to Mr Claybourne when we are alone.'

'Fine, prosperous family, the Claybournes, apparently—highly respected, powerful and wealthy—though your brother Charles was a mite wild by all accounts—and your father mad enough to take his own life. Yes,' he said with a smirk of satisfaction, seeming unconcerned with the tangible danger emanating from Kit, 'nothing to be proud of there, I can see that.'

Kit's hands blurred with the speed of their motion. His fingers closed around Ortega's throat, biting in. 'Shut your mouth, Ortega,' he snarled in a chilling voice as Ortega clawed at his hands, 'if you want to leave this cottage alive.' His gaze slashed over Ortega, shocking the Spaniard with its blazing contempt. 'When you insult my family you insult me, and no man does that and gets away with it.' He dropped his hands before Ortega's face turned blue.

Gasping for breath, Ortega fell back, clutching his throat. 'You'll regret that,' he whispered, 'I promise you. Is that how you murdered my sister—lost your temper and stabbed her to death? The price has gone up to thirty thousand—since you evidently have the means.' His thin nose pinched with unconcealed greed. 'Get me the money, Claybourne, and you will be rid of me. I have no intentions of returning to England in the foreseeable future.'

'Indeed?' Kit's mocking tone was incredulous. 'You can go straight to hell. You will gain nothing by coming here. Don't think you hold all the cards in this little game. You are either brave or extremely foolish. Direct threats take guts, especially when aimed at me. There will be no money, so go back to America and let your creditors do their worst. Knowing the kind of scum you owe, Ortega, they are not likely to let you escape what is clearly going to be an unenviable fate.'

Ortega's eyes narrowed and began to glitter dangerously. His smile was unpleasant as he smoothed his hair with a palm and brought his strident breathing under control. 'Aren't you forgetting something? By your subterfuge I can only assume you wish to keep your identity secret. How desperate are you, I ask myself?'

'Not that desperate—and not nearly as desperate as you. I shall take steps to ensure you get not a penny piece. Now, get out.'

Kit went to the door and opened it. Ortega smiled thinly, his gaze flickering past him to Amanda's coat draped over a chair. He raised his eyebrows as his gaze went to the slightly open bedroom door and then slowly back to Kit. 'I can see you have company,' he sneered. 'Far be it from me to keep a man from his wife, so I will be on my way. I'll give you two days to think about it, Claybourne. No longer.'

Closing the door, Kit turned and looked across the room to where Amanda stood, having heard every word that had passed between himself and Ortega. Beset with confusion, her face was pale, her eyes huge with horror and disbelief.

'You are the Earl of Rossington?' she said, the truth just beginning to dawn on her.

'One and the same,' Kit answered flatly as he moved closer. 'The title is an adornment I can do without, but I am stuck with it. You had to find out some time.'

'But not like this. I would rather it had come from you. I— I simply cannot believe it,' she uttered, her mind flitting about in a frenzy of confused thoughts and emotions. 'The revelation is so different from what I've assumed.'

'And what is that?'

'That you were a man of moderate means—a horse trainer, damn you,' she spat, her eyes brimming with angry tears. 'Never again will I listen to your lies.'

'I told you no lies, Amanda.'

'No. You merely omitted telling the truth. Oh, how could you?'

'Amanda…' He reached out to pull her against him, but she leapt back, evading his hands, unwilling to relent.

'Don't touch me,' she cried, her voice ragged with emotion. 'Don't you dare touch me. You tricked me into believing I was marrying a nobody. You should have told me. You should have eased my fears—and an earl, no less,' she scoffed contemptuously. 'Oh, how you must have laughed when I went to you in your prison cell, when I told you how my father wanted me to marry a man of title and wealth—and to think your eligibility far exceeded his desire and you kept it from me. And when I think how you took me into your bed and I didn't know who you were. How you must have laughed louder.'

Despite her haughty stance, Kit saw that her lovely olive-green eyes were glittering with unshed ears. 'I never laughed at you,' he said gently.

'But you should have told me,' she persisted, quite beside herself with fury.

'I couldn't tell you about something which I could not face myself,' Kit answered. 'When you came to me in Charleston Gaol I had the matter of a hanging to deal with, and I had no way of knowing if I could trust you with my daughter—but you were my only hope of bringing her safely to England and Victoria. I truly believed my life was over and at the time you had nothing to gain from knowing who I was.'

'What? Are you telling me that the fact that you made me the Countess of Rossington meant nothing to you? Had your sentence not been repealed, I would never have known the truth.'

'Yes, you would. In the letter I wrote to Victoria I explained everything. I also included a letter to my lawyers. My estate is entailed to the male line, so Victoria's son as next in line would have inherited—had I been hanged. Despite this, I left both you and Sky well provided for. So you see, Amanda, your father would have been proud of you. It was the kind of marriage he always wanted his daughter to make. He would have had everything he wished for and been a very happy man indeed.'

'Never mind what my father wanted, you played me for a fool. And that house I saw—Woodthorpe Hall. Is that your ancestral home?'

'Yes, and a fine house it is. Woodthorpe is where we shall live when everything has been sorted out. So you see, my dear wife, I shall be able to keep you in the style to which you are accustomed.'

'And Paul and Alyce? You knew them before we went to stay at Covington Hall, didn't you?'

He nodded. 'Paul and I have been friends all our lives. When I came here I wrote to them, telling them where I could be found if need be. When I arrived at Covington Hall, Paul told me that Ortega had been to see them, asking questions about the Claybournes—apparently they met him whilst in London at the same time as Henry and Caroline and invited him to call if he should find himself in the area. Somehow he must have found out there was a family by the name of Claybourne in Cambridgeshire, and thought he might find a connection to me.'

'That was my fault. When your name entered the conversation I unwittingly told Señor Ortega you came from Cambridgeshire. I'm sorry. It was stupid of me.'

'No, you weren't to know he'd go snooping about, digging up dirt to be used against me.'

Amanda glanced at him sharply. 'Is there dirt to dig, Kit?'

He shook his head. 'Who can tell what he found? Ortega is a desperate man, and a desperate man will take desperate measures. I explained everything to Paul and Alyce. I was aware they would have read the newspapers about what had happened in Charleston and my imprisonment and would be worried. It was necessary for me to swear them to silence. They were reluctant to be a part of the subterfuge—Alyce especially, because she cannot tolerate deceit, but when I told them about Quinn and the danger he posed, they agreed.'

'I sensed there was a familiarity between the three of you that went further than mere acquaintances.'

In an attempt to clear the chaos in her mind, Amanda turned her back on Kit and moved away. There was something else troubling her that had momentarily escaped her notice as she had listened to what Ortega had said. It was something about Kit's brother and his father. She turned and faced him, knowing that once again she was about to tread on forbidden territory. 'You told me you didn't have siblings, Kit. Were you lying about that?'

Kit reminded himself that the discovery of his identity had been a shock to her, and no matter what she said or did he would be patient and understanding. But when he looked into her accusing eyes, it was all he could do to bridle his temper. 'No—and I never lie intentionally.'

'But I heard Ortega say—'

Kit's amiability vanished. At once the expression on his face became hard and brittle and his eyes turned into shards of ice. 'Forget what you heard. There's nothing to be gained from dragging up the past, Amanda. I really do not wish to discuss it.'

His tone suggested such finality that Amanda stepped back. The harshness of his reply told her that whatever had befallen his family had left scars, as yet unhealed. What had happened to harden his heart? She stood there, looking at him for a moment. Whatever had happened in his past went deeper than she realised. Very quietly, she turned and picked up her coat.

'You are right. Don't feel you have to tell me anything you don't want to,' she said, forcing a calmness into her voice. 'And now I must go. I have to get ready for dinner.' Going to the door, she turned and looked back at him. 'Caroline told me to be sure to ask you to come—seven-thirty. I'm sorry. It quite slipped my mind to tell you. I know it won't be easy for you with Señor Ortega present, but I'm sure you'll cope. If you come early, you'll be able to spend some time with Sky before Nan puts her to bed.'

Amanda went out, dreading the dinner when the five of them would have to sit around the table and pretend that everything was all right.

Chapter Eleven

Kit watched Amanda go out and didn't try to stop her. When the door had closed he raked his fingers through his hair in consternation, compelling himself to reflect back on the last ten years, to think of the awful, tragic truth Amanda wanted him to reveal, to unlock the invisible door behind which lurked all the hurt and pain he had kept inside him, resolved never to let it out. It was hard thinking about what had happened to his brother and father all those years ago, and the torment had not diminished. To rake it all up would be like being back in that terrible time—alone, betrayed by his father whom he had loved, only to have that love rejected.

Kit knew he had to tell Amanda what she wanted to know, but dear Lord, he had never told anyone, never discussed what had happened, not even with Victoria, his cousin, to whom he had been close all his life. People around Woodthorpe had gossiped and whispered about it—still did, according to Paul and Alyce, but no one had known what it had been like.

Kit thanked God every day for bringing Amanda to his prison cell that day, and he felt that it was time for them to get on with their lives as husband and wife, but before they could do that he had to declare himself to Henry and settle this business with Quinn and Ortega. And so, having decided that before the day was out everything would be revealed and hopefully resolved, he grabbed his jacked and went in pursuit of his wife.

She was walking briskly past the stables with her head down. When Kit called her name she paused and turned, waiting for him to catch up with her.

'Amanda, I'm sorry. Too much has been said for me to keep silent any longer about my past—about my family—but I didn't want to examine the many feelings that compelled me to do so. I have never been able to trust myself to speak of a subject that brings me so much pain. But you are my wife, and you are right. I do owe you some answers. When I left England six years ago I put the past behind me—although God knows I could never put it from my mind. Come, let's walk. It isn't an easy tale, so I must ask you to bear with me.'

The wind was blowing quite strongly as they walked towards the park. Kit was looking ahead, looking dishevelled, wind-blown, and so utterly handsome that Amanda's heart ached for him. Falling into step beside him, she said, 'I told you, Kit, that you don't have to tell me anything if it is too painful.'

'I realise that if I am to lay the past to rest I must. I didn't lie to you when I told you I had no siblings, Amanda. I don't now, but I did. I had a brother. His name was Charles.'

Amanda turned her head to look at him with some surprise and said softly, 'Is he dead?'

'Yes.'

'Were you close?'

He shook his head. 'No—not as close as brothers should be. He was older than me by seven years. Actually he was a rogue with a list of transgressions as long as your arm—so long and so abhorrent to those with any kind of moral standards he would make the Devil himself blush. An explosive force sent my brother leaping and dancing through life, quarrelling, drinking, gambling with reckless extravagance over the wildest reaches of London and the Continent, seducing women he had no right to, until he was shot through the lungs by an outraged husband and coughed out his life before his time.'

Amanda stared at him, appalled, and put a tentative hand on his arm, causing him to pause. 'Kit, that is terrible.'

'Yes, it is. Charles had a cruel streak—didn't care that he hurt people or how many, as long as he got his way. He took after my father, who was wild and crazy in his youth and carried on like that until the day he died. Charles's mind was his own mind, the two of them being almost the same, except that Charles was colder, clearer of head, not given to Father's blustering and rages.'

Kit's smile was bitter as he continued to walk on slowly. 'In Father's eyes Charles was always his favourite and could do no wrong—a chip off the old block, so to speak. No matter how much misery Charles's behaviour caused my mother, Father never got worked up over Charles's sins of the flesh and the endless series of scandals that followed him through life. Father boasted about it to his friends—as though it were something to be proud of for all the world to see.'

His hazel eyes darkened with sadness for a moment, and then a faint smile curved his lips. 'Charles broke my mother's heart. I'm glad she didn't live to see what happened to him. Father never got over her death—though I don't think he ever looked to blame himself for a moment. When Charles died his grief was two-fold. He took to drinking heavily and, unable to go on, blew his brains out. Unfortunately it didn't go as he wanted. He didn't die immediately. It was ghastly beyond belief. He died in my arms—in great pain, choking on his own blood and crying for my brother.'

Amanda thought she had never heard such desolation, nor felt it. It was a story of pain and humiliation so great that she felt pity begin to melt her heart. 'Did you love your father, Kit?'

Pausing once more, he towered over her, and his lean, hard face bore a world of untold suffering. 'I did—and I wanted him to love me—desperately. God knows I was no plaster saint, but I wasn't Charles.'

There was a world of meaning in those final four words that struck deep into Amanda's heart. At last she began to understand how difficult it had been for Kit to live with what had happened. He knew she sympathised and understood the horror and the torment he had endured. It had been so hard for him to say these things about his father and brother—to confront his demons at last, each word a world of suffering and pain, the kind he had endured throughout his life.

Kit looked at Amanda, saw her concern for him in her eyes. He managed a fleeting half smile. 'Suicide—added to his other sins—is a dreadful, shameful business and doesn't sit well with some. I couldn't stay at Woodthorpe after that. There were too many bitter and ugly memories. So I went to America, leaving my affairs in the capable hands of lawyers, stewards and bailiffs. I intended coming back at some point, but at that time I wanted to put as much distance between me and Woodthorpe as I could. Victoria gave me tremendous support. She tried persuading me to stay, telling me that I was well liked and respected by the people of the domain I was destined to rule since the demise of my father and brother, but I was not convinced.'

'So you went to Charleston to heal your wounds. And are they healed, Kit? Do you feel that you can return to your home and live out your life there?'

'I can't wipe away the hurt my father and brother caused me, but life goes on. I have to bury the past. What is important now is to begin the long climb back to the place that is rightfully mine. I am duty bound to those who depend on me. I am single-mindedly committed to that—and with you by my side, how can I possibly fail?'

Amanda smiled up at him. 'It's a challenge—an arduous challenge, one I am looking forward to. Make it soon, Kit. I haven't had you to myself since our marriage, and the idea rather appeals to me.'

'It appeals to me, too, but what about your father?'

'He'll be completely won over when you wave your title under his nose and he sees the size and grandeur of Wood-thorpe,' Amanda said laughingly. 'When we were at Coving-ton Hall, did you go to Woodthorpe?'

He nodded. 'I'm sorry I had to insist on the subterfuge, but you must understand why now.'

'Yes, I do. Thank you for telling me, Kit. I know it wasn't easy, but I'm glad you did.' Linking her arm through his, she turned him about. 'Now come along. Enough doom and gloom for one day. You have to change for dinner and your daughter is impatient to see her father.'

Kit turned his head and looked into her eyes. Meeting his gaze, she smiled, a smile of such blinding sweetness and understanding that it almost sent him to his knees.

Amanda's apprehension about the evening had finally lessened now that dinner was over, but with the table between them, she saw the tenseness in Kit's face and manner. Despite the gloom Sadie's death had cast over the entire household, Caroline had been her usual cheerful self, keeping the con-versation flowing—though distantly polite to Rafael, for she could not stem the feeling that there was something sinister beneath all that charm—and giving no indication that she was any the wiser about Amanda and Kit's marital state.

Kit pointedly refrained from exchanging any form of gentlemanly cordiality with the Spaniard and anything he had to say he directed at Henry, who was fired up about the splendid new acquisition to his stable and seemed unaware of any undercurrents among the others present.

Afterwards Rafael excused himself and went out on to the terrace to smoke a cheroot. Amanda was suddenly alarmed when Kit rose and looked pointedly at her father.

'Might I have a word with you, Henry?'

Kit avoided Amanda's eyes. She sensed that something was afoot, and that whatever it was Kit wanted to speak to her father about had more to do with her than horses.

Wiping his mouth on his napkin, Henry heaved himself out of his chair and the two of them headed off to his study.

Kit declined a brandy, knowing he must keep a clear head for what he was about to disclose.

'Well, Kit, out with it,' Henry said, taking a cigar from an ornate box on his desk and lighting it. He offered one to Kit, but he shook his head in refusal. 'I can see something's bothering you.'

Without another thought, impatient only to have what he had to say out in the open and brave the explosion that was sure to come, Kit first of all began telling Henry of what his life had been like in America, gradually leading up to his imprisonment, the reason for it, and Amanda's offer of marriage.

Standing stock-still, not changing expression in the slightest, Henry listened to him. He went pale, and then a deep, painful red infused his face, matching the vivid colour of the carpet. When Kit had finished speaking Henry's mask shattered as he was overcome by a horrified awareness of all he had been told. He was greatly shaken, but he mustered his forces to bring himself under control. Putting the untouched glass of brandy he was holding on the desk, he took his cigar from between his lips and ground it into the ashtray.

'I am shocked—grieved, to learn of this,' Henry said at last. 'I had not the smallest idea. I cannot excuse what you have done or condone it, and if I were a violent man I would call you out.'

'It was wrong, I know that now, wrong to keep something of such importance from you.'

'Your reasons were valid and I respect them, and for all the things you may have been accused of, rightly or wrongly, I know you are not a murderer. But I agree it was wrong of you to conceal your attachment to my daughter. It was deplorable. As for Amanda, her conduct was disgraceful. Good God man, you should have refused her.'

Henry waited, demanding an answer with his silence. Kit reluctantly complied.

'At the time I had five days left to live. I was deeply concerned about my daughter. Amanda was my last hope. Besides,' he said with a warmth that did not go unnoticed by Henry, 'when a woman as courageous and lovely as your daughter comes to his prison cell, offering herself in marriage, any man would have to be a fool not to have done what I did.'

'You have come to care for her?'

'A great deal. Of all the women I have known, none has possessed the fire of heart and mind that she has. As it's turned out, marrying Amanda is the best and only decent thing I've done in my life.'

'And your first marriage? Do you discount that?'

Kit shook his head. 'Her name was Fern—a Cherokee. Her father saved my life and when he died she was alone and needed someone to take care of her.'

'So you married her.'

Kit nodded. 'She died in childbirth.'

'Leaving you with a beautiful daughter. Sounds to me like marrying my daughter is the second-best thing you've done,' Henry remarked with a note of approval and a smile that was suddenly warm and even paternal. 'Was she anything like Amanda?'

'No—the opposite.'

'Aye, well, Amanda can be too headstrong for her own good. Perhaps some of it was of my own doing and I drove her to do what she did. She was all I had, you comprehend that? I took no pleasure in playing the heavy-handed father, and when I wrote and told Quinn I had Lord Prendergast lined up for her to wed if she came back without a husband in tow, I can see it forced that impetuous, wilful daughter of mine to take desperate measures to seek a way out.'

'That's exactly how it was.'

'No doubt you will be aware by now that Amanda is a woman who likes to feel she has a will of her own. I can understand that—she takes after me. But in this world women should know where their duty lies, understand it and stick to it. Amanda is a member of a wealthy family and as such has an obligation to me not to be lightly dismissed. But Good God, man, for her to enter a prison full of desperados is a hard thing for a father to swallow.'

'I can understand that, and Charleston Gaol was a pretty grim place, but Amanda proved to be an answer to my prayers. We made a bargain. I agreed to her request to give her my name. In return, I extracted a promise from her that she would take care of Sky until she had placed her in my cousin's care in Chelsea.'

Henry nodded. At last everything that had puzzled him about Amanda's behaviour when she had arrived back in England was becoming clear. He sighed deeply. 'Go on, Kit.'

'Our marriage was legal and binding,' Kit continued, 'and Amanda gave me her word that if I secured my freedom she would acknowledge me as her husband and become my wife in truth. When we parted there seemed little hope that I would be reprieved, and when she came back to England she truly believed she was a widow.'

'Little wonder she was so put out when you suddenly appeared as my new horse trainer.' Henry's eyes narrowed as he gave Kit a quizzical look. 'Something tells me I was man-oeuvred into employing you. I never did take kindly to being outfoxed, but I have no regrets about setting you on, no matter how it was brought about.'

'I realise that this is difficult for you to accept, Henry—'

'Damned right it is.'

'But it will mean a great deal to Amanda to know that she has your support. It is important to her.'

'It happens to be important to me, too.' Striding to the door, he opened it wide and ordered a passing servant to have Amanda brought to the study.

Amanda came quickly. Having watched Kit disappear with her father, she had spent the time until she was summoned in a state of spiralling apprehension, and by the time she entered the study her stomach was churning. Her father stood behind his desk, stern as a guard, his fierce grey eyes gleaming intently at his daughter from under his bushy white brows. He knew. Kit had told him. Fear traced a finger down her spine. Immediately her eyes sought Kit and instinctively she went towards him, as if seeking protection. He put his arm around her slim waist, a gesture that did not go unnoticed by Henry.

'Well, miss,' Henry thundered, 'what have you to say for yourself?' When he saw her flash Kit a look of panic, he said, 'Kit's told me everything and, to put it mildly, I am appalled by your conduct. I am also shocked to learn my suggestion that you marry Lord Prendergast would provoke such a reaction.'

'It was more like an order than a suggestion, Father.'

'Do you deny that you went to Kit in Charleston Gaol and asked him to wed you? Which reminds me, I shall have some harsh words to say to Quinn when I see him. I sent him to Charleston to keep an eye on you, not to let you run wild and do as you pleased.'

Amanda searched her father's eyes, seeing displeasure but thankfully no contempt. 'No, I do not deny it—and Mr Quinn could not have prevented me if he'd tried.'

'Why the charade all this time? Did you not think I should be told?'

'Of course I did. I wanted to tell you—we both did, but we were trapped.'

'How so?'

Amanda looked at Kit. 'You haven't told him?'

'No, but I will.' He looked at Henry. 'When I came to Eden Park, not only did I come for Amanda, but also to find the man who murdered Mrs Rider and was callously prepared to let me hang for the crime. He will think the sentence has been carried out and that he is safe, so I considered it wise to keep my identity secret until I could confront him. I was afraid if he discovered who I was he might take drastic measures to silence me for good or disappear.'

'This man sounds dangerous. Have you found him?'

'I have.'

'Who is it?'

'I prefer not to say just yet. I regret having to ask you to be party to this, Henry. But the time is fast approaching when all will be revealed.'

Henry thoughtfully considered what Kit asked and then he nodded. 'Very well. You may rely on my discretion, but I hope your revelation will be soon.' He looked at Amanda. 'I don't like your way of acquiring husbands. You shouldn't have made promises if you didn't intend keeping them.'

'I know I shouldn't have,' Amanda said. 'But the fact remains that I did.'

'And you mean to keep your promise to Kit—to be his wife till death do you part?'

Amanda looked up at Kit. Wife. The word brought a soft smile to her lips. She recalled how she had once strained against it, but no more. It had a wonderful ring to it and she was proud to be Kit's wife. 'Yes,' she said slowly. 'Yes, Father, I do.'

As he met her gaze, Kit's mouth curved in that sensuous smile of his, instantly transforming him from a worried man facing the wrath of his father-in-law—a deeply concerned parent with strong principles about what was acceptable and what was not—to a lover.

'Thank the Lord for that, because otherwise it would mean a divorce—and divorce is a scandalous and shameful business,' Henry remarked forcefully. 'Besides, I don't approve of 'em.'

Henry looked at his daughter standing at Kit's side, pretty as a picture, quietly composed and certain of her absolute confidence in herself, and he thought what a fine pair they made, even though Amanda's lovely brightness was momentarily dimmed by her anxiety over how he would react to her deceit.

He thought of how she had been since Kit had arrived at Eden Park—all the small things about her he had seen and taken no notice of now came together and formed a logical pattern. The way she had acted, the look of her, her change of moods—one minute sprightly and animated and full of life, and the next deep in troubled thought. Often there was a quiet radiance about her, a glow to her face and in her eyes. He knew the look of a woman in the first throes of passion; if he had known about her and Kit before, he would have seen the change.

Before he knew what he was about, Henry felt the outrage, the anger and absolute appalled amazement at his daughter's disobedience and disgraceful behaviour diminish and leave him grounds for pity and exhilaration.

'I'm so sorry, Father.' Tears welled in Amanda's eyes. 'I'm sorry if I've hurt you—disappointed you and made you unhappy. I didn't mean to—truly.'

'Maybe if I'd not given you ultimatums, then none of this would have happened.' Suddenly he smiled. 'But looking at the two of you, something tells me you are glad it has.'

'Oh, yes—yes,' she sobbed happily, running across the carpet and throwing herself into her father's arms, clinging to him, tears of joy and exultation flowing freely now.

'Ah, well, my only regret is that I cannot give you the grand wedding I always wanted.'

'And you have no objections to me as a son-in-law?' Kit asked, beginning to relax.

With a smile of conciliation at the tall, good-looking man whom he hoped and prayed would take care of his precious daughter, he said, 'If you're as good at being a husband as you are at training horses, then I shall have no complaints.'

'And do we have your blessing?' Kit persisted. It was important to him that Henry welcomed the union before he told him the rest.

'Absolutely,' Henry said, striding over to Kit and vigorously shaking his hand. 'You're a fine man, Kit, no doubt about that, and I'm proud to have you as my son-in-law. We'll have to arrange for you to move in now you have family status.'

'That won't be necessary, Henry,' Kit remarked flatly. 'I have one or two things to take care of here and then I shall take Amanda and Sky to my home.'

Henry was taken aback. 'Home, is it? But this is her home.'

'Not any more. Amanda's place is with me now,' Kit said on a note of finality that brooked no argument.

Henry was undeterred. 'I don't deny that, but the way I see

it you want to take my daughter away from everything she knows to live in a cottage. Just what kind of life can you give her—as a horse trainer's wife? She is ill equipped for all that.'

Amanda saw Kit pale and she could have strangled her father for trampling on Kit's pride like that. 'Wealth isn't all there is to life, Father,' she interceded sharply.

'And how would you know that when you've never been without it? I have, and I can tell you that money matters. I know the flavour of poverty. It's as cold and sour as ditch water and drives people to an early grave.'

'As my wife, Amanda will be well provided for, I promise you that. I have come to care for her deeply, and I wouldn't hurt her for anything on earth.'

'And can you buy her all the fancy clothes and say that she will want for nothing?'

Amanda looked at her husband. When was he going to tell her father who he was and that his precious daughter was the Countess of Rossington?

Shoving his hands into his trouser pockets, he sauntered towards the desk, a cynical smile curving his lips. Pouring himself a brandy and handing Henry the one he had poured earlier, he drank deep. Putting the glass down, he moved to stand in front of Amanda, gazing intently into her eyes.

'A woman like your daughter, Henry, is born to sit in palaces, not to live in dark places and squalor with a man going nowhere. You are a queen, Amanda, and no man should demand less of you. Your good name and your honour deserve better—and had I been a man of little worth I would have released you from our bargain without argument.'

Deeply moved by Kit's words, Henry was watching him with a puzzled frown creasing his brow. 'What is it you're saying, Kit?'

'This, Henry. Since her marriage, Amanda has been addressed as Mrs Claybourne. Has it not occurred to you to ask why, since I am known to you as Benedict?'

Henry stared at him. 'Good Lord, so it is.'

'My real name is Christopher Benedict Claybourne of Woodthorpe Hall in Cambridgeshire. I am also Lord Wood-thorpe, the Earl of Rossington.'

Henry blinked twice and gaped at him. 'Well, I'll be blessed!' he gasped when his power of speech returned. Beyond the sheer unexpectedness of what Kit had disclosed, it was the change in him that stunned Henry into speechless-ness. It was one thing to have had Kit in his employ. It was another to be told he was a peer of the realm, his bold features suddenly transmuted into power by the stamp of office, and fronting a personality not only thoroughly masculine, but fierce in aspect. Kit had the kind of arrogance so supreme that it didn't need to express itself, and he always did have the easy, confident manner, cultured accent and casual air of au-thority that proclaimed a man of good breeding.

'Then—that makes Amanda a Countess.' He gazed at his daughter with wonder.

'And so I am—' Amanda laughed '—which is what you always wanted—for me to marry an aristocrat.'

'Did you know about this?' Henry asked her.

'Kit told me earlier today, but I'd already made up my mind to honour the promise I made and live with him wherever that might be.'

Henry looked at Kit. 'Woodthorpe Hall, you say? Isn't that the house we passed on the way to Covington Hall? Grand place by the look of it.'

'The same. I apologise for any distress I have caused you, Henry. You are in order to throw a punch at me. I've earned it,' Kit said drily.

Henry's scowl softened to a reluctant smile. 'I think my

days of throwing punches are long gone. You will find me the most forgiving of men,' he said magnanimously. 'I prefer a drink—champagne—to toast your union—and hopefully I can look forward to bouncing grandchildren on my knee before too long. The offspring of such a handsome couple will be such fine, pure-bred cubs as to make any man proud.'

Waxing gleeful and ecstatic when Amanda blushed to the roots of her hair, he crossed to the door. 'But I can't let it be known that my daughter was married in a prison—not if I can help it.' Frowning when a thought suddenly occurred to him, he paused and looked back. 'How many people know this?'

'Well, Mr Quinn and cousin Charlotte—though not until afterwards. No one else.'

'Because no alliance will withstand a scandal of this magnitude, I shall let it be known that you were travelling from America separately and that your ship went down in a storm and you were presumed drowned, Kit.'

'And how will you explain his change of name and the fact that he's been employed by you for the past few weeks?' Amanda asked, laughing lightly at the confusion of her father's busy mind.

'I'll think of something. Oh, and I shall insist on a church blessing—and a banquet—a belated wedding banquet, with everyone of social prominence invited. Now, where's Caroline? I must go and tell her the good news—she'll never believe it—Ortega, too—and the servants, and tomorrow the whole neighbourhood.'

The light touching Kit's eyes showed they were genuinely relieved, and the transformation to his lean, tense features was remarkable. He combed his fingers through his hair, looking oddly and uncharacteristically abstracted now he had told Henry everything.

Amanda felt unbearable relief stirring inside her. She remained silent as sweet warmth washed through her, and she felt unfamiliarly nervous as she stared at the handsome face of her husband whom she could now openly acknowledge. She loved him so much, more than anyone, more than anything. He was her destiny, her future. At that moment she wanted him so much, wanted to feel his arms about her, to feel his hard, muscular body pressed to hers. But she could only stand and watch him, distanced by his quiet manner.

'What made you decide to tell Father?' she asked, her soft voice disturbing the quietness of the room.

Kit's rigidity melted and he allowed the faintest of smiles to shadow his firm lips. 'It was time. I've had enough of subterfuge. Do you mind?'

'No, I'm relieved that he knows. How did he take it when you told him? Was he very angry?'

'He was—reasonable, considering the circumstances. What's done is done. Our marriage is out in the open now and we'll have to make the best of it.' Realising how insensitive he sounded, he took her hand and quickly added, 'We didn't have the best of starts, I know, and our future together is an uncharted path, but when I've settled this matter with Quinn and Ortega, we can make a fresh start at Woodthorpe.'

'Yes, I would like that,' Amanda said, thinking it was like being offered the cake without the icing. She assumed Kit loved her—he had never really talked to her about matters of the heart—but she needed to hear him say it, and until he did she wouldn't feel completely his. She loved him with a fierceness and desperation that made her feel helpless and vulnerable and completely under his control.

'What shall we do about Ortega? Now Father knows about us, he can no longer blackmail you. Will you tell Father?'

Kit shook his head slowly, deliberating over her question.

'Not immediately. I owe it to Carmen to see that her brother is kept out of gaol. He may be a reprobate, but she adored him—and he worshipped the ground on which she walked. Despite his attempt at blackmail, I believe he is harmless enough. When I was released from gaol he came after me in desperation. Deep down I think he knew I didn't kill Carmen, but he refused to believe it and hoped he could use my fall from grace against me. The man is constantly in debt, owes money all over the place—I imagine his creditors are on the lookout for his return to America. I shall give him an ultimatum. Either he leaves Eden Park immediately or I reveal all to Henry and he will order him off the place.'

'You are too generous, Kit. Blackmail is a criminal offence. He could be sent to prison.' Feeling the strength of his fingers still holding her own, all thoughts of Ortega flew from her mind. 'Will—you stay with me tonight?' she asked tentatively.

Releasing her hand, Kit shook his head, his expression suddenly grave. 'No, Amanda, not tonight.'

'I see.' She smiled cynically. 'So much for starting over.'

Immediately Kit reached out and pulled her into his arms and she found herself in a fierce embrace as he wrapped his arms around her.

'You little fool. Don't you think I would be with you every minute of the night and day if it were possible? But I need to confront Quinn and Ortega. I shall do that tonight.'

The thought that he might be in danger was disquieting. 'I hate to think of you being alone with them,' she murmured, resting her head against his broad chest.

Kit smiled grimly. 'Don't worry about me. Don't forget that I have the advantage. Quinn has no idea Ortega was Carmen's brother, and Ortega is ignorant to the fact that Quinn was her lover and killed her. Imagine the surprise on their faces when they find out.'

'Kit,' Amanda said very quietly, raising her head and gazing into his eyes, feeling herself being drawn into the vital, rugged aura that was so much a part of him. 'Please be careful. Remember that some things can only be accomplished when one's mind is at ease. I know how much you must hate Mr Quinn. Please don't kill him. It wouldn't help matters. Leave it to the police. I need you. Sky needs you. Promise me.'

'That,' Kit said slowly, softly, with the icy calm so characteristic of him, 'I can't promise you.'

There was no time to say anything else, for at that moment an exuberant Henry returned with Caroline. She was all surprise and beaming laughter, as though the conversation she'd had with Amanda earlier had never taken place. The butler came in bearing glasses and a bottle of champagne in a bucket of ice. Thankfully Ortega was not with them. When Henry had given him the good news, Ortega had offered stilted congratulations and feigned an excuse for not joining in the celebrations.

The moment Kit had waited for since coming to Eden Park had arrived. The hour was late; the place he chose was a barn used for storing hay and straw at the far end of the paddock—far enough away for no one to notice and interrupt their meeting. He sent two notes, one to Quinn and the other to Ortega asking them to meet him there at eleven o'clock, purposely arriving late himself. When he pushed open the door, Quinn was pacing up and down restlessly, while Ortega sat on a bench, not speaking, each curious as to the nature of the summons.

Having spent the two days since Sadie's body was found avoiding the constables, who seemed to have taken up residence at the house while they made their enquiries into her death, Quinn was pale and saggy red pouches underscored his eyes.

Kit stared at them both, the contempt in his eyes unmasked.

When he spoke his voice was like splintered glass. 'Welcome to my party, gentlemen. I'm so pleased you were able to come. It's a strange chain of events that has brought the three of us to this unlikely crossroads. Since I cannot abide the sight of either of you, my business here will be brief. I think it is time the three of us became better acquainted.'

Kit had the satisfaction of seeing Quinn blanch and his body tremble when he told him Ortega's true identity, and Ortega was close to killing Quinn when he learned he had been Ortega's sister's lover and murderer. Kit's proof of this was damning. When Kit introduced himself to Quinn as Christopher Claybourne, at first Quinn was disbelieving, incredulous—hadn't Christopher Claybourne been hanged in Charleston Gaol? When he realised Kit was deadly serious, fear burned away Quinn's acquired surface of reserve and his air of arrogance deserted him. Shocked, afraid and overwhelmed, his eyes blazing with madness, he confessed to killing Carmen Rider.

Kit moved towards Quinn, his tone soft, bland, almost pleasant, while murder lighted his eyes. 'You killed Sadie, too, didn't you, Quinn?'

Quinn's features had sharpened to a foxlike awareness of being trapped. 'Sadie? What has Sadie got to do with any of this?'

Kit looked at the older man, his eyes scornful. 'You killed Sadie for the same reason that you killed Carmen—because Sadie had started looking more favourably on someone else—on Ortega.'

All Ortega's attention was fixed on Quinn, his eyes naked with hate. 'You murdering dog. I'll kill you for this.'

'There's no need,' Kit informed him coldly. 'I informed the police of our meeting. They will be here any minute.'

'By then it will all be over.' Beyond all caution, Ortega

quickly produced a little pocket revolver that nestled in his shoulder holster beneath his jacket and pointed it at Quinn.

Kit stiffened. 'Put up your gun, Ortega,' he said quietly.

'Not a chance. I'll give this murdering bastard what he deserves.'

Quinn's lips moved in a snarl and he was electrified into action. He made a dash for the door. Kit exploded into motion. Bringing his arm down, he knocked the pistol from Ortega's grasp and stepped into Quinn's path, holding his own small pocket pistol, his finger on the trigger.

Breathing heavily, Quinn was seized with a sudden belief that for the first time in his life he faced one who could kill him.

'I should be glad to see you in hell,' Kit said quietly, his eyes glacial. 'And then only if I had had the pleasure of sending you there. However, I don't want to kill you, Quinn. Contemptible as you are I will not have your death upon my conscience.'

Moving quickly, Ortega picked up his pistol, blood boiling and mad as hell. His trigger finger trembled and he fired. The shot hit Quinn low on his left side. Blood spurted. Kit immediately threw himself at Ortega before he could fire again, and in that split second Quinn moved faster than he had for more that twenty years. Clutching his side, he pulled open the door and ran out into the night and disappeared before either Kit or Ortega could follow, running like a man in fear of his life.

Kit stared into the dark, straining his ears for a sound that might tell him which direction Quinn had taken, but, apart from his own heavy breathing, the twittering of a little owl perched on the barn roof and the sound the wind made rustling the tops of the trees, there was nothing.

At that moment the two constables appeared. Kit quickly told them what had happened.

'And Mr Quinn admitted to killing young Sadie, did he?' a rather portly constable with a harassed mien asked.

Kit nodded. 'Yes.'

'Ah, well, it might have helped matters if, instead of settling some kind of vendetta between the two of you, you'd have let us do the questioning.'

'He can't have gone far,' Ortega said. 'He was wounded.'

The other constable glanced at Ortega sharply. 'Wounded, you say. Would you mind telling me how he came to be wounded, sir?'

'I shot the bastard.'

The constable raised his eyebrows. 'I see. Then when we've done our search I'd like a word with you, if you don't mind. In the meantime, if you'd hand over your pistol, sir. Can't have you taking matters into your own hands now, can we?'

Reluctantly Ortega handed over the pistol.

Kit and the two constables left to scour the countryside, working with lantern light.

Ortega returned to the house in silent fury, and Quinn's escape did not give him the opportunity to dispel his rage. The house was quiet, all the servants having retired for the night. As he climbed the stairs his predicament weighed heavy on his mind. The shock of coming face-to-face with the man who had killed his sister was overshadowed by his need, his obsession for money, money he desperately needed to return to America. It meant everything.

On the landing he paused, sensing that someone was watching him. Turning, he saw Sky. She had let herself out of her room and was no doubt going in search of Nan next door. Suddenly an idea began to take root and the thought that everything might not be lost after all recharged his spirits.

Claybourne's child.

If he took her, Claybourne would give a king's ransom to get her back.

Chapter Twelve

It was shortly after midnight when Nan alerted Amanda to Sky's absence. Having gone to check on the child, which she was in the habit of doing every night, and finding her bed empty, thinking she had gone to Amanda's room, she went to make sure.

'But she isn't here, Nan,' Amanda said with the first stirrings of alarm. Getting out of bed, she donned her robe. 'We'd better look for her. Maybe she's gone downstairs.' The servants were woken to assist in the search, but there was no sign of the child. Nan was frantic with worry, which increased when she discovered Sky's coat and boots were missing. Kit was sent for. He came immediately.

'How long has she been missing?' he demanded.

'I don't know—perhaps an hour or more,' Amanda informed him. 'Nan went to check on her shortly after midnight, but she wasn't there. Oh, Kit, where can she have gone? We've looked everywhere.'

One of the servants handed Kit the note he had found on the tray. He tore it open. As his eyes scanned what was written he knew a wrath that was beyond anything he had ever felt in his life. 'Ortega! Ortega has taken her.'

'But what could possibly have possessed him to take Sky? Why? What does he want?'

'A ransom. Thirty thousand pounds. He'll let me know where it has to be delivered by first light. His first attempt at blackmail failed, so now he's thought of some other way of extracting money out of me. Damn Ortega!' he growled, his scowl taking on the deeper creases of his growing worry. 'Damn it, where has he taken her?'

That was the moment when one of the grooms—also roused from their beds to search for Sky—came to tell him that one of the horses was missing.

'Find the constables. Tell them what's happened,' Kit said in a voice of quiet command. 'They're looking for Quinn—though the Lord only knows where he's got to.'

'You saw Mr Quinn? What did he tell you?'

'The truth,' he replied with a slight twist to his mouth.

'What? That he killed Sadie?'

He nodded. 'He was wounded—Ortega shot him, but he got away. No doubt he's hiding somewhere on the moor. But my concern right now is for Sky,' he said, striding towards the door. 'Not a moment is to be wasted.'

'Kit, where are you going?' He spun round to look at her, and she felt a deadly chill creep up her spine and shuddered. Her husband's face was blank, his eyes ice cold and shining with a light that seemed to come from the depths of him.

'To look for my daughter. I will get her back. I swear I will,' he uttered with a steely determination.

'But she could be anywhere.'

'I'm almost certain Ortega will have headed for the moors,' he said pessimistically.

'Then I hope your prediction turns out to be correct and you find her.' The thought of Kit riding out to deal with Ortega terrified Amanda. From what she knew about Kit, there was no one better equipped to go after Ortega and track him down. However, beyond the question of skill, even though Kit was a man of conscience, what Ortega had done by abducting Sky was a crime that he would not forgive.

Kit took to the saddle and vengeance rode with him. His child had been taken and no man had ever set forth with a blacker rage filling his heart. His sights were solidly fixed upon the hills when he left Eden Park. Thankfully the clouds had drifted away from the moon and the night was clear. The stallion sensed his mood and pranced and galloped to do his bidding, its breath snorting out like a dragon's in the cool night air, its hooves striking sparks from rock as they thundered over them.

They rode over hills and through dales, scattering sheep and fording rushing streams, pausing to search caves and isolated barns, all to no avail. Kit's fury didn't moderate with defeat, and as he turned back to Eden Park when the sun was rising over the peaks, he would set off and search again if there was still no word of Sky.

Amanda was in the drawing room with Caroline and her father and a sad and frightened looking Nan when Kit strode in. Henry rose and went to him.

'Is there any news?' Kit asked hopefully. When Henry shook his head, naked pain flashed across Kit's face.

'Kit, I'm sorry about this. It's a terrible business, and to think I offered that man the hospitality of my home. Amanda has told me how he's tried to blackmail you from the start— that it was for this reason that he came here in the first place. I'd have taken a shotgun to him had I known. The police think he's hiding out somewhere on the moor. Men have been posted at intervals on the roads and others are out there looking.'

Amanda was awash with her own emotions and her anxiety

for Kit. With mud clinging to his clothes, she was shocked to see how strained and exhausted he looked, but the glass of brandy she gave him revived him instantly.

'Ortega won't harm Sky, Kit. We have to believe that.' She tried to sound calm and reassuring for his sake, but the fear in her voice was apparent to her own ears.

'Since he's kept my daughter out on the moors all night, I must say that I'm now beginning to believe him to be capable of anything.'

Suddenly a constable was admitted who told them that Ortega had been located three miles away. His thoughts running with the speed of light, some of Kit's urgency seized them all. Immediately Kit and Henry made for the door.

Amanda was determined not to be left behind. 'I'm coming with you.'

Kit rounded on her. 'No, Amanda. It's too dangerous.'

She thrust her chin determinedly, the light in her eyes telling him she was prepared to do battle if necessary. 'I'm coming, Kit. If you forbid me, I'll follow you anyway, so please don't argue. Come, we're wasting time.'

Kit strode ahead with swift intensity. Being beyond hunger and fatigue he hurled himself once more into the saddle, kicking the horse into motion before Amanda and her father had mounted. They were following within moments. Under her breath Amanda uttered a prayer that they would find Sky unharmed. The ground grew barren and rocky as they neared the granite bluff reaching high at its peak, then plunging in a sheer drop to the rocks below. Ahead of them, Kit was ascending, urging his horse over some awkward rocks with an intensity that suggested he would be better pleased to leap off the horse and drag it bodily up the hill.

On reaching the ridge they saw two of the constables were already there, keeping a safe distance from the edge, where

Ortega stood holding Sky by the hand. She was distressed and quietly sobbing. Kit dismounted, his eyes fixed on his little daughter. His shoulders were set like stone, braced to bear the burden of Sky's suffering.

Realising the danger Sky was in, Amanda slid off her mount and went to him, taking his hand in her own. He clutched it. She felt each bone and tendon. Love, fear and anger mingled together in a mix so strong her hand trembled in his.

'Stay calm, Kit. He'll let her go. He has to. Remember, you are not alone.'

Her words were no more than a whisper, meant to comfort, and they brought Kit's eyes to hers. Filled with a mixture of pain, suffering and outrage, they fastened on her upturned face for a moment. He nodded and then looked again at Sky. The child saw him and made a feeble effort of raising her free arm. Kit uttered a sound that might have been an oath or a prayer. Amanda, her heart in her throat, watched helplessly as Ortega drew Sky closer to him and she continued to weep.

From the ridge, Ortega had seen the police coming, but was unable to hide in time. His presence was noted and from that moment there had been no escape. He might be the world's most inauspicious, unsuccessful gambler, prepared to use any misbegotten, contemptible method to win, but he had never applied physical harm to man, woman or child. He had regretted taking the child as soon as he had ridden on to the moor. The dark and desolation had frightened her and she began to cry, asking to be taken back. But Ortega had gone too far to turn back.

He hauled Sky against him towards the edge. 'Stay back,' he shouted. 'Stay back or I swear I'll jump and take her with me.'

Everyone felt the instinctive need for caution. Amanda could barely move as she watched the scene unfold. Despite the horror and fear in her eyes, which were fixed on her beloved daddy, sensing the danger, Sky was being extremely brave. Amanda's heart went out to the child. She wanted to run forward and snatch her free, but such an action would be disastrous for Sky. All Ortega had to do was take one step and he would be over the edge with her.

'Damn you, Ortega. Take your filthy hands off my daughter. In addition to all the other vile and cowardly, despicable things you are, would you add murder to your crimes?' For all its quiet, Kit's voice was as sharp as a blade.

One of the constables came and stood beside Kit. 'Stand aside, sir, and let us deal with this.'

'No,' Kit said quietly. 'It's my affair and mine alone. I shall resent any interference that may endanger my daughter's life.'

It may have been something the constable saw in Kit's eyes or the air of authority that demanded instant obedience, but whatever it was it made him step back.

'You won't get the chance to jump,' Kit shouted. 'I'll kill you first.' He had a pistol drawn and aimed at Ortega's head.

'Let the child go,' one of the constables ordered, panicking at the sight of Kit's gun. 'It's over.'

'Stop,' Ortega shouted when the constable took one step forward. 'Don't come any closer.'

Suddenly a shadow moved from behind a rock and began to take shape. It was Quinn, his eyes wild and darker than blood, almost unrecognisable after his night on the moor, but the ferocious rage and hatred contorting his face told everyone that he was still very much alive.

He moved closer, furtively, his eyes fixed on the Spaniard's back. Ortega barely had chance to glance over his shoulder before Quinn, his face a hellish mask of rage and madness, lunged forward, reached out and caught Sky's free arm and flung her away. Kit was on her in a moment, scooping her up into his arms.

'Hush, sweetheart. It's all over,' he murmured. 'You're

safe now.' The ragged knot of relief in his voice was apparent as he pressed his cheek against her hair, offering strength, love and comfort to the weeping, trembling child.

Amanda had been holding her breath—she let it out with a gasp when Kit raised Sky up and crushed her to him as though he would never let her out of his arms again.

Ortega spun round and confronted Quinn, then, with a roar of rage, flung himself at his sister's murderer. The two men scuffled, becoming a twisting, writhing, struggling mass, knowing in their hearts it was too late for either of them. Too late for anything at all but the ancient, primitive drama of two men facing each other, condemned equally by their foolishness and pride.

Quinn stepped back. For a moment he looked at Henry, his eyes red from pain and exhaustion and tortured by a sense of sorrow that he had failed the one man he revered above any other. Teetering on the brink, he took another step back, but his foot found only air, making him lose his balance. His hands scrabbled wildly and the only tangible thing within reach was Ortega's flapping jacket, which he grasped in desperate self-preservation. The battle was lost. Crying their bitter tides of grief to the empty sky, the two of them went hurtling over the edge of the ridge together, on to the rocks below.

Unable to prevent it, everyone watched in silent horror, everyone except Sky, who was clinging to her father, her little face buried in his coat.

After a moment of stunned silence, knowing there was nothing that could be done for Ortega and Mr Quinn, Amanda was about to move away with Kit when she saw her father walk slowly towards the edge of the ridge. He looked stricken. She glanced at Kit. 'Take Sky back to the house, Kit. I'll be along with Father shortly.'

Kit looked back at Henry, understanding. 'Take as long as you have to. Quinn's crime and his death will have hit him hard.'

Amanda watched Kit ride away with Sky cradled in front of him, then turned to her father. How tired he looks, she thought. I have never seen him this way. A strong man, yet frail as well. Going to him, she averted her eyes from the two grotesquely sprawling broken bodies on the rocks below. Her father glanced round as she drew close, peering at her garments.

'The wind blows cold up here on the ridge. You should have worn a coat.'

'There was no time to look for one.' Tucking her hand through his arm, she said softly, 'This must have come as an awful shock to you, Father. I'm so dreadfully sorry.'

Looking down at the dead men, Henry shook his head as if to deny what his intellect knew, while pain, shock and fury at Quinn's betrayal and the taking of young Sadie's life tore through him. 'Quinn killed Sadie, did you know that?'

'Kit told me earlier.'

'We answer for our actions, Amanda. Oh, how we answer for them. No man escapes.'

'He also killed Carmen Rider—Rafael Ortega's sister— the woman Kit was accused of killing and almost hanged for the crime.'

'And Quinn would have let him?'

'Yes.'

'Then I don't know how he could have lived with himself.'

'When Kit was released from prison, to confront Mr Quinn was one of the reasons he came to Eden Park.'

'I never knew—never suspected Quinn had this dark side to his character—and I always considered myself to be a good judge of men. I was wrong. Of all the men who worked for me, I trusted Quinn the most—I even put you in his charge when you went to Charleston. I gave him everything.'

Amanda looked at him, sharply inquisitive. 'He worked for you a long time didn't he? How did you come to meet?'

'When he was just a navvy, working on laying rail track on the London underground. I'd never seen anyone work like him—every hour God sent he was there, doing the backbreaking, soul-destroying work that had killed his father and brother. I found out that he was working to keep his mother and young sisters out of the workhouse. There was a fierceness and determination about him in those days that I admired, and I was touched at how protective he was towards his family. In a queer way he reminded me of myself when I came from Ireland. I brought him to work for me, found a cottage in Rochdale for his mother and siblings so they could all be together—where some of them live to this day.'

'So that's the reason why he was always so loyal to you and would never hear an unkind word said about you. I did wonder.'

'Aye, I suppose it was. His mother's still alive. I'll go and see her—try to explain—though it won't be easy, mind. She was so proud of him. I must say something to the old woman—somehow find a way to vindicate the honour her son did not possess to ease her sorrow.'

They stood together in silence, feeling the tension eased by the beauty and quietude of the unbroken vista before them. They watched a hovering hawk overhead and the shadows play across the hills, then roused themselves when a chip of granite tumbled down the edge and disappeared from sight.

When Henry spoke again, his voice was stronger. 'Come along. Let's get back to the house. There's nothing more to be done here. What matters now is you and Kit and that little girl of his. I thank God she wasn't harmed.' He turned and looked at her when she linked her arm through his. 'But what of you, Amanda? Are you happy? It's important to me that you are.'

'I'm happy,' she said softly.

'You're quite certain?'

'Absolutely,' she assured him.

'And you love Kit?'

'Very much. More than my life.'

He patted her hand as they walked slowly back to their horses. 'Then there's nothing more to be said.'

The sun was riding high over the peaks when Amanda and her father returned to Eden Park. Everyone at the house was reeling with shock at what had happened to Señor Ortega and Mr Quinn, unable to believe that the coldly reserved Mr Quinn had killed Sadie. Caroline met them in the hall, looking most anxious. She took charge at once and ushered them into the drawing room.

'Where is Kit?' Amanda asked.

'With Sky, upstairs.'

'How is she?'

'Tired, mainly. She's been through a dreadful ordeal, poor lamb, but thankfully she appears to be unhurt. She must have been so frightened—to be taken like that and kept out all night on the moor. And when I think of what a man of Ortega's nature might have done—well—it doesn't bear thinking about.'

'Thank goodness it's all over—although I never envisaged it would end with the deaths of Mr Quinn and Ortega. Kit must be exhausted. I must go to him.' She looked towards her father where he stood quite still, his head slightly bowed and his shoulders drooping in dejection, gazing out of the window. 'Poor Father. Mr Quinn's death and what he did to Sadie have come as a terrible shock.'

Caroline's gaze settled on her husband with a deep compassion and tenderness. 'Yes, I know.' She smiled softly at Amanda and touched her cheek fondly. 'You look worn out, my dear. Go to Kit. I'll take care of Henry.'

Amanda was surprised to see Nan sitting on a chair outside Sky's room. Her eyes were bloodshot and red rimmed, and anxiety cried out in every line of her tired face. Amanda paused and knelt beside her, taking her hand in her own.

'Nan, why don't you go and get some rest? It's been a long night for all of us.'

'Not until I've seen for myself that Sky's all right. Her father's with her—has been since he carried her upstairs and closed the door. I can't bear to think what Ortega in his malevolence might have done to her,' she uttered fiercely. 'I should never have left her alone so long—should have looked in on her more often, but she's begun sleeping for longer periods now and I didn't want to disturb her.'

'You mustn't blame yourself, Nan. It wasn't your fault. Come,' she said, rising, 'don't distress yourself so. I am sure Sky is going to be perfectly all right. I'll go in and see Kit. Have some tea sent up to my room and you can sit with her while I talk to Kit.'

Amanda knocked softly on the door to Sky's room and quietly let herself in, leaning wearily against the hard wood. The curtains were drawn, but sufficient light filtered through the cracks to show the child fast asleep and Kit, a terrible fatigue about him, sitting in a chair by her bed, watching her. She wanted him so much then, wanted to feel his arms about her, to give him the warmth and love he deserved.

On seeing Amanda he rose and went to her, allowing the faintest of smiles to shadow his lips. She tried to speak, tried to express her relief, her joy that her husband and his child were safe, but her nightlong alternations of fear, hope, terror and shock had used up all her resistance.

Sensing what she was feeling, Kit drew her into his arms and for a long moment they clung to each other in silence, too happy and too deeply moved for speech. After a while he raised his head and looked down at her, his brows drawn together in concern.

'Are you all right?' he queried.

The tenderness in his eyes took Amanda's breath away. He was looking at her in a way that made her feel wanted, precious. She smiled and nodded. 'I'm fine—and like you a bit tired, I suppose, but it's nothing a few hours in bed won't put right. How is Sky?'

'Worn out, but Sky's resilient. She'll get over it. Apparently she went with Ortega willingly—he promised her an adventure—but she became frightened when he took her on to the moor in the dark. I swear that if Ortega hadn't fallen off the ridge, I would have killed him,' he uttered fiercely, a murderous gleam in his eyes.

'Then I'm glad you didn't have to. I wouldn't want my husband to be thrown back into prison—and this time with a legitimate reason. While Sky's sleeping, will you let Nan sit with her for a while? She's out of her mind with worry and won't rest until she's seen her.' He nodded, looking at his daughter. 'Come,' Amanda said, taking his hand, 'we'll only be next door.'

When Nan had seated herself in the chair Kit had vacated beside the bed, Kit nodded to her in silent gratitude and followed Amanda to her room. She poured tea for them both, feeling the hot, sweet beverage revive her a little as she drank it. After a few moments' silence Kit came to her. Taking her cup, he set it down and took her in his arms. Tilting her chin, he lowered his head and covered her mouth with his own. His kiss was hot and slow, almost lazy. Amanda melted under the heat of it, welcoming his intimate gesture. It buoyed her spirits after the dreadful night.

'How is Henry?' Kit asked when he found the strength to raise his head, still holding her in his arms.

'Like everyone else, he's relieved that Sky was unharmed and shocked to learn that Ortega could do such a thing. As for Mr Quinn—well, he's deeply shocked to know he killed Sadie. It's affected him terribly. We left the constables to arrange for the removal of the bodies.' She sighed, resting her forehead against Kit's chest. 'Who would have thought it would end like this? I don't think I shall ever be able to ride up to the ridge again, without remembering what happened today.'

'You don't have to. As soon as this has settled down, I intend to take you and Sky to Woodthorpe. It's time for us to begin the rest of our lives. Quinn, Ortega and Carmen are in the past, and there they will remain.'

Amanda glanced up at him obliquely. She wanted desperately to know about Carmen—or rather she wanted Kit to reassure her that there was nothing to substantiate her jealous imaginings about the Spanish widow.

'I—know this isn't the time to ask,' she said tentatively, 'but, what was she like—Carmen? Was she very beautiful?'

'Yes, she was, and treacherous into the bargain. No man in his right mind would put up with her tantrums, her sulky moods and vile temper.' He smiled. 'Many's the time I thanked God I was only her horse trainer. There were so many contradictions to her character—one minute she was as fiery as a tiger, the next as soft as a kitten. On the day I told her I was leaving she was the epitome of despair, and on the day I left she was dressed in the finery of a Spanish noblewoman. Her pride was colossal. It was all or nothing with Carmen. I wish I'd never met her—but then,' he murmured, his eyes caressing her face, 'I wouldn't have met you. Things have a way of working out.'

'Was she in love with you?'

He shrugged. 'She might have thought she was—she fell in love with every man who was unobtainable, and I'd made it clear from the outset that my work was with the horses and there would be no emotional entanglements. She bade me farewell—blithe and happy, thanking me for all the work I had put in with her horses.' He chuckled softly, shaking his head. 'Mother of God, there is no answer to the riddle of women.'

Amanda's smile was weak. Taking a deep breath and summoning her courage, she asked, 'Were you in love with her, Kit?' She waited expectantly, watching him.

He smiled at her, gazing down at her with a warm and tender light in his eyes. 'Would it matter to you if I were to say yes, I was in love with her?'

'Yes. Somehow I find the idea of you and her together objectionable.'

'Then I am happy to tell you that the answer to your question is a very definite no, my darling.' He breathed against her hair, his arms tightening about her in a fierce embrace. 'If I had loved her as much as I love you, you incredibly beautiful, brave, wonderful female, there would have been no power on earth that would have separated us.'

Amanda's breath caught in her throat. 'You—you love me?'

'Certainly I do. How could I not love you?'

'You—you never said so.'

'I have loved you for a long time, my darling,' he said tenderly, 'ever since you sought me out in my prison cell and asked me to marry you.' Lifting his head, he gazed down at her delicate, enchanting face, his brow raised in question. 'But what of you, Amanda? How do you feel about me?'

Amanda drew back a little to search Kit's strained face. She heard the uncertainty in his tone, felt the tension in his body, and her heart melted. His thick hair fell over his forehead and there was a sharp clarity in his eyes, making it impossible for her to deny the love she saw there, or to conceal her own.

'I have come to love you deeply, more than anyone and

more than you will ever know. You are everything I want and I shall love you always.'

His sigh was one of relief as he brushed her lips with his own. 'You can't imagine how I've longed for you to say that. We have a lifetime to spend loving each other and Sky and our future children.'

'I promise I shall be a good and loving mother to Sky, and I want so very much to give you more children, Kit—sons, who will look just like you.' The glow in Kit's eyes deepened to a bright flame as he crushed her to him. 'Father insists on having our marriage blessed, Kit—and so do I. With everything that's happened, we haven't had time to discuss it, but how do you feel about that?'

'I, too, would like our union blessed in church, but in the light of all that's happened let's keep it simple.'

'Where do you want it to be held? Here at Thurlow?'

'I know I run the risk of upsetting your father, but I'd like to start our life together where we will end it. I shall insist on having the blessing conducted at Woodthorpe in the family chapel. It is important to me. Just family and a few close friends—and afterwards a ball for everyone to celebrate a new beginning. Are you in favour of that?'

A shiver of pleasure ran through Amanda. The vision of a future stretching endlessly ahead was as golden and fertile as Woodthorpe itself. 'How could I not be?' she said, half-smiling, beginning to feel more alive with every moment. 'But how do you feel about returning to live at Woodthorpe after everything that happened?'

'It's my home, Amanda, where I should be. My father and Charles robbed me of my youth, my happiness, a way of life and my mother, surrounding me with an atmosphere I hated, one I had to escape from. But I've grown beyond anger and hatred—America and my time in the Smoky Mountains taught me that. I learned that the only person capable of destroying your immortal soul is yourself. I also learned that what other people do to you is not important, it's how you respond, how you deal with it that matters. In the end you learn.'

'What?'

'Forgiveness.' The word was spoken quietly and with enormous gravity, and then he smiled. 'So you see, my love, all things considered, I can put the past well and truly behind me. Despite my absence these past six years, Woodthorpe has not been neglected. It has been beautifully kept—clipped, pruned and taken care of by expert hands. I look forward to showing it to you.'

With tears shimmering in her magnificent eyes, Amanda's soft lips curved in a smile. 'And I am eager to see it. Everything I love most in the world is with you—where I belong, Kit, just as long as I can be sure I have your love.'

'You have that now and for always.'

Before all their guests descended on Woodthorpe to celebrate their union, those early, unfolding days for Kit and Amanda were a time of unimpaired delight. They rode together over the estate, wandered arm in arm together in the beautiful gardens with Sky skipping along ahead of them, watched from the terrace every night as the sun went down and the moon and stars came out.

Never had Kit known a time like it. Amanda was enchanting, delightful and divine, who in the night loved him like a pagan goddess, holding nothing back as she surrendered herself to him. He loved and adored her with a passion and devotion that was rooted deeply in his soul.

For Amanda, it seemed that she had never known such happiness. In the night Kit stirred her to impassioned heights she could not have imagined, and when he wasn't doing that she would simply nestle close, content to bask in the warm security of his embrace.

Three weeks passed in this heavenly peace. Amanda began to smile secretly. A suspicion had come into her mind, one she hardly dared believe. And now it had become a certainty.

She was going to have a child.

When she told Kit he was overwhelmed with joy and held her to him, deeply moved.

'This is most dear to my heart,' he whispered against her hair. 'But you must take care.'

Bending back her head and meeting the warmth of his gaze, she laughed lightly. 'Nonsense. I'm as strong as an ox. And if it's a boy, he'll be just like you, Kit—tall and fine when he grows.'

'Boy or girl, my love, our child will be well loved.'

Smiling tenderly, Amanda brushed a light kiss on his lips. 'I know.'

The blessing of their marriage was performed in the small chapel at Woodthorpe by the local rector. It was a solemn though happy occasion. Seated in front of Lord and Lady Covington and their enthralled daughter, Jane—who along with Nan had taken charge of an awe-struck Sky dressed in a pretty white dress and bonnet to match—with Caroline by his side, resplendent in a coat of pale lavender trimmed with fur, and a hat adorned with lavender flowers, Henry beamed throughout the service. His eyes were suspiciously moist and bursting with pride, the same as any father of a beautiful bride—even though Amanda, attired in a simple gown of cream silk and Belgian lace and the deep red mane of her hair hanging like a gleaming sheath down her back, was anything but.

Standing beside Amanda, there was a quiet reverence in

Kit, a sense of quiet joy, as he looked down at his bride—for that was what she was to him that day and always would be. The setting was so very different from the one inside Charleston Gaol, but never had he felt the rightness of what they had done that day as he did now. Her face was aglow, and in her eyes he saw the promise of a lifetime filled with love.

It was warm and sunny when they stepped out on to the terrace, where, against a backdrop of trailing roses, they posed for photographs—in later years their offspring would comment on how unnecessarily prim they looked as they gazed at them with wonder and awe. As the photographer folded his tripods and packed away the last of his wetplates, Kit took hold of Amanda's hand and drew her to one side.

'Happy?'

A thrill shot through Amanda as she gazed up at her supremely handsome husband—elegant, sophisticated, powerful and boldly masculine. She had borne his name for so long, but only now did she come to realise it. She nodded in answer to his question. 'Blissfully.'

The celebrations held at Woodthorpe to welcome home the Earl of Rossington and his Countess would be talked about for many years to come. It was a time for a new beginning, when ghosts, old sins, old hatreds, of the dead and the living, were laid to rest. Gaiety and festivities were the order of the day, when everyone in the surrounding neighbourhood came to assure themselves that all was well with the Claybourne family and to join in the merrymaking.

Everyone agreed that Lord Claybourne, unlike his father and brother before him, was a good man, deserving of their loyalty and respect. Speculation as to where he had been for the past six years and how he had come to sire a beautiful Indian daughter was rife, though many forgave him his absence—had he not considered their welfare by leaving stewards in charge to see that they were dealt with fairly?

And to be sure, the new mistress of Woodthorpe was as gracious and lovely a lady as any had known. Not one of them found her wanting.

Friends and relations had come to Woodthorpe for the ball to honour the occasion. The house was a buzz of voices and music, and guests came forward, bestowing good wishes and clasping Amanda's hand in ready friendship. Throughout it all Kit, looking incredibly handsome in formal black, remained beside her, his arm about her waist, claiming her as his possession, all the while aware that somewhere up above, Sky and Victoria's children were looking down on the festivities through the banisters.

When Kit paused to renew old acquaintances, taking Amanda's hand Victoria drew her aside, smiling gently. 'This is indeed a happy day, Amanda. Woodthorpe is such a lovely house and deserves better than to stand empty. It needs a family to bring it back to life, and I'm certain you and Kit will do that. His mother would have been so proud of him.'

'You knew who I was—that I was Kit's wife—when we met in Chelsea, didn't you, Victoria?'

'Kit told me in his letter, but he asked me not to say anything. Will you forgive me for the deception?'

'Of course. I understand why he did it.'

'I know Kit well. We've always been close. It was hard for him growing up with his father and brother behaving as they did—he told you about that?'

'Yes, everything. They must have been difficult times.'

'They were—for Kit and his mother. It was like a sickness with them—their mania for gambling—and—well, everything else. There were times when Kit used to disappear, when no one could find him, but he always came back. And there were other times even in the midst of social events—balls, parties and race meetings that his father and Charles were particularly mad about—when he'd grow strangely silent.'

'Why?'

'Because he had a brain. I think he could detach himself from the world and see it as it actually was—crude and ugly, without glitter, without polish. The people who surrounded his father and brother were silly, empty headed, going nowhere. I think he knew in his heart that it wasn't for him— wasn't what he wanted. After Charles died and then his father, the extent of his grief was colossal. I wanted him to stay, but we had reason to fear that if he remained at Woodthorpe, surrounded by objects, scenes, people, all of which reminded him of his father's last days—it might unseat his reason.' Suddenly she smiled and tears appeared in her eyes. 'But all that is in the past now and we can look forward to better times. You will be so good for Kit. I just know you will.'

Excusing himself from a boisterous group of young males, Kit looked around for his wife. In the fashion of the day, her gown of a pastel shade of lemon silk that matched her hair, dressed in a high chignon, to perfection and bared her shoulders sublimely, was simple and elegant. It had been pulled in to a mere twenty inches and her hips accentuated by the ruffles of her gown gathered at the back of the skirt into a bustle. She was dancing with Lord Bennet, a good-looking young man with more brashness and charm than was good for him, laughing at whatever he was saying to her. Taking a glass of champagne from the tray of a passing footman, he stood, content to look at her.

'You'll have to get used to the competition, Kit,' Henry remarked with an approving grin, coming to stand beside him. 'My daughter's a beauty and no mistake. She will grace

Woodthorpe splendidly and make you a good wife, but she's hot headed and strong willed and no matter what steps I've taken in the past to curb her, it's made no difference. She always has her way in the end. Don't be deceived. Beneath all her frills and flounces and heart-melting smiles, her wilful heart is unchanged. So beware. Her head may be filled with romantic notions for the present, but when the honeymoon's over she'll lead you a merry dance before she's done. Keep her with child, that's my advice. That'll tame her wild ways.'

It was said proudly. Kit turned and looked at him and saw the older man's eyes gleaming with wicked delight. Kit slapped him good humouredly on the back and they stood together, content to watch the woman dear to both their hearts dip and sway in time to the music. Pondering Henry's words and smiling secretly at his wife, Kit thought it would be a long while before Amanda led him a merry dance. Already the serenity of pregnancy had settled on her.

'She is all the things you say she is,' Kit murmured, 'there is no doubt about that—with a fire and a spirit which is all her own, but I wouldn't change one whit of her, Henry. Not one whit.'

'Nay—neither would I. I cannot find words to express my joy in your marriage, Kit. Amanda couldn't have chosen a finer man—which she managed to do without any help from me and with less effort than it will take me to find a new horse trainer,' he joked. 'See how everyone watches her. She's captivated the lot of them.'

'Especially that particular young man,' Kit observed, noting how well she danced with young Bennet and trying not to note how closely he was holding her. Handing his glass to a footmen, he said, 'I think it's time I claimed a dance from my wife and sent Lord Bennet on his way.' So saying, he went to retrieve his wife.

At that moment the musicians began to play another waltz.

Amanda looked towards her husband and smiled, and it was as if the whole room brightened in the dazzling radiance of that smile. Moving towards her, Kit felt the weight of her beauty. To his immense relief she abandoned Lord Bennet with gratifying speed.

'I believe this is our dance.'

'What took you so long?'

Filled with a feeling that was part-joy and part-reverence, with love passing between them in silent communication, Kit took her hand and led her into the middle of the dance floor, aware that they were the centre of attention and that everyone had paused to watch them. Drawing her into his embrace, he gazed down at her as he swept her along with the music.

'You are a success, my love,' he murmured. 'Everyone is in love with you and saying how fortunate I am to have found such a wonderful Countess.'

'And what of you?' she teased. 'Do I meet your standards of what a Countess should be?'

The heat of his eyes seared her and lent weight to the truth of his words when he gave his answer. 'Were we alone, I would show you and quickly prove the ardour you have stirred in me. But for now I must content my mind with gorging my rapacious senses on how it will be later, and the wondrous sensations I shall experience when I touch you, all of you, all over.'

Amanda's lips curved in a smile serene and mysterious and elementally feminine. She had never felt such softness in her before. There was an elation, born of the knowledge that all she felt he was feeling it, too. 'I can see you have a problem we must discuss, my lord. In our bedroom, perhaps—later?'

'Much as I would have it otherwise, so it must be.'

And so it was that seven months later their son was born—following what Nan proclaimed was an indecently short labour. Standing over the cradle where the sleeping infant lay, Kit looked down at him with wonder and awe, his eyes soft with love for his son. He was a beautiful child, with rosy, rounded cheeks and black fluffy hair clustered upon his head in curling whorls.

Raising his head, he gazed at his wife resting against the pillows. There was a reverence in him, a sense of quiet joy. 'Thank you,' he said, his voice aching and tender. 'He's a fine boy, my love. Perfect.'

From where she lay, Amanda lifted her thickly lashed eyelids, and the dazzling brilliance of her olive-green eyes fell lovingly on her husband's handsome face. 'Didn't I say he would be? Just like his father.'

Sky adored him, and when Amanda placed him in her father's arms he was so proud and profoundly moved that in the midst of one of the most achingly poignant moments of his life, he was rendered speechless.

A Scoundrel
of Consequence

Chapter One

1813

Thundering down the length of track in a deserted Green Park as dawn was breaking filled William Lampard with exhilaration. A stiff breeze was rolling away the early morning mist and the park stretched out in shades of green and brown and grey. Stabs of sunlight between the clouds edged the colours in bright gilding, and birds were waking in the foliage. For those few minutes as he raced along, there was just him and his horse—no duties, no expectations, just sheer abandon and forgetfulness of all the obligations that awaited him.

Slowing his horse to a more sedate trot, he left the track and directed it beneath some sheltering trees, thinking how good it felt to be back in London after three years as a soldier fighting the war in Spain. Suddenly, the serenity of the early summer morning was shattered by the explosion of a gunshot. A force hit him in the shoulder and the world hurtled in a slow tumble as he toppled out of the saddle on to the dew-soaked grass, where he sank into a black hole and everything ceased to exist.

Cassandra was travelling to her place of work earlier than usual and taking a short cut through the park when she heard the shot. Seeing a horse and rider leave the shelter of the trees and ride as if the devil himself was after him, she urged Clem to drive the carriage into the trees to investigate. On seeing the wounded man she immediately climbed out, believing he had been shot in a duel, since Green Park was often a venue for those sinister appointments in the dawn mist. Coming to her side, Clem bent and rolled the limp form over, nodding his head in relief as he took in the slow, shallow breathing.

'He isn't dead, thank the Lord.'

When sanity returned to William, somewhat hazily, it was to find a young woman in a dark grey coat kneeling beside him, and a short, stout man holding his frightened horse. There was a dull throbbing in his head, and an ache in his shoulder that pulsed in unison with it.

Cassandra gazed down into two crystal-clear orbs. There was a vibrant life and an intensity in those eyes, dark, brilliant blue, like the sea in a summer storm that no one could deny. 'I'm happy to see you are still with us,' the woman said in a soft, well-bred voice. She held her head gracefully, the brim of her bonnet casting a light shadow over her face. 'You have been shot. Let's hope your wound is not serious.'

William returned her smile with difficulty and tried to allay her fears by pushing himself up against a tree. He winced as pain—red hot and piercing—shot through his shoulder, then closed his eyes and rested his head back. Without more ado the woman briskly unfastened his bloodsoaked jacket, removed his crisp white cravat and opened his shirt, her expression schooled to a nun-like impassivity as she examined his wound. William's gaze flickered to the slender fingers pressing a wad of cloth against the torn flesh to staunch the flow of blood.

'You've done this before, I can see that,' he remarked, his voice deep and strong.

'I have, but usually my patients haven't been shot and they are much smaller than you.'

As she worked, Cassandra noted that the wounded man's clothes were of expensive elegance that could only have come from one of the *ton*'s foremost tailors. Having lost his hat in the fall, his hair, thick and dark brown, fell in disarray about his head, shading his wide brow and brushing his collar. About thirty years of age, his face was handsome, recklessly so, lean and hard. His nose was straight, his jaw uncompromisingly square. He had fine dark brows that curved neatly, and a firm but almost sensuous mouth. Everything about him was elegantly aristocratic, exuding power and a sense of force.

When the wad was secure she rested back on her heels and met his gaze. 'There. I think you'll live. Not much damage done—more to your pride I'd say. When will you gentlemen learn to settle your quarrels in a more civilised manner? Duelling is certainly not the answer.' Without giving William a chance to utter a reply in his defence, she got to her feet. 'Now come along. Try to stand. I think a doctor should take a look at that shoulder.'

'There's no need for that. If you'll get your man to bring my horse, I'll be on my way.'

'The bullet's still in there. It will have to be extracted and the wound dressed properly.' William uttered a protest, but it emerged as little more than a croak and when he tried to move, his limbs would not obey. Cassandra looked at him crossly. 'Please don't argue. You are in no position to object.' She turned to Clem. 'Come and help Mr…'

'Captain. I am Captain William Lampard,' he provided with difficulty as a fresh wave of pain swept through him.

'Oh!'

William saw an odd, awed expression cross her face as she scrutinised him, and in her eyes a momentary flash of a deeply rooted dislike. 'You've heard of me?'

'Yes, your name is familiar to me—although you are better known as Lord Lampard, the Earl of Carlow.'

Cassandra had heard all about Captain Lampard. He was

an arrogant lord who thought he could do as he pleased with whomever he pleased. For years, gossip had linked him with every beautiful female in London. His scandals were infamous. Whenever he was on respites from his military duties he was the talk of the town, and any sensible young woman mindful of her reputation kept well out of his way. The same could be said of his young cousin, Edward Lampard, who she had already decided possessed the same traits—for hadn't he tried to compromise her own sister, and the silly girl would have let him if she could have had her way?

'You've recently returned from foreign parts, I believe.' Her expression did not alter, but something in her eyes stirred and hardened and she compressed her lips.

'Spain.'

'Yes, well, I'd have thought you would have had enough of fighting in the Peninsula,' she remarked haughtily.

William had to stifle the urge to smile at her tart reprimand. 'I have, more than enough. By your reaction to my identity, I strongly suspect my reputation has gone before me, but let me tell you that it is much a matter of gossip and wishful dreaming.'

'If you say so, Captain Lampard, but it really is none of my business.'

'Would you think it forward of me if I were to ask you your name?'

'Not at all. I am Cassandra Greenwood.'

'Miss Greenwood, I am most pleased to meet you, and I'm thankful you came along when you did.'

Cassandra slowly arched a brow and her smile was bland. 'So you should be. Now come along and I'll get Dr Brookes to take a look at you.'

'Dr Brookes?'

'He's a doctor at St Bartholomew's Hospital. He comes to help out when I need him at the institute. I'm expecting him first thing, which is why you find me out and about so early.

Don't worry. I have every faith in his ability as a doctor. He'll soon have you fixed up.'

Observing the stubborn thrust of her chin and the glint of determination in her eye, William raised a brow in amusement. 'I see you have no intention of relenting.'

'Quite right, sir. When Dr Brookes has finished with you, Clem will take you home to Grosvenor Square in the carriage.'

William gave her a quizzical look. 'You know where I live?'

'Oh, yes, Captain Lampard, I do know that much about you—and some more,' she uttered softly, which brought a puzzled frown to William's brow, 'but we won't go into that just now. It would be inadvisable for you to ride after sustaining a wound that rendered you unconscious. There is every possibility that you would fall off your horse and incur a more severe injury, which would incapacitate you for some time.'

'Perish the thought,' William said wryly.

'Quite,' Cassandra replied. 'After awaiting your return from Spain for so long, no doubt the entire female population in London would go into a decline. Now come along. See if you can stand.' She would have liked nothing more than to help him on to his horse and send him on his way, but that would be a cowardly thing to do simply because he had a poor reputation.

Impressed by her efficiency and naturally authoritative tone, William tried to get up, but fell back as a fresh haziness swept over him.

Without more ado, Clem took the wounded man's arm over his broad shoulders and hoisted him unceremoniously into the carriage. After securing the Captain's horse to the back, he set off towards Soho, where they drew up outside a grim-looking building among streets where poverty and disease ran side by side. A score or more of undernourished children dressed in rags, their legs bowed and eyes enormous in pinched faces, were hanging about. William was helped out of the carriage and Clem again took his arm. With Cassandra leading the way, Clem half-carried the wounded man inside and into a room, where he lowered him on to a narrow bed, obviously not made for a man as tall as the Captain.

Taking deep breaths in an attempt to remain conscious, William was aware of dim forms moving about the room. Turning his head on the pillow, he saw a child lying in the bed next to him. Whimpering in his sleep and no more than seven years old, his stick-thin legs were poking out from beneath a blanket. Both his feet were bandaged. His face was an unhealthy grey, his skin ingrained with dirt, and his knees scraped raw.

Dragging his gaze away from the pitiful sight of the child, he took stock of the room, which looked like a small infirmary. It was quite large with five bunks and sparse, stark furnishings. With small windows and a stone-flagged floor, it was scrubbed clean. There was a stone sink in which a trim, white-aproned young woman was washing utensils and a fire burned in the hearth. The air was tinged with the aroma of food cooking—not unappetising—plain, mutton stew, he guessed. Suddenly a cup was pressed to his lips.

'Drink,' Miss Greenwood commanded.

Doing as he was told, William gulped the water down gratefully, letting his head fall back on the pillow when replete. 'Where in damnation am I?' he breathed, his curiosity aroused.

'Please don't swear,' Cassandra chided, having discarded her outdoor clothes and fastened an apron about her slender waist. 'I'll have no obscene language spoken here. You are not in damnation, but a small infirmary in a house that is a place of refuge for destitute children.'

William's lips twitched with a suppressed smile. 'I stand rebuked. I did not mean to be disrespectful.'

'Yes—well, keep a close rein on your tongue, Captain Lampard, lest the children overhear—although sadly some of them use a few choice words themselves and might be able to teach even you a thing or two. Ah, here is Dr Brookes.' She stood back to allow a good-looking man in his mid-forties enough room to make his examination.

'Good day, Captain Lampard.' Dr Brookes proceeded brusquely and cheerily as was his custom. 'It's not every day I get a distinguished patient to attend—especially one who's been shot.'

Cassandra brought a tray of salves and implements, placing them on a small table at the side of the bed.

Dr Brookes wrinkled his nose as he glanced at the injury. 'That looks to be a nasty wound. Right, we'd better get to work before you bleed to death. I don't think the shot's too far in so it shouldn't be especially difficult getting it out. There'll be a bit of digging around to do though. Can you stand it?'

'Captain Lampard has recently returned from the war in the Peninsula, Dr Brookes,' Cassandra provided. 'I'm sure he's had to endure worse.'

'Spain, eh?' Dr Brookes remarked, impressed. 'Would have gone myself—had I been years younger.'

'Miss Greenwood speaks the truth. I have seen and endured many things during the war, but this is the first time I've been shot—so get on with it, Dr Brookes.' William looked at the young woman who had taken a stance beside him, a wicked twinkle in his bold, appraising eyes. 'Are you to stay and hold my hand, Miss Greenwood?'

'No,' she replied primly. 'I shall stay to assist Dr Brookes.'

'Pity. Here is my last scrap of dignity. Enjoy it while you can, but I would advise you to step back, Miss Greenwood,' he said, eyeing with trepidation the probe Dr Brookes was holding. 'My temper is about to take a decided turn for the worse.'

Cassandra spoke no word, but stood aside while Dr Brookes began his work.

William gritted his teeth against the white shards of pain that were shooting through his shoulder as Dr Brookes probed the wound. Mercifully, within a matter of minutes the shot was located and removed.

'There—all done,' Dr Brookes said with a satisfied smile,

showing his patient the round ball. 'The wound's clean so it should heal nicely—though you should keep it rested for a time.'

'Thank you for all that you've done. You won't go unrewarded, I shall see to that.'

Dr Brookes nodded, and there was a gleam in his eye when he glanced at Cassandra. 'A small donation to the institute wouldn't go amiss, is that not so, Cassandra? Have your own physician keep an eye on the wound—and perhaps take some laudanum if the pain becomes severe. Now excuse me if I leave you in Miss Greenwood's capable hands. I must fly— patients to see at the hospital.' Hesitating by the young boy's bed as he began to mumble and mutter, to twist and turn, he placed a hand to the child's forehead. Shaking his head, he turned to go. 'I'll be in tomorrow to take another look the boy.' He paused a moment longer before enquiring haltingly, 'Will—your mother be at the institute?'

Cassandra lowered her head to hide a knowing smile. She had long suspected that it was her mother, as well as his concern for the children, that drew Dr Brookes to the institute. 'Yes, she should be—around midday, I think.'

Looking pleased, Dr Brookes nodded and hurried out.

Cassandra turned back to Captain Lampard to dress his wound, amazed that he had endured the whole procedure without a murmur.

'What happened to the boy?' William asked. 'How did he come to be in that state?'

'That's Archie,' she answered, her expression softening when her gaze rested on the child's face. 'His mother sold him to a sweep for a few shillings, poor mite.'

'How old is he?'

'Six years. Climbing boys don't stand a chance, any of them. So many die of consumption and they are never washed except by the rain. No one knows the cruelty that they undergo. Bullied and beaten by their masters, they rub their poor elbows and knees raw climbing the dark flues. Their flesh must be hardened. This is done by rubbing it with the strongest brine. But often their skin—if they survive—doesn't harden for years.'

'And Archie's feet?'

'Burnt by the fires—which aren't always completely out.'

If William was disturbed by this, apart from a tightening of his features he made no comment. Though her voice was without expression, before Miss Greenwood turned her face away, he was startled to see tears in her eyes mingled with compassion for the child.

'He doesn't complain, but I know he's in constant pain. It is my intention to find him a situation—but it will be weeks before he is fully recovered. One thing is for certain, it will not be with the sweeps—although it will be hard to place him. Your coat is ruined, I'm afraid,' Cassandra said, picking it up and placing it at the bottom of the bed with his equally ruined shirt.

'I'll get another.'

'Yes, I suppose you will,' she said, smiling then and forcing her eyes from the bronzed, dark, fur-matted muscular chest. The shoulder muscles jerked as she proceeded to dress his wound. This close he smelled of shaving soap and sandal-wood. Overwhelmed by every scandalous tale she had ever heard about him, she willed herself to ignore the strength of the lean, hard body stretched out on the bed beneath her, to complete her task and send him on his way.

William caught his breath at her unexpected glowing smile and started in amazement when he felt a peculiar, inner tingle from her touch. Light fell on her face only inches away from his own. She really was the most glorious creature, even in her sombre dark grey dress buttoned up to her throat. Her softly scented skin glowed like silk, and her mouth was a soft coral pink. Her hair was honey gold, pulled up to a chignon, but from which endearing rebellious tendrils escaped. Her blue-green eyes gleamed as she smiled.

'Do you work here all the time?' he asked.

'No, not all the time. I do have a life away from here.'

'I'm glad to hear it. It would be a crime for you to spend your entire life in this dreary place. There are better areas of London to focus your energies on. I would have thought young ladies could find more interesting and exciting ways of passing their time.'

Giving her a long, leisurely look, there was a twist of humour around his attractively moulded lips. The smile building about his mouth softened the hardness of his jaw and made him appear in that moment the most handsome man in the world to Cassandra. Then, suddenly, his direct, masculine assurance disconcerted her. She was acutely conscious of his close proximity to her and she felt a mad, unfamiliar rush of blood singing through her veins.

Instantly she felt resentful towards him. He had made too much of an impact on her and she was afraid that if he looked at her much longer he would read her thoughts with those brilliant clever eyes of his—which he did when her cheeks pinked, bringing a darkening to his eyes and an amused, satisfied smile to his lips.

'I am sure you're right, Captain Lampard, but not nearly as rewarding or as worthwhile. What I do here is more than a pastime for me and I am content with the way things are. The institute was brought into being by my father with the intention of providing aid and provision for destitute children—a place of Christian charity. He died three years ago. Like Dr Brookes, he was a surgeon at St Bartholomew's hospital. It's quiet just now, but it gets busier towards supper time. My mother is keen to carry on what my father began and devotes many hours to the institute. We also have volunteers who come to help for what they can do, not for what they can get. The institute really couldn't manage without them—or the benefactors, who help fund it. We feed the children, provide them with articles of clothing, which are donated to us, and if they are sick or injured we patch them up as best we can.'

'Even though some of them are criminals, uncivilised and riddled with vermin and diseases they might pass on to you?' William asked, raising himself up so she could pass the bandage over his shoulder.

'Yes, and since that is exactly the kind of children who come here, we have all the more reason to try and make their young lives more bearable. The place might not look much, but times are hard just now. However, we do have plans and raise funds in many ways to enable us to find larger premises and hopefully found an orphanage.'

'And are you successful in your fund raising?'

'Sometimes. You see, I make it my business to know the names of wealthy people I can approach for monetary contributions.' She smiled when she saw his eyes register surprise. 'You must think me terribly mercenary to go around trying to extract money from people like I do, but it's because I care for the children.'

'You are so hungry for their money?'

'Oh, yes—and I am not ashamed to say so.'

'Just remember that greed is a terrible thing, Miss Greenwood.'

Cassandra started at his statement, her gaze darting to his enigmatic dark blue eyes. 'Please don't look at me like that, Captain Lampard. I'm not greedy—at least not for myself. Only for the children. Money means nothing to me, but you have to agree that it is a useful commodity, and a few pennies can be the means of life or death to a starving child.'

'Maybe so, but for a young lady to tout for money by herself is highly irregular I would have thought. It is also a dangerous game you play.'

'Nothing is only a game, Captain Lampard.' The sparkle was gone, leaving only a frosted blue in Cassandra Greenwood's eyes. 'To many people, the notion of becoming allied with a woman in such a way is so extraordinary as to be laughable—and distasteful when they realise I am indeed serious.'

'Do you not think you should take what God sends you and be thankful?'

His words were so glib and offhand that Cassandra gave him a rueful stare. 'Try telling that to the children. You look surprised by what I do, Captain.'

'Surprised, yes—and appalled to a certain extent. You are an attractive young woman, and why your family has allowed you to become involved in this unusual and somewhat dangerous enterprise, I cannot imagine.'

'My work at the institute is often hard and intense and keeps me away from home for long periods, but I take pride in what my father began and in my work and what I achieve— that the children who come here go away with full bellies and, if they're lucky, a pair of boots, even though I know that in all probability they will sell them for a few pennies when they are back on the streets. A great many of them are orphans, others are unwanted, having been turned out by parents who have too many mouths to feed already, and others have been sold to chimneysweeps and the like for a few shillings. The children who come to us have nothing—and very little hope. Someone has to watch over them.'

'And you think you can make a difference to their lives?'

'A few of them, yes.'

'There are always the workhouses—and the charity schools—and the hospital for those who are injured.'

'The workhouses are appalling places, but better than living on the streets, I do agree, but they don't house all the children and the hospitals exclude children under the age of seven—except for those who require amputations.' Her lips curved in a wry smile. 'How sad is that? Are you aware that out of all the people in London who die, almost half of them are children?'

'No, I was not aware of that,' William replied stiffly, never having thought of it since this was the first time he'd had contact with anything to do with destitute children. He scowled. Cassandra Greenwood had an irritating tendency to prick his conscience and to make him feel inadequate in some way, which he was beginning to find most unpleasant.

Having finished her task, Cassandra looked him straight in the eye. 'I'm not proud, sir, just determined to carry out what my father started, and if you can find fault with that then I am sorry for you.'

'No, Miss Greenwood, I can find no fault with that. You speak brave words. Such sentiments are highly commendable and admirable to say the least.' Swinging his long legs on to the floor and standing up, he was relieved that the last vestiges of haziness had left his mind.

Cassandra's breath caught in her throat, for the lean frame unfolded until the man stood a full head and shoulders taller than herself. Assisting him into his ruined jacket, collecting the soiled dressing and instruments Dr Brookes had used, she moved away from him.

As she busied herself with the task at hand, William watched her, his eyes roving approvingly over her lithe figure, stopping at the swelling breasts beneath the restricting fabric, then straying back to the shock of honey-gold hair. His fingers ached to release it from its strictures, to run them through the luxuriant softness and kiss the shaded hollow in her throat where a small brooch was pinned to the neck of her dress. He studied her stance and the language of her slender form. Despite his experience with the opposite sex, he wasn't familiar with women of her class. He'd made a point not to be, but this one made him curious.

All of a sudden warning bells sounded in his mind with such unexpected force that he knew he had to get out of that place, to dispel the unwelcome, unpleasant thoughts as he tried to understand what it was that made an attractive woman like Cassandra Greenwood want to waste her life in this sorry establishment for underprivileged children.

He was a shrewd and rational man, a man of breeding and style who understood his motivations and knew his goals. He prided himself on his good sense not to be swayed by emotion or flights of fancy, so it came as a shock that he wanted to know more about Miss Greenwood—and that was the moment he realised what was happening. He—the ruthless and heartless Lord William Lampard, Earl of Carlow in Hertfordshire, with a distinguished army career, who kept London alive with gossip and scandal when he was in town—was afraid of the effect that this place and Cassandra Greenwood was having on him.

'Tell me, is there no board of trustees you are answerable to?'

Cassandra stopped what she was doing and turned her blue-green eyes on his with a candid air. 'Trustees? Oh, yes. There are four on the board—Dr Brooks and a colleague of his at St Bartholomew's, my mother and me.'

'I see. I was beginning to think you were your own woman, Miss Greenwood.'

'I am, in every other way, answerable to no one. Very much so.'

'And there is no prospective husband in the offing?'

'No. I like my freedom and independence—which is something a husband isn't likely to give me.'

'That depends on the husband. No doubt, given time, things will change.'

When Cassandra met his gaze she experienced a shock of something between recognition and a kind of thrilling fear. Those eyes, deep blue and narrowed by a knowing, intrusive smile, seemed to look right past her face and into her self. For that split second she felt completely exposed and vulnerable—traits unfamiliar to her, traits she did not like.

'Not if I have my way, Captain Lampard. And I always do.'

'I can see that. However, I am not here because I want to be convinced of the merits of children's charities. I am here because I was shot and in no condition to object—although I do thank you for all you and Dr Brookes have done.'

'Don't you like children, Captain Lampard?' she asked suddenly.

'It's not a case of not liking them. I've never had anything to do with them.'

William became thoughtful and a heavy frown creased his brow. It was an expression those who knew him well would recognise, for it indicated his interest. His curiosity was aroused. Cassandra Greenwood was a woman who lived and breathed her cause and he did not know how he knew, but he knew he was looking at that rare individual who would tell the whole world to go to blazes should it get in her way.

As the initial shock of his assault by an unknown assailant began to wear off, an instinct, a built-in awareness that thrived inside the soldier in him and was essential if one was to survive, told him that here was the dedication, ambition, determination and a sense of purpose of one who meant to succeed. There was an air about her, in the set of her chin and the firmness of her lips, a resolve so obstinate and positive that he found if difficult to restrain himself from showing the same enthusiasm as she did.

Donning his hat, he turned from her, his gaze resting for a brief moment on the child. He seemed to hesitate before coming to a decision. Looking back at her, he said, 'The boy—Archie. When he is recovered, send him to my house in Grosvenor Square. I'll have a word with Thomas, my head groom. If the lad likes horses, Thomas might very well set him on in the stables. I'm sure we can find him something to do that will keep him off the streets. I shall also make sure you are repaid for your kindness.'

'Thank you,' she said, her expression registering surprise as he moved towards the door. 'It would be much appreciated,'—but he must not have heard her words, for he did not turn to look at her again. Unable to believe he had offered to provide Archie with work and a home, she stood staring at the door through which he had disappeared for several moments.

Just when she was beginning to believe that every scandalous thing she had heard about him was true, he had to do something nice.

It would appear Captain Lampard had hidden depths. By offering to provide Archie with work and a home, he had exposed one redeeming feature to her. Was it possible that the renowned rake had returned to England a reformed character?

As William sat in Miss Greenwood's carriage taking him to Grosvenor Square, his horse tethered to the back, he tried to define what had been so attractive about her. She certainly wasn't plain. Her real physical confidence was sensual and there had been an assured innocent vanity in her smile. He smiled to himself, remembering it, but then a more pressing matter entered his thoughts and he became preoccupied with discovering the identity of whoever it was who had tried to end his life. A cold, hard core of fury was growing inside him, shattering every other emotion he'd ever felt, leaving him incapable of feeling anything other than the need to find the person responsible.

Cassandra, her mother and her eighteen-year-old sister Emma lived in a house of modest proportions in Kensington compared with Aunt Elizabeth's grand residence in Mayfair. Cassandra's parents had been well matched in character, but they came from different backgrounds. The Greenwood family belonged to the entrepreneurial and professional classes. Her mother was of the landed gentry with aristocratic connections. What Cassandra's parents did have in common was that they came from the poorer branches of their respective families. Neither of them had a private fortune.

Deeply concerned with the sorry plight of the City's destitute children, James Greenwood had opened the small institute in Soho. Since his death three years earlier, Cassandra and her mother had struggled to keep it open. They were constantly short of funds. Dr Brookes, who had been Dr Green-wood's close friend and associate, generously gave up his time to tend the seriously ill or injured children who came to them, and raised funds on their behalf.

Bereft after the death of her beloved husband, Harriet Greenwood, not content to lead a quiet life, had become involved in the running of the institute and was willing to allow her eldest daughter to work alongside her, even though twenty-year-old Cassandra's break from convention shocked friends and acquaintances and brought severe disparagement. But Cassandra, undeterred, refused to allow a lot of small-minded, ignorant people to take from her all that she and her mother were trying to accomplish.

Harriet's cousin Lady Elizabeth Monkton, a widow, child-less and a wealthy and extremely popular socialite, had taken both girls under her wing when James had died and done her utmost to guide them in the way she thought was best for them. Eager to give them each a Season, she had been disap-pointed when Cassandra, who had her own ideas and quietly despised the useless frivolity of the social scene, had declined her offer—although she was not opposed to using Lady Eliz-abeth's position to her advantage. In her own subtle and charming way, Cassandra was successful at coaxing money out of the well-to-do at the balls and parties she attended.

Tonight, Aunt Elizabeth—as she liked to be known to Harriet's girls—was to give a ball to mark her fiftieth birthday. Cassandra was to attend and, as a special concession, Emma, too, despite not having made her curtsy. They were at Monkton House, getting ready for the ball, and Emma was irritatingly out of sorts—one of the reasons being that she had earlier received a severe scolding from her mother for going riding in the rain and arriving back at the house soaked to the skin.

'It isn't fair,' Emma wailed, pouting petulantly, bemoan-ing the fact that Edward Lampard, the young man she was enamoured with, would not be at the ball. Ever since he had left London three weeks ago she had been restive and impatient for him to return. Flopping into a chair beside her sister seated at the dressing table as she put the finishing touches to her *toilette,* she scowled her displeasure.

'Please stop it, Emma. No good can come of your seeing that particular gentleman and I'm tired of discussing it. I've told you before that young man is a scoundrel in the making and will not be content until he's compromised you so completely that your reputation will be beyond redemption. Then no gentleman of worth will want you,' she finished severely.

Emma was stricken as she stared at the sister she loved and admired more than anyone else, whose strength and force of character were so much greater than her own. 'Scoundrel?' she protested heatedly, two high spots of colour burning on her cheeks. 'How can you possibly know that?'

'Because he happens to be the cousin of that renowned rake Captain William Lampard—a man with a string of broken hearts and shattered marital aspirations that would make any level-headed young woman steer well clear of him.'

'That's an awful thing to say, Cassy,' Emma retorted indignantly. 'Just because his cousin's a renowned libertine of the first order does not mean to say that Edward will follow suit. He is a decent, upright and honourable man—a gentleman.' There was a look of acute dismay in her eyes. She was bewildered by pain and confusion—anxious for Cassandra's approval and agonisingly aware that she did not understand her sister's antagonistic behaviour. 'He loves me and values what I think and feel—and raises me above all other considerations.'

'Well, with all these attributes he must be quite unique,' Cassandra said drily, unconvinced by her sister's defence of Edward Lampard. 'But he should not be saying these things to you, and to respond to a gentleman's attentions before his intentions are known is to risk the ridicule of others. I do wish you would behave with more propriety, Emma.'

'Really, Cassy, considering your limited experience, I need no instructions from you on how to behave in society.'

'It's not society that concerns me and you know it. I worry that this preoccupation you have with Edward Lampard will frighten away all the eligible young men before you come out—which Aunt Elizabeth seems set upon—although why she allows you to go out in company so much when you have not yet made your curtsy is quite beyond me.'

Emma stared at her. Their ability to communicate was truly broken down. 'Really, Cassy, what man could be more eligible than Edward?'

'I'm only trying to warn you of the dangers of you showing favour to any one man before your début, and you must not allow yourself to be alone with him.'

'Kindly keep your warnings to yourself. I am quite capable of taking care of myself.'

'How do you know he isn't merely toying with you, Emma?'

'Because he cares for me. Anyone would think you're jealous because you've failed to arouse any man's passions yourself,' Emma uttered petulantly.

'Passions? My dear Emma, I sincerely hope Edward Lampard keeps his passions under control when he is with you.'

'Cassy, will you please listen to me? I am in love. Really in love.'

'You think you are. Whatever the sentiments that young man has created, I have no doubt that in time the true nature of his character will be revealed. Now please go and get ready before Aunt Elizabeth comes looking for us.'

'You go to the ball, I don't feel like it,' Emma snapped petulantly.

Cassandra sighed and looked at her sister. Bold, open and loving, full of confidence and life, her green eyes set off by the lustrous gold of her hair, her nose pert and cute and her lips soft and full, at just eighteen years of age Emma had attended few social events. As a rule she looked forward to them and enjoyed them, always wearing her best gown and preening in front of the mirror like a bird of paradise determined on a grand display. Cassandra had thought tonight would be no exception, but she was wrong.

Emma had known Sir Edward Lampard for several weeks, meeting him at the odd soirée and the theatre, visiting neighbouring friends with Aunt Elizabeth in the mornings, and on outings in the park. Cassandra was not unaware that friendship of a certain kind was beginning to grow between them. At first she had considered it to be nothing more than youthful attraction, but Mr Lampard was persistent and always sought Emma's company, which, fearing he was intent on compromising her vulnerable and naïve sister, gave Cassandra cause for concern—particularly since he was closely related to the notorious scoundrel Captain Lampard—the man who had promised her a donation for the institute and had apparently reneged on his word. Now the thought of Emma having anything to do with that family did not sit easy.

'You're mean, Cassy.' Emma pouted. 'I don't know why you always have to say hateful things about Edward. You're spiteful.'

'No, I'm not. I'm just being realistic.'

Emma sulked for a moment longer, but, realising a fine pout would not sway her sister, she changed her tactics. 'Very well, I'll go and get ready. Perhaps his cousin, Captain Lampard, will tell me when Edward is to return.'

Cassandra swung round. 'Captain Lampard? He's coming here tonight?'

'I believe so. I know Aunt Elizabeth invited him.' Emma got up and, gathering up her skirts, flounced to the door. Ignoring her sister's perplexed frown, she rushed on. 'As well as being a magnificent combat officer, a man without fear and already a veteran of at least two campaigns— which Edward proudly told me about—he's extremely handsome, too, by all accounts. I've never seen him myself, but all the ladies positively drool over him.' She was the epitome of angelic goodness now her tirade was spent. With a delicious giggle she kicked the hem of her gown and opened the door.

'Emma, wait.' Getting up, Cassandra crossed to her sister. 'I want to be at the institute early tomorrow, so I don't intend being late to bed. I don't think you should be late, either.'

'I won't be, and I know you need your rest to pander to all those uncivilised children and to scrub the floors.' Perceiving that her thrust had hit its mark, Emma turned away.

Bruised by Emma's manner, the thoughtless insults cutting her to the quick, Cassandra drew a long breath, striving to get control of her temper. When she spoke again she was more composed and put her hand on her sister's arm.

'Please don't be angry, Emma. I'm sorry if I sounded harsh. Edward is handsome enough, I suppose, and I can understand why you are attracted to him. Such infatuations are common, but you are just eighteen and he is what—nineteen? You are an attractive and intelligent girl. Have you absolutely no idea of the harm this will do to your reputation? The way you have behaved with Edward Lampard is not a desirable mode of behaviour, and I know how much it upsets Mama.'

Cassandra's mention of their beloved mama made Emma look contrite. Their mother was a hard-working woman who doted on her daughters. 'I don't mean to upset her, truly. I know she desires me to be more like you—to take an interest in the institute that was so dear to Papa's heart—but I can't. It's just not in my nature.'

'I know, Emma, and it doesn't matter. I enjoy what I do; if I didn't, I couldn't do it, so I don't blame you. Only I do wish you'd listen to me when I attempt to advise you. I do have your best interests at heart, you know. Now go and get ready.'

On a sigh she watched Emma go out. She could only hope that, beneath her indignation, Emma had sufficient common sense to heed her words.

* * *

Escorted by Aunt Elizabeth, when Cassandra and Emma entered the large, mirrored ballroom with French windows leading out on to balconies, it was already congested with over two hundred of the *ton*'s most illustrious and sophisticated personages. Dancing was in progress, with ladies dipping and swaying, talking and laughing with their partners. Around the room were enormous bouquets of flowers and the immense chandeliers, dripping with sparkling crystals, reflected the dazzling kaleidoscope of colourful gowns and jewels.

Lady Monkton, a widow of ten years and one of society's most respected and influential ladies, was standing behind her charges like a protective mother hen, her chest puffed out, her back ramrod straight, her eyes proudly resting on her lovely girls.

There was little opportunity for the chaperons to relax and enjoy themselves at a ball, for they felt compelled to keep an eye on their charges at all times—to know who they were dancing with, and who they were dancing with too often.

Cassandra paused to casually overlook the throng to see who was present. Full purses would be plentiful. She never openly asked anyone for money—that would never do—but there were several here who were sympathetic to her cause and subscribed on a regular basis. She observed that Lord and Lady Ross were present. They were extremely wealthy, and Lady Faversham's husband was an influential London property owner who had frequently made generous donations to the institute in the past. Cassandra glanced at Emma when she gasped.

'Oh, look, Cassandra,' she remarked excitedly. 'It's Edward—over there. I had no idea he was back in London—and see, he's coming this way.'

Dismayed, Cassandra saw that the young man in question was indeed wending his way towards them, his blond hair falling attractively over his forehead and a smile on his lips.

She saw the pleasure that lit up his youthful face, warming him with astonishing intensity.

She sighed, defeated. 'So he is, Emma. I do so hope he is not going to be persistent and that you do not forget how to behave—and it is undignified, as well as unattractive, to stand with one's mouth open,' she chided, leaving her sister in Aunt Elizabeth's charge and strolling to the edge of the crowded dance floor to accost and charm anyone she thought would benefit her cause.

Alluring, fiery, and with an unshakeable sense of her own worth, Cassandra was bright and unpredictable—often playful and engaging, just as often frostily aloof. She drew men to her side almost without benefit of conscious effort. But those who fell victim to her potent magnetism soon learned to their cost that the fascinating Miss Cassandra Greenwood, while accepting their masculine admiration as both her right and her pleasure, kept herself beyond their reach.

An uncertain future loomed ahead of her, this she knew, but she was going to meet it squarely in the eye. She would not be looked over like ripe fruit on a costermonger's stall. There would be no inept youth with groping hands and wet kisses for her but a man, someone to love her with all the masculine authority at his command—experienced, bold and dashing— like Captain Lampard perhaps? She was shocked and instantly ashamed of the way her mind was working. Captain Lampard was totally unsuitable in every way and it was a ridiculous thought which she dismissed at once—but she could not deny it.

Chapter Two

Since his return to London and conscious that someone was trying to kill him—the reason why still eluded him—William had lost interest in society events. When the invitation to Lady Monkton's birthday ball had arrived he'd given it a cursory glance and was tempted to instruct his secretary to send a polite refusal, despite any social occasion at Monkton House reputed as being exceptional. It was Edward, having returned to London from visiting friends in the country, who'd persuaded him to attend. In fact, young Edward seemed to be in an exuberant mood of late and William was curious as to the reason for it—a young lady, perhaps?

Arriving at Monkton House, he entered the ballroom, impatient to get the evening over with; since he had no desire to strike up a conversation with any of the people who seemed eager to talk to him, in particular the ladies who were delighted to see him back in London after so long an absence, he stepped into the shadows at the back of the room and lifted his champagne glass to his lips.

With one shoulder nonchalantly propped against a pillar, from his vantage point he idly watched the crowd. A smile curved his lips when Edward waltzed a small, exceedingly pretty and engaging young thing around the dance floor.

She was dressed in a white silk gown with a blue sash tied at one side in two small bows. The look of complete absorption on both their faces as they gazed into each other's eyes told him that here was the cause of Edward's recent preoccupation.

Not best pleased, a troubled frown furrowed his brow. Anyone with eyes in their head could not fail to notice that almost invisible aura with which two young people in love seemed to surround themselves. William had certainly seen it, and because of Edward's young age and William's expectations for his cousin to enter his own regiment, he had strong objections to his cousin forming a match with any woman just then. Influenced by his hopes and fears, he would observe his cousin's behaviour attentively and discourage any entanglement.

His eyes did a slow sweep of the room and came to rest on a young woman on the edge of the dance floor. He looked away, but his gaze was drawn back to her, for there was something about her that kindled his interest—something familiar—her stance, the tilt of her head. Recognition flowed across his face and pleasure lit his eyes, followed by pure masculine admiration as his gaze drifted over Miss Greenwood. The effect of seeing her surprised him.

Instead of the stiff and aloof young woman he remembered in an unflattering drab grey dress, she was now draped in the palest off-white gown, the satin clinging to her, hugging her waist and accentuating her rounded bosom. With regal poise, Miss Greenwood, a proud, striking young woman with large luminous eyes beneath thick dark lashes and exotically winged brows, moved serenely from group to group, untouched by the noise and bustle all around her.

Observing her with the impartiality of a connoisseur, looking for flaws that others would miss, he found only perfection. Her colouring was more vivid in this glamorous setting, William thought. Her hair was the same vibrant honey-gold glistening with innumerable shades beneath the light of the chandeliers. A delicate necklace of diamonds lay against her throat in perfect complement to the gown.

She belonged in beautiful gowns and glittering jewels, he decided. They suited her far better than the sombre grey. But who was she really and what was she doing among the cream of London society? He continued to stand in the shadows, admiring the alluringly beautiful woman, but far more intrigued by the indefinable but unmistakable presence that made her stand out so clearly from the rest.

'So, William, I trust you will enlighten me as to what your thoughts are as you look at the thoroughly enchanting and delectable Miss Cassandra Greenwood with that possessive gleam in your eyes. Damned engrossed you are.'

William turned and regarded Sir Charles Grisham, decked out in rich peacock-bright satins and velvets—obviously chosen to create an eyecatching display—with a bland expression. His manner was so indolent that he always gave the impression of being half-asleep.

'My thoughts are my own affair, Charles—though favourable,' he added with a cynical curl to his lips and an appreciative gleam in his eyes.

'Singled her out for yourself, have you?' Charles said in a bored drawl, raising his jewelled quizzing glass the better to study the lady under discussion, the rings on his fingers glinting in the light from the chandeliers. 'Can't say that I blame you, and if you are contemplating making her one of your amusing bed warmers, then you are going to be disappointed. Many have tried and all have failed. There are certain things you should know about that adorable creature, since you've been absent from the *ton* pursuing those damned Frenchies in the Peninsula for the past few years.'

'Go on,' William said, lifting his arrogant brows and waiting, his look both suspicious and intrigued. His curiosity was piqued, but he'd be damned if he let Charles see it. Well acquainted with Charles Grisham, who in spite of his affectations was one of the most intelligent and erudite of the Corinthians, William knew perfectly well that the man was one of the most influential members of the *ton*. At twenty-eight, fair haired, of a slender athletic build and fastidiously tailored, he was much envied for his ability to tie a neckcloth into perfect folds. He had an acid wit that accepted no boundaries and was able to shred a reputation in minutes, when he chose a human target. William deduced from his remarks about Miss Greenwood that he had made her just that.

After helping himself to a pinch of snuff, Charles went on to regale William with Miss Greenwood's attributes and shortcomings, much to William's irritation. If Charles were to be believed, the lady was as cold as an iceberg and set with wilful thorns—one of nature's disagreeable blunders, in fact.

'As a result she has been dubbed the Ice Maiden. And the unkind—though appropriate, some would say—sobriquet has stuck. It's unfortunate since the filly has spirit. She should prove highly entertaining in a chase. Miss Greenwood is one of those rare eccentrics who attend society events and rarely dances except to please herself—which makes her something of a challenge to the likes of me. In fact, she doesn't go out in society at all unless it's to tout for funds for that wretched institute of hers—you know about that?'

William nodded, languidly listening, turning his sardonic gaze back to Miss Greenwood at the same moment as she bestowed a melting smile on a smitten elderly gentleman who was handing her a glass of champagne.

'Lady Monkton—her aunt—takes an understanding view on the matter. Some might think it admirable—personally, I consider it a damn waste of both time and a beautiful woman. Her mama and Lady Monkton let her do exactly as she likes with relative impunity, the result being she has become an object of ridicule.'

William's brows lifted imperturbably. 'Which in your opinion she rightly deserves.'

'Exactly.'

William looked at Miss Greenwood with renewed interest. 'She is Lady Monkton's niece, you say?'

'Not quite. Her mother and Lady Monkton are cousins, but she has taken on the role of aunt to the two Misses Greenwood. The grand lady took both Cassandra and her sister under her wing when their father died. Intending to give both girls a Season, she was disappointed when the older girl declined—being of the unconventional type, if you see what I mean. It's hard to believe that any man's hands have ever touched that delectably soft skin of hers—and I doubt she knows what it feels like to be kissed.'

Though he would dearly like to silence Charles, from William's own dealings with Miss Greenwood it was obvious that what he was saying was mostly true.

'Any unattached bachelor who is foolish enough to show an interest in her, she sends packing.'

'Including you, Charles, which is why you are so ready to point out her faults to me.'

Sir Charles Grisham lifted his arrogant brows, drawling, 'Including me.' He admitted, chuckling softly, 'Indeed, I confess to having been afflicted with a touch of frostbite. Being a notorious rake, I naturally assumed I could seduce her—to initiate her into the art of love. It did nothing for my self-esteem when she added me to her string of rejections. Now you are back in town I can see that I and every other male smitten with the charming Miss Cassandra Greenwood will have to look to our laurels. With your breeding and looks—not to mention your wealth—your potent attraction to women has always been a topic of much scintillating feminine gossip. You do seem to have an extraordinary effect on them, William, but I very much doubt even you will melt that particular iceberg.'

Mild cynicism marred the lean handsomeness of William's features as he refused to be drawn on what his thoughts might be concerning the young woman who had in all probability saved his life.

'By the by,' Grisham went on. 'I saw Mark in town recently—upholding the family name while you've been chasing the Frenchies. I have to say he doesn't improve with age—still the same old bore he was at Cambridge. With so much starch in his veins, it's a miracle the man can sit down. It's difficult to believe he's your cousin. Is it true that he jumps to the tune of his wife?'

William smiled mildly, knowing of Grisham's intense dislike of Mark—in fact, Mark's austere, intolerant attitude did seem to put most people's backs up. There were certain things about Mark that irritated even him—and the same could be said of his acerbic wife, Lydia. But being possessed of a fierceness to protect any member of his family, which had sadly dwindled to just Mark and Edward during the past five years, with the demise of both his parents and older brother in a riding accident, William would not therefore, speak against his cousin.

'If he does, then it is entirely their own affair. I couldn't have left my affairs in better hands, Charles. My cousin is a man of steadfast character and unimpeachable honour, and I would be grateful if you did not cast aspersions.'

'I applaud your loyalty—though in my opinion he doesn't deserve it. Loyalty is a rare virtue in either sex these days.'

'Besides, Mark is next in line to the title and the estate—unless I marry and produce an heir.'

'And is there a possibility of that on the horizon?' Charles enquired, his eyes lighting with obvious interest, for with this devilishly handsome lord off the social scene, the likes of himself and his associates would stand in better favour with the ladies.

William's eyes suddenly glinted with amusement. 'Marriage is not high on my list of things to do just now. When I feel inclined to pledge my hand in order to produce an heir,' he replied with grim humour, 'I'm sure you will be one of the first to know.'

'I shall be journeying to Hertfordshire tomorrow—I'm to stay with my aunt for a few days. I've neglected her disgracefully of late,' Charles confessed. 'I'm quite fond of the old dear.'

'And her money,' William uttered pointedly.

'I admit it does hold some attraction,' he said without shame. 'I shall be close to Carlow Park and I've arranged to ride over to see Mark—though I intend the visit to be of short duration.'

'Then, feeling as you do, why do you visit him at all?'

'Two rather splendid horses you have in the stables—saw them on the hunting field in January and I was impressed. A chestnut full of quality took my fancy, although the grey was damned fine, too. I heard Mark's selling them, so I approached him with an interest to buying one. He invited me to Carlow Park to look them over.'

William's expression was bland when he turned and fixed him with a quizzical stare. 'And these are Mark's horses to sell?'

'Damned if I know—although I don't suppose they are, seeing as they're stabled at Carlow Park.'

'Their names?'

'Monarch and Franciscan.'

William's expression hardened. On learning of his brother's death, from Spain he had asked Mark to keep an eye on the estate until his return. He hadn't given him *carte blanche* to do as he pleased and he felt a faint stirring of antagonism over Mark's having usurped his position by selling off his horses—in particular Franciscan, his brother's horse. Although, on second thought, perhaps it had more to do with Lydia than Mark.

'The horses are not for sale.'

Not to be outdone, Charles's eyes narrowed and a calculating gleam shone in their depths as he moved close to William so that what he was about to say would not be overheard. 'A wager I will make, William.'

Apart from one sleek dark brow cocked in question, William's features remained impassive. 'A wager? I wonder what you're intending to propose, Charles. I'm listening.'

'A wager that you fail to seduce the delectable Miss Greenwood before the Season ends in June.'

'And why should I want to seduce her?'

Charles shrugged. 'To prove that you can—that you haven't lost your touch.'

The challenge was thrown lightly and William teetered on the brink of accepting when caution reared its head. Seducing virgins wasn't his forte—never had been—but the lovely Miss Cassandra Greenwood had captured his attention and the challenge was intriguing. He was a man who must conquer, must win, whatever the odds stacked against him. Whenever he set his mind on having something, he was not easily dissuaded.

'And if I don't?'

'Then one or the other of those splendid beasts in your stable will be mine.'

'And what's in it for me—besides the delectable Miss Greenwood, of course?'

'A thousand guineas if you succeed.'

William rose to the challenge with a confident smile. 'That's unfortunate for you. If there's one thing I dislike, it's seeing my opponent lose.'

'So do I. Think on it, William. To seduce a woman famous for her strict morals—a virgin, I have no doubt, and as yet untouched by world's cynicism—a lovely rose, just waiting to be plucked. What could be more prestigious?'

'What more, indeed?'

'A wager it is then. No need to put it in writing. A gentleman's agreement will do.'

When a well-satisfied Sir Charles Grisham had moved on, William watched Miss Greenwood move about the room with renewed interest. So, she was untouchable. Suddenly she had become an exciting enigma, a mystery, which had multiplied tenfold. Gentlemen of the *haut ton* hesitated to go near her, to take liberties with her. Suddenly she had become a challenge he could not resist.

William watched her pause to speak to this person and that, careful to be as charming and polite as her nature allowed, for it did not do to antagonise. She was well versed in taking hold of a situation and bringing it round to her advantage, since the future of the institute might depend on people such as these. Sharp and witty, she sparkled, encompassing them all with her brilliant smiles and laughter—a light and joyous sound that caressed him, enticed him—and animated chatter, all serving to project the persona of a confident and capable young woman. These people were like children, thrilled and flattered to the core to be noticed by this gorgeous woman. It didn't matter if she schemed to capture their attention. She had it.

Miss Greenwood was quite exquisite, William decided, with an air of fragility about her, but she reminded him of a rapier blade, a sliver of silver made of steel. He wanted to laugh out loud. So this was how she extracted donations for her precious institute.

Moving out of the shadows, completely impervious to the stir he was creating, since it was the first society event he'd attended since returning to London, William advanced towards her, the crowd parting as if he had ordered it.

Cassandra was in the process of deciding who to approach next when she saw him moving in her direction. He was tall, with an authoritative air of breeding and command and an unconscious swagger of arrogance, which spoke of generations of influence and superiority and advantage. With wide shoulders and a hard, stern face and iron jaw, his bright blue eyes beneath fine dark brows were disconcertingly amused as they gazed into hers. When he was close a strange, unfathomable smile tugged at the corner of his mouth, and he slowly inclined his head towards her.

'Hello, Miss Greenwood,' he said, in a deep, resonant and incredibly seductive voice.

His very nearness had her stiffening. The sensation unnerved her. His towering figure left her no avenue of escape. She wished she were nearly a foot taller so she could meet him eye to eye. He was too attractive and had too much charm for his own good. Some people were born like that. It was as if they had a magnet inside them.

'Why, Captain Lampard. This is a surprise.'

A crooked smile accompanied his reply. 'For me rather more than it is for you, Miss Greenwood. You look ravishing, by the way. That colour is far more flattering to your colouring than the diabolical grey dress you were wearing on the day we met.'

Resentment coursed through Cassandra's veins. It dawned on her as his gaze dropped to her breasts in a leisurely perusal that he was far more interested in what was beneath the gown than the gown itself. He raised his eyes to her face where they captured hers and held them prisoner until she felt a warmth suffuse her cheeks.

'What are you doing here, Captain Lampard?' she asked, her smile deliberately cold and ungracious.

'Your aunt invited me.'

'So, you are aware that Lady Monkton is my aunt. Really she is my mother's cousin, but she has always been known as aunt to me and my sister. How long have you known?'

'About ten minutes.' If she had suspected his presence at her aunt's ball had been staged with her specifically in mind, then she was mistaken—disappointed, too, he hoped. 'I grew bored watching the world go by in my town house so I came to see if the sights were any better here at Monkton House.' He spoke with slow deliberation and the corners of his lips twitched with amusement. His eyes gleamed into hers as he added softly, 'I am happy to report they far exceed my expectations and I'm glad I came.'

Cassandra turned aside, tossing him a cool glance

askance. 'Have you nothing better to do than ogle the ladies, Captain Lampard?'

'It might look like that, but in truth I was watching just one.'

Cassandra ignored the remark, but she could not ignore the seductive lowering of his eyelids or the quickening of her heart. 'The gaming tables seem to attract a good many gentlemen. Why don't you try that?'

'Because I find talking to you more enjoyable than anything else I could come up with.'

'Your shoulder is healing well, I trust?'

'Apart from the occasional twinge it is almost back to normal. Your Dr Brookes did a fine job. I am in your debt, Miss Greenwood.'

'Yes, you are, Captain Lampard,' she replied coldly, not having forgiven him for not having sent her the promised donation.

As though reading her mind, he said, 'You received the bank draft I sent to the institute?'

'I cannot recall having done so.'

William frowned, averting his eyes in angry disgust. He would have a few choice words to say to his secretary. Damn the man and his incompetence. 'Then I can only assume there has been a mix up somewhere. I gave it to my secretary to deliver in person. I apologise most sincerely that you have not received it. Rest assured that I shall look into the matter first thing in the morning.'

'Thank you. It will be appreciated,' she said coolly. 'Following that unfortunate experience, perhaps you will think twice before you fight a duel to settle a score—be it a difference of opinion, cheating at cards, or a case of adultery—which, if what I have heard about you is to be believed, was more than likely the reason that took you to Green Park that day.'

'You are mistaken, and it is clear to me that you know nothing about the rules of duelling.'

'I don't?'

'No. For one thing, the normal practice when a duel is arranged is for witnesses—seconds—to be in attendance, and possibly a physician. Do you recall seeing any?'

'Why—I—no, I do not.'

'And for another, I do not hold with the practice. Perhaps you would care to take a walk outside in Lady Monkton's exquisite gardens and allow me to enlighten you on the finer points of the art of duelling.'

Cassandra drew back. 'Certainly not. I refuse to go anywhere with you, sir.'

A mildly tolerant smile touched his handsome visage, but the glint in his blue eyes was as hard as steel. 'Very well, Miss Greenwood, but I would appreciate a word with you in private.' Placing his hand firmly on her elbow, he led her to a small recess and looked down at her, his expression hard. 'You are under a misconception as to what occurred when you came upon me in the park. There was no duel. I was there to enjoy the exercise and solitude of an early morning ride, nothing more sinister than that. In short, someone tried to kill me.'

Oddly enough, Cassandra's first fleeting thought was that he was joking, but, when she saw the firm set of his jaw, she was inclined to believe he was deadly serious. 'To kill you,' she repeated quietly, unable to entirely absorb such a macabre event taking place so close to herself, yet been unaware of it. 'But why would anyone want to kill you?'

'At the moment, the reason is unclear, but I will find out, that I promise you. Someone tried to bring my life to a premature end and I damned well intend finding out who and why. Did you happen to see anyone acting suspiciously that morning?'

'Why, yes. Now I come to think of it, a man rode out of the trees close to where we found you. I didn't see his face. He was wearing a hat pulled well down over his face, and a cloak.'

'His horse? What colour was it—brown, black, grey?' William demanded, sounding sharper than he intended, but he was impatient to discover any clue that would lead him to the culprit.

'Dark brown—but on hearing the shot, I was more concerned about what had occurred than to take note of what the man and his horse looked like.' She paused, becoming trapped in his blue gaze. 'Do you think whoever it was will try again?'

Expression grim, William nodded. 'When I'm in London, I frequently ride in the park at that time. He must have been waiting for me—he didn't try to rob me, so I can only assume he had murder in mind. There was no warning. Nothing. If he was prepared to try once, he'll not let it alone. The question is, when.'

'Then you will have to look to your safety and take all due care.'

'I intend to. I am not the sort who jumps at shadows, and nor do I run from threats. As a soldier on campaign I learned to watch my back—I didn't realise I would have to continue doing so in London.'

'It would seem you have an enemy, Captain Lampard, one who hates you enough to want you dead.'

'It looks like it.'

'So, you are the innocent party and didn't provoke a fight.'

His eyes glowed in the warm light as he gave her a lazy smile, his mood reverting back to what it had been a moment before. 'I cannot claim to be innocent, Miss Greenwood, but neither am I the black-hearted scoundrel I have been painted.'

'I would hardly expect you to admit it if you were,' Cassandra retorted crisply. 'However, I've heard stories to convince me that you are.'

The tantalising smile grew wider in the face of her derisive stare. Folding his arms, William leaned his back nonchalantly against a pillar. 'I am deeply curious about you, Miss Greenwood. Tell me, have you always rebelled against the fashionable world?'

'I suppose I have. I attend these affairs not because I enjoy them particularly, but because they are a means to bring about that which is closest to my heart.'

'I'm aware of that. When you told me how you collect donations for your cause, I was ready to question your methods, but now I can see that with a flash of your eyes and a few chosen words you have them reaching into their pockets.'

'That is my intention.'

He gazed at her for a long moment, his devilish, sensual mouth turning upward in the faintest of cynical smiles. 'You are an extremely forward, quite outrageous and outspoken young woman, Miss Greenwood.'

'If you got to know me, you would have to become used to my manner and the way in which I deal with people.' She met his gaze candidly. 'You don't approve of what I do, do you, Captain Lampard?'

'It is not for me to approve or disapprove of what you do, Miss Greenwood.'

'Nevertheless you're quick to voice your opinion.'

'That is in my nature—and my right.'

On a sigh and letting her expression slip to one of utter boredom. Cassandra looked around. 'I do so hate these occasions. I find little interest in society's entertainments. I wish I could leave right now. See all the mamas watching their offspring with eyes like hawks, Captain Lampard. Launched upon Society and made to parade for inspection like so many fillies at an auction. They will be sold to the highest bidder— to the largest title and the most wealthy.'

'I confess I haven't really thought about it,' William remarked, not really interested. He preferred looking at her. Her blue-green eyes, attentive, observing, carried a brilliance that held him transfixed. 'It must be horrendous for the young ladies.'

'Don't waste your pity. It's all they want from life— pretty gowns, jewels. They have no notion of anything else. Their mamas are obsessed with etiquette, fiercely concerned with morals and the approval of their friends and acquaintances, determined that their daughters do and say the right thing—not to dance more than two dances with any one gentleman, and so on. How tedious and tiresome it all is.'

'I have already decided that you are a very unconventional young woman, Miss Greenwood.'

'I am concerned with none of that. I do so detest all the restrictions of the social system that enslaves women.'

'Are you suggesting that you would care to redress the wrongs of our misguided society? Are you so uninhibited by the prejudice of class that you would break the mould of convention that has encased women for centuries?'

'I despise convention; as you will have gathered, I live very much as I please, but without causing offence to those I love and those who love me.

'And to add to all that, you rarely dance,' William said, pushing his long frame away from the pillar and moving close to her, his gaze capturing hers. 'Will you step out of your self-imposed restrictions and do me the honour of dancing with me?'

Cassandra stared up at him. Those glowing eyes burned into hers, suffusing her with a growing aura of warmth. 'I—I do not care to dance.'

'I insist. After all, this is a ball and that is what people do. You—do dance?'

Her smile was feral. 'Of course I do. I prefer not to.'

'You distress me, Miss Greenwood.' His mouth twisted in a lightly mocking grin. 'You give me no grounds to hope for better things.'

'Nor should I,' she returned pertly. 'I've told you, I do not like these occasions.'

He laughed briefly. 'You seem to take special delight in reminding me. But I am not convinced. There isn't a woman alive who doesn't like to dance—and I do not believe you are any different, Miss Greenwood.' William peered at her closely and took note of her uneasiness. 'I'm right, am I not?'

Cassandra tilted her slim nose upward as she turned it in profile to him. 'I meant what I said.'

'Tell me, Miss Greenwood. Why do you resent me? Can it be that it is because my secretary failed to deliver the donation—or is it more of a personal nature?'

Indignant colour stained Cassandra's cheeks. 'You're right, of course. I do resent you, but not for the reasons you state.'

'Then would you please enlighten me.'

She looked at him direct. 'It is to do with my sister.'

'Your sister?'

'And your cousin.'

'Edward?'

'Yes.' She turned towards the dance floor and observed Emma about to take to the floor in a lively country dance with Edward Lampard. Her annoyance was raised to new heights. 'It may have escaped your notice, Captain Lampard, but your cousin and my sister have danced two dances together and are about to embark on a third. My sister is just eighteen years old and her reputation is about to be ruined before she has been launched into society.'

Totally unprepared for the turn the conversation had taken, William's eyes sought out Edward, seeing him with the same young woman he had been dancing with earlier. 'That young lady is your sister?'

'Yes. Unfortunately, the two of them have developed a fondness for each other.'

'A fondness?'

'Exactly.'

'Edward is a sensible, sensitive young man. Speaking as his older cousin, I can only applaud your sister's taste.'

'He is neither sensible nor sensitive if he cannot see that he is in danger of ruining her reputation,' Cassandra argued. 'Because of the time they spend together, I believe my sister is about to be compromised by your cousin. Everywhere we go we bump into him—be it in the park, at a soirée or the theatre.

I am certain these meetings are not coincidence and are pre-arranged in some way known only to Emma and Edward.'

'Pardon me, Miss Greenwood, but you are contradicting your own words. Did you not imply that you find the rules and restrictions that govern polite society utterly ridiculous? If you feel that way, then why should your sister's reputation matter to you so much?'

Cassandra sent a cool glance skimming over him. Having her own words quoted back at her was disconcerting. 'What I said applies to me, Captain Lampard, not my sister. She is a different matter entirely. When I said what I did, I was giving an honest opinion.'

William's lips twitched with ill-suppressed amusement. 'Do you have an aversion to my cousin, Miss Greenwood? If so, I find any preconceived ideas you might have about him being a scoundrel insulting and deeply offensive. Perhaps you're afraid that scoundrels run in the Lampard family—and maybe you see him as some kind of threat?'

'I do not consider him as much a threat as an inconvenience.'

Laughter twinkled in his eyes. 'I can see how confused you must be. It is a wholly perplexing problem you have there.'

Cassandra's cheeks became flushed with indignation. 'Are you laughing at me, Captain Lampard?'

'Heaven forbid, I wouldn't dare. Now, shall we dance? I will even say please if that will persuade you.'

Cassandra did not want to be persuaded. She did not want to dance with him. She did not want to become better acquainted. Still, if it meant a large subscription to the institute, then she could at least be pleasant to him for a short while. Besides, if sufficiently provoked, he might be tempted to risk creating a fuss to gain what he sought.

When William saw her hesitate, he smiled. 'Come, Miss Greenwood. People are beginning to stare. Your reticence only heightens my determination. I will have this dance, otherwise I might very well change my mind about the size of my donation. The amount will be considerably smaller than it would be if you were to partner me on the floor. Should your colleagues at the institute find out, they would never forgive you.'

Quite unexpectedly she smiled pleasantly and William almost reeled under the impact. Her eyes seemed to contain sparkles of light and a soft rose tinted her cheeks. Her lips parted over even, white teeth that shone, and a small dimple in her cheek caught his eye. Her smile deepened, and so did the dimple. He was momentarily transported and utterly speechless.

'I suppose I could dance with you for the sake of civility.'

'And a generous donation,' he was quick to point out.

'Of course—but this sounds very much like blackmail to me, Captain Lampard.'

'*You* might say that,' he murmured softly. 'I would prefer to call it persuasion.'

'Very well. I am persuaded. I surrender.'

Decorously presenting her with his arm, he laughed. 'I was hoping you would,' he said quietly. 'If we continue in this fashion, Miss Greenwood, we might even become friends.'

Cassandra smiled thinly. 'I would advise you not to place any wagers on that, Captain Lampard.'

'I might be tempted,' he said, with more meaning than she realised, leading her forward on his arm as the musicians played a waltz. 'I am not averse to the odd gamble.'

A sudden hush settled over the guests as those present turned, anxious to appease their curiosity. What they saw amazed them. Cassandra Greenwood was taking to the floor with Lord Lampard—well, he always had been able to charm every female within sight—and it went to prove that the prim Miss Greenwood was no different from the rest after all. But the fact that she was to dance with Captain Lampard—his first dance since returning to London—caused other gentlemen she had declined to dance with in the past to consider their attraction. Aware of his reputation as a rake, they were admiringly speculative.

Taking Cassandra in his arms, William's hand slid slowly, possessively, about her trim waist, drawing her close. 'I sincerely hope you were telling the truth when you said you do know how to dance, Miss Greenwood, otherwise you will make a laughing stock of us both,' he murmured, his wicked, sensual mouth turning upward in the faintest of cynical smiles.

'Just because I don't usually dance, doesn't mean that I don't know how to, so lead the way, Captain, and I will follow.'

'My pleasure, Miss Greenwood. My pleasure. For this one dance, forget your institute, your children and your fund raising and be a young lady of the *ton,* intent on enjoying herself. Take it from me, it's more fun than trying to extract money from society's elite.'

So saying, William whirled her round the floor. His senses were alive with the elusive perfumed scent of her, to her supple young body. Getting to know Miss Greenwood could be very pleasurable indeed. Deliberately, he drew her closer so that his hips brushed hers and he felt a tremor pass down her spine. His imagination began to run riot and he dwelt on the thought of what it would be like to plunder those soft lips and make love to her. His blood stirred hotly and his body was beginning to react in such a way that he had to force the thoughts aside.

It would have surprised—and gratified—him to know that Cassandra's thoughts were not so very different from his own. Beneath her fingertips, his beautifully tailored claret jacket was without a crease. Smelling pleasantly of sandalwood and brandy, he moved with elegance and grace, but, light as his arms were, she could feel the steel beneath.

Her eyes were level with his broad, muscular shoulders. Every inch of his tall frame positively radiated raw power and leashed sensuality, causing her to remember every scandalous story she'd ever heard about him. Handsome, sinful—

strangely the thought excited her. How could she claim unin-
terest in the man when his mere presence could so effectually
stir her senses? Lifting her gaze to his ruggedly hewn features,
she met his knowing eyes, seeing something relentless and
challenging.

'You dance well, Captain Lampard.'

'Suddenly you're an expert?'

'I know the difference between good and bad. Tell me, do
you always get what you want?' Cassandra asked.

'Usually,' he replied. 'Perhaps because I'm totally selfish,
arrogant, inconsiderate and a complete scoundrel—or so I've
been told by those who know me. It's the way I was raised,
you see—having people pander to my smallest needs, to
gratify my every whim.'

Cassandra slanted him an arched glance. 'What you really
mean is that you were a spoilt child. Still,' she quipped,
'you're a male, so I would expect no less.'

The dance ended and he released her, but the warmth of
his touch lingered. He escorted her to where Lady Monkton
was seated beside other matrons who had gathered to
gossip and nibble on sweets. A tall woman, with the
family's fairness and a majestic bearing, Lady Monkton
looked up when they approached, pleasure lighting her
features.

'Cassandra, my dear, how nice it is to see you take to the
floor at long last—and with Captain Lampard. I had almost
given up on my niece,' she said not unkindly, although she
never stopped reiterating her disappointment that Cassandra
refused to let her arrange her début. 'You must excuse her. She
has no social graces—only social causes.'

'Which is to be admired, Lady Monkton.'

'I'm happy you think so, Captain Lampard. You know,
you are far too handsome for your own good. You are enjoying
yourself, I hope?'

'Indeed, Lady Monkton. Thank you for inviting me.'

William's smile and the way he bowed over the elderly lady's hand was the epitome of politeness and charm. 'May I say that you are more beautiful than ever.'

Lady Monkton laughed lightly, and Cassandra was certain her cheeks flushed beneath her rouge.

'Flatterer. I must say that I—and every lady present—are delighted by your reappearance in the *ton*. It's long overdue. London will be a far more exciting place with you in it. Thank goodness you have Bonaparte beat.'

The musicians were beginning to play another refrain. Not to be let off lightly, William turned to Cassandra.

'Miss Greenwood, may I have the pleasure of dancing one more waltz with you?'

Cassandra drew back, intending to decline. 'Why—I—'

'Of course you must, Cassandra,' Lady Monkton was quick to interrupt, relieved to see her niece taking an interest in the frivolous things other young ladies seemed to delight in. 'Two dances with the same partner is socially acceptable, so off you go now and enjoy yourself.'

Cassandra shot a look at her aunt, seeing the shrewd, uncannily knowing expression pass over her. Beaten, on a sigh she turned and moved away.

'I'm only asking for another dance—one more dance, Miss Greenwood,' William murmured, taking her arm and propelling her back towards the dance floor. 'Nothing more intimate than that.'

'It's a good thing, too, Captain Lampard. No matter how generous your donation, anything more intimate than a dance is definitely out of the question. I don't think I even like you.'

'Who said anything about liking?' he remarked, laughing lightly as he took her in his arms. 'It's the act that's pleasurable.'

'Captain Lampard,' she chided, feeling her cheeks flush rose-red as he whirled her round, 'you are embarrassing me. Kindly stop it or I shall be forced to leave you standing on the dance floor—which would never do.' Observing the humour in his eyes, she scowled, struggling to prevent her lips from smiling. 'Are you teasing me, by any chance?'

'Most assuredly.' He laughed, the sound low and so seductive that several people dancing close turned to look at them.

'Then please don't.'

His teeth flashed white in a lazy grin, but his gaze dipped lingeringly to her soft lips. 'I enjoy teasing you. I find it—intriguing and pleasurable.'

'And I don't like being teased. If you think I do, then you've taken leave of a major portion of your senses.' His smile widened and it was such a wonderful smile. Captain Lampard exuded provocative charm. He could probably charm the birds out of the trees, but this particular bird wasn't about to tumble for that silky voice. But she was not nearly as immune as she thought—as she wanted to be. He was a magnificent male, and she was human—flesh and blood—and his sexual magnetism was overwhelming, dislike him though she might.

'As soon as the dance ends I must circulate,' she told him. 'I must also have a stern word with my sister. In fact, I do believe your cousin is now escorting her into the buffet.'

William glanced across at Edward and the young woman, who was gazing up at him adoringly. Experiencing a sharp stab of unease, he frowned. 'You sister looks sweet and very young.'

'Don't let her looks deceive you. She has a romantic mind and your charming cousin has somehow managed to captivate my dear, gullible sister. They do say that love is blind, and it seems Emma has no sight when it comes to Edward. However, I will not let him take advantage of her and cast her off—which will most certainly get her banished from polite society before she has the chance to make her début. She's hellbent on holding on to him. I do expect Emma to behave with discretion and propriety, but unfortunately she is strong willed and the very opposite of biddable.'

William's brow lifted in amusement. 'Then perhaps she takes after her big sister.'

'She most certainly does not. She does not respect my opinion and she never listens to any edicts from me or Mama.'

'I can understand your anxiety, and, if it will put your mind at ease, I strongly disapprove of Edward forming any kind of liaison at this time.'

'You do? Then if we don't do something to discourage it at once, things could become complicated. Once Emma gets some maggot into her head, there's no stopping her.'

'What do you suggest I do?'

'Can't you order your cousin to avoid her, or failing that, send him away somewhere?'

'Your anxieties and fears may soon be at an end. Edward is shortly to enter the Military Academy as a cadet, with the hope of purchasing a commission. In the current climate it's inevitable that his regiment will see service overseas.'

Cassandra's relief was enormous. 'Oh—thank goodness. That would be the answer to everything. What you may do for me in the meantime is to speak to him, keep an eye on him. I don't relish the idea of having a Lampard as kin.'

A pair of cool blue eyes regarded her dispassionately. 'How extraordinary,' William mocked. 'All my life I have harboured the delusion that all young ladies yearn to snare wealthy husbands—and, despite having made his home with me on the demise of his parents, Edward is wealthy in his own right. I am amazed that you have objections to my family's suitability, for their breeding is unexceptionable and they are better connected than most.'

Cassandra was so carried away with making sure that he understood her concern, and that her sister's reputation must be protected at all costs, that she didn't heed the muscle that was beginning to tick in his tightly clenched jaw.

'I'm sure you're right, Captain Lampard,' she hurried on, her tone straightforward, not facetious, 'and that your family's credentials are impeccable, but wealth and an illustrious name does not give a man the right to do as he pleases and to do it with impunity. I am sorry to have to say this, but if Edward turns out to be anything like the hellion you are reputed to be—for I do understand that you have great experience in living—then he will make an exceedingly bad husband.'

William heard the insult in her smoothly worded statement, and any amusement that was left vanished from his expression. In one swift movement he whisked her off the dance floor and released her. He then looked down at her with hard, unforgiving eyes, a scowl drawing his brows together.

'Miss Greenwood,' he said in a voice dangerously low, 'if you imagine for one minute that I would approve of Edward marrying your sister, then you are living under an illusion. However, there is a whole procession of society matrons who are eager to lure me into marrying their daughters and who are perfectly willing to overlook my excesses in "living," as you so baldly put it. I'm beginning to realise that I do not rate highly in your estimation. As a rule I have never cared for anyone's opinion, and I most certainly would never let them influence my actions—and this includes you.'

Stung at being manhandled from the dance floor and offended by the tone of superiority with which he delivered this lecture, Cassandra gave him a lofty look, but on searching his shuttered features and taking judicious note of the taut set of his jaw, she realised that she had gone too far in voicing her disapproval of his character and was unable to retreat from a predicament into which she should never have put herself in the first place.

Biting her lip, suddenly feeling very small and very foolish, she said, 'I—apologise if I have offended you, but I only said what I thought out of concern for my sister.'

'You have said quite enough, Miss Greenwood,' he snapped, irrationally angry at her unprovoked attack on his character. 'If it is your intention to humble me, then you can forget it. Rest assured that my donation to your institute will be with you in the morning, and let that be an end to the matter. And now I bid you good night.'

William turned on his heel and strode purposefully from the ballroom, leaving Cassandra staring in his wake. Mortified, shocked and bewildered by his sudden departure, these emotions were banished in a blinding flash of fury. How dare he walk away from her like that? The man was rude beyond bearing, too full of himself, affecting pompous poses and delighting in turning the head of every female in the room.

As the music died she became aware of being stared at and noticed the whispered conferences as people gathered in groups, having witnessed the altercation that had taken place between Cassandra Greenwood and Captain Lampard. With as much dignity as she could muster, she lifted her head and returned to Aunt Elizabeth, and it wasn't long before she left the ball and went home without seeing anything more of the arrogant and pretentious Captain Lampard.

Then why, as she climbed into bed, did the thought of his smile and the remembered touch of his hand make her heart beat faster? Suddenly at a loss, she blew out the candle.

Chapter Three

Seated in his carriage taking him back to Grosvenor Square, the anger caused by Miss Greenwood's censure to his character continued to burn inside William. Normally he would have smiled and shrugged such comments off as being of no consequence, whereas this time the self-confident, invulnerable Lord Lampard, who always treated women with amused tolerance, had been driven to walk away from Miss Greenwood because she had artlessly spoken the truth.

The wager he had made with Charles against his better judgement bothered him, and his conscience that he thought long since dead chose that moment to resurrect itself. Realising the enormity of what he'd done, already he was regretting it. He had taken the wager to seduce and dishonour a woman he had found to be full of goodness, trusting and candid, with a combination of wisdom and naïveté and undeniably lovely. Miss Greenwood was above a mere dalliance. May God forgive him. It was madness, and he hated himself with a virulence that nearly knocked the breath out of him.

For the first time in a long time, he had met a woman without guile. Her young innocent face passed before his mind's eye, a face of much seriousness, a ripe, opulent beauty that made his blood stir hotly. Never in his wildest dreams had he imagined anyone like Miss Greenwood. What an enchanting creature she was, artlessly sophisticated, part-angel, part-spitfire. For some peculiar reason that was quite beyond him, it mattered to him what she thought of him.

By the time his carriage drew up outside his residence, his anger had abated and his stomach clenched at the unmannerly way in which he had left her. He had decided not to pursue Miss Greenwood. She would be in no danger from him. There was no room in his life for women like her—not even her blue-green eyes, her face of an angel and a body to rival that of Venus, would make him change his mind.

To hell with Grisham and his wager, he thought as he shoved open the carriage door and stepped down into the street. It was off. He could have the damned horse.

The following morning Cassandra left for Kensington, leaving Emma to spend the rest of the day with Aunt Elizabeth, who, according to Emma, was to indulge her young charge in her favourite pastime of shopping. Not having retired until the early hours, Aunt Elizabeth had not surfaced from her bed so Cassandra had to take Emma's word for this—although she had no reason to doubt what she said, for Emma spent a good deal of her time at Monkton House being pampered by Aunt Elizabeth.

When Cassandra bade her sister farewell, she thought how pale Emma looked. There was also a strange, vague look in her eyes that told Cassandra her mind was on other things. She did not pay any heed to it just then, but she would have reason to remember it later.

Cassandra and her mother had just finished their evening meal when a flustered and highly distraught Lady Monkton arrived.

'Oh, my dears, something quite dreadful has occurred—

something so dreadful I don't know how I am ever going to tell you.'

Concerned, Cassandra immediately went to her, anxiously studying the worried lines on her face. 'Dear Aunt Elizabeth,' she said, taking her hand, 'you are upset. Come and sit down.'

When her ample body was comfortably ensconced in a large winged chair, Lady Monkton snapped open her ivory fan and began to agitate the air close to her face. 'What I have to tell you will come as such a shock to you. I wonder how to break it.'

Instinct told Cassandra that her aunt's distressed state had something to do with Emma. 'It's Emma, isn't it? Tell us quickly, Aunt Elizabeth.'

'It's not good news, is it, Elizabeth?' Harriet whispered, her hand clutching the collar of her dress at her throat.

'She's—she's gone—run away—eloped—with Edward Lampard.'

'Run away?' Harriet recoiled, her voice incredulous. 'Oh, dear God.' She sat down, her colour gone, her eyes haunted.

Incensed, at first Cassandra couldn't form a coherent thought. Not until she looked up and saw her mother's pale face beneath her lace-and-ribbon cap did she collect her scattered wits.

Deeply shocked, reaching for Cassandra's hand, Harriet stared at her cousin. Her mother was a strong woman, renowned for her ability to maintain her composure even in times of stress, and through her work at the institute accustomed to hard work. Having dealt with the grief and heartache she had suffered on the death of her beloved James, she had thought she could deal with most things, but Emma's unpardonable, inconsiderate and shocking behaviour had come as a hard blow.

'Believe me when I tell you that I had no inclination she would do this,' Lady Monkton said in a broken voice, dabbing at her moist eyes with her handkerchief, 'and I am so sorry. I hold myself entirely responsible. Oh, I know she is fond of that young man—flattered by the attention he showers on her—what eighteen-year-old wouldn't be? He is handsome and exciting—first cousin to Lord William Lampard, whose lineage is impeccable. Their fathers were directly descended from one of England's oldest families, as was Lord Lampard's mother.'

'Yes—the ideal man for her to become acquainted with after she has made her début,' Harriet said quietly. 'But not at this time. I do so want her to meet other eligible young men before she settles down to marriage. Oh, the stupid girl. I knew Edward Lampard had drawn her attention, but I had no idea she had any partiality for him. Why could she not have waited? But patience never was one of Emma's good points. None of this is your fault, Elizabeth.'

'You are too kind, Harriet, but how could this have happened?' Lady Monkton wailed. 'All my hopes, all my plans—and then she elopes.' She shook her head dejectedly. 'I just can't believe it.'

'You have shown Emma nothing but kindness, doing all that could reasonably be expected of you—always steadfast and reliable. Since James died, you have been such a great comfort to me and made a real difference to all our lives—especially Emma's. For that I shall be eternally grateful. No, Elizabeth, I do not blame you—only my silly, wilful, Emma, and myself. I spend so much of my time at the institute that I failed to see what she was up to.'

'Ungrateful, foolish girl,' Cassandra retorted, seething, mentally berating her sister. 'I always said her forward behaviour would bring her grief. I knew how she felt about Edward Lampard and I tried talking to her, but where that young man is concerned she will not be reasoned with. Still, I never dreamt she would do something like this.'

'I truly believed Emma had returned home with you, Cassandra. It wasn't until one of the maids was tidying her room and came upon a note left on her dressing table that I became aware of what she had done.' Plunging her hand into her reticule, Lady Monkton produced the note.

Cassandra took it and scanned what was written in her sister's untidy handwriting. Her mind seized what Emma had done and her blood ran cold. 'She writes that she is leaving London, that she is running away with Edward Lampard. They are in love and cannot live without each other. They are to be married in Scotland.' The missive was signed with a flourishing, *Emma*.

'But where in Scotland can she have gone?' Harriet asked.

'Gretna Green, I would say,' her cousin answered, 'that is the first changing post over the border. The marriage of a minor without parental consent is illegal in England, but there is no such barrier in Scotland—and it does seem to be fashionable and romantic for young people to elope to Gretna Green at this time.'

'That young man must have arranged everything,' Harriet said. 'Emma wouldn't know how. Dear God in heaven, Cassandra! What are we to do? We must get her back before it's too late—before—before he...'

'There's only one thing we can do, Mama. I'll go and see Captain Lampard. If he knows about this, then he may already be halfway to Scotland in pursuit. My guess is that he doesn't. Edward wouldn't want him giving chase. If he decides to go after them, I'll go with him.'

Her mother was appalled. 'But—you can't go calling on a gentleman, Cassandra, and most certainly you cannot go all the way to Scotland. I forbid it.'

'Mama, this is no time to concern ourselves with such trivial matters. In this case I have no qualms about going against the rules of protocol. Emma's reputation is at stake so not a word of this must get out, otherwise she will never be able to show her face in society. Please don't worry. I'll bring her back.'

'I'll come with you,' Lady Monkton volunteered, trying to rise out of her chair. A pained expression crossed her features and her hand went to her chest. 'Oh, dear. My dyspepsia's beginning to trouble me again.'

'Please don't worry yourself,' Cassandra said, her jaw set as she stuffed Emma's note into her pocket. 'Stay and take care of Mama. I'll have a stomach powder and a glass of warm milk sent in.'

Harriet went to her daughter. 'Cassandra, when you see Captain Lampard, promise me you will watch that temper of yours. I know what you are like when roused.'

'I can't help it. I know what these hellraking lordlings can be like and I will not be patronised.'

Hurrying to her room, she quickly put some items of clothing she would need for a long journey—of short duration, she hoped—into a bag and within minutes she was in the carriage and heading for Grosvenor Square.

When Cassandra arrived outside Captain Lampard's London residence, she hardly noticed the grandeur of the house. Telling Clem to await further instructions, when she was admitted she couldn't fail to take in the breathtaking splendour.

William wasn't in the best of tempers and in no mood to be charitable or accommodating when Siddons flung open the door to the huge green-and-gold salon to announce a visitor. It was eight o'clock in the evening and Edward had been expected at the Military Academy at ten o'clock that morning, but the youth had mysteriously disappeared at nine o'clock and had not been seen since. William was at a side table, about to pour himself a calming glass of port when he was interrupted.

'I beg your pardon, my lord,' Siddons said, usually stiff and unflappable, but now looking extremely harassed, 'but this young lady insists on seeing you. I told her she would have to be announced, but she would not wait.'

With narrowed eyes, William looked beyond his butler into the stormy eyes of his uninvited visitor. 'Thank you, Siddons. It's all right. Miss Greenwood and I are acquainted, so you can leave us.'

'His lordship knows why I am here.'

'I do not recall inviting you.'

'I always was impetuous,' Cassandra retorted, striding purposefully past Siddons without taking her eyes off Captain Lampard, the man she considered to be the source of all her family's woes. His tall frame was clad in impeccably tailored light grey trousers and a white shirt and neckcloth at his throat. She didn't stop until she was just inches away.

William's eyes, glittering like hard metal, narrowed even more. At close range he saw the burning, spitting rage that fairly sizzled in her wide, clear eyes. 'Miss Greenwood,' he said when Siddons had closed the door, 'if you are here to collect the donation I promised, you are wasting your time. It was delivered to the institute first thing this morning.'

Thrown off track, Cassandra stared at him in stupefied amazement. 'Donation?' She moved a little closer. 'I did not come here for that. Do you think that's my only concern? Money?'

His lip curled derisively. 'What else? If it isn't money, then what is it that's got you all fired up and ready to explode?'

'My sister.'

'Blast your sister.'

'My sentiments entirely, Captain Lampard. She is the problem and I am having to deal with the consequences of what she and that conniving, smooth-talking cad of a cousin of yours have done.'

William could hardly believe his ears. 'What the hell are you talking about?'

'I am here to ask you why you did not heed my warning. Was it too much to ask that you take your cousin in hand and keep him away from my sister?'

Something unpleasant began to uncurl inside William. 'What are you saying?'

'Your precious cousin has run away with her. They have

eloped—gone to Scotland,' she informed him coldly, enunciating each word she uttered. 'More than likely to Gretna Green, where all young romantics flee to get married.'

William faltered. His surprise was genuine. He thought he could not have heard her correctly. 'Eloped?' His voice sharpened. 'Good God! Are you mad?'

'Mad? No, I am not mad, Captain Lampard. I am furious—as is my mother. She is quite beside herself with worry. Where is your lecherous cousin? Do you know?'

William shook his head. 'No, I confess I do not, and it is hardly my fault if your sister is too much for you to handle.' Surprise and fury made him brutal.

'Why, you conceited, unmitigated boor,' Cassandra fumed, her anger full bodied and fortifying. 'If I could stop her doing anything, I wouldn't be here.'

'And your mother, does she know you are here?'

'She knows I came here to speak to you. Since your cousin resides in your house, you are to a certain extent responsible for his actions.'

'And how do you know they have eloped? Have you proof of this?' William demanded.

'Emma left a note. Here.' She pulled the paper from her pocket and thrust it at him. 'Read it. See for yourself, and then tell me what you intend to do about it.'

Quickly William scanned the missive, which was concise and to the point, leaving him in no doubt that his cousin had indeed run off to Scotland to wed Emma Greenwood.

'The damned fool,' he growled, raking his hair back from his forehead. 'How long have they been gone?'

'Since nine o'clock this morning.'

'Eleven hours start. How are they travelling?'

'We don't know that.'

'Lady Monkton's carriage?'

'No.'

'Then they must have hired one. Knowing I would give

chase, to make good their escape, Edward will have hired a coach and four, which will mean a faster journey.'

'And frightfully expensive. No wonder only the very rich can afford to elope to Gretna Green,' Cassandra retorted drily. 'Are you going after them?'

'The young fools leave me with no choice.'

'Then you'll take me with you?'

William had turned to the door, ready to stride out to the stable yard to order his carriage to be made ready at once, but her voice halted him and he spoke quietly as he turned to answer her question. 'No. All you will be is a hindrance. I want neither you nor your company.'

Cassandra's face whitened, but she would not give way. She took a deliberate pace closer to him. 'Do you really think I will let you go alone? Do you think I would trust you to bring my sister back safely? Oh, no, I think not. For all any of us know she may have come to harm; should that be the case, then, when she is found she will have need of me.'

'I know you're upset,' William said, trying to moderate his tone to placate her, but there was a thrust to her jaw that told him she was ready to fight. She had an untamed quality running in dangerous undercurrents just beneath the surface that warned him to be wary. 'You have every right to be, but you are not going with me.'

Cassandra's chilled contempt met him face to face, and then, tossing her head, she turned from him and stalked towards the door. 'Very well. I certainly have no desire to accompany a man on a journey when he has no desire to have me along.'

William strode after her. 'Where, in heaven's name, are you going?'

'After them. I'll take Aunt Elizabeth's carriage.'

'I can appreciate your concern, but you cannot embark on this mad escapade alone.'

'Oh, no?'

His arm shot out, his fingers closing cruelly on her upper

arm, spinning her round to face him. 'You little idiot,' he seethed. 'Allow me to advise you to forget this foolish notion.'

'Advice? If I wanted advice, you would be the last person on earth I would ask,' Cassandra retorted, a flush of anger having spread over her cheeks and icy fire smouldering in the depths of her eyes. 'This is my business, as well as yours. How are you to stop me going after them? You must surely know by now that I do as I please. Now kindly release my arm before I scream the place down.'

William felt the situation slipping rapidly from his grasp. Whatever he threw at her she had an answer. Despite his intense anger—directed at her and his irresponsible cousin, and also at himself for not having heeded Miss Greenwood's warning—he did not have the mental capacity or the right to forbid her to journey to Scotland alone. Releasing her arm, he stepped back.

'You beast. How dare you lay your hands on me?' she fumed, glaring at him and rubbing her arm.

'Miss Greenwood, you are being quite unreasonable.'

'Unreasonable? Because I am worried about my sister? You, Captain Lampard, are the one who's being unreasonable.'

'If you go tearing off to Scotland, what about your institute? Are you not needed there?'

'I am always needed, but there are others to do the work in my absence.'

'Then consider the impropriety of travelling alone with me to Scotland. What will your mother have to say?'

'Mama is so upset about Emma absconding that she won't care as long as she is returned—unmarried.'

'I cannot believe that any parent in their right mind would let their daughter venture forth alone on the road to Scotland. Don't you care how much scandal it will cause?'

'My reputation is the last thing on my mind just now. I don't care that it's not the done thing for a young woman to go careering off with a single man unescorted. Nor do I care about the scandal that will be sure to ensue. Do you, Captain Lampard?'

Her question was thrown down as a challenge, one he could not ignore. For the first time he looked at what she was wearing. Attired in a sapphire-blue travelling costume and matching hat perched at a tantalising angle atop her coiffured hair, it occurred to him that she was dressed for travelling.

Cassandra watched him studying her as if seeing her for the first time. She held her breath expectantly, letting it out with relief when he put his hands up in surrender.

'Very well, we will go together. I'll order the carriage and perhaps you should call at your home to collect a few things you will need for the journey.'

'There's no need. I came prepared.'

William's eyes shot to the leather bag by the door and then back to her. For a moment he looked blank. He simply stared at her, then he shook his head as if trying to clear it. 'Why, you scheming minx!'

Planting her hands on her slim hips, calmly drumming her fingers, her smile was sublime. 'Aren't I just—I'm rebellious, too, in case you haven't noticed.'

'You knew I'd agree for you to accompany me.'

'Oh, yes, Captain Lampard. I was certain of it.'

Despite his fury, William experienced a mixture of disbelief, amusement and admiration as he gazed down at the exquisite young beauty who had skilfully managed to manipulate him into doing something he didn't want to do. He laughed out loud, the tension falling from him like a silken shroud.

'Miss Greenwood, you are incorrigible.'

'Yes, I know. Do you mind?'

He laughed some more. 'Not a bit. In fact, I suddenly find myself looking forward to our journey together. The company will be most welcome. It will be interesting to see which of us will have expired before the journey's end.'

'Oh, you never know, Captain Lampard—perhaps we'll be getting on so well by the time we reach Gretna Green, we too might recite our vows over the anvil.'

'I doubt it, Miss Greenwood. I really do.'

'So do I. Now, shall we go? I think enough time has been wasted.'

William's emotions veered from fury to mirth as he followed her out of the house, thinking Cassandra Greenwood to be the most provoking, insufferable female he had ever had the misfortune to meet. The idea of being bested by a twenty-year-old female in his own house was unthinkable and humiliating. In the course of twenty-four hours, she had gone out of her way to anger him and incur his displeasure with a rebellion and impertinence that both infuriated and exhilarated him.

She was also captivating and alluring, with the kind of face and body that stirred his blood. A reluctant smile curved his lips as his eyes focused on the impudent sway of her skirts. Despite his decision not to have anything more to do with her, her sudden appearance at his home had changed everything. She was a challenge, a challenge he couldn't resist, and the fact that she was determined to stand against him only spiced his interest.

Ensconced in Captain Lampard's sleek, well-sprung travelling coach drawn by four splendid bay horses and with two armed grooms in the driver's seat, they were soon heading up the Great North Road. Fortunately, the roads were dry and relatively quiet, so they should make good time.

'Make yourself comfortable,' William had said when he had assisted her into the spacious conveyance, the very height of luxury. 'Apart from the stops we make to change the horses, we'll travel throughout the night.'

She cast an apprehensive glance at him as he climbed in, but much to her relief he seated himself across from her. As he caught her gaze a slow smile touched his lips.

'It's safer if I sit here. I fear the nearness of you will destroy all my good intentions.'

'Then I can only hope that your good intentions will continue all the way to Scotland, Lord Lampard,' she replied archly.

Leaning back, they made themselves comfortable against the cushions. William stretched his long legs out in front of him, wondering how he was going to endure the journey. He wasn't made of stone, and the delectable young woman was so lovely she'd tempt any man who was alone with her for five minutes.

One of his legs almost touched Cassandra's own. Silently he dared his companion to object, watching her as one might observe a dew-laden flower, awed by its fragile beauty. Cassandra's dark lashes fluttered downward self-consciously as he continued to watch her, uneasy with his boldness and his close proximity in the confines of the coach. Too masculine, his potent virility made her feel entirely too vulnerable. Furtively she glanced at the offending lean and muscular limb, casually moving further into the corner to avoid contact.

Watching her from beneath lowered lids, William made no effort to move away, and grinned lazily when she spread a thick fur rug over her knees.

After they had travelled some distance in silence, the thought came to Cassandra that if she wanted to survive this journey with her sanity intact, they must have some conversation. It was dark outside and the lanterns' rays bathed the inside of the coach in a soft, golden light. She felt a sudden stillness envelope them. Vividly aware of the confined intimacy, she was overwhelmingly conscious of the man facing her.

She knew so little about Captain Lampard, only the unsavoury side to his character. As he stared intently out of the window at the starlit night, his granite face was in profile. There was indomitable pride and arrogance chiselled into his handsome face, along with intelligence and hard-bitten strength. His jaw was set in a hard line, his brow furrowed in angry preoccupation, and it suddenly occurred to her that this elopement was as much a shock to him as it was to her.

Taking a deep breath, she said, 'I'm sorry. I realise this is difficult for you, as well. I have been wondering where Emma and your cousin are just now. Do you think we will catch up with them, that we'll be in time to stop them marrying?'

Drawing the velvet curtain to shut out the night, William turned to look at her. 'Unless they meet with some mishap or decide to spend the night at a coaching inn, then I very much doubt it. Edward will know that your sister left a note telling her family what they intended, and will be afraid that I will have been made aware of that fact and will give chase—I am certain they'll go direct to Scotland.'

'Do you get on well with your cousin?'

He nodded. 'I do, but there'll be a reckoning when next we meet. I've always been too lenient with him. When his parents died it hit him hard. I don't know how he would have coped if he hadn't come to live at Carlow Park.'

'How old was he?'

'Just fourteen. Because I was away with the army a great deal, Robert, my older brother, saw to his well-being and education. Robert was killed in a riding accident two years ago.'

'I know. I'm sorry. What was he like—your brother? You—were close?'

'As close as brothers can be,' William said quietly.

Meeting his gaze, Cassandra saw the reflective, almost tender glimmer of light in his eyes.

'I was the lucky one,' he went on.

'Why do you say that?'

'Our parents loved us equally, but because Robert was the elder—the heir—he was singled out for special attention and made aware of his importance. It was hard for him. He wasn't allowed to climb trees, to take the boat out on to the lake without someone to watch over him, to realise his ambition and join the army as I did, which he would have loved to do. When our parents died and he came into his inheritance, I was away with my regiment.' The flexed muscles in his cheek gave evidence of his constrained grief. 'I was in Spain when I was notified of Robert's accident.'

'Did you come back?'

'No. I was in the thick of it at the time. I knew the estate was in good hands. Mark, my more-than-capable cousin, the son of my father's younger brother—there were three of them, Edward being the son of the youngest of the three—ran things until I resigned my commission and came back.'

He sighed, closing his eyes and resting his head back on the upholstery. 'I sometimes wonder if the very fabric of the Lampard family is not cursed. There is an unfortunate dark thread running through it, and who knows where the next tragedy will occur. My own life has been threatened, as well you know, Miss Greenwood. For what reason I still have no idea, but if whoever it was is intent on killing me, then perhaps the next time he attempts it he will succeed.'

'Please don't say that.'

He smiled a cynical smile, half opening his eyes and looking across at her. 'Why? Would you be sorry, Miss Greenwood?'

'I hate the thought of anyone being murdered—no matter who it is. You must be on your guard. Remember there are more ways to kill a man than by shooting him.'

William looked at her. 'I know.' After a moment's silence, to change the subject, he said, 'Are you and your sister close, Miss Greenwood?'

With surprise, Cassandra was conscious that he was now studying her with a different interest. 'Yes, I suppose we are—although Emma can be difficult at times. Family, especially sisters, can be complicated. Most of the time I think of Emma with exasperation. She's a trial. Papa was a quiet, hardworking, tolerant man, dedicated to his profession. When he died, Aunt Elizabeth, with no children of her own to spoil, stepped in and took us both under her wing. She is so looking forward to giving Emma a Season and will be extremely disappointed if she goes ahead with this foolish notion and weds your cousin. Both Mama and Aunt Elizabeth are devastated by their actions.'

'Then let us hope they see sense and have a change of heart.'

'In which case we should meet them on the road returning to London—although if this should get out, then the consequences for Emma will be dire indeed. In the eyes of polite society she has broken all the rules and will be shunned because of it. And then there is the delicate matter of—of...' She averted her eyes, feeling her face prickle with the heat of an intense blush. She was too embarrassed to voice what she had been about to say.

William knew exactly what was on her mind and that for her it was a delicate issue. 'Worry not, Miss Greenwood. Despite your opinion of him, my cousin has many fine attributes, one of them being that he is a gentleman. Deflowering gently reared virgins would violate Edward's code of behaviour.'

Cassandra flushed scarlet, embarrassed that he should phrase it so bluntly. 'Oh—I—I see. Then I am relieved to hear it.'

William found himself enjoying her discomfiture. 'My own code of honour is more relaxed—which you know all about.'

'Yes, so it would seem.' Looking at him, with his arms crossed imperturbably over his chest, his legs stretched out and his eyes glowing darkly in the dim light, there was something undeniably engaging about him. He made her feel alert and alive, and curiously stimulated. 'Now your military career is ended, will you take up your inheritance?'

He nodded. 'It's a pity, really. Mark would have been more suited to the inheritance than either Robert or me. He's very solemn—takes life seriously, has rigid ideas about behaviour and doesn't know how to enjoy life.'

'Does he approve of you, Captain Lampard?'

'Not a bit, but we've always rubbed along well enough. Unfortunately, he always gave credence to gossip and was too ready to believe what he heard.'

'Are you telling me you are not the libertine, the despoiler of women, you are portrayed as being?'

'No one is ever quite what they seem, Miss Greenwood. Not even you. You know,' he said, his gaze never leaving hers, 'you have a unique distinction.'

'What's that?'

'You have the distinction, apart from my mother, of being the only woman to have listed the failings of my character to my face.' His lips twitched with ill-suppressed amusement. 'When I left Lady Monkton's ball I felt wounded to the quick and deflated, as though I'd been pricked all over with thorns.'

'You have a hide thicker than an oxen's, Lord Lampard. I'm sure you'll heal.'

His amused laughter removed the sting from her words. 'Nevertheless I was curious as to how I had allowed such a feeling to come about. I find you an immense challenge.'

'You do?'

'Indeed. Aren't you afraid of being confined in this coach—alone with me all the way to Scotland?'

'Should I be?' Although she could feel her pulses racing, she somehow managed to maintain her calm expression.

He arched an eyebrow. 'No. However, considering my reputation as a scoundrel of the first order, don't you think you *should* be?'

'As you said yourself, Captain Lampard, no one is what they seem. Perhaps you are a scoundrel with a sudden urge to reform.'

A low chuckle preceded his reply. 'Heaven forbid. I confess that I find this unfortunate development a nuisance, but one good thing has come out of it.'

'Oh?'

'I get to spend time getting to know you better.'

'Why? Do you find my company pleasant?'

'When you're not being stubborn and temperamental.'

'I am never temperamental.'

'I disagree. There's no question about it.'

'Only if you drive me to it.'

'Tell me, Miss Greenwood, is there no young man in your life?'

'Of course not. I—have distinctive tastes.'

'Why of course not?' His eyes gleamed with devilish humour. 'A lovely young woman like you should be surrounded by doting swains.'

Cassandra was glad the light was so dim inside the coach that he couldn't see the blush that infused her cheeks and neck. 'I have my work at the institute, which is important to me. I will allow nothing to interfere with that.'

'Not even love,' he murmured softly, his gaze capturing hers.

'No.'

'Are you scared of love, Miss Greenwood?'

'No, I am not.'

'I don't believe you.'

'Believe what you like. It's true,' she retorted, feeling as if she were under attack.

'Then if you are not afraid of love, why do you hide behind your children and your institute?'

'I am not hiding and they are not my children. The institute is not mine, either.'

'Now you're prevaricating, Miss Greenwood. I think if you didn't have to mix with the *ton* in order to raise funds for your precious institute, you would be quite happy to make yourself invisible—to fade away into obscurity.' He smiled at her sudden look of indignation that his words had provoked. 'I apologise if my opinion is unkind—which is no more unkind than when you listed some of my shortcomings to me last night—but you must admit that it does have the ring of truth about it.'

'Whether it is true or not, I would not admit such a thing to you. I am not afraid of love, it's just that I have no experience of the kind of love you speak of and, at present, I am not interested in that sort of thing.'

'Then as a woman you are truly unique.'

Cassandra looked at him warily. 'You are not trying to seduce me, are you, Captain Lampard?'

'Would you allow me to seduce you, Miss Greenwood?'

In spite of the fact that his eyes were touching her like she had never been touched before, Cassandra gave him a defiant look. 'Now you're mocking me.'

'I wouldn't dream of doing that. You're far too adorable to mock.'

How could she be angry with him when he smiled that engaging smile? It was no longer possible. Her lips curved in a smile of her own. 'And you really are a complete rogue, Captain Lampard, arrogant and overbearing.'

He grinned. 'I am. I admit it. What I need is a lovely, patient and extremely tolerant young woman to take me in hand, to make me see the error of my ways and reform me.'

'Then I wish you luck. Intolerance and impatience have always been two of my failings, but there must be a female somewhere who will fall for a silken tongue and an accomplished womaniser, who will be willing to expend so much energy, time and effort on such an unenviable task.'

'Aye, but she will never be bored, I promise you that.'

Reaching up, Cassandra removed her hat and placed it on the seat beside her. 'How conceited you are, Captain Lampard. You rate yourself too highly. Now, if you don't mind, I'm going to shut my eyes and try to get some sleep.'

Resting her head against a cushion, she closed her eyes, thinking of the strange, easy conversation she had engaged in with her companion. Had she been too ready to judge, to believe the gossip she'd heard about him? Was he so different from what she had assumed? For the short time she had known him, she decided that none of it described him or did him justice. There was a powerful charisma about him that had nothing to do with his powerful physique or mocking smile.

There was something else, too, something behind that lazy smile and unbreachable wall of aloof strength, behind his piercing blue eyes, that told her that Captain William Lampard had done, seen and experienced all there was to do and see, that to know him properly would be exciting and dangerous, and therein lay his appeal—an appeal that frightened and unnerved her. She told herself that he was nothing to her, just a spectacularly handsome man who happened to be helping her solve a family crisis; as soon as this business with Emma was resolved, she decided that any association between her and this infamous captain would cease.

Eventually the gentle rocking motion of the coach, combined with the warmth, made her drowsy and she drifted into sleep. The night was hushed and still around them, the only sounds being the hoofbeats and the creaking of the coach as it progressed north.

William crossed his legs and looked over at the sleeping young woman. What a glorious creature she was. Her lips were moist and parted slightly, the thick crescent of her lashes sweeping her cheeks. He watched the slow rise and fall of her chest. Attired in her conservative travelling costume, the thought of all her soft, warm flesh beneath was causing his imagination to run wild.

Something in his heart moved and softened, then something stabbed him in the centre of his chest. What the hell was wrong with him? He had been angry and offended by her antagonistic manner at the ball, and at the same time overwhelmed by the realisation that if he didn't take care, she would come to mean something to him, and he wasn't ready for that. Miss Greenwood was an unusual female, intelligent, opinionated and full of surprises. She was also the epitome of stubborn, prideful woman. Yet for all her fire and spirit, there was no underlying viciousness. She was so very different from the sophisticated, worldly women he took to bed—experienced, sensual women, knowledgeable in the ways of love, women who knew how to please him.

No, Miss Greenwood was different, a phenomenon. She

had a touching belief in her cause. He sensed a goodness in her, something special, sensitive—something worth pursuing. There was also something untapped inside her that not even she was aware of—passion buried deep. What would happen if she allowed it all to come out? In sleep she looked like a child. He was dangerously fascinated by this vulnerable side to Miss Greenwood, he realised, and settled down to observe her sleeping profile. Nothing made sense, for nothing could explain why he was beginning to enjoy being alone with her.

Chapter Four

When Cassandra stirred and opened her eyes, dawn was breaking. Stretching her aching body and covering a yawn with the back of her hand, she glanced at her companion, who was now seated beside her. Apart from having removed his jacket and loosened his neckcloth, he looked exactly as he had when she had gone to sleep, watching her. Not all night, she hoped, and why had he changed his seat? There was a quiet alertness in his manner and his gaze was fixed warmly on her face. Self-consciously she tucked a stray silken lock of curling hair behind her ear.

'Do you feel rested? You've slept most of the night.'

Cassandra started at the sound of his deep voice. 'I do. Where are we?'

'Cambridgeshire.'

She sighed and made to move away from him, but his arm reached out and drew her to him and he smiled lazily.

'What are you doing?' she gasped, trying to pull away, but he held her firm against him. 'Have you been sitting there all night?'

He nodded with infuriating calm. 'You looked uncomfortable and your head was lolling about all over the place. You slept much better with it resting on my shoulder.'

A blush stained her cheeks, partly from indignation and partly from embarrassment. 'Oh, you really are quite insufferable. How dare you take liberties when I was asleep? Please remove your arm and allow me to sit up. I don't like being mauled.'

William's mouth curved in that faint, cynical smile of his and he kept his arm where it was. He liked the feel of her in his arms. 'Why are you so stubborn?' Tipping her chin up with his finger, he looked deep into her eyes. 'When a woman is willing to risk herself alone in my company, she has to expect certain consequences. I think it is time I adopted a different approach through the thick mire of our disagreement. It's time I tried a little persuasion of a different kind.' His eyes pinned hers and held them.

'Persuasion?' she asked, helplessly staring at him, heat running down her spine and her heart taking chaotic flight.

William noted the pulse beating in the long curve of her throat before his gaze settled on her lips. Placing his hands on her upper arms, he pulled her hard against his chest, his hands gentle and controlled, yet unyielding.

Cassandra had no time to protest before he lowered his mouth and took her lips with a gentle expertise that made her gasp. Stunned into silent quiescence, at first she froze at the initial shock of the contact, then a sense of wonder stirred within her subconscious mind, rousing her to a dazzling awareness of what he was doing to her. The assault on her senses was immediate and immense as she caught the clean, masculine scent of him, the feel of him, the taste of him. Often she had dreamed of such a kiss, but the experience of it made those insubstantial dreams seem like shadows.

Temporarily divested of the anger that had fortified her earlier, her body lost its resistance and relaxed. Sliding her hands up over his chest to his shoulders, feeling his body's heat and vibrancy through his clothes, she unwittingly moulded her melting body to his. He kissed her long and lin-geringly, a compelling kiss, his lips moving back and forth, exploring with slow, searching intensity, gentling imperceptibly, and beneath the demanding persuasion was an insistence that she kiss him back that was almost beyond denial, and a promise that if she yielded it would become something quite different.

Any warning that her mind issued was stifled by the blood pounding in her ears and the shocking pleasure of being held in the arms of the man whom she had decided she would not allow to breach her self-control. His arm tightened, forcing her closer, while a large masculine hand curved round her nape, long fingers caressing and soothing her flesh.

William was both surprised and devastated by her response to his kiss, and when she began to kiss him back with more ardour than he had expected, her tongue became a flicking firebrand as his mouth consumed hers. With desire surging through him and pounding in his loins, he had to fight back the urge to lay her down on the seat and take there and then. Dragging his lips from hers, he gazed down at her upturned face. She was wide-eyed, vulnerable and trembling, her face flushed a glorious pink, and her lips moist and parted.

He lightly traced the curve of her cheek with his forefinger, admiring her freshness, her spirit, her innocence. She was everything he had known she would be, and much more. He was astounded to discover he wanted her with a fierceness that took his breath away, and he was impatient to waken all the passion in her lovely, untutored body.

'Do I see in your warming behaviour, in your response to my kiss, some glimmer of hope for a much more pleasurable understanding between us in the future? And do not deny what you feel, because I will not believe you.'

'It is possible,' Cassandra murmured, basking in the warmth of his smouldering gaze and the lazy smile that curved the firm sensual mouth, which had gently, then fiercely, explored hers. Unsteadily, she fixed her gaze on his mouth, not comprehending why he had broken off their kiss.

Tipping her chin up, he looked deeply into her eyes and quietly said, 'What do you think of my method of persuasion?'

Cassandra drew a long, steadying breath and slowly expelled it. She hesitated before answering, her magnificent eyes searching deeply into his. 'In truth, I do not trust my heart and mind to withstand the barrage of your persuasion.' Her feelings were nebulous, chaotic, yet one stood out clearly among all the others—desire. She had not wanted him to stop kissing her, and she was impatient for him to repeat the act. Something had happened to her while she had been in his arms, something quite splendid, daunting and exciting.

William glanced out of the window and released her. 'I'm happy to hear that, but we'll have to discontinue our amorous interlude. We're about to stop for breakfast.'

The coach was passing through the tall gates of a substantial coaching inn.

'I thought we'd stretch our legs and get some breakfast while the horses are being changed. However, time is precious. I don't want to waste one minute of it.'

Reaching for his jacket, he shrugged it on and solicitously helped her to alight from the coach. Aching in every limb and still in a state of shock about what had just happened, telling herself that she should have slapped his face, Cassandra disappeared to attend to her personal needs and to collect her scattered wits, while William stopped to issue instructions to the grooms.

Passing through a covered doorway, they entered the inn together. The general air was one of comfort and respectability. The stout landlord greeted them. Seeing the young couple were people of quality, he led them through the common room where several patrons were already eating breakfast, and ushered them into a low-beamed dining parlour, which provided a semblance of privacy.

The acrid odour of ale and the appetising aroma of hot food pervaded every corner and started Cassandra's mouth watering. Settling themselves at a table in a window recess, William stressed to the landlord their need for haste, and in no time at all, Annie, the landlord's plump and cheerful spouse in a starched cap and smelling of freshly baked bread, laid out a sumptuous breakfast in front of them.

Cassandra's stomach groaned for sustenance, and without wasting time she began to do the food justice.

'You're hungry,' William remarked, watching her with an amused gleam in his eyes as she munched on a piece of bacon.

'Ravenous, and this bacon is simply done to a turn. It's delicious,' she said, piercing a steamed mushroom. She paused just long enough to take a gulp of her coffee and glanced across at him to see that he was consuming his food more leisurely, savouring each taste fully. 'You really should eat plenty. Mama always says you should eat a hearty breakfast to start the day. She always says we do not eat to satisfy our appetite. Food is strength.'

'Wise woman, your mama.'

'So you must have something inside you to fortify you on the journey, Captain Lampard.'

'William.'

She stared at him. 'I'm sorry?'

'I would like you to call me William. I have left the army. My title is Lord Lampard—but I would like it if you would call me William.'

'I do not think that would be appropriate—in fact, it would be highly irregular—but Captain Lampard is such a mouthful.'

'There you are, then. You have my permission to call me William.'

'That is generous of you.'

'I have my good points.'

'I agree,' she said, laughing softly. 'Why—even scoundrels must have some somewhere.'

'Then I have managed to vindicate myself to you—just a little?'

'Yes—a little. Despite your earlier transgression—you know, kissing aside—so far you have been most courteous.'

'I do my best. And you will call me William?'

'Well, as you are already aware that I am the unconventional type, very well—William.'

A tremor ran through him when she spoke his name for the first time. 'That's better. Are you going to grant me permission in turn to use your Christian name?'

She shrugged. What did it matter what he called her since she had resolved never to see him again after this unpleasant business was done with—although his earlier assault on her lips almost made her wish he would do it again. 'I have a feeling that if I don't, you will use it anyway.'

'I take it that's a yes.'

She nodded, taking a bite out of her bread.

'Thank you—Cassandra. Now that is out of the way, enjoy your breakfast.'

'I intend to, even though you're thinking that I really ought to be worrying about getting to Scotland post haste and not stuffing myself with eggs and bacon.'

He smiled that slow smile of his, calmly slicing through his egg. 'Not at all. I'm glad you can live for the moment.'

'You mean I should not think of what will happen?' She sighed. 'Unfortunately, I do worry. Quite frankly, I find it depressing to contemplate all the fuss there will be when we do catch up with the runaways. If they are already married, then the scandal that will ensue when we all get back to London will be horrendous.'

'It can do no good worrying, so eat your breakfast.'

At that moment the landlord brought in a pot of fresh coffee and placed it on the table. 'Is everything to your liking?'

'It is. Thank you, landlord,' William answered.

'You and your lady wife are out and about early, sir,' the landlord said by way of conversation—as well as being inquisitive. 'Travelling far, are you?'

'Some considerable distance, yes. It's been a long night, landlord, and my *wife* and I would like to partake of this excellent breakfast and be on our way. Will you excuse us?'

'Of course, sir,' the landlord said in a flat tone, backing towards the door. 'Didn't mean to impose. Enjoy your breakfast.'

When he had closed the door, with a mischievous smile tugging at his lips and one eyebrow cocked, William looked at Cassandra, who was staring at him accusingly.

'You really are the limit,' she gasped, unable to believe what had just happened. 'I gave you freedom with my name, but now I think you are again taking liberties. You let that man think I am your wife.'

William shrugged indolently. 'Merely to quell the gossip. Consider the situation as it will look to him—a young woman travelling with a man unaccompanied. If you are not my wife, then in his eyes that makes you my mistress.'

Her eyes opened wide. 'Mistress? I will be no man's mistress.'

'Which is why I told him you are my wife—to avoid any embarrassing speculation, you understand.' He reached for the coffee pot. 'More coffee?' he offered with a lazy grin.

Meeting his clear blue eyes with their wicked sparkle, unable to keep a straight face Cassandra laughed and shoved her cup forward. 'I am quite overwhelmed by your consideration and, yes, thank you, I would like some more coffee.'

Eager to be on their way, with fresh horses harnessed to the coach, the two grooms replete after a hearty breakfast, William and Cassandra were about to leave the inn when a soberly dressed gentleman carrying a small brown leather bag came hurrying in, almost knocking Cassandra over in his haste. Immediately he reached out to steady her, apologising profusely for his clumsiness and hoping she was not harmed in any way. Cassandra laughed it off and assured him she was quite all right. At that moment the landlord appeared out of the common room and hurried over to the stranger, seeming relieved to see him. William took Cassandra's arm and they proceeded towards the door.

'Thank the Lord you're here, Dr Wade. I apologise for having to send for you, but the young lady's still very poorly. Her companion is beside himself. 'Tis to be hoped it's not infectious,' he said, shaking his head solemnly. 'Bad for business that would be.'

'I'll go straight up. Runaways, you say?'

'Aye, it appears so—not that they've said as much, but my Annie has a nose for these things. Arrived late last night.'

Having listened with little interest to the interchange between the landlord and Dr Wade, upon hearing the word 'runaways', William paused, suddenly alert, and turned back to them as they were about to climb the stairs.

'Wait!' he called, striding towards them.

The two men turned and looked down at him.

'There are a couple of runaways staying here?'

'Aye, there are,' the landlord replied. 'What of it?'

'What are their names?'

The landlord rubbed his chin. 'Well, now, I'm not sure—'

'It's all right landlord,' a quiet voice said from the top of the stairs. 'I'll speak to the gentleman.' The young man who suddenly appeared looked at Dr Wade. 'You must be the doctor. Please go and tend the young lady. She really is quite ill. I would be grateful if you could give her some medicine to make her feel better.'

As the doctor went to tend his patient with the landlord to show him the way, the man came slowly down the stairs. His attractive face was grey and drawn, his eyes shadowed with fatigue. Not until he stood in front of William did he speak.

'Hello, William. I knew you'd come.'

William's face darkened for an instant as he strove for control. 'Well, Edward,' he said, his voice coated with ice, 'what the hell do you think you're playing at?'

* * *

Noticing they were attracting curious glances from the other patrons, William requested a private room. The landlord immediately put one at their disposal.

When the door was closed, concern for her sister propelled Cassandra to Edward's side. 'Is it Emma who is ill?' she asked, deeply concerned that this was indeed so.

Edward nodded. 'She began feeling unwell shortly after we left London.'

'Then why on earth didn't you take her home? What could have possessed you to embark on this mad escapade when she was feeling unwell?'

'I wanted to go back, but Emma wouldn't hear of it. She said it was nothing more than a chill, that she would soon feel better and that we should go on to Scotland.'

Cassandra drew back angrily. 'Shame on you that you think to place all the blame on my sister. You knew perfectly well what you were doing when you arranged this elopement. The two of you have been alone together for twenty-four hours—spending the night with her in a sordid tavern room as if she were some common drab,' she fumed contemptuously. 'Are you like the rest of London's young rakes—play with women, make them fall in love with you, seduce them, and then tell them you have no need of them?'

Deeply offended, Edward's eyes flamed with anger. 'First, I am no rake, Miss Greenwood. I honour your sister and I would not lay one finger on her until she is my wife.'

'Wife? Ha! Any aspirations you might have to make her your wife you forfeited the moment you absconded with her.'

'Cassandra, enough,' William said quietly but firmly, taking her arm and drawing her to one side.

Furious, she shook her arm free. 'Enough, you say. That silly, impressionable girl, who is my sister, was so flattered by your cousin's attentions that she would foolishly allow him to talk her into anything. How do we know he hasn't seduced her already? His treatment of her has been abominable to say the least.'

'Stop it, Cassandra,' William said sharply. 'Calm down. I will listen to what Edward has to say while you go and see your sister.'

She glared at him. 'Since it is my sister he abducted, then I will stay to hear what he has to say. I shall go and see Emma when the doctor has examined her.'

William nodded. 'Very well, if you must, but please sit down and be quiet.'

As she perched on the edge of a chair, Cassandra's heart was beating in rhythmic thuds, but, difficult as it was to remain silent, she did as she was told and did not speak. William stood with his back to the fire, tall and impressive in his dark green cutaway coat and highly polished brown boots. He did not look like a man who had been travelling all night. His immaculate appearance made his cousin's dishevelled state more obvious. Edward's coat was unbuttoned, revealing a pale grey satin waistcoat. Though elegant, the clothes looked as though he had been wearing them a couple of days, and his white neckcloth was loose and rumpled.

As William's cold eyes flickered over him, Edward attempted to straighten his neck-linen. Knowing William's set-downs were lethal, he was filled with dread as he waited for his blistering tirade to begin, but all he could think of was his dear, sweet Emma lying ill in bed.

'I hope you'll pardon my appearance, William,' Edward said. 'With Emma being so unwell, I've been up all night.'

William nodded grimly. 'So have we, thanks to you. Well? What have you to say for yourself?'

Edward flinched before his cousin's controlled rage. He was ensnared in the web of his own folly, he knew that.

'You've been a fool, Edward, a stupid, self-indulgent bloody fool,' William went on furiously without giving Edward time to reply. 'I am disappointed in you—deeply disappointed. What in God's name made you do it? You have known Miss Greenwood—a well brought-up and guarded young girl—for such a short time.'

'Three months. I was drawn to her from the start, and in the time I have known her I have come to hold her in high esteem,' Edward said, doing his best to smile in an attempt to lighten the serious tones and harsh lines of his cousin's face. 'I did try to stay away from her, but fate intervened and kept throwing us together.'

William gave a brief, humourless snort. 'So, your ardour ran away with you and you began to woo her, beginning the pattern, the customs that a gentleman pursues with the lady of his choice, which eventually leads to marriage,' he rapped out, walking up and down the room in earnest frustration.

Edward swallowed hard and stepped back from the furious blast of those steely blue eyes. 'Yes—something like that.'

'What a load of mawkish rubbish. You must have been off your head. Did you not consider the young lady's age when you began trailing after her petticoats like some lovesick calf? For God's sake, Edward, she is just eighteen years old—seventeen when you first knew her—still a child in some people's thinking.'

'I know, but it made no difference to the way we felt about each other. We decided we wanted to be together, and, knowing both our families would be set against it—'

'Damned right we would,' William growled, his gaze relentless.

'We decided to elope—to bring forward what is inevitable.'

'And what about your army career? Did you not concern yourself with that when you were making declarations of love to Miss Greenwood and preparing to elope?'

Lowering his head in contrition, Edward said in a low voice, 'I didn't think it would matter if I put my career on hold for a while. I've done wrong, I know that, and I would like to put it right—so far as I can.' Raising his head, he directed his gaze at Cassandra. 'When we arrived at the tavern last night,

Emma was so sick and frightened, and there was nothing I could do to help her. I apologise most sincerely for any hurt I have caused you and your family, Miss Greenwood. For what satisfaction you may want of me later, I will bide by it. But I would ask you to let it wait until Emma is feeling well.'

Cassandra rose. 'Yes, you are right. Emma must be our main concern.'

'Wh-what is to be done, sir?' Edward asked his cousin haltingly.

'I have decided that you will leave for the army immediately when we return to London,' William informed him, turning his back and looking out of the window. 'It is where you should have been yesterday. There will be no further discussion on the subject. You will remain with your regiment until it is time for it to leave the country. To spare Miss Greenwood's reputation it is imperative that we avoid a scandal. I insist that we keep this unpleasant business between ourselves, and in this you will assist us by maintaining a discreet silence. You will have no further contact with Miss Greenwood. Is that understood?'

Edward stepped forward in alarm. 'But, William—you can't do this. I beg you to hear me out...'

William spun round. 'I can and I will, Edward. Until you are both of age and until her mother gives her consent, you will sever all ties. Finally, I expect your total cooperation. Do you agree?'

Edward capitulated before the seniority and the wrath of his cousin. 'Yes, sir.'

As he shoved his fair hair off his brow, Cassandra saw that his hand was trembling, his face set pale with deep emotion. Strangely, her heart welled with pity. He was crushed by the wave of events that had overtaken him. There was moisture in his eyes and he blinked rapidly, leaving her in no doubt of this young man's tender feelings and deep concern for Emma. The truth was, she had disparaged him because she did not want Emma to form an attachment to any man before she had made her début, and her sceptical attitude, once adopted, had stuck.

The anger that had consumed her from the moment she had learned of the elopement evaporated, along with her belief that Edward Lampard was anything like his cousin William, and nor would he be if he lived to be a hundred.

Cassandra was startled by Emma's condition. Nothing more than a severe chill, Dr Wade had said, and in his opinion it was safe to take her home. In Cassandra's opinion, she though her sister was extremely ill. Her cheeks were flushed, her skin beaded with perspiration. Resting against the pillows with her eyes closed, she looked so very young and vulnerable. Cassandra's heart went out to her.

Sitting on the bed, she took her hand. Emma opened her eyes. They were very bright and feverish, and there was a desperate look about her. Emma started when she saw her sister.

'It's all right, Emma,' Cassandra was quick to reassure her. 'Please don't upset yourself.'

Tears formed in Emma's eyes. 'Are you very angry with me, Cassy?' she whispered with difficulty. 'I know I must have put you to so much trouble. I am so sorry.'

'I'm not angry, although you do seem to have got yourself into something of a pickle. What you and Edward have done is very foolish, but at this moment all I am concerned about is you.'

'Poor Edward. Is he all right?' No longer able to hold her tears at bay, she began to weep.

'Yes, though he's worried about you.'

'I—I've been at my wit's end all night and I feel so poorly. Please be kind to him, Cassy.'

'Shush, not now, Emma.' Cassandra held her sister's feverish hand until her sobs subsided and she slept.

Getting up, she quietly left the room. William was waiting for her at the bottom of the stairs. His face was strained, as if he had been waiting for her in wretched suspension.

'How is she?' he asked. His voice was surprisingly gentle.

'Very ill indeed.' Suddenly feeling tired, she bent her head, putting the back of her hand to her eyes. 'I'm sorry, but I am so worried about her.' William's eyes were warm with concern—not for her, she knew that, but for her sister.

'That is completely understandable in these circumstances. You are upset. What can I do to help?' His offer was made in a tone of gentle commiseration.

Cassandra lifted her head, her eyes searching his. 'She can't stay here. I have to get her home where she can be properly looked after. Can it be done?'

He nodded. 'I don't see why not. The landlord isn't happy about her being here. Doctor Wade has stressed she has nothing infectious, but the landlord thinks a sick woman on the premises will put travellers off staying here.'

'Poor Emma. She was terribly glad to see me. She was so upset that I hadn't the heart to berate her.'

William's brow arched and he smiled. 'You are a very understanding woman.'

Cassandra was warmed by his smile and his solicitude. 'My sister is often of a different opinion.'

'Siblings usually are. We shall leave right away. You and your sister must travel in my coach—you will be more comfortable. I will accompany Edward. Get her dressed. I'll settle the account with the landlord and make sure the coaches are made ready to leave.'

'Where's Edward?'

William's eyes went to the closed door to the private room. 'Shall I go and tell him how Emma is?'

'No. Leave him,' William said curtly. 'Our main concern is to get your sister into the coach and be on our way.'

'Will—will you come up in a few minutes? Emma is terribly weak and she may need helping down the stairs. I'd be most grateful.'

William nodded, his expression grim. Turning from her, he strode out of the inn.

* * *

When he knocked on the door to Emma's room fifteen minutes later and entered, it was to find Cassandra struggling to get her sister into her coat. The girl was sitting on the bed, swaying as she tried to keep awake.

Cassandra shot him a beseeching, apologetic look. 'We're almost ready.'

When Emma tried to stand, in her weakened state she flopped back on to the bed. All the life seemed to have drained out of her, leaving her like a mechanical toy.

'Here, let me.' Without more ado, William strode to the bed and lifted her into his arms—so easy and quick. The weight that Cassandra had scarcely been able to move was casually carried across the room. 'Bring her things. I'll carry her out to the coach.'

Hastily gathering together Emma's few possessions, Cassandra followed him out of the inn.

After easing his burden into the coach, William turned to Cassandra. 'I believe your sister will be more comfortable with the cushions placed round her. I would advise you to sit beside her to prevent her rolling around. The day's warm enough, but wrap her in the blankets. Have you got everything?'

'Yes—I think so. Oh, I do hope she's going to be all right. We have such a long way to travel.'

'Don't worry. We'll drive the horses into the ground if need be. She'll be home and tucked up in her own bed in no time. We'll be travelling behind, so if you have to stop we'll know.'

As she was about to climb inside the coach, Cassandra hesitated and looked to where Edward was standing, observing the proceedings. He was motionless save for the steady movements of his breathing. His ashen face was a solemn, sad mask, his heart in his anguished eyes as, shoulders slumped with dejection, he turned and climbed into the other coach.

William watched Cassandra shake out a rug and tuck it around her sister. 'Will you be all right?' She nodded and in

her face he saw grim resolution. 'Good girl. Order the coach
to stop if you must. We'll be close behind.'

The driver whipped up the horses and the carriage sped
and rocked along the main highway, passing slower convey-
ances. Cassandra did as William had suggested and sat
beside Emma and with infinite tenderness held her slender
body, which trembled against her own steady one as Emma
slept fitfully. Her concern for her sister deepened when
Emma began to mumble incoherently, but after a while it
was as if the effort of speaking weakened her and her head
fell sideways and her voice suddenly disappeared. She began
to tremble, which increased, and her teeth began chattering
violently.

Tucking another rug about her, Cassandra knew Emma
was getting worse. She felt a wave of desperation as she strove
for control and to calm her mounting fears. Nevertheless,
panic lashed at her; worried to death, she ordered the coach
driver to stop. The accompanying groom jumped down and
lowered the steps. William's coach halted behind.

Jumping to the ground William strode towards her, taking
her hand and drawing her close, his handsome face set in
anxious lines. 'What is it?'

'Emma is much worse. She's delirious and all of a-tremble.
We really must get her into a bed   anywhere.' She sighed,
trying to keep her voice level, but William heard the quiver
in its depths. 'I'm sorry. You must think I'm mad worrying
like this.' William smiled almost…affectionate, she thought.

'I think you're doing splendidly.' William gazed at her
strained features and felt a resurgence of the peculiar tenderness she sometimes seemed to evoke in him. 'It's inevitable
that the strain of the past twenty-four hours is beginning to get
to you, but I am certain your sister will be fine.'

'Please, William, London is hours away. Do you think we
could find somewhere?'

William drew in a breath, his eyes meeting hers. After a

moment of thoughtful silence, he nodded. 'I know the very place. We'll be there shortly.'

Glad of his strength and reassurance that everything would be fine, Cassandra seized on that and clung to it for all the comfort it offered. Returning to the carriage, she felt enormous relief from knowing William was close. She remembered the moment when he had taken her hand, as if he hadn't been aware that he had done so. Her gaze had been drawn to it. There was something so masculine in the strength of that hand and the long fingers that made her heartbeat quicken at the memory. She sighed, gazing out of the window as villages, scattered cottages and a patchwork of fields flew past, realising that there were times when William Lampard was far too attractive for her peace of mind.

After travelling a few more miles they turned off the main thoroughfare into narrower, twisting lanes. Cassandra had no idea where they were going and she didn't care. She could only hope, when she looked at Emma lolling in the corner of the coach, that they got there quickly.

As her eyes searched ahead she was disheartened. There was nothing but parkland with browsing deer that seemed to go on for ever. A long avenue lined with tall trees led away round a bend and crossed a humpbacked bridge. After passing through some high gilded gates, she saw it—a house, old and imposing and of honey-coloured brick, with many windows, long and gleaming, unlike any she had ever seen before.

When the coach drew up at the bottom of a flight of steps leading up to the front door, she was aware of people— servants, male and female—coming out of the house and throwing up their arms in alarm.

Standing in the drive, Cassandra was awestruck as she looked at William striding towards her. 'William—who does this house belong to?'

'Me. Welcome to Carlow Park. Now, let's get your sister inside.'

Seemingly indifferent to the panic taking place on the steps, immediately he took charge of Emma. Gathering her into his arms, he went up the steps and into the house. Cassandra was behind him, her whole being concentrated on her sister.

Striding past the thunderstruck servants, who were speechless with shock at the sight of their master with a drooping young lady in his arms, his eyes lighted on an officious-looking woman dressed in black.

'Mrs Henderson, is there a room prepared?'

'Welcome home, my lord—and yes, the green room is always made ready for the unexpected guest.' Totally unprepared, Mrs Henderson, the housekeeper, was not at all pleased with his lordship's unexpected arrival after two years' absence. Her eyes glanced curiously from the unconscious young woman in his arms, to the young woman looking on anxiously and back to Lord Lampard.

'Thank you. Get someone to fetch Dr Tomlinson at once. They are to tell him it's urgent.'

Effortlessly climbing the stairs and walking along thickly carpeted landings hung with family portraits, he eventually shoved a door open to what Cassandra assumed must be the green room, and went inside. With infinite care he laid his burden on the bed and stood back to let Cassandra take over.

'I'll get her undressed and into bed,' she said, beginning to unfasten Emma's coat.

'I'll send one of the maids in to give you a hand.' He strode to the door.

Cassandra paused and looked at him. 'William.' He turned. 'Thank you. I really am grateful to you for letting us come here.'

'My pleasure. It was fortunate that Carlow Park was so close. And don't worry. The doctor will be here shortly.'

Half an hour later, having got Emma undressed and into bed with the help of an obliging maid called Molly, Mrs Henderson ushered Dr Tomlinson into the room.

Doctor Tomlinson confirmed what Dr Wade had said, that Emma had a severe chill. When the crisis was past he was sure the chill would leave no ill effects. He departed, ensuring she had a cordial to drink and prescribing mustard plasters, rest and warmth.

Having spent the time he had been back at Carlow Park settling in and familiarising himself with the order of things, William went to see Cassandra later that evening and to enquire after her sister. He'd hoped Cassandra would have left Emma in the care of one of the maids and joined him and a subdued Edward for dinner, but she had declined and dined in her room.

When he knocked she opened the door. He hesitated and stared at her. Her face glowed pale in the dim light. Seeing her unbound, honey-gold hair falling in a gentle cascade over her shoulders, he drew in a quick breath. For the space of half a dozen heartbeats he didn't move. Then slowly he smiled.

'I've come to enquire after your sister,' he said softly. 'May I come in? I am aware of the impropriety of such a visit, but these are hardly normal circumstances. I thought you might like some company.' Cassandra returned his gaze, wide-eyed and uncertain, then, opening the door wider, she invited him inside. 'How is she?' His eyes were drawn to the young woman in bed, but they did not linger. They preferred to dwell on the older sister.

'She is easier—slips in and out of sleep, but she's cooler and no longer delirious. I think she's over the worst of it.'

'I'm glad to hear it. Have you everything you need?' he asked, moving away from the bed to the fire so as not to disturb Emma.

'Yes. Everyone has been most kind. I can't thank them enough.' Cassandra stared at him, standing with his back to the fire, and she experienced such a rush of excitement it caused her to become tongue-tied. She was affected strongly by the force of his presence and the memory of his kiss and, studying him, was all too aware of the strength of his attraction. Overcome by tiredness, she sat in the chair she had been occupying when she'd heard his knock.

William was standing over her, looking down at her with concern. There were dark shadows beneath her eyes and she was pale. She had become soft and quiet in her distress for her sister. It was hard to believe that this was the same rebellious spitfire who had confronted him so courageously at his London residence.

'How are you, Cassandra?' he asked quietly.

The gentleness and warmth in his tone brought the heat creeping into her cheeks. 'Me? I'm all right.' She smiled tiredly. 'It's been quite a day.'

'You really must try and get some rest. A room has been made ready. One of the maids can sit with your sister.'

She shook her head. 'No. I would not consider it. Emma is my responsibility. If I'd spent more time with her, watching over her, perhaps we wouldn't be in this mess.'

'You shouldn't blame yourself. None of this is your fault. You are not your sister's keeper, Cassandra. She does have your mother and Lady Monkton.'

'Since Papa died, Mama spends a good deal of her time at the institute. Emma spends most of her time at Monkton House, but even Aunt Elizabeth would never have expected her to do something so stupid as to elope.'

William nodded towards the inviting green-silk winged chair positioned across from her own. 'Do you mind?'

She shook her head. 'Not at all.' Resting against the back of the chair, she half-closed her eyes. 'Please sit down, William. You must be feeling as exhausted as I do.'

He sat down, stretching his long muscular legs out in front of him and crossing them at the ankles.

The atmosphere was relaxed between them. There was silence inhabited by the living presence of the fire. In spite of herself, Cassandra found her eyes captured and held by William's dark blue ones. With his brown hair curling softly into his neck, the same magnetism she had seen before was in his eyes. The room seemed to come to life with his presence, infusing it with his own energy and vigour.

'Are you glad to be home?' she asked.

'I am, but I've been away a long time. It takes some getting used to.' He smiled and there was a suggestion of mischief in his eyes. 'My untimely arrival with two lovely ladies has set the house in turmoil and certainly given the servants something to gossip about.' He laughed softly. 'No doubt my return to Carlow Park with two female companions will spread through Hertfordshire like a wind through a hayfield.'

Cassandra was suddenly alarmed. 'I sincerely hope not. Emma's reputation is already teetering on the edge. I was hoping we could return to London with no one any the wiser.'

'Then allow me to allay your fears. Sticking close to the truth, I have told Pearson, my butler, and Mrs Henderson that I encountered you and your sister on the road and that you were travelling to London. When your sister became ill you sought rooms at a coaching inn, but the landlord was reluctant to accommodate you. I offered you my assistance.' His eyes glowed in the warm light of the fire as he gave her a lazy smile. 'I only did what any self-respecting gentleman would have done in such circumstances.'

'Thank you. You seem to have thought of everything.'

Silence reigned once more as they stared intently into the glowing heart of the fire, and then they looked at each other. Drawn by the depths of her eyes looking into his and by the soft freshness of her lips, William contemplated her for a moment.

Cassandra sat, riveted by the warm gaze. She had a strange idea that if she moved or spoke the rare moment would be broken and something precious lost. In the end it was William who sighed and spoke first.

'Tell me about your father,' he said, reluctant to leave her just yet. 'He must have been a remarkable man.'

'Yes, he was. I always looked up to him and admired him greatly for all he achieved. His death came as a terrible blow to us all. The institute was very important to him—his ultimate dream was to open a hospital for children in London. Sadly, he didn't live long enough to realise it—but one day it will happen.'

'And you say your mother works there.'

Cassandra nodded. 'She works extremely hard—I wish she didn't,' she said quietly. 'When my father died, Mama went all to pieces and we were so worried about her for a time. The institute became her salvation—mine, too, in a way. Together we did all we possibly could to keep it open—raising funds was difficult and a worry. We desperately needed more benefactors—we still do.'

'Is Lady Monkton a benefactor? But I suppose she must be, being a relative and extremely wealthy.'

'As a matter of fact, she isn't—though she has offered to make a sizeable donation many times. Mama refuses to take a penny of her money for the institute. She's so grateful for everything she's done for all of us since Papa died that she insists it stops there. When I approached the wealthy for donations, at first I was painfully aware that I was a social outcast. The *ton* patronised me, were amused by what I do. Some treated me with outright scorn, and I was miserable— and then angry that I allowed those people and their comments to upset me. Realising I was about to fall at the first hurdle, I took firm hold of myself and set about trying to change their opinion of me.'

'And you succeeded.'

'Yes. I practised detachment, I learned how to laugh, how to read people, how to charm.'

'What you really mean is that you became a virtuoso of deceit.'

'Yes, I suppose so. I had to win them over. I harbour no grudge against them for their ignorance.' Afraid that William might feel sorry for her, she smiled and shook her head dismissively. 'They soon began to accept me and what I do—thanks to Aunt Elizabeth.'

William thought it more poignant than funny. At that moment he felt an inexplicable surge of anger at all those small-minded people who had ostracised her. Deep inside he felt a stirring of protection towards her that surprised and disturbed him, and he turned his face away to cover his own bewildering emotions.

'It's late. I shall leave you to get some rest. Tomorrow I will escort Edward to London. It's time that young man began his army career—a spot of discipline will do him good.'

'Poor Edward. I'm beginning to feel sorry for him. He is hurting so much—and he is in love. People do foolish things when they are in love—so they say.' She flushed and laughed softly. 'Of course, I wouldn't know. Don't be too hard on him—otherwise you'll probably drive him to desert the army.'

William shot her a look of mock offence. 'I resent that. I have been the very soul of patience with the youth. Besides—I seem to recall you accusing him of being a lecherous, conniving, smooth-talking cad.'

'That was unpardonable of me—it was also before I knew him and saw how genuinely fond he is of Emma.'

William's look was one of incredulity. 'Miss Greenwood, I do believe you are becoming soft.'

Her lips curved in a smile and the dimple in her cheek deepened. 'Do you know, Lord Lampard, I do believe I am.' Cassandra tilted her head to one side and her eyes quizzed him.

'What?' William asked, suddenly wary of her. 'What's going through that busy head of yours now, Miss Greenwood?'

'I am wondering if this quiet, almost retiring man sitting opposite me really can be the arrogant rake I've heard about.'

'Retiring?' His chuckle sounded low and deep. 'Heaven

forbid! Are you trying to ruin my image, Miss Greenwood? How have I allowed you to imagine I am any less dangerous than society has painted me?' On a more serious note, he said, 'I did a lot of growing up in the army. It teaches you things you can't possibly learn in ordinary life. And now I've returned to Carlow Park to settle down and take an interest in the estate—and maybe find myself a wife.'

There was a sudden sparkle in his eyes that Cassandra prudently ignored. 'Then I am sure you will enjoy being pursued by women who fancy the title of Lady Lampard, Countess of Carlow, and have a respect for this beautiful house. The pursuit will be hot and strong. But what kind of marriage will it be? I suspect that you would not allow marriage to impair your freedom. Will you pay attention to your wife and doing what you call your duty, and then be off to London to take pleasure with your mistress?'

'That depends on the woman I choose to wed. There isn't a scoundrel alive who can't be tamed by the right woman, and I firmly believe that one should constantly strive to improve oneself.' He raised one sleek, well-defined eyebrow, watching, waiting for her reaction. A faint half-smile now played on his lips as if he knew exactly what was going on in her mind.

'I have a distinct feeling you are trying to proposition me, Lord Lampard.'

'Ah, now there's a thought. Scoundrel I may be, but I am a fairly honest person. Shall I convince you of my merits?'

'You've already tried that,' she quipped, reminding him of his assault on her lips in the coach. 'I should have slapped your face for your impudence.'

'Why? You enjoyed kissing me just as much as I enjoyed kissing you.'

'Nevertheless, marriage à la mode would not be for me. I think what I do is preferable to an unhappy marriage.' Cassandra looked at him and felt a curious warmth for the man whose profligate reputation gave her every reason to despise him. She considered it rather odd that she didn't. A woman was always flattered to learn a man was attracted to her—as remarkable as it might be. She sensed William was completely sincere, and she wasn't at all displeased.

William heaved himself out of the chair and stretched his aching body. A slow roguish grin moved across his features. 'Then I feel I shall have to persuade you—and enjoy doing so. But for now I will bid you good night. I intend to be away early. I'll call on your mother and explain everything.'

'Thank you. I'd appreciate that. She'll be out of her mind with worry over Emma, and will be so relieved that we reached her before she got to Scotland. Of course, we won't impose on you for longer than is necessary.'

'You are not imposing. Hospitality is one of my strong points.'

'Nevertheless, we'll be going home just as soon as Emma is fit to travel—perhaps in a couple of days, so if you would be so kind as to ask Mama to send Clem with the carriage, I would be grateful.'

'There won't be any need for that. I shall see you get back to London myself.'

As he left her, William reluctantly faced the fact that Cassandra Greenwood was a far cry from the women he usually associated with. What an enchanting, intriguing creature she was. In reality, she was warm, caring, sensitive and intelligent, but she was also a natural temptress, captivating and enchanting, alluring and vibrant, with a ripe beauty that heated and stirred his blood—and she had the softest, most appealing mouth he had ever tasted, and the largest blue-green eyes.

Chapter Five

The dark of the night crept around the house and the moon shone like an orange globe. For Cassandra, the hours flowed together, and when Emma rested in the quieter state of fevered sleep, she curled up in a chair in front of the fire, sometimes dozing, sometimes just staring into the glowing embers, trying to understand the turbulent, consuming emotions William Lampard was able to arouse in her. When she was with him there was an element of danger, which only added to the excitement.

How carelessly and artfully he was beginning to weave his web about her. She had not intended to become so ensnared. She knew him for a practising philanderer, so why had she allowed herself to be attracted by him? Why had she let her emotions become involved? The fact was that she had, and she greatly feared that she could be overwhelmed by him.

Early the next morning, opening the door to a quiet knock, Cassandra wasn't really surprised to find Edward standing there.

'Pardon my intrusion, Miss Greenwood. I have come to enquire after Emma. I do so hope she is no worse.' His tormented eyes went beyond her to the young woman in the bed.

Cassandra smiled understandably and stood aside for him

to enter. 'No, she is no worse. You will be relieved to know my sister is a little better,' she said in a quiet, reassuring voice.

Edward moved slowly to the bed. Bending and leaning forward, his eyes soft with love, he whispered her name. Emma's eyes flickered open. When his features came into focus her face lit up with the flame of her love.

'Edward,' she whispered hoarsely. 'Oh, Edward—my love.' Then her eyelids fluttered and closed and she settled against the pillows.

Cassandra turned away from the beseeching urgency in his eyes, unable to look upon their hot brown sweetness when he looked at Emma.

Seeing that she slept, Edward straightened and crossed to Cassandra, his expression one of deep concern. 'William and I are to leave for London shortly. It may be some time before I am able to return, depending on where my regiment sends me. I know we did wrong, Miss Greenwood, but please believe me when I say that I care for Emma deeply and intended no harm to come to her.'

'I know.'

'Will—will you allow me to write to her?'

'Unfortunately I cannot do that. It's not my place. It is my mother you will have to approach for any future association with Emma. And I must warn you that, because of your un-acceptable behaviour, she may very well refuse.' When she noted the dismay this caused him, she smiled. 'Emma is very young. If her feelings for you are unchanged when she has made her début, then who knows. My sister is wilful and headstrong, and usually gets her own way in most things. I ask you to be patient, to give this unfortunate business time to settle down.'

He nodded, trying his best to hide his pain. With one last look at Emma, he opened the door and glanced back at Cassandra. He smiled a shaky smile. 'Emma is indeed fortunate to have such a loyal and caring sister. Goodbye, Miss Greenwood, and thank you.' And so Edward took his leave of Emma sadly, but with hope in his heart.

The next day, after partaking of a light breakfast and pleased that Emma had managed to eat a little, Cassandra left her resting peacefully and with Molly to sit with her. She walked in the grounds, relieved, after her confinement, to stretch her legs.

Carlow Park, the ancestral estate of generations of Lampards, green and full of life, was comprised of hundreds of acres of game-filled woods and rolling parkland, fertile fields and sheep in the meadows. It was pleasantly warm and the sun shone forth with splendour. Cassandra caught her breath at the sight of it stretching far into the distance beyond the gardens. Descending a low flight of steps from the terrace, she leisurely followed a path around the immaculately clipped velvet lawns, admiring the borders gloriously abloom with late spring and early summer flowers.

Carlow Park was more beautiful than any place she ever imagined. In the distance, down a gentle slope, the gardens gave way to an enormous lake. Swans and water fowl drifted on the tranquil surface, and it was overlooked by an ornate stone summerhouse. She began walking towards it, enjoying the gentle breeze that came off the water, feeling it blow through her hair, which fell loose about her shoulders.

From the corner of her eye she glimpsed a movement. Halting her step and half turning, she saw William astride a magnificent chestnut horse riding towards her. Her heart gave a leap of surprise, consternation and she admitted, a certain excitement. He was one of the most striking looking men she had ever seen—a man of power who set himself above others, as accustomed to obedience from those about him as he was from his horse, which he sat as though he were part of it.

When he was close his broad smile gleamed with a startling whiteness against his lean, tanned features. Short heavy wisps of his dark hair curled slightly about his face. There was a health and vitality about him that was almost mesmerising.

'I'm happy to see you taking the air, Cassandra, which can only mean that your sister is recovering, since I cannot imagine you leaving her alone otherwise.' He dismounted, thinking how ravishing she looked with her face all rosy from the sun's warmth. Her hair fell in a cascade of waves, with thin strands teasing her cheeks. Its lustrous simplicity gave her the look of a young innocent—which was precisely what she was. He had been unable to put her face from his mind since he had first seen her. It was the most compelling face he had ever seen and full of contradictions—open, yet guarded, anxious, determined, and so very vulnerable.

He still couldn't believe how he had left Edward at the academy and raced back to Carlow Park like a besotted idiot in his eagerness to see Cassandra. Unfortunately, a disturbing incident had occurred on the road that had delayed him and by the time he'd arrived home it had been too late to call on her. For the time being he decided to keep what had happened to himself, but one thing he was sure of—it had been another attempt on his life.

When the shadowy figure of what they thought was a masked highwayman had appeared in the road in front of them brandishing a pistol, the driver had pulled the coach to a halt. The man then rode to the side of the vehicle, his pistol aimed at William. With his reflexes honed to perfection in Spain, where he had dealt with men seeking to kill him on a regular basis, William was prepared with his own gun. He fired before his assailant could do so. Unfortunately, the shot terrified the horses and they bolted, leaving his assailant clutching his arm and disappearing into the dark.

His mood on returning to Carlow Park had turned bleak. He had pondered the silent admission that he was helpless before whoever it was who was trying to kill him, that he knew neither where to find him nor how to stop him trying again.

'Emma is a little better,' Cassandra replied, ignorant of his thoughts. 'It's such a glorious day—I thought I might walk to the lake.'

'Then if you don't mind the company, if you will allow me, I will join you.'

'There is no need. I'm sure there are many things you have to do.'

'Nothing that can't wait—and not nearly as interesting.'

Meeting his gaze, Cassandra saw the reflective, almost tender, glimmer of a warm light in his eyes.

'I insist,' he said.

'How was your journey to Woolwich yesterday?' Cassandra asked, falling into step beside him.

'Well enough. It was late when I got back.'

'And how was Edward when you left him? Do you think he'll settle down to military life?'

'I hope so. Edward is patriotic, with a tremendous regard for loyalty and honour. He has the makings of a good soldier—although the boy's in love, enraptured by the lovely young creature who has slipped so effortlessly into his life. I can only hope it won't be a handicap.'

'So do I. Did you see Mama?'

'I did. When I arrived at the house, fearing the worst, her distress was great. However, she was most relieved when I told her we had apprehended the runaways—although she was most upset to learn of your sister's illness.'

'Poor Mama. I know how this will have affected her—and Aunt Elizabeth. Emma was staying with her when she disappeared, and she blames herself entirely.'

'I can understand that. Now the shock is over, your mother longs for your return—but in the light of your sister being unwell, she does not press for it.'

'Emma will be well enough to travel tomorrow. I—think we should go home.'

'Shouldn't you stay another day or so—just to make sure?

Won't you let me try and persuade you?' He cocked a brow, humour dancing in his eyes.

She gave him a wry smile. 'I am well acquainted with your powers of persuasion, my lord, and I would appreciate it if you would keep them on a tight rein. I think we've imposed on your hospitality long enough.'

'Very well, if you must. I offered to take you back to London myself, but your mother would not hear of it. Clem will be arriving with the carriage tomorrow—around midday.'

'And the elopement?'

'You may rest assured it has not been circulated and remains a private matter among ourselves.'

'I am relieved to hear it.'

Reaching the water's edge, from beneath the heavy boughs of an elm they stood looking across the lake. The water was dark and still, shining silver here and there where it caught the sun. Moorhens drifted by and a heron on its stilted legs pierced the water with its long beak in its search for food.

'This is so peaceful—perfect,' Cassandra murmured. 'You are so lucky having all this—to grow up in such wonderful surroundings and to know it's yours.' She turned her head and looked up at him, seeing at once that he'd fallen in with her mood. How remote he looked, how detached.

'The fortunes of birth,' he answered quietly. 'Thank you for the compliment to my estate. I'm glad you like it. I feel an aching nostalgia when I remember the years I lived here as a child. I only wish my brother could have lived a full life to enjoy his inheritance.'

'I'm sure you do. I—if you would rather not talk about him,' she said, sensitive to his changing mood, 'there is no need to.'

William knew he would, but he didn't want to examine the myriad feelings that were compelling him to do it. 'I feel the wrenching loss of my parents and my brother. The poignancy of being here after Robert's loss is difficult. He was several years older than me—quiet, serious, duty bound.' He smiled down at her as his mood lightened. 'Unlike me—fun loving, reckless—'

'Impossible and irresponsible, to boot,' Cassandra added, laughing lightly.

'And charming,' William finished with a confident, amused lift to his brow.

'But of course.'

'I was always very much Robert's younger brother, but he was always willing to let me tag along. The village over there is Carlow, and the church you see is where generations of Lampards are interred—Robert, too.'

'And that rather splendid house?' Cassandra asked, pointing to a stately manor house that stood on the outskirts of the village, its tall graceful chimneys rising like dark fingers into the sky.

'That's Littleton Manor. My cousin Mark and his wife Lydia live there. Lydia was to have married Robert. After the accident, when Robert was killed, she married Mark.'

'And—do you mind about that?'

He shook his head and smiled. 'No. I thought they were ill suited. Mark is more her type—although I do not think theirs is a happy marriage.'

'And what type is she?'

'If the two of you should meet, you'll know what I mean—although I have to say that I know very little about her. Mark is rigidly upright, extremely competent, sound headed and was just the man to keep order at Carlow Park while I was in Spain.'

'And now you're no longer a commissioned officer having to take orders from your superiors, how do you think you will settle down to being a country gentleman? I don't suppose you've had time to reacquaint yourself with the people who live and work on the estate.'

'Not yet.'

'Well, like your ancestors, you must watch over them—and lead by example,' she told him with a forceful laugh.

His expression was one of mock horror. 'You mean I will have to reform?'

'Will that be so very difficult?'

'Impossible—but I value your advice.'

'I believe you are actually extremely good at what you do, with your sharp mind and commercial sense. Are you going to stay at Carlow Park—or do you intend returning to London?'

'I'll stay here for now. There's much to do, and people to see. I never sought the title or the estate. It suited me well enough being a soldier, but I suppose I'll soon get used to all the hard work that has to be done.' He looked at her seriously. 'You'll know all about that with what you do at the institute. You've made quite a life for yourself in London.'

'I work very hard.'

'I admire that,' he said quietly.

She smiled nervously. 'You must think I'm dreadfully ill-bred.'

'I think,' he said softly, 'that you are magnificent.'

'You certainly know how to flatter a woman.'

'It isn't flattery, just an honest opinion.'

The husky sincerity in his deep voice and the way he was looking at her snatched her breath away. His well-tailored jacket and buff-coloured trousers accentuated the long lines of his body, and she noticed again how incredibly blue his eyes were in the brightness of the day. It was impossible not to be drawn and respond to this man. A curious sharp thrill ran through her as he looked down at her, his eyes alert above the faintly smiling mouth, and she promptly forgot everything.

And so they faced one another—the soldier and libertine, and the gently reared young woman—and, despite Cassandra's opposition, the attraction between them was almost palpable. He looked at her, the sun filtering through the boughs of the elm sending prisms of light dancing around them, flickering on William's thick dark hair, outlining his strong face.

Raising his hand, he gently brushed the backs of his fingers over her warm cheek, relieved that she didn't resist. 'Has anyone ever told you how lovely you are, Miss Greenwood?'

Cassandra felt a sudden stillness envelope them. Vividly aware of the heat of the sun, she was overwhelmingly conscious of him, of the way his gaze had dropped to her mouth. Confused, and feeling her heart begin to pound with helpless anticipation, she looked away, but he placed his finger beneath her chin and turned her face back to him.

'What's the matter? Don't you like being complimented?' His voice was low and husky.

She shook her head slowly, feeling a surge of irrepressible excitement rising in her. His eyes met hers in silent, half-challenging amusement, saying things she dare not think about. She struggled impotently to maintain her hold on her thin control, feeling it weaken under the strain as he studied her, unabashed.

Gently he pushed a stray strand of hair from her brow. She leaned her back against the great elm, grateful for its support. She was no more capable of telling him to stop than she was of sprouting wings to take flight. When he put his hand upon her waist she leaned into him, and when he lowered his head and touched his lips to her cheek, she sighed and softly spoke his name. And when he began to kiss her with sweet demand she clung to him, wishing with all her heart it would never end.

Suddenly his arms were around her, the strength of them shattering her calm, her senses erupting. He kissed her with slow ardour, his hands moulding her close, stirring the passion in her blood. The fragrance of his cologne and skin pervaded her senses. She could not free herself from those sultry kisses and nor did she desire to. Her body was caught in a web of enchantment.

The moment was shattered when a footman seemed to appear from nowhere. They were so absorbed in each other that neither of them had heard him approach. They drew apart.

'I'm sorry to intrude, my lord, but Mr Palmer has arrived.'

William nodded. 'Thank you, Myers. I'll be there directly.'

He looked at Cassandra as the footman headed back to the house. They smiled at one another, aware suddenly of an intensity of feeling between them. To Cassandra it was new and exciting, as though the future held a secret and a promise.

'Mr Palmer is my lawyer. It quite slipped my mind that I'd arranged for him to come this morning.'

'You go. I'll stay here for a while longer.'

Cassandra watched him mount his horse and ride off before turning back to the lake. So many conflicting emotions swirled inside her, fighting for ascendancy. For just a few brief days they had been together and he was becoming more attractive by the minute. She was finding it impossible to shake off the effect he was having on her. A few moments ago before he had kissed her she had felt alarmed, particularly as she realised that it was not so much of him that she was afraid, but of herself.

After a while she turned away and slowly made her way back. Seeing a rose arbour ahead of her and a wooden bench, which she thought would be a nice place to sit a while to absorb the ambience of the gardens, she headed towards it, enjoying the warm feel of the sun on her face.

Something moved among the greenery—she felt eyes on her suddenly, and her flesh tingled warily. A man appeared in front of her, come from nowhere, it seemed. Plainly dressed in black, which threw up the whiteness of his cravat, tall and thin, he looked to be in his early thirties. His chin was strong and there was a scornful curl to his lips that gave him a somewhat proud and insolent appearance. His skin was pale and so were the hard, grey eyes, seemingly half-asleep beneath heavy lids. He had about him an extraordinary air of quiet power.

Cassandra shuddered, feeling trapped like a fly in the web of his gaze as he stared at her with intense, unwavering—and perhaps resentful, she thought—curiosity. He came towards her, leaning on the gold-knobbed cane he held.

'Miss Greenwood.'

Cassandra nodded briefly, calmly, considering him. 'You have the advantage. That is more than I can say of you, sir.'

He inclined his head ever so slightly. 'Mark Lampard— Baron Lampard of Littleton Manor, which is situated on the outskirts of Carlow village. I am Lord Lampard's cousin.'

Cassandra thought he was not dissimilar to his cousin. Both wore the look of the well-bred of generations, and possessed the complex traits that thrive in the families of those who are born to govern. But there was a fastidious air of supercilious taciturnity about Mark Lampard that William did not possess.

'For the past two years,' he went on, 'since the demise of Lord Lampard's brother, I have been acting steward to his estate. There is very little I do not know about what goes on.' He spoke in a slow, deep voice, essentially undramatic, conveying the perfect measure of its owner's self-control. 'William told me of your distressing circumstances. I hope your sister is feeling better.'

'She is a little better, thank you, which is why you find me taking a walk. I felt a need for some air after being confined to the sick room—and I have to say Carlow Park is indeed a lovely place.'

'There is none finer in these parts.'

'You—have spoken to your cousin.'

'I have, indeed—yesterday, before he left for London with young Edward. He recounted to me in detail his elopement with your sister, and I have to say I was shocked to hear it— very shocked indeed. Tell me, Miss Greenwood, does your sister usually give your family so much trouble? I do realise that young ladies of her age are often difficult to manage.'

Cassandra's heart swelled with indignation. 'Emma is the most tractable of young ladies and has never given my mother cause to worry. I believe in this case she was much influenced by your cousin Edward, who, do not forget, almost ruined her reputation beyond redemption. Does he usually get into scrapes of this sort?'

The arrogant Mark Lampard was undaunted by her show of indignation or her slight directed at his young cousin. 'As a rule, no. It is a blessing and a profound relief that you caught up with them in time, thereby avoiding a catastrophe of immense proportions. Edward has a military career mapped out. Marriage at this stage of his life would not be appropriate.'

Roused to anger and resentment by his insult, Cassandra did her utmost to retain her composure when she spoke. 'And does that apply to my sister or to any young lady Edward might be drawn to? From what you say, Mr Lampard, you seem to have strong objections to Emma's suitability. Are you objecting to my father having been a professional man and not a titled gentleman? Do you consider us to be inferior?'

'Not at all. I have great admiration for your late father's profession, and indeed I am certain your sister is most charming. I am merely pointing out that it would have been a most imprudent marriage.'

Cassandra was not so sure she believed in his admiration of her father. 'Next you will be accusing her of tricking Edward into eloping so she could ingratiate herself into your family.'

'Not at all, and I beg your pardon if I have upset you, but it is all so unsatisfactory.'

'I could not agree more, Mr Lampard. Do you often decide on the propriety of your cousin's inclination, and determine the manner in which he is to be happy? He is about to embark on a military career, where he may be called upon to lay down his life for others, so is he not old enough to decide for himself how to conduct his private life?'

'Miss Greenwood, are you saying that you would not have objected to a marriage between them?'

'Had I not objected, I would not have gone chasing off to Scotland to prevent it. However, since nothing has come of it we can put it behind us. As soon as Emma is well enough to travel, we will return to London.'

'That would be best,' he said with haughty composure.

'Pardon me, sir, but I will be the judge of what is best for both my sister and myself. Now, if you will excuse me, I will return to the house.'

He stiffened, but appeared to accept his dismissal. His eyes met hers coldly. 'Of course. I will detain you no longer. Good day, Miss Greenwood. It was interesting meeting you.' With these words he went on his way.

Cassandra's mind was in turmoil. Feeling a weakening in her legs, she sat on the bench and reflected on her highly charged encounter with Mark Lampard. Normally in control of her emotions, she was simmering, seething with anger. The meeting had been sudden, surprising and antagonistic—although why Mark Lampard had such strong feelings on the elopement she could only put down to concern for his cousin Edward. But that did not excuse his insufferable rudeness. His manner had been insulting and unacceptable and she sincerely hoped she would not have the misfortune to come into contact with him again.

Feeling a sudden chill, as if a shadow had passed in front of the sun and robbed her of its warmth, she stood up and headed back to the house.

It was early evening when Cassandra opened the door to William's knock. He was standing with his shoulder propped casually against the door post and his arms crossed over his chest, looking at her with a lazy smile. With his hair still damp from his bath and dressed in an olive-green jacket and light grey trousers, he looked incredibly handsome and completely at ease. Trying to ignore the treacherous leap her heart gave at the sight of that captivating, intimate smile and warm gaze, she invited him inside.

'I came to enquire after your sister's progress.'

'Emma is much recovered—so much so that she's been out

of bed this afternoon.' She tilted her head to one side, her eyes enquiring and her lips smiling slightly. 'Is that the only reason why you came calling, William?'

'I've grown used to having you around—I was missing you.'

Mesmerised by his tone and the expression in the fathom-less depths of his eyes, Cassandra's pulse tripped. 'I am immune to your flattery, Lord Lampard,' she said, not unkindly and with a teasing light in her eyes.

'Then I am sorry to hear that. I shall have to try a differ-ent tack if I am to succeed in getting you to change your opinion of me. I have come to invite you to dine with me. Mrs Henderson tells me you have not yet eaten?'

'I really don't think that would be a good idea. Besides, I haven't seen the inside of a bed for two nights.'

'Then I'll forgive you if you nod off during the soup course.' His eyes held a challenge and a provocative smile curved his lips. 'Are you afraid of being alone with me, Miss Greenwood? Nervous, perhaps?'

'Lord Lampard, for the past two days you have been saying and doing things that make me extremely nervous.'

'Cassandra,' he said in a smooth, deep voice that had a dangerous effect on her heart rate, 'I am only asking you to have dinner with me—nothing more intimate than that.' He smiled. 'I think it's the least you can do in return for your board and lodging.'

Seeing the wicked mischief alight in his eyes, Cassandra laughed softly. 'Then, since you put it like that, how can I possibly refuse without appearing rude.'

Amusement touched his lips. 'You can't,' he said, pushing himself away from the wall.

'Although, with only one change of clothes, you'll have to take me as I am.'

His look became positively seductive. 'It is not your clothes I'll be looking at. I'll expect you in the dining room in a few minutes.'

* * *

When Cassandra entered the dining room, William was waiting for her, looking disgustingly relaxed with a glass of wine in his hand. When she appeared in the doorway his eyes appraised her. Her face flushed warm.

'You look enchanting, Cassandra. Hungry?' Handing her a glass of wine, he gestured towards the table.

Hearing the husky intimacy in his voice, Cassandra's heart rate increased. 'I confess that I am.'

The dining room was very grand. The long dining table and the chairs of dark blue velvet, gilt-edged mirrors, white marble columns and patterned ceiling, did not induce a relaxed atmosphere, but within a circle of candle light, the servants having been dismissed after serving the food, with William seated at the head of the table and Cassandra close to him on his right, the atmosphere was comfortable and intimate.

It was when they were on the sweet course that Cassandra remembered her encounter with Mark Lampard.

'I—I met your other cousin today—Mark.'

William raised his brows and glanced across at her. 'And?'

'And what?'

'Did you—have a conversation?'

She nodded. 'You—are not alike.'

'If you mean he isn't a scoundrel of the first order, then you're right. We're as different as chalk and cheese, but we rub along well enough. Mark is my heir, a pillar of the community, and has never made any secret of his disapproval of my easygoing ways.'

'He is also very—direct,' Cassandra remarked. Aware that she was a guest in his house, good manners made her choose her words with care so as not to give offence.

He arched his brows in question. 'Direct? In what way?'

'He—he told me how relieved he is that we reached Edward before he married Emma. At first I believed he was shocked by the elopement, but he soon made his sentiments known to me. He was most—explicit.'

William frowned, suddenly thoughtful. 'Please don't misunderstand Mark.'

'I don't. I think I understand him perfectly. He harbours a mistaken belief that Emma's allurements, in a moment of infatuation and weakness, made Edward forget himself. The long and the short of it is that I believe he would never consider my sister a suitable match for Edward. We belong to the professional class, you see—no wealth, no title.'

'Did Mark upset you?'

'No. He was perfectly civil to me, but the substance of our conversation made me angry.'

Having finished his sweet course, William pushed the dish away from him. There was an odd expression on his handsome face. 'I'm sorry about that, Cassandra,' he said grimly, 'and I apologise for my cousin. I'll speak to him, and I promise I will set matters right.'

'Please don't—not on my account. The last thing I want is to cause a rift between you and your cousin. Emma and I will be gone tomorrow, so let that be an end to the matter.'

William said no more on the subject, but he was concerned about what Mark could have said to upset her, and he was determined to have a word with him.

'How is Archie, by the way?' he asked, remembering the young boy with the burnt feet he had seen at the institute. 'I've been meaning to ask, since he hasn't appeared at my London residence as yet.'

'Archie? Oh—his feet are much better. He's almost recovered. Doctor Brookes removed his dressings a week ago and he's walking with the aid of a crutch at the moment. As soon as he feels he can do without it he will be well enough to leave the institute.'

'Then don't forget to send him to Grosvenor Square. I've told Thomas, the head groom, to expect him.'

'Thank you. I do appreciate it. You've no idea how difficult it is trying to find places for the children who pass through our doors. Archie's a quiet boy. He won't give you any trouble,' she said, spooning up the last of her fruit.

Cassandra looked lovely and vulnerable in her pale, high-necked muslin, her hair coiled softly about her head. William couldn't tear his eyes away from her. Moving his chair away from the table, he leant with his arm draped across the back, his foot propped casually atop the opposite knee, relaxed, indulgent and very attractive as he watched her dab her mouth with her napkin and place it on the table.

In thoughtful silence, Cassandra sipped her wine, while contemplating the man reclining close to her, completely at ease. Everything about him bespoke power. His shoulders were broad, his chest well muscled under his jacket, and the muscles in his legs were outlined beneath his trousers. Years of fighting and army life had toughened him and she suspected that he would prefer to be with his fellow soldiers on campaign than mixing in society.

'Will—will you miss the army?' she ventured hesitantly.

'I already do,' he replied, distracted by the myriad emotions playing in her expressive eyes.

His admission struck Cassandra's tender heart. 'I get the sense that you don't feel comfortable when you're out in society, and that you think all the nonsense that goes with it as pointless as I do.'

'Occasionally—although it does have its compensations.'

'Such as?'

'I get to meet lovely young ladies I would not meet otherwise—proper young ladies with active, clever minds, other than those who think no further than how they look, the next society event and snaring the right catch. It may surprise you to know how bored I am with all that.' He smiled. 'I seem to have grown more particular in my tastes with age. Here, have some more wine,' he added smoothly, reaching for the bottle and pouring some into her glass.

'Do go on. I'm all attention,' Cassandra said, taking a sip of her wine. 'Although I must warn you that you are the kind of man my common sense and Mama tells me to avoid at all costs.'

'And do you always listen to your mama?'

'Of course. Her advice is always sound—it is the kind of advice that applies to all well-bred ladies who have very definite ideas of the way they wish to be thought of and treated by gentlemen. By well-bred, I mean different from the sort of ladies you normally associate with.'

Suppressing a smile, William smoothed his expression into an admissible imitation of earnest gravity. 'And how does a well-bred young lady wish to be treated by a gentleman?'

'He must have eyes for no one but her, he must be devoted to her—and be of a romantic nature, otherwise you haven't a prayer of success.'

'Romantic! Now there's an interesting word.'

Cassandra saw humour lurking in his eyes. Her delicate brows drew together and amusement teased the corners of her generous mouth as she surveyed him. 'Can you say that applies to you, Lord Lampard?'

'Oh, I've had my moments.'

Aware of what she regarded as his deliberate, unprecedented efforts to charm and disarm her, Cassandra met his gaze direct. 'Are you trying to seduce me, by any chance?'

The laughter left his eyes and he stood up. 'You are a naïve, idealistic young woman, Cassandra Greenwood. However, you are not a child and neither am I. Do you want me to spell it out so there's no mistaking my motives?' Taking her hand, he drew her to her feet, watching a heated flush stain her cheeks.

'Motives? And these motives you speak of—are they noble?' His eyes raked her face with the leisure of a well-fed wolf. She felt a tremulous feeling stirring inside.

His long, strong fingers cupped her face. 'They are adult and perfectly natural, and it's a foregone conclusion that any moment now I am going to kiss you. You know, you are a mystery to me, Cassandra Greenwood.'

'I cannot think why,' she remarked, as she sought to forestall what her heart knew was inevitable.

'You're also very beautiful.'

Thrown completely off balance by this unexpected turn of events, alarm, hot and fierce, sped through Cassandra's mind. He was being so tender, so gentle, so persuasive, and his gaze was warm and sensual. 'Please, let me go, William. I—I think the wine must have gone to my head. I am not in the mood for any of this.'

'Then we'll have to do something about that.'

'I—I must go and see if Emma is all right. I've been gone so long,' she said, her voice quavering.

'She'll cope.' Running the tip of his finger down her cheek, he felt it was warm and soft, like satin.

'William—I am extremely tired and would like to go to bed.'

'So would I. With you.'

'Please…'

'Are you going to get angry—to reject my advances?' Her eyes were dark, full of indecision. He smiled seductively. 'Come, Cassandra, you have been dubbed the Ice Maiden by every rake you've spurned. Prove them wrong. Shall we continue from where we left off earlier?'

'And I'm supposed to melt into your arms and sigh simply to prove I have blood in my veins and not ice? Please, William, my patience is wearing very thin.' Her words were definite, but her voice sounded unconvincing.

He laughed softly, his hooded eyes full of sardonic amusement as his arms went round her and pulled her close, moulding her body to his. 'I've certainly given you provocation.'

'I agree.' In his arms he was more attractive than ever, and despite her protestations the urgency to be even closer to him was more vivid than before. She watched him, anticipating, entranced, hardly breathing.

Bending his head and nuzzling her neck beneath her ear, hearing her gasp, in his sublime male arrogance, William knew her resistance was beginning to crumble. 'I'm difficult and impossible, I know, but that's because I'm attracted to you. I want you, Cassandra.'

'Want? There's nothing wrong with wanting, but it is a sin to take what is not offered.'

He laughed low in his throat, 'I have been sinning all my life, so there is nothing new there. I'll do my penance later. I do want you. I have from the first moment I laid eyes on you.'

'And you're sure of that?'

'Absolutely,' he murmured, nibbling her ear. 'I am sincere.'

Feeling divine sensations shoot through her body, Cassandra closed her eyes. 'You haven't a sincere bone in your body.'

'But I have an overwhelming need for you.'

Feeling her legs tremble and the back of her knees ache, Cassandra leaned into him. He was as smooth as silk, an accomplished womaniser, but he was so appealing, and she was no longer a child. For the first time she felt the deep pull of physical desire, and here was the danger. She no longer feared a man's touch—instead she feared her own weakness.

When he raised his head she was unable to look at anything other than his lips hovering close to her own. She was shocked by how much she wanted to feel those lips on hers once more. She breathed out slowly as excitement and longing almost overwhelmed her. The touch of his hands inflamed her. Lowering his head, he kissed her gently, his mouth beginning a slow, unbelievably erotic seduction, and Cassandra felt the power of him, real and tremendous, in his restraint.

There was pleasure at the feel and taste of his lips. It was exhilarating, thrilling, agonising, all at the same time, and she was lost in a sea of sensation. Excitement gripped her and there was terror of the unknown. His arms went round her, drawing her close, his hand sliding slowly down her spine as he moulded her to his body. As his lips moved on hers, those lips and his touch unlocked something within her, releasing all the repressions and restraints she had imposed on herself for so long. Cassandra's breathing quickened and her body began to speak a language new to her, a language William understood perfectly.

When she melted against him, sliding her hands slowly up his chest and around his neck as she returned his kiss, William experienced a burgeoning pleasure and incredible joy that was almost past bearing. Minutes later he finally forced himself to lift his head and gaze down into her eyes, feeling them pulling him inexorably into their depths. He saw something there that reflected what he was feeling—desire. It was the way she stood—still, poised, willing him to kiss her again. Tenderness began to unfold within him—a sensation that had been as foreign to him as the voice of his conscience until he'd met this truly remarkable person and he asked himself how it was possible that this one woman could make him lose his mind.

'Have you any idea how lovely you are, Cassandra Greenwood—how incredibly desirable and how rare?'

Seduced by his mouth and caressing hands, the feel of his long legs pressed intimately to her own, Cassandra felt her body brought vibrantly to life. Drawing a shattered breath, she whispered, 'This is madness, utter madness.'

'I couldn't agree more,' he breathed, his mouth opening hungrily over hers once again.

As he continued to kiss her thoroughly, endlessly, producing a knot of pure sensation in the pit of Cassandra's stomach, the passion that ignited between them surpassed even William's imaginings—it surpassed anything he'd ever felt. Lust hit him with such unexpected force. His conscience stirred. Could this warm, incredibly beautiful and physically aroused creature be the Cassandra Greenwood the rakes of the *ton* had dubbed the 'Ice Maiden', and not a goddess by any means? But, by God, when she pressed herself against him and he felt her soft, ripe curves, she had the body of one. She was telling him silently, with her lips, her body, that she was definitely not made of ice.

When he finally released her lips he gazed down into her upturned face. Her eyes were liquid bright, and her lips, slightly parted, trembled and were moist from his kiss. 'So, the Ice Maiden melts. You want me. You can't deny it.'

'I suppose I am human after all. You've just proved that.'

'You're afraid.'

Disorientated and bewildered by what had just happened between them, Cassandra let her forehead fall against his chest. 'Yes.'

'You've nothing to fear from me.'

Raising her head, she looked at him, seeing no teasing light in his eyes. 'I hope not.'

'Cassandra, do you want to talk?'

She shook her head.

His lips quirked. 'I don't usually render a woman speechless when I kiss her.' He sighed, placing a gentle kiss on her lips. 'You are tired. Go to bed. We'll talk in the morning.'

Disengaging herself from his arms, she stepped back. 'Yes—I am tired. Please excuse me.'

Cassandra looked in on Emma before climbing into the bed in the room next door, but, as exhausted as she was and try as she might, she lay awake until the early hours, trying to understand the disturbing and consuming emotions William had aroused in her. How could she possibly understand this mindless, wicked weakness he seemed to inspire in her? Did skilled libertines make every woman feel that she was special? The wonderful memory of his kisses sent happiness spreading through her that was so intense she ached from it.

Was it possible to be so happy, to feel such joyous elation shimmering inside? At that moment she felt like the most beautiful woman in the world. She savoured again that feeling of exhilaration she had experienced in his arms, a sensation as heady and potent as good wine. She felt a melting sensation in her secret parts. Her thoughts began to travel beyond the kiss, and she felt the madness and the delight of secrecy at her forbidden thoughts. How she wished she could feel the strength of his arms around her now, loving her. She knew he was a man she could love, a man she could happily spend the rest of her life with.

She also knew William was a skilled rake and an accomplished flirt, but at that moment when she felt as if she was special to him, her heart rebelled against believing it. But she was no fool. Compared to him, she knew she was as naïve and unsophisticated as the proverbial newborn babe.

The following morning, William received Sir Charles Grisham in the library, his expression one of bland courtesy. 'What brings you to Carlow Park, Charles? Isn't it rather early in the day for a social call?'

'Dear Lord, William, have your wits become addled since you quit the army? Don't you listen? Why, only several days ago I told you I was to visit my aunt in Hertford.'

William's expression showed nothing more than mild surprise. Was it really only a few days since Lady Monkton's ball? It seemed a lifetime away. 'Yes, of course I remember. You told me Mark had invited you to call—something about a horse.'

'Two, actually, but that was before our wager concerning that paragon of virtue, the ravishing, sophisticated and highly desirable Miss Cassandra Greenwood.'

William's eyes narrowed, and there was no humour in his expression. 'Yes, isn't she.'

'Your interaction at the ball and the way you stalked off and left her standing has become the talk of the *ton*. They're still trying to figure it out. London's abuzz with rumours.'

'And no doubt they'll put two and two together and make five,' William remarked drily. 'The rumours will soon be forgotten when some new scandal comes along to take their interest.'

'When I left Monkton House for White's, I had a mind to record our bet, but on second thoughts I decided against it, since a horse and no money is involved—except for the thousand guineas I shall have to part with if you win. I decided to keep the wager a private matter between ourselves.'

'I'm relieved to hear it.' This was one wager William wanted kept out of the exclusive gentleman's club White's famous betting book, in which its distinguished members recorded wagers on virtually everything, not only sporting events, but political and all manner of happenings whose outcome was unknown.

'Well, old man,' Charles said, sprawling, rather than sitting on the chaise before the fireplace, 'may your expectations be fulfilled—and my own—but if you're going to seduce the gently reared, unsuspecting Miss Greenwood before the Season ends, you're hardly going to carry it off buried in the country. The lady lives in town.'

'As if I need reminding.' On no account must Charles know Cassandra and her sister were residing at this very moment beneath his roof. Charles had many admirable traits, but discretion wasn't one of them.

'It's doubtful she's going to develop a *tendre* for you anyway in such a short time. Best get back to London, eh—otherwise that splendid beast you have in your stable will be mine. I think it will be anyway—so nothing to worry about there. You may have unscrupulously flayed the reputations of more pretentiously proud females than you can recall, but I told you when we made the wager that Miss Greenwood is made of different stuff.'

'Women fall for the most unlikely men, Charles,' William drawled, wearing a mask of genteel imperturbability, while becoming more irritated by Grisham's presence by the minute.

'There's no accounting for taste, I suppose, but in this instance you will fail—unless, of course, you have a strategy, Lampard. If so, be a good chap and pour me a brandy—and a cigar wouldn't go amiss—and I will listen with interest while you tell me all about it.'

Chapter Six

A wager! A horse!

Cassandra stood like a pillar of stone behind the slightly open door, her mind numb, unable to remember why she had been so eager to see William, to seek him out and look upon his handsome features once more, for him to confirm that she hadn't dreamt what had happened between them last night.

The conversation she had overheard hung in the air like a bad smell. No one had insulted her as much as this and it was more than her pride could bear. Dazed and unable to form any coherent thought, she backed away from the library door, and turning walked towards the stairs, wanting nothing more than to seek the refuge of her room. As the full realisation of what she had heard sank in and renewed life began to surge through her, her magnificent eyes shone with humiliation and wrath. She was appalled and outraged; there was no excuse, no possible way to deny the awful truth.

The unspeakable cad! The lecherous libertine! The man would seduce a nun in a nunnery if he had a mind. And just when she was beginning to trust him, to respect him and believe he had been unfairly maligned, to think that there was little truth in all the disgusting and immoral things she had heard about him—all her tender feelings were demolished.

William Lampard was a heartless beast and she could not believe that she, sensible and intelligent Cassandra Greenwood, had let him kiss her—and shame on shame, that she had wantonly kissed him back. What a fool she had been, a gullible, stupid, naïve fool.

Her mistake was that from the moment they had been thrust together, his easy banter and relaxed charm had completely disarmed her. She knew that men took advantage of foolish, innocent girls, so how had she allowed herself to fall into that trap? She had enjoyed his company, had melted into his arms like some besotted idiot, and had felt gratitude for his immense generosity in bringing them to his home, when all the time he had been playing a game with her. She was his prey, and he was intent on seducing her, dishonouring her, and to win his bet nothing was going to deter him from trying.

He had made a wager with Sir Charles Grisham to seduce her before the Season ended; should he fail, Sir Charles would be so much richer by a horse.

A horse, for heaven's sake! It was more than her lacerated pride could withstand. Her face blazed with fury. Oh, the humiliation of it. And if he succeeded, what would her life be like, following a tainted liaison with a renowned rake? The discovery of his treachery had destroyed all her illusions. She'd never trust him again, ever. How could she? He would never redeem himself from this.

As she went back upstairs, all these thoughts marched through her tormented and rage-filled mind. She would never forget what she had heard—ever—nor did she want to. She wanted to remember it so that never again would she be taken in by the likes of William Lampard. Of course, if she wanted to avenge herself, she could play him at his own game and he would have no idea of it—but, no, she wasn't like that and she had no time to waste on such foolishness.

By the time she reached her room an icy numbness had taken over and she was surprised to find she was no longer in the throes of heartwrenching pain. Stiffening her spine, she decided not to let him know what she had overheard, but this had given her an advantage and she was determined that she would outmanoeuvre him. Immediately she began planning a way to thwart and foil and exasperate the plans of this infuriating lord. She was strong and resilient and would get over this. They would leave Carlow Park just as soon as Clem arrived.

Back in the library, William poured a couple of brandies and handed one to Charles. Raising his own, he proposed a toast to Monarch.

'The horse is yours.'

Charles was incredulous, and then a slow, disbelieving smile broke across his face. 'But the wager? Good Lord! Have I heard right? Have you lost all reason?'

'I have never been more sane in my life.'

'So I am to assume you've had a change of heart and no longer wish to seduce Miss Greenwood? That you're folding—as easy as that?'

'Absolutely.'

'Then you're the most peculiar player I've ever had the pleasure of opposing,' Charles remarked, sensing something crucial was going on here that he knew nothing about. 'Unfortunately, I enjoy a challenge and the pleasure is somewhat muted by the wager's outcome.'

'Then I am sorry to disappoint you. I have developed a deep regard for Miss Greenwood. I will not dishonour her. However, I have no intention of reneging on our wager. You can take the horse with you today if you wish, Monarch—I refuse to part with Franciscan. He was my brother's horse, so I'm sure you will understand my reluctance to part with him.'

When Cassandra went in to Emma, she found her up and dressed and sitting on the window seat, her knees drawn up to her chest. She was staring bleakly out over the gardens, her eyes, soft as velvet, looking at nothing. She looked pale and fragile, but, when she saw Cassandra, she managed a weak smile.

'How do you feel?' Cassandra asked, sitting beside her, facing her.

'I have felt better.'

Cassandra squeezed her hand affectionately. 'We're going home shortly. Clem will soon be here with the carriage. You'll start to feel stronger when you're home with Mama to take care of you.'

'Is she very angry with me, Cassy?'

'Mama has been extremely concerned, Emma. She loves you very much and is sorry you're ill.'

'But is she angry,' Emma persisted, 'because I eloped with Edward?'

'Naturally she is upset by the whole dreadful event. She wasn't best pleased when she found out—and poor Aunt Elizabeth blamed herself most wretchedly.'

'Where is Edward?'

'He went to Woolwich with Will. Lord Lampard.'

Emma looked stricken. 'He's—he's gone to the academy—to be a soldier?' Cassandra nodded. 'Oh, I see.' She bent her head. 'It isn't fair. I wanted to be his wife so much. I shall be lost without him. How can I possibly carry on?'

'You are stronger than you know. In two or three years this will seem a small thing when you look back. Don't let it hurt so much, Emma.'

'But it does and this is now.'

'If you truly love Edward, it will endure.'

'You would, Cassy, I know. I have not your endurance. I— I won't give him up. I know you think I'm young and silly and that I don't know my own mind, but I do love him.'

Emma's face had taken on such a look of agony and despair that Cassandra softened involuntarily. 'I know you do,' she said gently and sighed. 'I know you're grown up, Emma, but do you really think you're ready to be married?'

'Yes, of course. Eloping was all my idea. I persuaded Edward. You mustn't think badly of him.'

'I was wrong about Edward, I realise that now. I misjudged him completely and I apologise for ever doubting him. You are right. He is a fine young man.'

Emma lifted her head, relief and hope lighting her eyes. 'You do? Oh, Cassy, I can't tell you what it means to me to hear you say that.'

'He loves you—genuinely loves you. Despite this foolish indiscretion, I believe him to be a good person—destined to be wounded by those harder, more selfish and less sensitive than he. I'll tell you what I said to him—give it time. Leave it for a while. I am of the opinion that things should be temporarily held in abeyance. Only until after you have come out, you understand, and this unfortunate business is behind us. Perhaps then, if you both still feel the same, then Mama will have no objections.'

Cassandra wished she didn't have to face William before she left. She remained with Emma for the rest of the morning. When it was time to leave, with her head held high and her delicate chin stubbornly set, she accompanied her sister downstairs. William was waiting for her in the hall. Outwardly she was composed and very calm, but inside she was seething.

William came towards her, curious as to why she had not come down earlier to see him. He ached for her—to touch her, to gaze on her lovely face, to hear the sweet, soft sound of her voice. When he had held her, she had touched a tenderness and protectiveness within him he hadn't known existed. After she favoured one of the footmen with her broadest smile, William was taken aback by the courteous and impersonal smile she gave him.

He wasn't to know how all her senses were crying out for him, how she was slowly dying inside. He had callously set out to dishonour her, and yet it was all Cassandra could do not to humble herself at his feet. With tremendous will she knew she would have to be strong to withstand a man of his character. William Lampard had no claim to being a gentleman in her interpretation of the word, but she knew him to be a proud man, and she intended to trample his pride to pieces.

'Did you sleep well?'

'Like a babe,' she quipped, trying to sound cool and amused. 'Indeed, I slept so well I failed to wake until a couple of hours ago.' She was surprised that her voice didn't shake.

Her tone, her very posture, were cool and aloof. William peered down at her, trying to read her expression. He wasn't sure what he had expected. An acknowledgement of what had passed between them, he supposed. His gaze went to Emma, who was hovering several paces behind, unsure how to approach Edward's imperious cousin who must be furious at their elopement. He took pity on her and softened his expression. 'Your sister looks pale. I told you I would be delighted to have you stay a while longer until she is fully recovered. I would not have said it if I did not mean it.'

'I know—and thank you,' Cassandra answered, her manner brusque, causing a flicker of consternation to cross William's face, 'but I am anxious to get home.' Only once did her composure slip a notch, and that was when Mark Lampard and a woman emerged from the study and came to stand behind William. Her bright smile faded uncertainly.

William turned to acknowledge them. 'Mark, you have met Miss Greenwood.'

'I have had that pleasure,' he replied, his eyes never leaving hers.

His hard, direct gaze told Cassandra their encounter had given him as little pleasure as it had her. 'It's good to see you again, sir,' she said politely.

He turned to the dark-haired woman standing beside him. 'Allow me to present my wife, Lydia.'

'I'm pleased to meet you, Lady Lampard,' Cassandra responded.

'Likewise,' Lydia replied smoothly.

Cassandra could read no expression in the woman's clear, attractive features, and as she regarded her closely, she felt her thoughts probed by careful fingers. She suppressed a shudder. Tall and slender, her nose aquiline and her hair perfectly coiffed, Lydia was quite beautiful, as a statue is beautiful— remote and cool. Her features were finely moulded and her lips showed a bitter twist. There was an indefinable poise about her, a certainty, and she had power. One thing Cassandra ascertained when she met her cold grey eyes—the coldest she had ever seen—was that this woman did not like her.

'Please excuse us. My sister and I are just leaving. We hope to make London before dark.'

'Then I wish you a safe journey.'

'Thank you. I'm sure it will be. Please excuse us.'

Taking Emma's arm, she led her outside to the waiting coach. William held out his hand to assist her down the steps, but she turned away. He was certain she had seen his hand, and he frowned in puzzlement as he watched her walk away. After a moment he realised she had an obligation to attend her sister, who still looked poorly, and he felt slightly easier. When Emma was inside the coach and it looked as if Cassandra was about to climb in without saying anything more to him, his face darkened and he took her arm.

'Cassandra, a moment, please.' He drew her aside out of earshot. 'Why are you doing this? Why are you angry with me?'

Her wide-eyed look was one of complete innocence. 'Angry? I am not angry,' she replied with a brittle gaiety, trying to harden herself against him, to forget his kiss and the way he had held her.

'I thought after last night—'

'Last night should never have happened. It was a mistake. We both lost control.' She looked up at him, looked away and back again. 'I should have known better than to submit to the charms of a philanderer.'

'I'm sorry you feel that way, because I think you are the loveliest, most courageous young woman I have ever met.'

Cassandra felt as if her heart was breaking. His gaze was one of consuming intensity, his mouth all wilful sensuality. 'Please stop it. Your compliments smack of insincerity. What happened was nothing more than an amusing diversion. It was just a sophisticated flirtation—the rule being the one you, a skilled libertine, usually play by—that no one takes anything seriously.'

He frowned. 'Are you afraid of what happened between us?' he asked in a voice of taut calm, wondering why she was behaving like this.

'Afraid? No, of course not. Why should I be? It's just that I do not want you to be courtly or romantic. It's not you. Why—before I know where I am I might start falling for it and believe you truly care.'

'You cannot mean that.'

'Why not?' she said, struggling valiantly to sound flippant.

'It meant nothing to you?'

'Shall we leave out the dramatics?'

William's face hardened into an expressionless mask, but his eyes were probing hers like daggers, looking for answers, as if he couldn't really believe this was the same woman who had melted in his arms with such sweet, innocent passion and yielded her lips to his. His disappointment made him carelessly cruel. 'You would do well to remember how you responded to my kiss—willingly—and how you enjoyed kissing me.'

'That was last night. This is now—and I didn't enjoy kissing you,' she lied primly, doing her utmost to avoid his eyes as a change came over him. In all her life she had never encountered such controlled purposeful anger.

William stared at her. 'Forgive me if I appear dense, but you gave a fair imitation of it last night.'

She smiled. 'And no doubt after all your conquests, you're surprised to discover there's a female who finds you resistible.'

Reaching out, William gripped her upper arms and jerked her against him. When he spoke his voice was dangerously low. 'I would like to convince you that you can overcome that problem—to persuade you.'

'Try as hard as you like, but you will not succeed. I will not allow it.'

His features were as hard as rock, his eyes like ice. 'And I thought you were different from the rest—fool that I am,' he said with biting sarcasm that made Cassandra's heart squeeze in the most awful, inexplicable way. William was no longer able to find her either amusing or admirable. His eyes moved over her face as if he were memorising it. His hands slid down her arms and abruptly he released her as he stepped back.

'I will detain you no longer. You'd best get into the carriage. Your sister is waiting. Goodbye, Cassandra. I hope you have a safe journey.'

The regret in his voice touched her to the core of her being. She would have turned back, but she sharply reminded herself of what she had overheard. But as she settled herself beside Emma, she experienced a sharp tug of loss at the realisation that she might never see him again. Her heart ached with the desolation of it.

His face inscrutable, his eyes as dark and ominous as the Thames on a stormy day, William stood and watched the carriage disappear down the drive. Truly believing that he was the injured party, he turned and stalked into the house, determined to purge her from his mind—purging her from his heart would not be so easy.

During the days that followed, he gave himself up to adjusting to life at Carlow Park and the day-to-day running of the estate. Bailiffs were called to give an account of their management, accounts gone into, acres of land ridden over, meetings with his tenant farmers—when he was finally satisfied that everything was as it should be, his thoughts turned unwillingly to Cassandra.

Alone in his elegant house, he restlessly wandered from room to room, unable to escape the throbbing emptiness that was gnawing away at him with a pain that increased unbearably with each passing day. He missed his military life and his fellow soldiers, and now that he was home the absence of his family cut through him like a knife. But what surprised him most was how much he missed Cassandra. She had entered his life like a breath of spring, and had left it after just a short time like a violent winter storm. With each hour that passed, the more impatient he grew to see her again.

How had he allowed her to get that close? A faint smile touched his lips as he remembered how heartbreakingly young and lovely she had looked at Lady Monkton's ball as, with intelligent logic, she had charmingly touted for donations for her precious institute, donations that would bring a small degree of humanity to children's lives. She was courageous, spirited and incorrigible. Only Cassandra would have dared do such a thing at a society ball, and only Cassandra would have taken him to task over what she considered to be his licentious ways.

The truth was that neither time nor distance had blunted the feelings he had for Cassandra Greenwood. From the moment he had set eyes on her she had bewitched him, cast a spell on him from which he could not set himself free. She had come between him and everything that up to meeting her had formed his pleasant and harmonious life.

But he could not understand why she had melted into his arms one minute and then, for no comprehensible reason, had treated him as if he were contemptible, as if she were trying to teach him some well-deserved lesson. Unable to concentrate on his work and becoming more frustrated by the day, he knew he was losing the battle to forget her. And so, after notifying Mark of his departure, he left for London with the hope of seeing her, and to fill the gaping emptiness of his life.

Harriet made a huge fuss when Cassandra and Emma arrived home. Between severe castigation, concern for Emma's health and tears of relief that she had both daughters secure beneath her roof once more, Harriet ordered Emma—penitent, pale and tired—to bed. Harriet was a sensible woman, but she was soft where her younger daughter was concerned.

Later, seated in front of the fire, Cassandra talked quietly to her mother, giving her an account of all that had transpired. When she rose to go to bed, Harriet said, 'Don't go yet, Cassandra. There is another matter I wish to discuss with you.'

'Oh?' Cassandra sat down again. Ever since they had arrived home she had known something other than Emma was worrying her mother. 'It's about the institute, isn't it?'

'I'm afraid it is.'

Harriet's eldest daughter worried her greatly. Cassandra's single-mindedness, her sense of purpose, was so strong, so directed, it was frightening. Ever since her dear papa had died she had dedicated all her time and energy to the institute. What Harriet was about to tell her would wound her deeply.

'As you know, things have been difficult for a long time. Despite Lord Lampard's generous donation, the funds are rapidly drying up. If—if things don't improve, then I fear that we will have to close the institute.'

Cassandra stiffened. 'Lord Lampard? I knew he had made a donation, but I have no idea how much.'

'A hundred pounds.'

Cassandra's eyes opened wide. 'That is a generous sum indeed.'

Maybe, she thought wryly, it would not have been so generous were it not for the wager he had made with Sir

Charles Grisham. She was beginning to realise that William Lampard never did anything without a motive, and she strongly suspected that his generous donation was all part of his seduction.

But what was to be done about this other matter? She was willing to tout for funds, but apart from that she left the financial side to her mother. Things had been serious for a long time, but she had not known how serious. Suddenly, despite the warmth of the room, she felt chilled to the bone, numbed by the enormity of what this could mean. Her mother was a gentle lady, with an aura of unflustered serenity. Yet below that surface was a quiet steeliness. Everything about her was ruled by the love she had shared with her husband.

'I can't believe things are so bad. We can't close the institute, Mama. The children rely on us. All Papa's hopes and dreams are wrapped up in that place.'

'I know. It pains me, too. The institute is very important to me. I feel as if, while ever I carry on with your dear papa's work, I still have a part of him with me. I wish there was some other way.'

'What we do makes such a difference to the children's wretched lives. We must find a way to keep it open. What are we to do?'

'I don't know. We should be able to keep going for a month or so. In the meantime I'll try and think of something.'

'We need to redouble our efforts. First thing tomorrow I'll write to the benefactors—maybe they will be extra-generous and give more. Things will work out for us,' Cassandra promised unconvincingly. 'Have you not considered accepting Aunt Elizabeth's offer?'

'No. We agreed in the beginning never to ask Elizabeth to donate money—even though she would be willing to do so. I am grateful for all she's done for us as a family—for her to fund the institute is one step too far.'

'I do agree with you, Mama. It was but a thought. I'll see

if we can get some government funding—although Lord knows how hard I've tried and failed in the past—but—Mama, will you write and thank Lord Lampard for his donation?'

'Yes, yes I will. I intended to, but this shocking business of Emma's elopement wiped it clean from my mind. She has broken all the rules governing moral conduct. Let us hope that none of this comes out. If it does, in the eyes of the *ton,* she will be considered shameless and wanton—soiled—unfit company for unsullied young ladies, gullible heirs and polite society. In short, her reputation will be ruined. What happened to the young man—Edward Lampard?'

'Lord Lampard took his cousin to the Military Academy at Woolwich, where he hopes he will settle down to soldiering.'

'Do you think he will try to see Emma?'

'Not unless you grant him permission. I have to say, Mama, that I misjudged him. He's a serious-minded, personable young man. It is plain that he loves Emma—and she him.'

'Nevertheless, we cannot escape the unforgivable fact that he compromised Emma most disgracefully. And Lord Lampard?' Harriet asked after a moment's hesitation, peering at her daughter's face with curious concern. 'You must have spent some considerable time alone with him—and—I know he has a certain reputation with the ladies. I may spend a great deal of my time at the institute, but I've heard endless gossip about him—rumours—not altogether favourable.'

'Whether they are true or not, Mama, what difference does it make? We were thrown together out of mutual concern for our respective relatives, nothing more. He was polite and attentive towards me, when Emma took a turn for the worse, I was indeed grateful that he put his house at our disposal.'

'Then that is to his credit, and perhaps his character is not as black as it has been painted after all.'

Cassandra lowered her eyes. How could she say to her mother that men like William Lampard brought nothing but anguish to any woman foolish enough to fall for their attractive looks and silken tongue? He was devilishly appealing, yes, but dangerous and destructive.

Two weeks had passed since that conversation in which Cassandra and her mother had decided to write letters to all the institute's benefactors, as yet, they had not received a single reply. All those who had made donations in the past were no longer dedicated to their cause.

Cassandra threw herself into her work, going about her duties with a calm demeanour that belied the multitude of emotions raging inside. No matter how adamantly she tried not to think of William Lampard, he had ways of creeping into her mind.

It was time for Archie to leave the institute. A rule Cassandra had made when she had first become involved with the institute was not to become too attached to any of the children, but because of the severity of Archie's injuries, which had made his stay at the institute longer than most, she had become extremely fond of him and would be sorry to see him go.

A timid, quiet body, he'd been terrified that he'd have to go back to work for the sweep when his feet healed. When Cassandra told him she had found him a place working with horses in Lord Lampard's stables here in London, he was overwhelmed with a mixture of relief and delight. Cassandra went to great lengths to groom and dress him for the occasion. His fair hair was cut and he was dressed in some decent second-hand clothes. And so, proudly wearing a new pair of boots and with his young face shining with excitement, Cassandra took him to Grosvenor Square.

The day was a brilliant blue, with a fresh warm breeze that carried the scent of flowers from Green Park. Full of trepidation in the carriage, Cassandra hoped fervently that William was still at Carlow Park, although, even if he had returned to London, she was hardly likely to encounter him in the stables. On Cassandra's instruction, Clem did not stop in front of the house, but went round to the back. They were directed to the stables by a kitchen maid.

Crossing the stable yard, they gingerly entered the stable's dim interior, the smell of hay, horses, manure and leather strong, though not unpleasant. Cassandra observed several people at work. Her gaze became focused on a man instructing a young stable boy on how to groom a tall bay mare in one of the boxes.

Tall and thin, Thomas was in his late thirties, yet he had a boyish look about him. When he saw them standing in the doorway, there was an unmistakable look of admiration in his eyes as he left off what he was doing and strode towards them.

'My name is Miss Greenwood. Lord Lampard told me there is a place for Archie here in his stables.'

Thomas looked at the young boy, whose wide-eyed gaze was fixed on the many horses in wonder. He smiled. 'I was told to expect him; with so many horses, there's always a need for an extra pair of hands. Do you like horses, lad?'

'Oh, yes, sir,' Archie was quick to respond, his reply coming straight from the heart.

'That's good, because his lordship likes his mounts to be well taken care of.'

'And what splendid mounts they are,' Cassandra remarked.

Hearing the voice of the woman who had been occupying his thoughts for the past two weeks, the man in the next stall jerked erect and swung around.

From the corner of her eye Cassandra glimpsed a tall man in the box to the side of her, and an uncontrollable tremor of dread shot through her. She could have sworn she saw him stiffen with shock, but in that instant she was absolutely besieged with cowardice and kept her head averted, her face hidden behind the brim of her straw bonnet.

'Miss Greenwood!' William's voice rang out.

As she turned her head their eyes met instantly, and so abrupt was William's appearance that Cassandra started. A world of feelings flashed across his face—surprise, disbelief, admiration—but only for a moment. Astonished and confused, she looked away and back again.

'A pleasure seeing you again, Miss Greenwood,' William said with grim formality.

The scathing tone of his voice, and the fantasy of seeing him remorseful following their bitter parting at Carlow Park, collapsed the instant she saw his face—it was as hard and forbidding as a rock. When they had parted she had not expected to feel the awful lack of him in her life. For a short while he had filled every moment of it, with his often difficult, sometimes passionate and demanding self. He had angered and amused her, aroused her, made her feel and think… and hurt, shamed and humiliated her. She would never forgive him.

He stood with his arm resting negligently on the back of a horse without bothering to come forward, watching her through narrowed eyes. His white shirt hung loosely about his wide shoulders and his thick hair was tousled and almost black in the dim light. His face was one of arrogant handsomeness with its sculpted mouth and striking eyes, but there was cynicism in those eyes and a ruthless set of his jaw. Everything about him exuded brute strength, and as she searched his features there was no sign that he had actually held her and kissed her with seductive tenderness. She flinched at the coolness of his eyes as they raked over her.

'How is your sister?' he enquired.

Cassandra swallowed and was surprised that she managed to reply without her voice shaking. 'She is very well, thank you. A—and you?'

'As you can see, I have survived our last encounter without scars.'

Thomas, who had observed the exchange and noticed Miss Greenwood's nervousness, found the incident as odd as his lordship's coldness towards her. However, it wasn't for the likes of him to criticise or speculate on what was between the two of them. 'Miss Greenwood has brought the lad Archie that you spoke of, milord.'

Coming out of the box, William looked down at the boy he had last seen stretched in bed with his feet bandaged. 'So, you are Archie. And are you recovered?'

'Yes, sir—milord,' Archie said, in awe of the towering man and having a hard time keeping his eyes off him.

'Well, then, I am glad to hear it. Welcome to my home, Archie.'

Archie flushed gratefully.

'Thomas will teach you all you need to know. You'll soon settle in and learn all about horses.'

'Thank you, sir,' Archie said, unmistakable eagerness in his young voice.

Looking on, Cassandra knew that a word from Lord Lampard had made Archie his servant for ever. Grateful to him for putting Archie at his ease, all the bitter heartache of the last two weeks began to lose its biting edge.

William addressed Thomas. 'Have Tim show Archie where he will sleep.'

Observing Miss Greenwood's worried look, Thomas was quick to reassure her. 'Don't worry about him, Miss Greenwood. He'll be perfectly all right. He'll share a room with young Tim here,' he said, drawing the lad forward. 'As you can see, they're of an age and I'm sure will become friends in no time.'

To confirm Thomas's words, an amiable-looking Tim took Archie's hand, and, with a smiling look at Cassandra, Archie followed his new friend up some wooden steps to the quarters above.

Thanking Thomas, Cassandra left the stable with William hard on her heels. 'Thank you. By treating Archie with courtesy, you have engendered his respect and you can be assured of his life-long devotion.'

'Pity the same cannot be said of you.'

Cassandra ignored his remark and averted her gaze. 'I am grateful to you for giving him a place. I only wish I could place others so well.' She looked back at him, meeting his gaze directly. 'I didn't expect to find you here, otherwise I would have asked Clem to bring Archie.'

'And deprive me of the pleasure of seeing you again? Shame on you, Cassandra.' The humour in his voice was disguised by a disapproving frown.

'Have you been in London long?'

'No more than twenty-four hours.'

'I see.'

The words were commonplace, such as might have been exchanged by virtual strangers.

'Please excuse me,' Cassandra said, her manner brusque. 'I must go.' She began to walk across the cobbled yard. Suddenly William's tall figure appeared in front of her, barring her way to the gate and freedom.

'And where are you off to in such a hurry?' he asked, taking her arm and halting her in her stride.

The touch of his hand made her breath come faster. It had always been so. It was beyond her power to control—but conceal it she must. The magnetic attraction still remained beneath all the irritation—she both hated and wanted this detestable man.

'Please release my arm,' she said stiffly, the wager he had made with Sir Charles Grisham at the forefront of her mind. Her mind still burned with the memory of what she had overheard at Carlow Park that day and she wasn't ready to be forgiving. 'I have brought Archie and now there is nothing more to be said.'

William had no mind to let her off lightly. He laughed, and it was such a warm, throaty laugh that ended in a smile, the kind of smile that would melt any woman's heart if she didn't know him for the arrogant, heartless libertine he was. His grip on her arm did not slacken, but it was painless.

'You think not? It seems to me we have a great deal to say to one another. When you left Carlow Park I was quite put out that I had been rebuffed by you. I couldn't help thinking about you—a great deal, as a matter of fact. I haven't been able to get you out of my mind. And now—here you are.'

'You are very convincing and you have a flattering tongue,' Cassandra uttered scathingly. 'In fact, I could actually believe you are speaking the truth, but then you have undoubtedly had a great deal of practice.' He raised a handsome brow as he gave her a lengthy inspection. 'Has anyone ever told you how infuriating you are?'

His white teeth gleamed behind a lopsided grin. 'Thus far, my dear Cassandra, every female I've ever encountered. I'm quite nonchalant about these things. For some reason unbeknown to me, I believe you are somehow testing me.' His blue eyes glinted like hard metal. 'I think this may bear further investigation and we must discuss the matter.'

It dawned on Cassandra as his gaze fastened on her lips that he was remembering their kisses. For a man who had received such a crushing let-down when they had parted company, William Lampard seemed disgustingly at ease.

'I don't think so. Anything I have to say to you I said when I left Carlow Park—and go and fondle someone else,' she retorted, dragging her arm from his grasp, her eyes flaring with poorly suppressed ire. 'I'm sure the kind of woman you usually consort with would welcome your attentions.'

He laughed softly at her condemning tones. 'I'd rather be fondling you.'

'Why?' she scoffed. 'Because you want to add me to your long string of conquests?'

Her chilled contempt startled him, and his eyes narrowed. 'Conquest! Now there's a controversial word. You're mistaken, Cassandra. To conquer is to overpower, to take and force one's strength on another. I do not ask you to yield to me and nor do I take anything that is not freely given. I know how you reacted when you were in my arms—I felt your desire. You enjoyed kissing me.'

'No,' Cassandra whispered, shamed by the memory of her own response.

'Do not deny it. I know the truth.'

'No, you don't. You don't know me,' she said furiously. 'And I don't know you. I don't trust you.'

'But you do want me, Cassandra,' he told her with a knowing smile.

Despite the fact that she shook her head, she knew it was true, but she wouldn't give him the satisfaction of saying so.

His gaze dropped meaningfully to her lips. 'When I kissed you, you found me very desirable.'

Cassandra jerked her face away. 'Stop looking at me like that. It isn't seemly. The yard is full of stable boys and we are in full view of your neighbours,' she stated, glancing at the many windows of the surrounding stately houses that overlooked the stable yard.

William looked at her flushed, entrancing, rebellious face and a reluctant smile tugged at his lips. 'You have no idea what I would dare do to you,' he warned with a lazy, suggestive smile. 'And do you have any idea what will happen if I follow my inclinations and kiss you? For a start, we will be talked about and you will be off limits to every respectable male in London.'

Her eyes shot daggers at him. 'I'm off limits anyway—of my own volition, as well you know. Just leave me alone. I'm going now.' She backed away and put her hands up defensively to ward him off when he took a step towards her. 'And if you come near me I shall scream and tell your servants you are molesting me. Goodbye, William. I really don't think I want to see you again.'

As she climbed into the carriage and ordered Clem to take her home, she refused to look back, so she didn't see his expression of quiet determination as he stood and watched her go. She felt her eyes sting. She must cling to the thought that she was extremely fortunate to have found out about the disgusting wager before she had made a complete fool of herself, that she had realised the full extent of his profligacy, and that the original rumours, which had told her to avoid him, had been correct. But it was all so dreadful and painful beyond anything she could have imagined.

When Cassandra's carriage had disappeared, William continued standing there, deep in thought. He gave up trying to understand the reason for what he was about to do. He wanted Cassandra Greenwood and that was reason enough. She represented everything most desirable in a woman. When he had taken Charles's wager, she had merely been the tantalising object of his lustful thoughts and he'd thought of little else but possessing her, but after giving it careful thought he'd quickly changed his mind.

Seducing gently reared virgins was not his style—he preferred the women he made love to to be experienced, sophisticated and undemanding of himself and his time, but that did not lessen his obsession with Cassandra in the least. The effect she had had on him then had been as unsettling as it was now, and he was unable to analyse the raw heat that ran through his veins whenever she was near him.

Since he had dispensed with his military career and returned to the responsibility of his inheritance, it was his duty to marry and provide an heir, a responsibility of which he had been constantly reminded from the day he learned of Robert's death. And now, when he thought of Cassandra—lovely to look at, a temptress, enchanting and alluring—he wanted her badly. She had inflamed him and stirred his lust without intention. He smiled, for he could not blame her. Beauty, combined with charm and sweet innocence, would sway any man.

The fact that she had determinedly begun to oppose him— the reason for which remained a mystery to him—did not deter him. Had he not felt her body's reaction, her desire for him when he had held her and kissed her? He did not have the slightest doubt that he would be able to lure her back into his arms. His mind made up, he turned and strode briskly back into the stables. His decision to make her his wife was one that brooked no further debate.

When Cassandra left Grosvenor Square, firmly believing that her association with Lord William Lampard was well and truly over, she was unprepared for what happened next.

The secret of Emma's elopement with Edward Lampard was revealed and the public and very unsavoury scandal that ensued was enormous. Harriet and Elizabeth were devastated. All their hopes and carefully laid plans to give her a Season were dashed. Cassandra scanned what was printed in the newspapers, her stomach churning.

Her eyes wounded and glazed with shock, Emma was seated on the sofa, shattered by the weight of responsibility for her foolishness. 'I'm sorry,' she whispered helplessly, looking from her mama to Aunt Elizabeth, speaking through the tears of shame and sorrow choking her. 'I'm so very sorry. I didn't intend any of this.'

Peering from her mother's face to Emma's stricken one, Cassandra said, 'Don't worry, Emma. We'll stand together on this.'

'Thank you,' Emma said. 'At a time like this, loyalty counts for a lot.'

Harriet and Elizabeth exchanged sympathetic glances, and Cassandra headed for her sister, sinking down beside her. 'I'm sorry,' she murmured, wrapping her in a fierce hug. 'You're not the first female to lose her head over a handsome young man, and you certainly won't be the last.'

'It's more than that, Cassy. I told you how I feel for Edward. I haven't changed and I miss him dreadfully—especially now, with all this going on.'

'I know. I wish I knew how details of your elopement were leaked—who is spreading these stories.'

Emma shook her head dejectedly. 'I suppose social prejudices will exclude me from respectable *ton* events—but none of that seems to matter any more without Edward.'

'I can't condone what you and that young man did, Emma, behaving with such indiscretion,' her mother said gently, deeply worried by the change in her daughter. 'But from what Elizabeth has told me, elopements are fashionable—why, there have been several already this year.'

'And all the couples succeeded. If Edward and I had reached Scotland and married, I might have been hailed as a heroine—just as Henrietta Kirkbride was when she eloped and wed Viscount Swinburn. N-nothing untoward happened between us. You do believe that, don't you, Mama?' Emma sounded as meek and bewildered as a child who has been punished for something it didn't do.

'Of course I do.'

Cassandra sighed. 'Whether it did or not, I'm afraid you are ruined just the same.'

Cassandra was right. Lurid versions of the elopement were spreading like wild fire through the *ton*. More damning by far was the story circulating that the young lovers had spent a night alone at a coaching inn before an irate Lord Lampard and Emma's sister had caught up with them—which was another intriguing story that people were beginning to get their teeth into and chew. And so, deciding that Emma's character must be of the blackest nature, she was summarily dropped by the *ton* before she'd even made her curtsy.

Chapter Seven

William arrived at the institute when a motley assortment of street children were partaking of their one proper meal of the day. He pushed his way inside a communal room and stood looking round at the uneven walls, sagging ceiling and old pitted beams, and yet, despite the dilapidation of the place, everything was scrubbed to a high quality of cleanliness.

Two of Cassandra's helpers had their arms in a bucket of water at a large pot sink, washing crockery. Children lined up eagerly with their bowls, all eyes on the huge steaming pot from which a cheerful, middle-aged woman, wearing a mob-cap and a huge apron wrapped round her rotund middle, was ladling out an appetising stew. Snatching up a hunk of bread to go with it, the children went to sit at a long table where some were already bolting their food under the watchful eyes of Miss Greenwood.

William's attention was drawn to her. Her hair was pinned up, her face all rosy from the steam of the cooking, but it was tense, which told him she was under great strain. He was anxious to fathom her mood, but where he had known her before as a quick-tempered, provocative and passionate young woman, he now perceived an air of quiet seriousness about her. Perhaps the tribulations of the past week had stripped all humour from her. She bore no hint of the happy, charming Cassandra he had seen at Lady Monkton's ball, or the feisty young woman who had courageously told him their association was over. He braced himself, but could not shrug off a dismal frame of mind. The outlook seemed far from bright.

As if she sensed his presence, Cassandra looked towards the door. If she was surprised to see him there, she didn't show it. He expected defiance, hauteur, but there was neither. She moved towards him, her eyes broodingly sad.

Gazing up at him, noting his usual careless elegance, Cassandra thought he was so like she remembered that she expected to feel the familiar warmth flow from him, but his eyes were fathomless and gave nothing back.

'You've come at a busy time,' she said. 'As you can see, this is when we prepare a meal for the children. They're so hungry they'd eat anything. At least what we give them is wholesome and nourishing.'

'I called at your home, hoping to see your mother. When I was informed she had gone away I thought I'd seek you out. I hope you don't mind me coming here.'

'No, of course I don't—it wouldn't take much working out where I would be. Mama and Aunt Elizabeth have taken Emma to the country—to Netherton Hall, Aunt Elizabeth's house near Guildford. A time spent out of town at this time will be a relief—you understand.'

William nodded. 'I'm here to help. It's an appalling state of affairs. How are you coping?'

'Not very well.' Sighing with great weariness, she bent her head, putting the back of her hand to her eyes for a moment. 'It's all such a dreadful mess.' She had tried so hard not to let her worry over Emma get to her, and she had succeeded to a certain extent, but she was storing up a terrible burden of emotion.

William's eyes were warm with concern. She looked tired and worn out, and behind her calm exterior he sensed she endured a nauseating turmoil of distress. He stood with his hands in his pockets, his face carefully blank, while all the time he wanted to reach out and take her in his arms, kiss and soothe her and tell her he was going to make everything all right, and yet, remembering the deep division that stood between them, how could he?

'Can you get away?' he asked quietly. 'I've got my carriage outside. We should talk about this. I would be grateful if you would grant me a little of your time and listen to what I have to say.'

She gave a wry smile. 'Talk? How will talking solve anything? Whatever you have to say to me can be said while I am working.'

'I came to talk with you privately. Please, Cassandra, I am in earnest. I'm sure they can manage without you for half an hour while we take a walk in the park.'

Cassandra stared at him for a long, indecisive moment. Since she must discuss this unfortunate business with him because it involved his cousin, she must at least be civil. 'I suppose I could, but as you can see I am not dressed in any proper state for a walk in the park.'

'You could be wearing sackcloth and ashes for all I care. I assure you that dress beneath your apron is most appropriate,' he said with that gentleness that always surprised Cassandra at unexpected times. 'That colour blue suits you—it matches your eyes. I am sure your bonnet will complement the look.'

She glanced at him, the black wave of despondency that had engulfed her for the past week lifting a little. 'Since it's only an old straw bonnet that I wear with almost everything, it will be an odd combination, but one I am sure will make me the envy of all the other ladies in the park,' she remarked with wry humour.

Admiration swelled in William at how valiantly she was rallying.

'I'm just slipping out for a while, Agatha,' she informed the woman ladling out the stew. 'There's something I have to do. Will you be all right?'

Agatha smiled broadly and nodded, openly admiring of their handsome, elegantly attired guest. 'Aye, lass. We'll manage. You go on. A break will do you the world of good.'

'Agatha's a true gem,' Cassandra said as she removed her apron and donned the aforesaid bonnet. 'Having lost her husband in the Peninsula and with no children of her own, she devotes all her time to the institute. She cares deeply for all the children who come here, and gets through as much work as anyone in an easy and efficient fashion. I don't know what we'd do without her, although she's not the only one. Several women come to help out. They are good women, charitable and respectable.'

The two women at the sink turned to watch her leave with William, their mouths agape. Never had they seen such a handsome gentleman at the institute, and already they were speculating as to who he could be and how close his association was with Miss Greenwood.

William handed Cassandra into the carriage and climbed in after her, instructing the driver to make for Green Park. She sat beside him perfectly still, her hands folded in her lap, her face now pale but composed. Several people were strolling in the park, governesses with their young charges and nursemaids pushing perambulators. Acquaintances exchanged greetings and children bowled hoops along the paths. Sweet scents of early summer, of flowers and cut grass drifted on the light breeze.

Not until they were walking slowly along a path did Cassandra find her voice. 'How has this happened? How did everyone find out about the elopement? Who saw—who told?'

'I have no idea. These things have a way of leaking out. Other people's love lives are endlessly fascinating to others. The stories thrive under the complicit though theoretically unseeing eyes of servants.' His lips curved in a wry smile. 'The servants' hall at my house here in London is privy to more secrets than the Prime Minister's cabinet. But no matter how it came out, it is done and we must deal with it.'

Cassandra stopped and looked at him in an agony of exasperation. William saw her defences rise as she said, 'We? How are you affected? It is Emma who is affected. Emma who is ostracised. Her own foolishness and that of your cousin has endangered her future—as a man it will not affect Edward the same and you know it. It never does and it is so unfair. Emma is young—young and deeply hurt.'

'You're not exactly in your dotage, Cassandra,' William murmured gently.

'Emma is not as strong as I am. I can cope with most things. My heart is filled with rage against a society that could treat a young woman who has done no wrong so harshly. They are savages. Personally I wouldn't care less if I was cut. As if I care a snap for the *ton*'s approval—but I care that Emma minds. She is so sensitive. When she read the awful things that were written about her in the newspapers she went to her room and stayed there for two days, weeping inconsolably.'

'I am sorry to hear that,' William murmured, genuinely moved by Emma's distress. 'She deserves none of this.'

'Knowing people are talking about her, laughing at her— she can't stand it—it's destroying her. Her future is in ruins. No decent gentleman will associate with a young woman of questionable virtue. And she is missing Edward dreadfully, not knowing if she will ever see him again. Mama is devastated and doesn't know how she will endure it. Thank God Aunt Elizabeth took them to Netherton Hall to get away from London and the gossip.'

Seeing a bench away from the path and prying eyes, and doing a quick scan of the area to make sure no one was about to take another shot at him, William took her elbow and led her towards the seat. They sat down and half turned to face each other. Cassandra was twenty years old and still unmarried—no one had offered for her, though she was a better woman than any of the women he had known. Naturally enough this had engendered in her contempt for men's opinions—her manner told them she could do without them and their help. But she had a fierce pride, so what he had to suggest must be approached with caution.

He stared at her very seriously. 'Edward is also suffering most wretchedly—mainly because he knows how the scandal will be affecting your sister. I can see how it is affecting you, too, Cassandra.'

'I can't pretend that I don't mind Emma being the object of derision, and myself for that matter, but I have to get on with things. Unfortunately the institute is doing badly—it has been for some time—because of lack of funding, and since the scandal broke the money's dried up completely. It's only a matter of time before we will have to close it down.'

'I am genuinely sorry. I do understand the gravity of the situation.'

'It's a merciless world,' she murmured, shaking her head sadly. 'There are so many unwanted children sleeping anywhere they can. I have to think of the streets and hovels where they struggle in dirt and filth such as no human being should endure. It's a wonder any of them survive. I try not to be too emotional about it, but I cannot bear to look upon the face of a starving child while the rest of the world goes by. Mama always tells me not to get too emotional, but I can't help it.'

'What a sensitive soul you are, Cassandra Greenwood. One day you will get your orphanage and then you can fill it with as many destitute children as you like.'

She shook her head and smiled. 'No. It's just a dream. I'm sorry. I've been talking too much. I'm often criticised for being too outspoken.'

'Who criticises you?'

'Mama and Aunt Elizabeth, but when I feel strongly about something I can't help it.'

William moved a little closer to her and took her hands in his own, both surprised and relieved that she didn't object, noting her eyes richly lashed under excellently marked eyebrows. The way in which she was looking at him, she suddenly seemed very young and defenceless.

'This is how I regard it. What is the very worst that can happen? What do you fear most?'

She swallowed hard and tried to speak as calmly as he. 'That Emma's reputation is ruined beyond redemption and that she has no future—and that the institute will have to close and the children who have come to depend on us will have nowhere else to go.'

William smiled—it was so like her to think of others before herself.

'Why do you smile?' she asked.

'Because that's your woman's heart speaking. Speaking as a soldier, I can think of no worse fate than death. So be it. Now, what is the best thing that can happen? What do you most desire?'

'That the two things I have just mentioned will be resolved,' she whispered fervently.

'Both are likely, and nothing is beyond one's strength, if the need is great enough.'

Cassandra looked startled. 'How can I believe that? I think you speak more to comfort than from belief.'

'I've got a suggestion that might appeal to you and your mother.' His smile widened and his blue eyes sparkled. 'It will certainly appeal to Emma. There is a solution, you know.'

'There is?' Unconvinced, her voice sounded flat. 'Then please tell me what it is so we can all be put out of our misery.'

'Edward and Emma could get married.'

Cassandra stared at him in amazement. 'Married?' This was not what she had expected him to say.

'I am cautiously optimistic that we can turn this around. If I doubted it, I would not suggest it, and nothing will be as effective at tossing aside the *ton*'s reticence. I'll admit I haven't given a great deal of time to working out all the details, but allowing for the scandal hanging over our heads, there is no reason in the world why Emma can't be introduced into society as a married woman. It might even offer her a certain notoriety, with everyone falling over each other to invite the newly-weds to this and that.'

Cassandra studied him. This was a different William Lampard from the one she had seen before. His easygoing manner, his ready understanding, his quiet attitude, brought calm to her troubled mind. But why was he doing this when he could so easily turn his back on them all and walk away? Did he still hope to win his part of the wager he had made with Sir Charles Grisham and turn this unfortunate situation to his own advantage? If so, he was going to be disappointed—for she would not fall for the soft words of a seducer—but she would willingly accept any suggestion he could come up with if it would solve the crisis. Aware that he was still holding her hands, his touch awakening her senses from their blissful anaesthesia, she slowly extricated them from his grasp.

'Why are you doing this? It's only a short time ago that you would have done anything to prevent Emma marrying your cousin.'

'If I did, that had nothing to do with your sister. Edward was due to begin his military career. Marriage was out of the question. As a soldier he will most certainly be sent abroad at some point—it would be a lonely time for a young wife.'

'Which will happen anyway if the marriage goes ahead.'

'Then that will be something for them to work out. Plenty of young ladies marry at eighteen. It is not unusual. Edward and Emma may be young, but they are in love, and if it lasts they'll be happier than those whose marriages are arranged with sole regard to the increase of family fortunes and no mutual affection between them.'

'Why, Lord Lampard! I never took you for a romantic.' Despite her family's dire predicament, and deeply suspicious of his motives for helping her family, Cassandra gave a teasing smile.

A rogue twinkle sparked in his eyes. 'Oh, I have my moments, but I would be obliged if you would keep it to yourself. Should it come out, my male pride would be wounded to such an extent that it will be irretrievable and my reputation as one of the *ton*'s most disreputable rakes will be in ruins.'

'So you do admit it—that you are just as disreputable as society says you are.'

He laughed good humouredly, relieved that her distress had lifted and she could indulge in light banter. 'No human being is perfect, Miss Greenwood.'

'You are quite right. Have you discussed this with Edward?'

'No. No one. If Emma and Edward decide marriage is what they want, then, since Lady Monkton can no longer bring Emma out, let her arrange the wedding—a truly splendid affair that will certainly give the *ton* something to gossip about—providing your mother is in agreement, naturally.'

'I think she will be thankful to have the situation resolved amicably—and Emma won't take any persuading. Aunt Elizabeth will be delighted with the outcome.'

'I'll write to my grandmother, the Dowager Countess of Carlow, and ask her to come to London. She is a lady of tremendous consequence.'

'Do you think that's necessary?'

'Absolutely. The more weight we have behind our campaign, the greater the chance of success. Society will soon change its attitude when they see not one, but two of the most influential ladies in London are championing Emma.'

'Does you grandmother live at Carlow?'

He nodded. 'I wanted her to move back into Carlow Park where she spent many happy years with my grandfather— Lord knows it's big enough—but she won't hear of it. She has a house on the estate, a companion and housekeeper and servants to look after her. She is content to remain where she is and make room for another generation of Lampards.'

'She sounds intriguing.'

'She is. She doesn't often come to town, but she will if I ask her. In her day she was one of the golden girls of society and never out of the newspapers. She's a bit of an eccentric and was something of a rebel in her time. She leaned towards the unconventional, running close to the limit, and never failed to disappoint either her fans or her critics. Until a few years ago she shamelessly adored forcing society to bend to her will. No one will dare say a word against Emma in her presence.'

'Oh, dear. She sounds quite formidable.'

'She is—in fact, you'll probably get on remarkably well,' he said with a reassuring, meaningful smile.

Cassandra stared into his compelling eyes incredulously. 'You really have thought all this out, haven't you?'

William laughed shortly, his eyes glowing in the warm light. 'Don't underrate my genius for strategy and subtlety. Since we cannot stop the gossip, we will redirect it. I'll prove to you how easy it will be to manipulate the *ton,* and to honour the Lampard tradition, it will have to be a church wedding done on a grand scale, with a vast number of relatives, friends and acquaintances from both sides—about seven hundred, I should think, maybe more—so as not to offend and alienate the *ton.*'

'Emma is passionate about everything spectacular and will relish any opportunity to be the centre of attention, so she will approve of that. Have you given any thought to the wedding breakfast, by any chance?'

'The venue can be left to your mother and Lady Monkton— perhaps Monkton House or my home in Grosvenor Square. Either will be suitable for such a large gathering.'

'A wedding on such a grand scale cannot be planned in a hurry. There will be so many arrangements to make—gowns to be made, invitations to be written, sent out and acknowledged. Why, it will take months.'

'Weeks,' William stated irrevocably. 'It must take place before the end of the Season, when everyone retires to their country estates for the summer. I shall put my entire staff at your disposal and I am certain Lady Monkton will waste no time in seeing her niece wed.'

'She'll love every minute of it…but…won't people talk and wonder at the need for such haste? I—I mean…' A light embarrassed flush suffused her, but she could not resist the query.

Knowing exactly what she was getting at, William's eyes narrowed and he smiled devilishly. 'I do know what you mean and I have considered that. Should it be true that Emma is *enceinte,* I doubt that either Edward or Emma would want a grand wedding, but a quiet affair out of the public eye. In any case, those who suspect this might be the case will be proved wrong given time.'

'Yes—of course, you're right.' She sighed, standing up, reluctant to leave the park, but there was so much to do at the institute. 'I must be getting back. How is Archie, by the way? Has he settled down?'

'He has. He's taken to his work well and likes being with the horses. He's become a favourite with cook, who says he's far too thin and needs fattening up. He's already put on weight. You wouldn't believe he was that scrawny scrap of a lad I saw at the institute that day I was shot.'

'I'm glad. He deserves a chance in life and I thank you for giving it to him.'

When they reached the carriage William handed her inside. 'The walk has done you good,' he remarked, noting the blooming rose colour in her cheeks as he settled himself across from her.

'I do feel better.'

'Good. Cassandra, when last we met you told me you never wanted to see me again—or words to that effect,' he said on a more serious note. 'If Edward and Emma agree to wed, I'm afraid you are going to see a good deal more of me. Will that be a problem for you?'

Across the distance that separated them, their gazes met and held, the silence punctuated by traffic and the clopping of the horses' hooves on the cobbled road. As they had talked, for Cassandra it was like taking a great burden and placing it on his strong shoulders, and she could breathe again. She was beginning to regard him with a new respect—and he had insinuated himself into her heart in a way she had never sought. But she could not forgive him that dreadful, shameful wager he had made and never would, but she was not about to be churlish about it now.

'Not if that's the way it has to be. It's a terrifying possibility,' she said with a hint of humour, 'but I'll risk it. When will you speak to Mama?'

'When will she be back in town?'

'That depends on Emma—a week or more.'

'Then perhaps we should drive to Guildford. The sooner the wheels are put in motion, the better—although I must speak to Edward first. I'll travel to Woolwich tomorrow and talk to him, and, if you can manage it, we can go to Surrey the day after.'

After seeing Edward and obtaining his ecstatic agreement to the suggestion that he marry his darling Emma, the following morning found William and Cassandra travelling to Guildford. It was a lovely day, warm and with fleecy white clouds drifting overhead on a gentle breeze.

Settled into the plush interior of the chaise and happy to have left the bustle of London behind, feeling unusually at ease following the tribulations of the past days, Cassandra let her gaze stray across to her companion. Attired in a cream-silk shirt and olive-green jacket, his muscular legs clad in calf-coloured superfine and shiny brown boots, William Lampard was the image of casual, relaxed elegance. Even his expression was casual—too casual, she thought. He seemed larger in the close confines of the coach, his shoulders broader, his face one of leashed sensuality and arrogant handsomeness, and there was a cynical twist to his sculpted mouth. Everything about him was forceful and exuded brute strength, and was most unsettling to her virgin heart.

'It's a pleasant day for a drive to Guildford,' William commented at length. 'I hope Lady Monkton will not mind us arriving unannounced.'

'She will be surprised, to say the least, when we arrive together—and will no doubt lecture me most severely on my lack of protocol for travelling with a gentleman alone. I suppose I must thank you for all you are doing to help Emma.'

'That is not my prime reason for doing it,' William answered smoothly.

Cassandra did not miss the meaningful glint in his eyes watching her from beneath hooded lids and was prompted to ask warily, 'Then what is your prime purpose?'

A slow smile curved his lips. 'Why, to get to know you better.'

'I think you know me well enough, Lord Lampard,' she retorted sharply, suddenly irate since his statement confirmed he intended to win the wager he had made with Sir Charles Grisham. 'And do you have to watch me so closely?'

'I like watching you. You are a stubborn woman, Miss Greenwood.'

'That's right. I am.'

'Beautiful, too. You look radiant this morning, by the way. The dress you are wearing is quite becoming— peacock-blue, I'd say.'

'Thank you. Every woman loves being likened to a bird,' she said drily.

'I meant it as a compliment,' he assured her.

'That's what worries me.'

William's eyes burned hotly behind his dark lashes. 'You know, you tempt me sorely, Cassandra.'

His gaze sparked a quickness within her, and she averted her eyes. No one before William had ever had such a turbulent effect on her. What was there about this man that aroused her so? There had been other handsome men—dashing, daring, some she considered intelligent—but not one had touched her like this man did and just the memory of his kiss filled her with delicious excitement, leaving her hungering for the consuming heat of his passion.

Greatly disturbed by the path her mind was taking, she turned away and gazed at the passing scenery, but after a moment's contemplation, she found herself looking back at him and inquiring, 'Have you ever been in love—really in love, I mean?'

William cocked a wondering brow at her and a lazy smile tugged at the corners of his mouth. 'There have been times when I thought I was, but now I'm beginning to realise I was mistaken.'

'Be serious,' she rebuked. 'Either you have or you haven't. It's as simple as that.'

He shrugged slightly. 'Nothing is that simple. There was a woman in Spain once—but I realise now that what I felt for her was only infatuation.' He smiled and his voice grew soft with the memory, as though remembering gave him pleasure. 'She was a widow woman, with the blackest hair and the darkest eyes. She taught me much—but it was a long time ago and best forgot.'

'I suppose you were besotted. Was she pretty?'

'She was very beautiful,' he conceded. 'Well-rounded in all the right places—twenty-five—worldly…'

A light blush touched Cassandra's cheeks and she quickly turned away, not wanting to meet his close perusal. 'You needn't go on.'

William chuckled softly. 'You did ask.'

'And I regret doing so.'

William sighed, folding his arms and leaning into the corner of the seat, wondering what she would have to say if he told her that the thought of other women soured in his mind when he contemplated her. 'Why have you grown averse to me of late, Cassandra? I am curious as to the reason.'

'I do not wish to encourage you in your blatant disregard for my status as an independent woman. I meant everything I said that day I took Archie to work for you. Nothing has changed.'

He laughed briefly. 'And you seem to take special delight in reminding me. Are you aware that there is a rumour spreading through the *ton* that I am trying to draw you into my clutches?' he said, watching her from beneath lowered lids. 'Our association has raised a few eyebrows.'

'Really,' Cassandra replied drily. 'I hadn't realised our acquaintance would cause such speculation.'

'People are talking.'

'It's not uncommon. It's how they communicate,' she retorted flippantly in an attempt to hide her unease about the direction the conversation was going.

'They're talking about us.'

'And what are they saying?'

'That you are about to become my mistress—if you are not already.'

Cassandra's eyes sparked angrily. 'Indeed! It's all very well for you. Your reputation isn't at stake. Nobody cares if you go about seducing every woman in London. It's what men do. But it's different for me. If people think you have seduced me, then I am ruined.' The words tumbled out.

William cocked an eyebrow, his eyes dancing with amusement. 'Ah—and all of a sudden you care what people think, do you?'

'Yes—in this instance I do.'

'And you wouldn't if it were some other man doing the seducing?'

'Perhaps not.'

'Then you will be relieved and happy to know that there are some members of society who credit you with more sense than to be caught by me.'

'I'm glad to hear it. As if I haven't enough to contend with right now.'

'The fact that the two of us left London to prevent the

runaways from reaching Gretna Green has been classed as compromising circumstances. It was my fault. I knew what the rules were and broke them when I allowed you to accompany me and later took two unchaperoned young ladies to my home.' His grin was devilish. 'Imagine—if we found ourselves in the same situation as Emma and Edward.'

Cassandra gave him a dire look. 'I am—it is my worst nightmare and it won't happen.'

Cassandra was unconscious of the vision she presented with her skin aglow, her lively eyes and the material of her travelling dress straining over her breasts. Her delectable face fed William's gaze, and his eyes passed over her shapely figure with warm admiration, creating a sweet, hungering ache inside him. He couldn't think of anything more pleasurable at that moment than having her warm and willing in his arms, soft and yielding, as she had been when he had kissed her at Carlow Park. He burned with a consuming desire for her, and he would be satisfied with nothing less than her complete submission. His intense physical attraction to her continued to surprise him.

Gazing out of the window, Cassandra expressed to her companion the wish that he had selected to travel in an open carriage.

'You're right, of course.' His smile faded, and he grew serious. 'But there is need for caution. My life may depend on it.'

'Have you found out any more about the man who shot you that day?'

'Twice.'

She met his eyes with an unwavering gaze. 'Twice? You mean he has tried again?'

He nodded, his face grim. 'When I was returning to Carlow Park after taking Edward to Woolwich.'

'But—you never said anything.'

'There was no need.' He went on to recount what had occurred and she listened in horror. 'Ever since that first attempt I no longer ride out alone and I am constantly looking over my shoulder. I've employed someone who specialises in investigating matters such as this, a Mr Jardine. Hopefully he will come up with something before whoever it is trying to kill me succeeds.'

'Wouldn't you be safer at Carlow Park, in the country, where you will know if there is a stranger loitering about?'

'You forget that I have spent precious little time at Carlow Park these past few years. Nearly everyone is a stranger to me. Besides, it was in the country the last time my would-be assassin tried to dispose of me. I just wish I could think of a reason why someone is so desperate to have me dead.'

The look that appeared on his face gave Cassandra a chill, but it was briefly seen. 'Jealousy, hatred, greed…someone from your military past, perhaps—someone out for revenge,' she suggested.

'I've thought of that—gone over and over it in my mind. I admit I've made enemies in the past, but I can't think of one who would want to kill me.'

'Then the only other motive I can think of is for personal gain. You—told me your cousin Mark is next in line to inherit your estate.'

'He is.'

'Since he is your cousin and you are close, I know how you will react when you hear what I have to say, but…' She hesitated, afraid of the risk she took, but somehow she found the courage to ask him, 'Do you think it's Mark who is trying to kill you? After all, he has much to gain.'

The muscles in William's cheeks tensed and flexed as he met her eyes. 'No. Never. Is that what you think, Cassandra?'

'Well—I don't know, but I suppose it is a possibility.'

'No one who knows him would think so.'

'Perhaps you do not know him well enough.'

Anger darkened Williams eyes. 'I believe I do. Take it from me, it is not Mark.'

'Well, I think you should keep a close eye on him all the

same.' She had only met him briefly, but there was something about him that told her Mark Lampard was not entirely to be trusted.

Not wishing to pursue that particular line of enquiry, William sat in brooding silence for the next few minutes, but the mere fact that Cassandra had suggested his cousin in connection with the shootings gave him a feeling of unease. Unconsciously he massaged his shoulder, which ached when he was tense.

Cassandra noticed. 'Does your shoulder still pain you?'

He shook his head. 'No more than a slight discomfort.'

The tranquillity of the journey was shattered when they left the London Road and turned into a narrow lane. Cassandra's gaze was drawn across some fields to a wooded hill and there, on the skyline and where the trees parted, was a lone horseman. The sun caught and glinted on an object he was holding up to his face. She was sure it was a telescope and that it was focused on them. She gave a gasp and her head spun round to William. She could tell by the expression on his face that he, too, had seen the horseman.

'William,' she said in alarm, 'I think that horseman is watching us.'

'So do I. Unfortunately he's too far away for us to see his face.'

'Do you think it's the same man who's been trying to kill you?'

'We'll soon find out. If it is, he's damned persistent. He must have followed us.'

William urged Boulting, the driver, to go faster. The horseman disappeared into the trees and, as the chaise lurched on, William expected him to reappear at any second. He looked ahead and peered into the dense woods on either side of the lane, but his sight could not penetrate the dark interior. Coming to a tight corner, the horses took it fast. The chaise lurched, two of the wheels running on to the verge, one of them sliding into a deep rut obscured by long grass. Boulting hauled on the reins, the chaise tilted. The spokes of the wheel took the weight and snapped, and the wheel rim shattered.

Miraculously Cassandra managed to stay in her seat. Panic threatened, but she steeled herself against it. His taut features clouded with grave concern for her safety, after assuring himself that she was all right, William jumped down into the road to join Boulting. He had alighted and was staring at the broken wheel in dismay.

'Now what do we do, milord?' he said, scratching his head, his hat having come off when he'd been thrown to one side.

Steeling himself, William stood and looked around, his senses alert. He stared down the lane, listening. The wheel was shattered, the body of the chaise lurched to one side, and the horses, half out of the traces, were restive—and he was sure he could hear hoofbeats in the wood and he couldn't see a damned thing.

Drawing his pistol from a holster beneath his jacket, he dove down. 'Cassandra,' he snapped, 'stay inside and keep down. You, too, Boulting. I believe we are about to have a visitor.'

Now the sounds coming from the undergrowth were getting closer. Crouching low, William cocked the pistol and strained to see into the blackness beyond the lane from which emanated tangible danger and waited. Boulting did the same, but had decided to reach for his hat, which lay in the grass in front of William, when the shot rang out, filling the air with a deafening crack and causing roosting birds to take flight. He cried out and fell backwards, clutching his head. William fell to one knee beside the wounded man at the same time that Cassandra, her heart racing and assailed by a terrible concern that William had been shot, flung open the door and climbed out.

'William!' Her eyes were wide and fearful, though a great flood of relief and joy swept through her to see he looked unharmed.

His expression grim, he shot her a glance. Her face was ashen. 'I'm all right, but the same cannot be said of Boulting.

He's been shot.' His eyes met hers. 'We both know it was meant for me.'

Without wasting a second, he hauled Boulting towards the protection of the carriage and urged Cassandra to do likewise. Giving himself no time to deliberate his actions, in a running crouch he ran several yards down the lane before disappearing into the dark interior of the woods.

Trying not to panic, Cassandra looked down at the driver. He was unconscious but alive, thank goodness. She knelt to tend him. There was so much blood. It was a head wound and she knew they always bled a lot. Immediately she lifted her skirt. Ripping a length of cloth from her petticoat, she made a wad from part of it and pressed it over the wound to staunch the flow of blood, winding the rest round his head to secure it. She then knelt beside him to wait for William to come back.

With the stealth of an Indian, William moved through the riotous undergrowth, careful not to trip on trailing briars. The conifers gave out a sweet resinous smell. Their needles were soft underfoot, the straight trunks rising up all round him like a body guard. He watched carefully for any movement that would expose his quarry. And then there he was, a dark-garbed figure sitting atop a dark brown horse, watching and waiting, his eyes intent on a small circle of light showing through the trees.

'I believe you are looking for me,' William said, his voice like steel. 'What kind of niggardly coward is it that shoots a man in the back?'

The assailant had been aware of no sound or movement. Now he spun round to see the tall figure of his prey, his arm raised, and at its end a pistol stared back at him. He raised his own, prepared to fire. There was a flash and then another. The sounds rent the air and there was a half-screaming grunt as the horseman fell from his mount and smashed face down to the ground. The horse bolted with fright and went crashing through the undergrowth. Going to his assailant, William turned him over with his foot. The man was of heavy build, his face that of a man in his mid-thirties, a complete stranger—and unfortunately he was dead.

Cassandra kept her eyes fastened on the woods, her ears straining to the slightest sound. She'd heard the shots and her heart had taken up a frantic beating while she waited. Tiny shards of fear pricked her spine while a coldness congealed in the pit of her stomach when she heard someone moving through the undergrowth in her direction. Shaking with apprehension, she crouched beside Boulting, not daring to breathe. Her skin crawled on the nape of her neck. Perhaps it wasn't William. Perhaps he was lying wounded or dead in the woods.

When William suddenly appeared, she experienced a rush of mixed and complex emotions, and her relief was so great she almost expired.

'William?' His name came in a tentative question.

He moved quickly towards her. His face was grim, but he managed a smile in an attempt to allay her fears. 'There's no longer any need to be afraid.'

'Why, what—what has happened?'

'The man's dead. I'd rather he wasn't, so I could have asked him what all this has been about—but it was either him or me.'

'Dead?' she whispered. 'Did—did you recognise him?'

'No—but that doesn't surprise me. I have no doubt he was paid to kill me—by whom I have yet to find out. There was nothing on him to identify him—no name, nothing.'

'What will you do? You can't leave him in the woods.'

'I don't intend to. I'll ride into Guildford later and speak to the authorities. But first we must get Boulting to a physician before he bleeds to death. How far do you think we are from Netherton Hall?'

'About two miles, I would say.'

'We need help. I'll unhitch the horses. You'll have to ride for help.'

Cassandra stared at him and shook her head. 'Ride? But— I don't,' she confessed, suddenly feeling totally inadequate and wishing she'd learned. 'Unlike Emma, I never took to horses. I've never been on a horse in my life.'

William's face was incredulous. 'You haven't? Damn. And I thought there was nothing you couldn't do. I can't leave you here alone with Boulting.'

'There's no need,' Cassandra said, looking back down the lane with relief. 'I think I can hear someone coming.'

An open carriage with a driver and a single male occupant was heading towards them. When the driver saw the chaise blocking the road, he slowed down and stopped. The man climbed out and hurried to William, who had managed to quieten the horses. William introduced himself and gave the stranger a brief account of how the chaise had come to grief. The shooting of Boulting and the dead man in the woods he preferred to keep to himself, his explanation for Boulting's injury being that he had been thrown from the box when the chaise had swerved.

'Where are you heading?' the gentleman asked, who had introduced himself as Mr Loftus, a businessman from Guildford.

'Netherton Hall. Do you know it?'

Mr Loftus nodded and smiled broadly. 'Indeed I do, sir. I have the honour of being acquainted with Lady Monkton. Very fine lady. I'll take you there directly.'

'I would be most grateful.'

Together they managed to lift the now semi-conscious Boulting—thankfully a small man of light weight—into the carriage.

William turned to Cassandra. 'Go with Mr Loftus, Cassandra. I'll stay with the horses. Send someone as soon as you reach Netherton Hall.'

'But—what about—?'

He placed a warning finger to her lips to silence her before she said too much. 'We'll discuss that later. Don't worry,' he said quietly, for her ears alone. 'I've told you. The man's dead. He won't be coming back.'

She stared up at him. When she had heard the shot, for a terrible stabbing moment she had known a tightening of fear so strong it seemed to take the breath from her body. For a moment she was held in a space of frozen time, unable to drag her eyes from the ones that commanded her attention. Swallowing her fear, she whispered, 'I know, but I feel he is still a threat. You will keep your pistol at the ready, won't you?'

Meeting her gaze, William saw her concern for him in her eyes. His smile was gentle, his eyes warm. 'Are you trying to protect me, Miss Greenwood?'

'You do seem to need it from time to time. Please take care.'

Taking heart from the lack of a threat, Cassandra climbed into the carriage.

Chapter Eight

Cassandra's unexpected arrival at Netherton Hall—and the manner of it—put the house in turmoil with servants hurrying all over the place. Aunt Elizabeth and her mother came out of the drawing room to see what all the fuss was about. Seeing a dishevelled and soiled Cassandra snapping out orders to the servants, they stood and watched in amazed stupefaction.

Boulting was carried to a bed in the servants' quarters, the doctor sent for and two grooms despatched to mend the broken wheel and assist Lord Lampard. Mr Loftus, happy to have been of help, went on his way after paying his respects to Lady Monkton. Not until they were in the drawing room did Aunt Elizabeth demand a full explanation of what had happened.

'An accident, you say,' Harriet said, her voice filled with concern. 'And did I hear you mention Lord Lampard?'

'Yes. He had to stay with the horses.' Cassandra decided it would be best for William to tell them about the shooting.

'I must say this is all highly irregular, Cassandra—travelling all this way, alone with Lord Lampard, without informing us of what you intended.'

'I know, Mama, and I'm sorry, but there was no other way. Lord Lampard has something of importance to discuss with you and Aunt Elizabeth and it couldn't wait.'

'But—just look at you,' Aunt Elizabeth remarked in shocked tones and slight admonishment. 'Oh, my goodness! Is that blood on your skirt? And just look at your petticoat—why, it appears to be in tatters.'

Cassandra glanced down at the sorry state of her clothes, seeing the torn hem of her petticoat peaking out from beneath her dress. 'I know I must look a sight, but poor Boulting bled quite profusely. I had to bind his wound—'

'With your petticoat?' Lady Monkton regarded her sternly.

'Some of it.'

'Well—I am all amazement and cannot wait to hear what you have to say.'

'How is Emma?' Cassandra asked, directing her gaze at her mother seated beside her on the *chaise-longue.*

'Better now she is away from London and the gossips, but her spirits are shaken. She spends most of her time in her room.' Equally concerned for her elder daughter, Harriet took Cassandra's hand. 'But how are you, my dear? You look tired and quite agitated. You work too hard at the institute, Cassandra. You really should let Agatha do more, especially when I'm away. Were you hurt when the carriage lost its wheel?'

'No, Mama, I am perfectly all right,' Cassandra was quick to reassure her. Forced to curb her agitation and anxious for William to arrive, her eyes kept flitting to the window that overlooked the drive.

Cassandra continued to answer their questions, striving to be composed, but her thoughts were elsewhere. Blue eyes invaded her unwilling mind, and a warmth slowly spread through her. They stared down to the depths of her being, stirring unwelcome longings. She sighed and looked out of the window once more. What was to be done?

The sooner William put forward his suggestion regarding Emma and Edward and left for London, the happier she would be. She would stay in Surrey and travel to London with her family in a few days' time. The institute was in good hands—

Agatha was more than capable of running things. If Emma agreed to marry Edward, then hectic preparations would begin in earnest as soon as they returned home, so a few days' respite would not go amiss.

William and the doctor—Dr Shaw—arrived within minutes of each other, both of them going straight to Boulting. William thought wryly that his demands on the medical men of late were happening all too frequently and he sincerely hoped this would be the last.

Later, when the doctor had left and William came striding in, he went directly to Lady Monkton. Cassandra stole a glance at his chiselled profile, marvelling at the strength and pride carved into every feature on the starkly handsome face.

'It's a pleasure meeting you again, Lady Monkton—and you, too, Mrs Greenwood,' he said with polite formality. 'I apologise for disturbing you like this and for coming here un-announced, but there is a matter of importance I wish to discuss with you. As Miss Greenwood will have explained we met with a mishap two miles down the road.'

'Thank goodness neither of you is the worse for your ordeal. Please sit down, Lord Lampard. Cassandra, ring the bell for tea. I do hope your man Boulting's wound isn't serious.'

'Not as serious as I first thought,' William said, selecting a chair close to Cassandra and sitting down. 'You should know that my driver was shot, Lady Monkton.'

William went on to give them a brief account of what had happened. Lady Monkton and Harriet Greenwood stared as if they had been struck dumb. Harriet was both alarmed and dis-tressed at the very idea that her daughter could have been hurt.

'And your assailant is dead, you say?'

'Unfortunately, he is. I would have liked it to be otherwise so that I could have questioned him. He carried nothing on his person to identify him.'

'No doubt he was some unmitigated rogue intent on highway robbery.'

'Yes—that's the conclusion we reached.' In keeping with his intention to keep quiet about the earlier threats to his person, William gave Cassandra a warning look that insisted on her unquestioning cooperation.

'If you would be so kind as to provide me with a horse to ride into Guildford to meet with the authorities, I would be most grateful. I shall have to offer some explanation to today's débâcle.'

When William returned to Netherton Hall he was shown into the drawing room where the ladies were gathered before dinner—all except Emma, who remained in her room.

Cassandra looked at him, her senses suddenly heightened by his presence. 'You saw the magistrate?'

He nodded, his expression closed as he accepted Lady Monkton's offer of a fortifying brandy. 'Everything is being taken care of. How is Boulting?' he asked, taking a large draught of the fiery liquid.

'He was sleeping when I looked in on him. I understand that Dr Shaw left him a sleeping draught. It seems to be working.'

'I use Dr Shaw myself,' Lady Monkton told William. 'I have absolute confidence in him, so Boulting is in good hands.'

William sat in the chair he had occupied earlier. 'I am sure he is. The wound is superficial and Dr Shaw is convinced there will be no permanent damage, but he has advised against moving him for a few days.'

'Then we shall ensure he is made comfortable while he is here—and you are welcome to stay as long as you like, Lord Lampard,' Lady Monkton offered, smiling pleasantly, hoping he would.

Alarm exploded within Cassandra. 'Oh—but I think Lord Lampard will have to return to London, Aunt Elizabeth—is that not so, Lord Lampard?'

He cocked a lazy brow, his look challenging. 'I do?'

'Yes. I am sure one of your grooms could take him back to town, Aunt Elizabeth.'

'That is up to Lord Lampard, my dear.'

William's eyes met Cassandra's squarely. She waited for him to decline the invitation, but he did nothing of the sort. A man to take advantage of all opportunities presented to him, he seized upon the offer. A smile played just behind his features and he gave a slow nod of what appeared to be acceptance.

'Because of my concern for Boulting, I would be happy to remain a few days, Lady Monkton, and I thank you for your kind invitation.'

'Good—that's splendid.' The elderly lady beamed.

'But…but your clothes…your wardrobe…' Cassandra retorted.

A roguish grin twisted his mouth. 'My military training taught me to always be prepared for the unexpected.'

Cassandra could only stare at him, and when she saw the satisfied smile sweeping across his face, she felt like telling him she could not possibly endure his presence at Netherton Hall indefinitely. It was only with great effort that she curbed her tongue.

Leaning back in his chair, a booted foot propped upon the opposite knee, supremely assured in his arrogance that he had scored a victory, he smiled across the distance into the less-than-warm depths of her eyes. In his own, there was a kindling fire that touched her like a hot brand. She glared at him. How dare he look at her like that when they were in the presence of her mother and Aunt Elizabeth? Cassandra had noticed the sharp glances that had passed between them during her exchange with William.

'Then I hope your stay will be a pleasant one,' she said stiffly, her cheeks burning as she endured William's mocking gaze. She had known instinctively that Aunt Elizabeth's warm and congenial offer would guarantee his acceptance, yet his visit would pose definite problems for her. 'Aunt Elizabeth is famous for her hospitality, but won't you be bored with only a house full of females for company?'

'Not at all. I'm sure I shall find plenty to occupy my time. I will start by teaching you how to ride. You're the only female I know who doesn't.'

Cassandra was astounded by his effrontery. 'Oh, no, you will not. I told you I have never been on a horse in my life and I do not intend doing so.'

'Come, Cassandra,' he said teasingly. 'Be adventuresome.' His laughing eyes communicated with hers in silent challenge. 'Afraid?'

'Yes—no—I don't know.' Why was he doing this? she wondered infuriatingly. The man was insufferable. He was positively revelling in her discomfort. 'I have a strong aversion to horses when they come too close,' she confessed.

'Then I shall help you to master your aversion. You'll have them eating out of your hand in no time at all. You might be a little sore from the experience at first, but I can assure you you will soon get the hang of it and enjoy yourself.' He switched his gaze to Lady Monkton, who, like Harriet, was listening to their exchange in quiet amazement. 'Do you have a suitable mount for your niece to ride, Lady Monkton?'

'Why, yes—a beautiful, gentle little mare called Jade. Emma used to ride her until she became more proficient. She will be perfect.'

'There you are then. I will give you your first lesson tomorrow morning.'

'You take too much upon yourself, Lord Lampard,' Cassandra replied stiffly. 'I shall think about it.'

William chuckled softly. 'Your daughter has a very strong opinion of me, Mrs Greenwood—unfavourable for the most part. She is also an extremely stubborn young woman.'

'I have no opinion of you whatsoever, Lord Lampard,'

Cassandra retorted, trying to ignore her mama's questioning eyes as she looked with curiosity from one to the other.

Harriet caught the intense look that passed between Cassandra and Lord Lampard. His eyes held a measure of admiration for her daughter, which asked a question—what on earth did this mean? She gave Cassandra a quizzical look, having observed her impatient fidgetings while awaiting Lord Lampard's arrival. Harriet was not very well acquainted with Lord Lampard, only having met him the once when he had called to tell her that Emily and Cassandra were at Carlow Park and to collect some clothes for Cassandra, but he was the first gentleman ever to show an interest in her elder daughter, so what was she to make of that?

When he had greeted her earlier and looked into her eyes, she had been struck by his great personal attraction. There was warmth about him and a sense of humour in his smile, yet his mouth was firm, with a twist to it that said he was not a man to be trifled with. She liked him and hoped she would see more of him in the future, although she was somewhat concerned by his unfavourable reputation and hoped he would not trifle with her daughter's affections.

'Cassandra does not have the slightest concept of the importance of appropriate behaviour, Lord Lampard,' Lady Monkton informed him. 'If she had, she wouldn't have travelled to Netherton Hall alone with you.'

'Why ever not?' Cassandra argued on a lighter note, having gathered her senses. 'I don't recall you voicing any objections when we went after Emma when she eloped.'

'That was a different matter entirely,' Lady Monkton reproached.

'If you say so, Aunt Elizabeth,' Cassandra conceded with a suppressed smile.

'Now, what is this matter of importance you wish to discuss with us, Lord Lampard?'

'I wish to confer with Mrs Greenwood and yourself on the

best way of solving this unfortunate affair concerning Edward and Emma—to salvage something decent out of this folly. I am thinking of their best interests. Please don't think I am interfering, but since Edward is my cousin and has no parents to advise him, I am involved. I am here to try and make an intolerable situation better.'

Harriet shot him a grateful smile. 'I won't pretend this is not an anxious time for me, Lord Lampard. Restoring Emma to society's good graces is important, so anything you can suggest is welcome. Elizabeth and I are at our wits' end over what is to be done so that Emma can hold her head up in society.'

William's smile was sympathetic. 'Then, since it concerns Emma, would you like her to be present?'

'No,' Harriet said quietly. 'I think we should listen to what you have to say first. My daughter is a complete innocent and a victim of her own foolishness. She is suffering because of it. I have no wish to add to her suffering until I know what it is you have to propose.'

'As you wish.' Leaning back in his chair, William steepled his fingers and regarded his audience seriously for several moments before he went on to put forward his suggestion. They listened intently without interrupting, their eyes opening wide with incredulity when they realised he was suggesting that Emma and Edward should be allowed to wed. Not until he had finished speaking did Harriet and Elizabeth look at each other.

'What are your thoughts, Elizabeth?'

Elizabeth looked immensely pleased and was almost bubbling with excitement. 'Why, I think it's a splendid idea. It is both bold and cunning, but what a splendid plan it is.'

Harriet sighed. 'I would have liked it better had Emma the chance of having more contenders for her hand.'

Elizabeth shook her head. 'Unfortunately, there never will be now. Edward is the only contender and the only one she wants. What do you say, Harriet?'

With no feasible reason to object, Harriet nodded. 'Very well. We will send for Emma and see what she has to say.' She shook her head and sighed regretfully. 'I only wish I had the funds to give her the wedding I know she will want.'

'Poverty is no barrier to social success, provided there is some other distinction to offer—be it brains or beauty,' Elizabeth retorted, 'and both your daughters have been blessed with both. Why, even the Prince Regent changes the accepted order of things when it suits him.'

'I dare say, but I'm not the Prince Regent.'

'It doesn't matter. Emma will not be alone. I will be with her, do not forget, and no one will dare ostracise her in front of me. I have no control over wagging tongues, but she has spirit enough to endure what they might put her through initially, knowing that the outcome will be favourable. No doubt the *ton* will enjoy dining out on her reputation until the betrothal is announced.'

'Which I think should be immediate,' William suggested quietly.

'I agree absolutely. My entire life has been scrupulously dedicated to the precepts of convention, but there are times when one has to go against the rules of the *ton*. This is one of them and I am prepared to fly in the face of decorum and convention. When we return to London we will begin with drives out, evenings at the theatre, shopping and exhibitions and the like. Oh, and one more thing—which concerns her dowry. I have decided to settle on her a generous sum, so that will no longer be a problem,' Elizabeth announced, looking extremely pleased by the way things were turning out.

Overwhelmed by this unlooked-for generosity, Harriet stared at her. Tears of gratitude swam in her eyes and tenderness welled in her heart. 'I don't know what to say. We are putting you to so much trouble already—it's beyond being kind of you to do this. Emma doesn't deserve it.'

'Nonsense. You seem to have forgotten that you are my

dear cousin and I am devoted to both your girls. Besides, it is what my dear husband would have wanted. He was extremely fond of Cassandra and Emma, you know—indeed, is Cassandra not our goddaughter?—and it is my duty to take care of you—all of you. What you don't deserve is what the *ton* is doing to you. You are coping valiantly and it does you credit.

'You are too good, Elizabeth,' Harriet murmured, reaching out and gripping her hand affectionately.

'Now, Harriet, don't come over all emotional. You know it gives me pleasure to do this for Emma, so indulge me.'

William looked from one to the other of the ladies with something akin to admiration. 'Edward's parents left him extremely well off—and their family home in Richmond, which has been closed up since their deaths, can be reopened. It's a splendid residence overlooking the park. Emma will love it and will want for nothing. If she wants to be close to Edward while he is doing his army training, then there is no reason why they can't take lodgings in Woolwich.'

Emma came in, looking wan and lifeless. She looked at her sister and Lord Lampard nervously. 'Why are you here, Cassy?'

'Because of you, actually.' Taking Emma's hand, Cassandra drew her down beside her and their mama on the *chaise-longue*. 'Please listen to what Lord Lampard has to say, Emma.'

Emma sat perfectly still, her hands clenched in her lap, her face pale but composed. Cassandra's heart went out to her, but she sincerely believed that, when she had heard what William had to say, they would see the old Emma restored to them.

What Lord Lampard suggested seemed so unlikely, so inconceivable, that Emma couldn't believe it.

'You have got your wish, Emma. What do you say to my suggestion?' William asked gently. Emma smiled, a smile that warmed his heart and promised her full cooperation.

'What does Edward say?' Emma asked. 'You have spoken to him?'

William nodded. 'It is what he wants.' Standing up, he

took a letter from inside his coat and handed it to her. 'Everything he has to say is in his letter.'

Emma looked at it as if it were the most precious gift. Excusing herself, she fled the room to read it in private.

When William began conversing with her mother, Cassandra watched him. He was the image of relaxed elegance, looking not only casual, but supremely self-satisfied, his expression so bland and complacent that once again she felt there was more behind this than bringing Edward and Emma together. She asked herself the question—how did she feel about this man who she seemed unable to banish from her life? She searched her mind carefully, frowning as she looked away from him, trying to be completely honest with herself. He was capable of plucking at the strings of her heart and turning her bones to water by simply kissing her—she already knew that, but what else did she feel for him?

Of course, she was extremely grateful to him for all he was doing for Emma, although at the back of her mind she knew he wasn't really doing it for Emma, Edward, her mother or Aunt Elizabeth, but to remain close to her in order to win his wager before the Season ended, and, despite her determination to steer clear of him, she had to go along with it for Emma's sake. He held all the cards and he knew it, and she couldn't walk away, not until Emma and Edward were married. Though it gave her no pleasure knowing she was indebted to him, she realised the generosity was all on his side and that one day soon he might extract payment.

When the evening meal was over the ladies retired to the drawing room to discuss Emma's forthcoming nuptials. After a while Cassandra rose and wandered through the long French windows on to the grey stone terrace. The air was soft and languid; the sweet scent of roses and honeysuckle hung heavily. The night was drawing in and already myriad stars shimmered in the dark blue velvet sky. The moon was a great yellow orb in the east, and to the west the dying sun blazed in the sky in a brilliant and dramatic display of crimson, orange and yellow.

Stepping down from the terrace, she strolled through the garden and sighed, thinking it was a time for lovers, yet she was thinking of the children at the institute and what would happen to them if it were to close. She had no doubt they would become lost in the alleyways and courts of wretched places like St Giles.

Slowly she wandered through the abundant rose bowers, idly fingering the velvety blooms, their scent heavy and erotic. All of a sudden, as she rounded a corner, she saw William. He had disappeared after dinner and she thought he had gone to his room, but here he was, seated on an ornate wrought-iron bench facing the crimson sky. He had one knee crossed over the other, the snowy whiteness of his elegant cravat shining bright.

Cassandra was struck by his stern profile and for a moment she was able to see a kind of beauty in it, but as quickly dismissed the thought. Her breath was suddenly caught in her throat and her heart was beating painfully fast. Not wishing to intrude on his solitude, she took a step back and was about to turn and disappear into the rose bushes, but she realised she must have made a sound or he sensed her presence, because without warning he turned his gaze directly at her. She felt heat in her face—felt it spread at that naked, desirous look. It was a look that spoke of invitation and need.

William saw her radiant gold hair, her cream dress that shaped the perfect form of which he was so enamoured and he had no mind to let her escape. When he looked at her, his eyes were as calm as the sea on a fair day.

'Don't go. Come and sit with me a while,' he said quietly.

'I—I don't wish to intrude.'

'You're not.' He sighed deeply. 'I think that when you found your way here, I was thinking of you. How lovely you look. I was half-afraid you were not real, but a ghost of the night.'

'No, I assure you I am flesh and blood.'

He nodded, his face expressionless. 'So you are. Come and look at the sky. Is it not beautiful?'

He calmly contemplated her for a moment before looking back at the sky, which he seemed to find so fascinating. Cassandra was drawn towards him and slowly made her way to the bench, seating herself a little way from him. She, too, gazed at the beauty of the sky. It was an intimate moment and she had the strange idea that if she made a sound something rare and precious would be broken. The silence was disturbed by the occasional call of a bird.

In the end it was William who spoke.

'I would sit and gaze at the sunset for hours in Spain. It always brought a sort of peace.'

'The war must seem very far away now.'

'It is. I spent a long time there.'

'What was it like?' she asked, trying to envisage him as a soldier, thinking how handsome he would look in uniform.

'Hot for the most part—dusty, although the winters, especially in the mountains, could be freezing. Food was frequently in short supply because supplies failed to get through.'

'How long were you in Spain?'

'Two years—most of it spent in the saddle.'

Cassandra gazed at him. He continued to look at the sky. She thought how different he was, how remote, how detached. She was baffled, then at a loss for words, for he was not usually like this—at least not the William she had come to know. And why did he not play the part she had assigned to him, and become the seductive scoundrel?

William turned his head and looked at her, and into his eyes, dark now, came a look like a sudden flame; he smiled slowly, as if in secret. 'You have no idea how lovely you look. The moonlight suits you. It makes you look fragile and vulnerable and very pliable, yet I know you are strong and determined— and more than a little obstinate.'

There was a caressing note in his voice, which at any other time would have brought a brittle retort to her lips. Instead, perhaps because of the quiet, the warmth and the beauty of the sky, she merely looked at him a little inquiringly and smiled.

'You are too free with your flattery, William, and I think you are teasing me.' She expected him to reach out and touch her hand, which lay on the seat between them, but he didn't, and she felt both glad and disappointed at the same time.

'Am I? I suppose I could be accused of worse.'

His voice was grave, quiet and compelling—almost mesmeric. Once again Cassandra felt that little flame flicker within her, making it all the more difficult for her to regard him as her enemy.

William said no more, and she, too, was silent, and he smiled to himself. He looked ahead of him, thinking of the woman beside him. The recurring images of her in his arms, of the kisses they had shared, drifted through his mind, still confused and contradictory—Cassandra by the lake at Carlow Park, her arms around his neck, her lips moist and willing, eyes shining under lids like petals; Cassandra turning away from him, distant and angry.

What was to be done? he asked himself. For she had wanted him. There was no mistaking that it had been a totally mutual thing between them from the very beginning, from the day he had taken her in his arms in the coach as they had chased after Edward and Emma. He smiled at the recollection. He had fully expected her to protest at the time and slap his face, but instead she had melted into his arms as if she belonged there. And she did. All he needed to do was make her realise it.

'Did you see much fighting in Spain?' Cassandra asked, breaking the silence.

'A great deal, as a matter of fact.'

'And did you suffer any injuries?'

'Several—minor ones. I was lucky.'

He turned away. It was hard to talk rationally when he remembered so much. How could he tell a gently reared young woman born and bred in England what it had been like—the nastiness of war, the terrible waste and slaughter, the long marches over mountainous terrain in pursuit of the enemy, the battles, the bombardment, the blood, the flies feasting on dead bodies? Most of the soldiers fought in a style that did credit to their training, but a great many of them were battle shocked, with a blank, haunted staring in their eyes—young men who had been forced to be brave for too long. Some had quite literally run out of courage—some had been too weary to bury the dead.

In the small circle of light that they inhabited, the warm, scented air lapping around them like a comfort blanket, binding them in a strange reserve, Cassandra was strangely sensitive to his thoughts and understood. 'You don't have to talk about it, William. I have spoken to a lot of soldiers who have returned from the Peninsula, so I do have a picture in my mind of what it was like.'

'Unless you were there, at Albuera or Badajoz, you can never know, Cassandra, and it's as well that you don't. Thank God we've seen the last of it. But there were times when we saw the real Spain, and at times like those, when the sun set over the brooding mountains and crimson lit the sky—like it does now, in a way that belongs to the radiance of midsummer—we saw the beauty of the country and it felt good to be alive.'

Again they fell silent and Cassandra felt strangely reluctant to break this magic moment. This was how she had often dreamed, sometimes when she had sat at home alone in the long evenings when her mother had been at the institute and Emma had been staying at Monkton House, that a man would talk to her and she would listen. She realised there was so much she didn't know about William. Who would have thought that one of London's rakes *par excellence* would sit looking enraptured at a sunset?

'How are you liking being back at Carlow Park?' she asked at length, tentatively.

'Well enough. It's very different from how I remember it. The covers have been taken off the furniture and the vases are filled with flowers, but the house seems empty to me—like a tomb,' he said quietly, almost to himself.

'All empty houses often feel like that,' Cassandra remarked, knowing how deeply he missed his family.

'You may be right. Carlow Park was always a happy house, full of laughter. It needs fresh life injecting into it, which is down to me—something for the future. Coming back from Spain, after being a soldier for so long, it's as if I've become somebody else and I'm still trying to find the old me.'

There was no mistaking that he was in earnest. His voice was full of an emotion Cassandra did not understand. 'It's bound to take time. And are you happy?'

'I suppose I am content.'

'What's the difference?'

'Contentment is a state of mind—when mind and body are compatible with each other. Happiness is something that comes and goes and has different levels. Music makes one happy, as does personal achievement; also seeing happiness in others—the birth of a child—knowing you have done something for others that improves their lives, like your work at the institute, the good you do for the children.'

Cassandra thought for a moment. 'I've never considered it like that before, but what I feel when I see the children go away from the institute with full bellies is more a feeling of satisfaction than happiness.' She looked at him curiously. 'Is it happiness you feel for what you are doing for Emma and Edward?'

They looked at each other across the short distance that separated them and William's eyes held hers for a long instant, with a light in them like the crimson flame in the sky.

He shrugged. 'Happiness, contentment and satisfaction— because it means I will see much of you, Cassandra.'

'And is that your reason for concocting this ingenious scheme?'

'One of them,' he confessed unashamedly. He stood up and smiled, his teeth gleaming white in the gathering gloom. 'Now come, enough open hearts and philosophising for one night. I'll walk you back to the house. I would like to keep you here, talking to you, but you have a big day ahead of you tomorrow. It is important that you have a good night's sleep if you are going to learn to ride a horse.'

Later, when she was alone in her room, Cassandra reflected on her encounter with William. To say she wasn't affected by it was a huge understatement. It had left her confused and slightly shaken. Just now as they had talked or just sat in silence looking at the sunset, when she had looked into his eyes they had been filled with such an enigmatic expression.

The whole incident had been incredible for her. For a time she had totally forgotten the gulf that yawned between them and she had responded with a spontaneity to his quiet thoughtful mood—a mood she wanted to capture and remember, which amazed her. When she had sat beside him it had felt so absolutely right, so amazingly natural she could feel it even now, as she prepared for bed, a warmth, a smoothness of something sweet running through her veins like warm honey.

The following morning Cassandra stood in front of the cheval mirror and cast a critical eye over her riding habit. She had borrowed it from Emma since she didn't possess one of her own. It was a little tight across her breasts, but apart from that it was a good fit everywhere else and rather chic, she thought approvingly, doing a twirl. After straightening the matching hat that sat jauntily on her fair curls, she slipped her hands into her kid gloves. Picking up her riding crop, she left the room and made her way to the stables, apprehensive about her first riding lesson and wondering why she had let herself be talked into it, but William Lampard had set the challenge, and, goaded by the mocking amusement in his eyes, she had refused to give him satisfaction by declining.

The stables were close to the house, but hidden from view by a tall box hedge. Sixteen stalls were set around the stable yard, not all of them occupied. Grooms and stable boys were going about their daily chores. William was there ahead of her, talking and joking with lazy good humour with one of the grooms.

Cassandra paused across the yard, slanting a long considering look at her tormentor; when she recalled their encounter in the garden the previous night and how drawn to him she had been, she felt a sudden warmth in her heart. In his tan jacket and white silk neckcloth, buckskin riding breeches and gleaming brown leather boots, his dark hair ruffled by the slight breeze, he was devilishly attractive to look at. Her pulse raced; she was unsure as to the cause—her handsome riding instructor or her fear of mounting the beast he was leading towards her.

Cassandra felt her legs begin to shake and cold fear race down her spine; her pulse accelerated wildly. All her life she'd been nervous around horses—she felt it was not about to change.

'Good morning, Cassandra. I trust you slept well?'

'Yes, perfectly, thank you.'

'I enjoyed watching the sunset with you.' His tone was intimate, his gaze warm and meaningful. 'We'll have to do it again.'

'Yes,' she replied, looking nervously at the horse.

Noting her apprehension and the way her eyes darted from the horse to him, William was determined that by the time he had finished she would have conquered her fear of horses. Like the countryside itself she was dressed in green with touches of gold setting off the rich shade. When he was close, a slow, lazy smile swept across his face and Cassandra braced her trembling body for him to say something mocking, but his deep voice was filled with admiration. 'You look lovely. Are you ready for your first lesson?'

'I think I'd prefer pistols at twenty paces,' she remarked, eyeing the mare suspiciously when it shook its head and snorted loudly.

'Whoa—easy, now,' William murmured soothingly to the mare. He smiled at Cassandra encouragingly. 'Try not to be nervous. Don't let the horse see your fear. Horses need to be taught obedience by their rider. Once that has been established, a good horse will always recognise its master—or, in your case, mistress. Come and make friends with Jade. See, she's as docile as a lamb.' Taking something out of his pocket, he offered his hand to the horse. Jade snorted and moved towards it, taking the piece of sugar and crunching appreciatively. William placed another piece of sugar in Cassandra's gloved hand. 'Now you try.'

Gingerly she did as he had done and was tempted to withdraw her hand at the last minute, but didn't, and her lips broke into a wondering smile when Jade nuzzled her hand and took the sugar.

'There, see how easy that was? Time and a lot of friendship can make anything happen.' William casually caressed Jade's nose, urging Cassandra to rub her neck. After several minutes more, in which Cassandra tried to familiarise herself with the horse, William said, 'Are you ready to mount her?'

Taking a deep, fortifying breath, Cassandra nodded. 'I suppose it's now or never.'

She was dreadfully nervous as William helped her settle into the side saddle. She felt so high up her head spun. The feeling passed after a moment. William let her sit there and get the feel for the horse before leading it out of the yard and down a path to the park. It was frightening at first and Cassandra was terrified she would fall off. Walking along beside her at a slow, measured pace and holding the side of the bridle, William was wonderfully patient, giving her instructions and correcting errors. Gaining confidence all the time, she began to relax and enjoy herself.

William stared up at her profile, tracing with his gaze the soft lines of her face, the brush of lustrous dark lashes, a stray strand of hair that rested against her cheek, her features rosy with the exhilaration of the ride. 'You're doing well. How do you feel?'

'Better than I imagined—although the horse has something to do with that. She knows how to be extra gentle with me and has helped me to build up my confidence.'

'She has a natural gift of patience, I grant you.'

Glancing down into his eyes, Cassandra saw the soft, smiling warmth there and the last of her fear evaporated. 'It is clear you have a way with horses.'

'I enjoy being with them. When I was in the Peninsula a good mount was worth its weight in gold. It could mean the difference between life and death.'

'Speaking of which,' Cassandra said, 'why did you give Mama and Aunt Elizabeth reason to believe we were set upon by a robber yesterday instead of someone who was out to kill you?'

'Because it is my business and also because your family is already overburdened with problems without adding mine to them.'

'Don't you think you should have told them the truth? After all, it was not only your life that was in jeopardy, but mine, too.'

William's head shot up and he looked most contrite. 'And that was my primary concern, you must believe that. The last thing I want is to put your life in danger, which is why I shall be returning to London tomorrow. I suspect the man who has been following me was a hired assassin.'

'Maybe whoever it is who is trying to kill you will give up now.'

William didn't think so. An inbred caution still told him to be wary until he knew for certain who was behind it.

'Perhaps Mr Jardine will come up with something.'

'That is what I'm paying him for.'

'How do you know that whoever is behind it hasn't hired someone else to execute the deed, and that they aren't watching us at this very minute?' Cassandra asked, her gaze travelling over the vast tract of parkland and imagining a murderer behind every tree.

'I doubt it. Don't forget, there was no identification on the man I killed. It will take some time—if ever—for the authorities to find out who he was. But after saying that, I have no doubt that the person who wants me dead will soon hire someone else when he fails to get results.'

Chapter Nine

Coming to some trees on the crest of a hill, they followed a path down a gentle slope to a brook. The sun was hot and only the gentlest of breezes stirred the trees.

'We should rest the horses. It would be a pity to ruin a good mount.' William reached up and lifted her down. Her perfume was reminiscent of a warm summer day, when blossoms surrendered their scent to the air.

'We should?' As soon as her feet touched the ground she moved away from him.

Fastening the reins loosely to a low-lying branch, William leaned against a tree and gazed at her, a half smile curling on his lips. 'I'm trying to be a responsible and considerate riding instructor,' he joked, his eyes twinkling with humour.

'But we've only ridden across the park—at a sedate pace, too, I might add.'

'True. In fact, you're doing so well, tomorrow we'll progress to a trot.'

'Don't you think that's a bit ambitious?'

'You can do it.'

'And you have more confidence in my ability than I have.'

'Tell me, Cassandra,' he said after a moment in which he

studied her thoughtfully, 'why did you want me to go back to London when Lady Monkton invited me to stay?'

The directness of his question brought the heat creeping into her cheeks. 'Was it that obvious?'

'Blatantly.' Shoving himself away from the tree, he sauntered to where she was standing.

He was looking at her with those seductive blue eyes and Cassandra felt all the power and provocation of that gaze. Feeling decidedly uncomfortable, she wished she hadn't got off the horse. 'Will—will you stop looking at me like that?' she said, devoured by his burning gaze. She walked in a circle to avoid him, but he followed like a predator, backing her up against the tree he had just vacated, his smile taunting.

'Why are you trying to avoid me?'

'Because I think you're playing a game with me and I don't like it,' she retorted, feeling her defences begin to crumble and seeking refuge in anger.

'No? Well—if I am playing a game, perhaps you should know that you cannot win, but I can teach you how to play.' His voice was low and seductive, his eyes fastened on her lips.

'Please stop it, William. I don't like playing games.'

'Why—are you afraid you will lose?'

'No, it's just that I want no part of it. You may want me, if that is what you desire, but I will be no more yours than any man's.'

'Don't you like relationships?'

'It's not forming a relationship I am against. It's the consequences.' His lips were only a few inches from her own and it was difficult keeping her eyes off them.

'Consequences? What do you mean?'

'The same consequences that compel me to avoid practised seducers like yourself. I am fairly independent and I prefer it that way.'

'You, my dear Cassandra, are proud and foolish,' he

mocked while his eyes bored into hers. 'I ask myself, can a young lady be tempting and alluring and still be proper?'

'Yes, of course.'

'Then what do you want from life, Cassandra—besides your independence?'

'I want what every woman wants—and that is not to become the victim of a philanderer who thinks he is some grand gift to womankind.'

'Believe what you will, but unfortunately I cannot undo the years I lived before I met you. I cannot understand why you are so against me when your family has been kindness personified.'

'Yes—well done. I must congratulate you for the way you have ingratiated yourself with my family. Why have you made it your business to befriend us? Emma now thinks the sun rises and sets with you, Aunt Elizabeth looks on you as some kind of saviour and is already making the guest list for the wedding—who to include and who to leave off because of past slights. Mama is relieved Emma is to be wed—and—and I am confused.'

'And am I the cause of your confusion?'

'Yes, you are. Why are you doing this? Why should you care about the ruined reputation of a young woman who is nothing to you? You have come home from soldiering to take up your inheritance—a colossal undertaking for any man— someone may still be trying to kill you and yet here you are, playing Cupid. Why? None of it makes sense.'

His expression became serious and his eyes burned into hers. 'Does it not? Very well. I will tell you. It is you I want. You, Cassandra. I have seen laughter in your eyes, though they have been far too serious of late. You are beautiful in a way that makes men's heads turn again once they have noticed you, even though you have built an invisible wall around yourself, which can be removed only for a man you truly love.'

'And do you think you are that man?'

'I do.'

'You are arrogant if you believe that.'

'That, too. There is something more that attracts me to you. Not only do I feel the urge to sweep you into my arms and kiss you senseless, but I'm aware of some hidden, enticing quality that carries an air of mystery about it and I will not rest until I have uncovered it.'

Cassandra made a move to turn away, but William caught her by the shoulders and forced her to face him, pressing her back against the tree. What he saw in her eyes, plus the slight trembling in her slender body, belied her words. Lowering his head, he covered her mouth with his, but he misjudged her. There was a sharp pain as her small teeth clamped down on his lip. He drew back, tasting blood. His eyes narrowed and his lips curved in a slow smile. 'Why, you little vixen. I always knew you had fire in your veins.'

Cassandra glowered at him, feeling her pulses quicken as she watched his tongue slowly lick the small droplet of blood from his moist lip—a provocative gesture by any means, but to her susceptible heart it could bring about her downfall. 'It serves you right. You take too many liberties. You may force me, William Lampard, if that is your desire, but I will be no more yours after than I am now,' she vowed, her voice ice cold. 'I am merely trying to spare you what will be a thoroughly embarrassing and completely futile effort at seduction.'

'It won't be futile.'

'Yes, it will.'

His reply, though spoken in a hushed voice, tore through her with force. 'That wasn't what you said when I kissed you at Carlow Park—twice, as I recall.'

The bold reminder of that time at Carlow Park, when she had willingly let him hold her and kiss her, was more than Cassandra's taut nerves could withstand. 'No matter how you connive and cajole to seduce me, it won't work. I'm immune.'

William retaliated by taking her face between his hands and forcing her head back. He looked down at her with eyes that were hooded with emotion. 'No, you're not. I remember, you see, how you melted in my arms, and I intend to see if I can still make you feel the same.'

Fires ignited inside her at the touch of his hands on her face that flared to a startling intensity. His taunting smile made her realise the folly of baiting him. 'You will be wasting your time,' she snapped, swamped with humiliation at the brutal reminder of how openly besotted with him she had been at Carlow Park, before…

'Shall I show you how thinly guarded your denials are?'

Cassandra tried to push him away, but his arms snaked around her waist and brought her full against his hardened frame. His mouth swooped down on to hers with hardened possessiveness and his fiery kiss warmed her to the core of her being. The contact was like an exquisite explosion somewhere deep inside her. It was unlike any other, because underlying the ruthlessness of it, there was flowing a demanding persuasion, an insistence that she kiss him back—and if she yielded to it there was a promise that the kiss would change and become something else, something different. The sensation of his hardened body pressing against hers was devastating and she was afraid that her will would crumble beneath the onslaught of his fervour.

She tried to turn her face aside in denial, wanting him to stop before she was consumed, before she forgot her vow to stand against him—before she forgot that shameful, humiliating wager he had made with Sir Charles Grisham. But still she let him kiss her, allowing herself, just this once, the forbidden, fleeting joy of his mouth and his body close to her—never had she been so conscious of the nearness of another human body. She was held in an unyielding vicelike grip, her soft breasts crushed against his chest. His lips left hers and traced a burning line down her throat, causing her senses to erupt. Temporarily robbed of the anger that had fortified her resistance, her traitorous body relaxed.

'Kiss me, Cassandra,' he breathed, his hand splayed across her lower spine, forcing her closer to him, and she unwittingly moulded her melting body to the hardening contours of his. The heat of his lips touched her own once more, his mouth insisting, stirring, demanding, working their pagan magic on the warm and supple woman in his arms.

Cassandra's mind cried out with agonised yearning and now, unable to withstand William's passionate onslaught, for a slow beat in time she yielded. Beyond her will, her arms snaked up and around his neck, her fingers feeling the thickness of his hair at his nape. With a small, triumphant moan he gathered her more closely into his arms. His lips moved hungrily over hers, relentless in their demand, forcing hers to open beneath his mounting ardour. Feeling her response, he deepened the kiss, devouring her sweetness, drugging her senses, setting her whole being on fire.

Fighting back the wild desire to thrust her down on to the grass and take her there and then, William dragged his lips from hers and drew a long steadying breath. He studied the flushed contours of her face, the thick crescent of her lashes and the fine line of her eyebrows. Her lips were soft and tender from his assault, her eyes warm and glowing with desire. He longed to run a fingertip down the slender column of her throat, and to continue downwards until his hand cupped her breast.

He imagined how it would be to have her in his bed, to take her in his arms and draw her to him and devour her with a passion he had not felt in a long time. What a glory that would be. She would make a magnificent bed partner—he had sensed it the instant her mouth had responded to his. It would happen. He would make it happen if he expired with the effort.

Surfacing slowly from the depths of desire, Cassandra dazedly rested her head back against the tree. She could only stare into William's hypnotic eyes—still dark from the mysterious forces of passion—as if she could not comprehend what had just happened between them. 'You beast,' she whispered. 'How dare you kiss me when you knew I didn't want you to?'

'Come, Cassandra,' he murmured lightly, though he himself was shaken by the moment. 'It was only a kiss—and you have been kissed before.'

'I have—by you, and not like that.'

'But you did enjoy it,' he stated assuredly.

Cassandra was furious with herself for not only responding to it, but also for liking it. The sensation she had felt when he put his arms about her and lowered his mouth to hers rippled through her body along with all the other strange things she had experienced. 'What if someone saw?'

'There isn't another living creature in sight except for the horse—and it's too busy cropping grass to pay any attention to what we might be doing.'

'Is it right what you said—that you intend leaving tomorrow?'

'Yes, that is what I've decided. I shall leave Boulting here for a few days more to ensure his complete recovery.'

Cassandra drew back and stepped towards the edge of the brook, where she paused and looked down into the shimmering water as it hurried on its way. She was confused and humiliated. What had she done? How could she have allowed such a thing to happen? She had let herself be carried away on a wave of passion. After her vow never to fall for his seduction, she had succumbed to the coercive, compelling force of his masculinity, melting her reason with his kiss, playing upon her vulnerable, naïve senses as a musician plucks the strings of a violin. He had made her a willing, ardent accomplice to his lusts, and she despised him for it. To William Lampard she represented nothing more than the object of a wager he was determined to win. Raising her head, she looked at the sky. Somewhere she could hear a lark. A blackbird warbled and insects hummed softly.

She was aware of William standing a short distance behind her, watching her so intently that he might have been trying to commit every detail to memory. She struggled to free herself from her trancelike state induced by the heat of the day and the intoxicating closeness of the irresistible man behind her; though she could not dismiss him from any part of her awareness, she managed an attitude of cool disdain.

The fragrance of her perfume drifted on the air and through William's senses. Seized by a strong yearning to hold her against him once more, he moved closer and slipped an arm about her slender waist, pulling her back against him as he bent his head and murmured close to her ear, 'Cassandra…'

'Don't touch me,' she retorted angrily and jerked herself away as his voice tore holes in the thin façade of her composure. 'I think we should go back.' She turned to face him.

William nodded and smiled, content in his belief that he had measured the weakness of her character in the strength of her passion. 'It's a bit late for that,' he told her softly.

'Don't twist my words, William. I meant back to the house and you know it. But you must accept this is as far as it goes between us. If you ever attempt to kiss me again, I'll kill you. Please don't anticipate events that will never happen. I don't want you now and I never will.'

The smile died from his lips and his eyes narrowed into glittering dark slits. 'Your lips have just told me otherwise and I already have the answers I sought. Don't fight me, Cassandra.'

'I will,' she flared, tossing her head and flashing her eyes in anger when she met his gaze, facing him with all the indignation of one whose innermost secrets have been exposed to the scrutiny of another. She shrank from him when he reached out to touch her, realising with a jolt that in the future she must avoid him at all costs. 'I will fight you with all the strength I possess. Do you hear me?'

He nodded. 'Every word.' Gathering the reins and drawing the horse towards her, he lifted her into the saddle. Placing his hand on the bridle, he looked up into her stony face. 'But one day you will come to me. You will be mine in the end, Cassandra.'

'Never. I want no part of you! Ever!'

He contemplated her for a moment, his face expressionless. 'Very well. It would seem that we must continue this at another time. Now—are you ready?'

She nodded and stared straight ahead as they set off back across the park.

His face turned from Cassandra's gaze, William was deep in thought, his lips were set in a tight line as he led her towards the stables. When he'd retired from the army and returned to civilian life, his future had been all mapped out. Now that future had been shaken to its foundations and a new aspect of life presented itself in the form of Cassandra Greenwood. He could walk away from her and pretend she never existed, but deep down he didn't want to, and nor did he intend to.

For the rest of that day, and the following morning when he appeared at breakfast, he was his usual polite, cheerful self, but both Cassandra and William knew things had changed between them. He was coolly remote towards her. It was as though an invisible wall had sprung up between them, and it had everything to do with her angry rejection of his kiss.

However, accompanied by Emma on a frisky bay mare, who kicked her mount into a gallop from time to time, William took Cassandra into the park as he'd promised and, true to his word, had her trotting back to the stables, praising her on her developing riding skills and saying she had the makings of a fine horsewoman, that she must definitely continue her lessons with Emma now he was no longer available to teach her.

After partaking of a light lunch and bidding Aunt Elizabeth and her mother farewell, he left for London.

True to William's predictions, the announcement in the papers of the betrothal between Sir Edward Lampard and

Miss Emma Greenwood hit society with all the force of a thunderbolt, along with the arrival in London of the Dowager Countess of Carlow, who had taken up residence at the home of her nephew in Grosvenor Square and immediately made her approval of the marriage known. Such an announcement bearing the Dowager Countess of Carlow's seal was not to be ignored by anyone wishing to remain on that lady's very exclusive guest list.

The morning following the announcement in the newspapers found William at Monkton House. Unaware that he would call without warning, Lady Monkton had taken Emma shopping in Bond Street. Having no wish to accompany them, Cassandra had remained behind—although when the butler announced the arrival of Lord Lampard, she wished that she'd gone with them.

When he strolled into the room she rose from the couch. Placing the book she'd been reading on a table next to her, she clasped her hands demurely in front of her. Splendidly garbed in a finely tailored coat of bottle-green, William crossed the room to where she stood. His chiselled features were touched by the warm light of the sun slanting through the windows, and the growing ache in her heart attested to the degree of his handsomeness.

'William—I—we were not expecting you. My aunt and Emma are not at home just now. If it is Aunt Elizabeth you wish to see, perhaps you could call later.'

'I am delighted to find you alone, Cassandra,' he said softly, his eyes plumbing the depths of her beauty. 'What I have to say you can relate to Lady Monkton later. But you may set aside your fear. I will not abuse you. You have my word that for the time we are alone I shall comport myself with dignity and propriety.'

She regarded him with a widely sceptical frown. 'In truth, William, I find that difficult to believe. Your persistence never ceases to amaze me. Please sit down.' As he seated himself in a comfortable wingback chair opposite her, there was no way to protect herself from his relentless regard. 'Are you as outrageous with other women as you are with me?'

His eyes took on a slumbering intensity. 'Only those I have a yearning for—and I have told you I have a yearning for you.'

'There you go again, reminding me of past foolishness.'

He raised a brow. 'Yours or mine?'

'Both. Those embarrassing moments I forgot myself I remember with clarity, and they cannot be called anything but foolish. I told you then I want you to leave me alone.'

For several endless, uneasy moments, he gazed at her with enigmatic blue eyes, an impassive expression on his face. 'And I wonder,' he murmured at length, propping one booted foot across his knee and steepling his fingers in front of him, 'if what your head tells you to do will outlast the testing of the flesh.'

'And there's nothing like a woman's reluctance to surrender her virtue to heighten desire, is that not so, William?' she retorted coldly. Placing her hands on the arms of the chair, Cassandra leaned forward to press her point home. 'And I will not have my virtue rent asunder in a rake's bed.'

'And therein lies the rub.' William laughed softly. 'But be at ease, Cassandra. Your virtue is safe with me. No one could be more concerned about it than I am.'

'Safe!' she derided. 'Forgive me, but I feel I must disagree. Whenever I am with you I feel there is but one thought on your mind.'

'And yours, Cassandra,' he countered bluntly, reminding her of her passionate response to his kisses. 'As for myself, perhaps I have something else in mind.'

Calmly Cassandra met his gaze, the outrageous wager he had made to seduce her before the end of the Season never far from her thoughts. Her own lack of discipline and restraint when he had kissed her angered her, but she wasn't entirely certain whether to blame it on him or herself.

'And I have no wish to hear it. Please tell me why you are here.'

'Now the betrothal has been announced, if Edward can be released from his military duties I think we should begin our assault on the *ton.*'

'Oh, and how do you propose we do that, pray?'

'I think we should start by visiting Almack's Assembly Rooms this coming Wednesday.'

Cassandra's stunned gaze shot to his. 'Almack's?'

He smiled. 'That's right—the temple of the *beau monde.* The most exclusive of London's clubs.'

'But we'll never get past the *grandes dames* of society. They guard the doors like formidable dragons.'

'I agree. The patronesses retain the right to blackball anyone they consider is in any way undesirable without explanation.'

'But won't we find it difficult obtaining vouchers?'

'That is where my grandmother's influence comes in. She is well acquainted with one of the patronesses and will prevail upon their friendship.'

'But what's the point? Almack's is known as the Marriage Mart, where girls are launched upon society by their mothers in the hope of them finding a rich and titled husband. Since the club's main function is to act as a showcase for débutantes, neither Emma nor myself come under that category. Emma will already be betrothed and I have no intention of being.'

'Nobody will know that.'

Cassandra stared at him in stupefaction. She knew what he was asking her to do and she would have none of it. 'Please stop it, William. I have expressed my feelings to you on this particular matter. I am not a débutante and I don't want to be.'

'Not for just one night—to help your sister become an accepted member of the *ton?*' he murmured in coaxing tones.

'At my expense.'

'Is it not what any caring sister would do to save a sibling from a lifetime of ostracism?'

'Do you think I don't know that?' she flared. 'How can I forget the real purpose of what will turn out to be an expensive charade? Ever since Emma eloped I have been aware of nothing else; now you are asking me to support her in her efforts to redeem herself in the *ton*'s eyes so she will no longer be scorned, ridiculed and snubbed—to make my bow, when all the time I want to bow out of polite society for good.'

'I know, and, for what it's worth, I'm sorry. I know how much the institute means to you and when Emma's future is settled you will be able to resume your duties.'

Wary of the machinations of William's mind, Cassandra slanted him a look. Why did she always feel that Emma and Edward played only a small part in his scheming and that he was more concerned with her? 'You are going to an awful lot of trouble—and please don't insult my intelligence by saying it is for Emma. You don't know her, so why should it matter to you what happens to her?'

'Because I want what is best for both Emma and Edward. Edward is important to me. Emma is important to him. Need I say more?'

'I will not be forced into this, William.'

'Not forced, Cassandra,' he hastened to assure her softly. 'Persuaded, perhaps.'

She glowered across at him. His flat conviction that she had no choice except to agree to this was almost more than she could bear. 'If I agree to this ridiculous scheme of yours—which I haven't, I hasten to add—how can you be sure it will work?'

'Oh, ye of little faith,' William said, a wicked, knowing gleam in his eyes. 'It cannot fail.'

Just then Lady Monkton, followed by Emma, bustled in. She was delighted to see William and, after ordering refreshments, lost no time in asking the purpose of his visit. At his suggestion that they attend Almack's she positively beamed, thinking it a splendid idea—Emma was less enthusiastic.

'But my betrothal to Edward has been officially announced. I cannot enter Almack's as a débutante.'

'That's right.' William's eyes settled on Cassandra. 'But your sister can.'

Cassandra's eyes shot to his with a flare of anger and found, as she suspected, the amused and mocking grin challenging her.

Emma's head spun round and she looked at her sister, her eyes shining with happiness and hope. 'Oh, would you, Cassy? Would you really do that for me?'

'You can surely see that this is the perfect solution,' Lady Monkton was quick to remark approvingly. 'Almack's will be the stage for you both to make your marks upon the world. The mystique of the club is based upon snobbery and social cachet and is more important than a presentation at court. To be admitted through the club's exclusive doors will set the seal on Emma's and Edward's betrothal and they will be virtually assured of acceptance at all the *ton*'s functions. You, too, Cassandra. I can't tell you how happy it will make me, how proud— to formally present you to society. It's unfortunate we didn't decide this earlier and had you fitted out with the whole new extensive wardrobe of a lady of quality, which is the custom.'

'But I am not a lady of quality, Aunt Elizabeth, and I maintain that it would be an unnecessary extravagance,' Cassandra retorted testily. 'I have enough day dresses, evening dresses, dresses for routs, balls, assemblies and cloaks and hats and all the necessary accessories to see me through to my dotage.'

'I would still have liked to have you properly fitted out.'

Cassandra looked at the three faces watching her expectantly, realising that it was quite useless voicing her objections. She sat perfectly still, her hands clenched in her lap, glaring at the clever, unscrupulous manipulator across from her. She was being tricked by a master player and there wasn't a thing she could do about it. She was trapped and he knew it.

'Are you familiar with Almack's?' Lady Monkton asked William, unaware of Cassandra's inner turmoil.

'I haven't set foot in the place in over a decade,' he told her, unable to prevent his distaste from showing.

'Why, when it's so popular?'

'Lord knows why it is since there's nothing particularly attractive about it or the entertainment it offers. Almack's is a place of insipid propriety. It may hold the most exclusive parties in London, but they are sedate to the point of boring.'

'Then, since you find it so dull, you needn't attend,' Cassandra suggested coldly, hoping he would do just that. 'Aunt Elizabeth will be more than happy to chaperon Emma and me.'

William looked at her. His smile was infuriating. 'What? And deny me the pleasure of escorting you? I wouldn't hear of it. I insist you give me two dances and you must promise there will be no touting for donations for your precious institute. Afterwards we will finish the evening off at my residence in Grosvenor Square. Grandmother will be entertaining a few friends and we are invited. She is most anxious to meet the young lady who is to wed her grandson.'

When William had departed and Aunt Elizabeth and Emma began excitedly making plans for the forthcoming event, the full realisation of what was expected of her hit Cassandra and it began to appear as if she could hardly avoid it. The thought made her breath catch. It was a realisation that against so much opposition there was nothing she could do. Her mind formed a vision of herself at Almack's as a débutante and she angrily shook her head to make the image depart. Her mind did not extend beyond her immediate escape, but there was none.

Her mother shared her doubts about what she was doing, knowing how her daughter felt about society's mores and how she mocked the ludicrous lengths to which people went in order to do only what propriety would allow. She had no wish, however, for Cassandra to set herself apart from it completely, and realising why her daughter was doing it, she gave Cassandra her blessing.

* * *

After prolonged, painstaking primping and preening in front of the cheval mirror, the preparations were complete. Exquisitely coiffured and gorgeously attired, in a gold-spangled gown of cream satin and lace and clutching her fan in her gloved hands, Cassandra joined a radiant Emma, Edward and Aunt Elizabeth in the carriage that was to take them to Almack's in King Street. Edward had come alone, explaining that William had been unavoidably detained and sent his most abject apologies. He would be along later—probably after ten o'clock—and Cassandra was to be sure to reserve a dance for him. Cassandra was both vexed and disappointed to hear this, but she was determined not to let thoughts of William occupy her evening.

Prepared to make her mark upon a world from which she sought to be excluded, when Cassandra passed through the exclusive, holier-than-holy portals of Almack's Assembly Rooms she felt the trap closing around her. Beneath her calm, controlled exterior she endured a nauseating turmoil of anger.

When they entered the huge ballroom, decorated with gilt columns and enormous mirrors, it was filled with animation, laughter and music, dancers and swirling dresses and sparkling jewels. Suddenly the conversation became muted as every influential head swivelled towards the new arrivals, then escalated to frantic whispers. The city was afire with talk of Emma and Edward's betrothal and Cassandra was aware of the amount of gossip and speculation their appearance at Almack's was causing.

There were so many people it was clear the ball was going to be a crush. Most of the débutantes were making their formal bow to the *ton* that night. Blondes and brunettes waited with heightened colour and eager gazes, while the hunting instincts of their mamas and chaperons for the male species were at fever pitch, which meant they had scented prime prey and were making sure their charges' cards were full, as young

swains—attractive, well-favoured and well turned out—
lavished attention on them.

Cassandra surveyed the scene with disdain. She sighed. It
was going to be a long night.

Having fully expected Cassandra—noted for her sobriquet, the Ice Maiden, and for the fact that she frequently
turned down prospective partners—to be escorted to Almack's
by the renowned Lord Lampard, the young bucks hung back,
expecting the illustrious earl to appear at any moment, but
when he failed to do so, within minutes she was creditably
besieged and her dance card began filling up.

'Miss Greenwood. I am both delighted and surprised to see
you here this evening.'

Cassandra started and took a step back as the indolent figure
of Sir Charles Grisham, who had just come out of the card
room, bowed before her. 'Why, good evening, Sir Charles.'

He beamed delightedly at her. 'Well, now you are here, if your
dance card isn't full, perhaps you would honour me with a
dance—or two?' he asked expectantly, a bold gleam in his eyes.

She looked at him—Sir Charles Grisham, the dashing and
flamboyant Corinthian, the other half of William's wager.
Her interest was pricked. Suddenly the evening might not be
such a disaster after all. Perhaps she could have some fun—
wield her wiles under Almack's glittering chandeliers.
Suddenly a cunning light entered her eyes, and she smiled
with deep satisfaction. She would make it doubly difficult for
William to succeed in seducing her by feigning an interest in
his friend. Anticipation laced with excitement flowed through
her, and determination to get her own back and bring the conceited William Lampard down a peg or two drove her.

Perhaps she could make him angry enough—or jealous
enough, she hoped—to lose control completely and confront
her with what he had done. And when he did, she would coldly
tell him that she had known about the wager all along and
make him grovel at her feet and beg for her forgiveness—

although a picture of William Lampard grovelling at anyone's feet was a difficult one to conjure up. It would be such a lark. Suddenly she brightened and gave Charles a favourable, dazzling smile.

'Why, Sir Charles, I would be delighted, although you must realise that it's a mistake to show partiality by dancing twice with the same partner.'

'As to that, I really could not care less,' he drawled.

'And I do have my reputation to uphold,' she teased.

His grin was impudent as he subjected her to a long, lingering gaze. 'I would not dream of doing anything to damage that. You will pencil me in?'

'You are a determined man, Sir Charles.'

'And you are lovelier than I remember, Miss Greenwood.'

'Flatterer. In which case I shall reserve two dances for you,' Cassandra heard herself say.

Within half an hour every dance of the night except the one she had reserved for William after ten o'clock had been claimed. The strict rules of the club stated that the doors closed at eleven and after that no one was allowed in. Under the watchful and profoundly proud eye of Aunt Elizabeth, both her charges took to the floor with their respective partners for a lively country dance.

When Cassandra had danced with more gentlemen than she could remember, gentlemen who flattered her outrageously, and she was dancing her second dance with Sir Charles Grisham, William arrived just before eleven o'clock. Unbeknown to him, he was too late to claim his dance with Cassandra—she had given it to someone else. At the sight of him she experienced a rush of feeling, a bittersweet joy in view of what stood between them and her intention to make him realise that there were several rivals for her company.

There was a whispered stir among those standing on the side lines of the crowded ballroom. Almost every eye turned towards the entrance as the man who had just arrived attracted their total attention. It was none other than Lord Lampard, the Earl of Carlow, who had not attended Almack's for many years.

Like every other male present he was attired in formal black tail coat, white waistcoat and neckcloth and regulation knee breeches. A tall strong-looking man, his brooding good looks turned heads wherever he went and caused several young women to heave a quiet sigh—and tonight was no exception. When his gaze swept the room, acknowledging his cousin dancing with his radiant betrothed with a slight nod, before coming to rest on the exquisite creature dancing with Sir Charles Grisham, they did not have to ask which female it was that had lured him to the club tonight. Was there any truth in what was being said about them? Were they really caught up in a torrid affair? It was clear from the way he was looking at her that Lord Lampard would not be inclined to ask anyone else to dance.

Completely impervious to the stir he was creating, excusing himself to Lady Cowper, just one of Almack's arbitrary and despotic patronesses trailing in his wake, William strolled further into the ballroom. He regretted being unable to escort Cassandra to the club, but, when he'd received Mr Jardine's note informing him that he was to call on him at eight o'clock with interesting news regarding the assassin, he'd been keen to know what he had found out, so he'd decided to let Edward do the honour of escorting the ladies.

The effect of seeing Cassandra dancing with Charles surprised him—the sudden tightening of possessiveness, the unexpected tug on his vitals. At the same moment, combining the perfect amount of boldness and maidenly demureness, Cassandra raised her eyes to Charles's attractive face and smiled favourably. It was a small encouragement of sorts, for William saw Charles's hand tighten about her waist as he spun her round. He felt a dart of anger course through him.

Had it been any other man she was dancing with he would

not have felt so put out, but, knowing Charles's penchant for a pretty face and how mischievous he could be, and that for some perverse reason of his own he might be tempted to mention their wager, he felt decidedly uneasy. Having completed his business with Mr Jardine, and eager to see Cassandra, he'd hurried to Almack's to be with her, but now, feeling thwarted, his high spirits faded.

Propping his shoulder against a pillar, he continued to watch her in brooding silence. Dazzling and vivacious, she shone out among all the débutantes, and she was smiling into Charles's eyes in a way that made him want to wring her neck. Considering her opinion regarding this kind of event, he'd fully expected to find her looking bored to death, but instead she was enjoying herself in a way that astounded him—a mite too much for his liking.

Cassandra was fully aware of William watching her from the sidelines and with glee she deliberately set out to put his teeth on edge by flirting quite shamelessly with Charles. When the dance ended and Charles escorted her back to Aunt Elizabeth, Cassandra, glancing in William's direction, felt the turbulence of his desire and the violence of his anger reach her with equal intensity.

There was not a man in the room to compare with him. She had not failed to notice the women who glanced his way, their glances lingering an extra fraction of a second. She should be flattered that a man such as he had come to Almack's because of her, but how could she be? Something cold fell in her chest. He wasn't sincere, she knew that, and that hurt.

Pushing himself off the pillar, William approached her. 'I'm glad to see you are enjoying yourself,' he commented with calm emphasis.

A brilliant smile dawned across Cassandra's features as she met his gaze. 'Yes, I'm enjoying myself enormously,' she replied, managing to look extremely innocent, despite the seductive allure of her gown and rosy face. 'It's the most wonderful evening I've had in years. It's a shame you couldn't come earlier. You've missed a splendid evening.'

His eyes narrowed as they looked pointedly into hers. 'It's not over yet. I have a dance to claim from you, don't forget.'

She managed to feign a look of disappointment and mortification. 'Oh, what a pity. I thought you must have forgotten. I did reserve one, but when you failed to arrive I thought you weren't coming so I danced with someone else. Unfortunately, my dance card is full and I'm afraid there's not a thing I can do about it.'

William's face darkened with annoyance, and Cassandra could almost feel his struggle to hold his temper in check, but before he could reply a smiling swain of medium height and pink-faced stepped up to her to claim her hand. With a dazzling smile on her pink lips, she turned her back on William and stepped on to the dance floor without a backward glance, leaving him to exist in a state of seething frustration.

William glared after her. His jealousy and fury mounted as he watched her throw herself into a Scottish reel. He saw how heads turned to look at her—honey-gold hair glowing like the sun, a gown of gold-spangled cream satin and swirling lace. For a moment she caught his angry eyes and smiled, secure in herself, secure in certain victory.

Gritting his teeth, William thought every unpleasant thing about the young man she was with. When the dance ended he advanced towards her, but before he could reach her she had been claimed by another swain.

'You are not gaining headwind tonight, William,' a calm voice said next to him. 'Cupid must have smitten you,' Charles observed, 'if you have to follow Miss Greenwood all the way to Almack's. Wouldn't have thought this would appeal to you.'

William whirled round, but stopped when he saw Charles's slumberous eyes watching him, and the unthinking response that sprang to his lips died. For, he thought angrily, Charles was right. He was bewitched and beguiled by the wench. In short, for the first time in his life his heartfelt emotions were overruling his head, and he didn't suffer the affliction well.

'She's out to collect as many fawning admirers as she can tonight,' Charles went on. 'You appear to have a great deal of competition—and small wonder. Miss Greenwood is quite out of the ordinary. She shines tonight. She is also warm, witty and an exquisite dancer—and she appears to be avoiding you.' Helping himself to a pinch of snuff, he lifted his arrogant brows and turned to William, his look both suspicious and intrigued. 'Why, I can't imagine. Would I be right in thinking you've had a change of heart and would like to seduce the lady after all?'

'Mind your own damned business,' William growled.

Charles smiled lazily, not in the least offended by his friend's offhand remark. 'If I didn't think you were after her, I'd make a play for her myself.'

William slowly turned his head and gave him a bland stare. 'If you value our friendship, Charles, you will forget you made that remark.'

Charles slanted him an amused look. 'You're beginning to sound like a jealous swain, William. Don't tell me your attentions towards Miss Greenwood are honourable. Good Lord, perish the thought. I am trying to imagine what the *ton* will make of it if the renowned Earl of Carlow, libertine *par excellence,* has decided to wed the daughter of a penniless professional.' Adopting a bored expression, he glanced around the room. 'I always find evenings at Almack's unbearably flat— don't know why I bother coming. Perhaps you'd care to join me in the card room.'

'If I'd wanted to play cards, I would have gone to White's,' William ground out ungraciously. He frowned. 'A drink wouldn't go amiss.'

'Forget it. Unless you have a fancy for lemonade and orange water, there's nothing else.'

William gave Cassandra another half an hour of flaunting

herself on the dance floor before he approached Lady Monkton and informed her it was time to leave for Grosvenor Square. He wasn't unpleasant and was amiable to everyone who spoke to him as they were leaving; in fact, Cassandra was put out that he didn't seem to mind that he'd missed dancing with her and that she'd totally ignored him.

Chapter Ten

Light blazed from every window of William's house in Grosvenor Square. In the large, sumptuously furnished white-and-gold salon, tables and chairs and sofas had been placed so that the thirty guests could gather in intimate little groups to chat or play cards. Several gentlemen were in the adjoining billiard room, wreathed in the smoke of their cigars. Into this serene company entered the newcomers. A hush descended as conversation ceased and every eye turned in their direction. When they saw it was the master of the house conversation and cards were resumed.

Lady Monkton paused to acknowledge an acquaintance, leaving William to escort Cassandra and Emma to be presented to the dowager countess, where she was seated at a small table playing bridge. She was a handsome woman with a majestic bearing, an aristocratic nose and imperious expression. Her eyes brightened as she observed her grandsons' approach—William, proud and arrogant, who attacked life with a vigorous purposefulness, and Edward, who was good-natured and easy to get on with. Edward had felt a wrenching sorrow over the demise of his parents, and the dowager had thanked God that he'd had William and his brother Robert to guide him.

'Ah, William, I'm delighted you were able to join our festivities, even if tardily.'

William bent and kissed her proffered cheek. 'I apologise if we've kept you waiting, Grandmother. The ladies were enjoying themselves greatly. It was difficult to drag them away.'

'I'm happy you were successful. I'm eager to meet the two young ladies who have so bedazzled my grandsons.' Completely ignorant of the unease her casual remark stirred in the older of the two young women, or the look of indignation she darted at William, the dowager watched them execute their flawless curtsies.

Taking Emma's hand, Edward proudly drew her forward and introduced her.

The dowager raised her lorgnette to her piercing eyes and inspected her from top to toe. She nodded her approval. 'Yes, you have chosen well, Edward. I must compliment you on your excellent taste.'

'You are very kind,' Emma said, radiant with happiness as she hung on to Edward's arm.

Not to be won over so easily, in response the dowager raised her brows and disdainfully looked at her. 'I have admonished Edward most severely and I will tell you, young woman, what I told him. I do not approve of couples eloping—unpleasantness always ensues. It was badly done by you both and was in danger of creating a scandal of the worst kind. Still, I am glad William decided to handle it. If one cannot stop gossip, it's as well to turn it in another direction—a feasible solution.' She looked at William. 'How did it go at Almack's? Have we pulled it off?'

William nodded. 'Just as I planned it would,' he told her, still seething over the let-down Cassandra had given him earlier and impatient to take her to task over it. 'The betrothed couple were a tremendous success. I have no doubt that tomorrow morning Monkton House will be swamped with invitations for them to attend every social event in London.'

'Splendid.' She looked at the butler who was bearing a tray of goblets. 'Bring in the champagne, Siddons. We will all raise our glasses and drink a toast to the happy couple.' Her gaze shifted to Cassandra. It was slow and pointedly bold as she perused the young woman. She carefully studied the blue-green eyes regarding her from beneath a heavy fringe of dark lashes. 'And you are Cassandra. You are very young,' the dowager countess observed, studying the lovely visage, 'and very lovely.'

Cassandra smiled at the elegantly attired woman while thinking that the Dowager Countess of Carlow was the most intimidating woman she had ever met—and that William was so like her. 'Thank you. It's kind of you to say so.'

The dowager looked at William with an expression of approval and satisfaction. William's reply to her look was merely a sardonic lift to his brows, which caused a *frisson* of alarm to shoot through Cassandra. Since leaving Almack's he was all charm and politeness personified, but she knew that beneath that veneer of calmness he was burningly angry.

'Now circulate. Introduce them to my guests, William,' the dowager ordered, picking up her cards to resume her game of bridge, a sudden humour lighting her eyes as they swept over the collected throng, 'before they expire with curiosity.'

William skilfully guided them from group to group and introduced them. As they mingled, all attention should have been focused on Emma as Edward's betrothed, but Cassandra had the uncomfortable feeling that she was the one under scrutiny and the dowager countess in particular was showing more interest in her than was acceptable to her peace of mind.

When introductions had been duly made the champagne was brought in. There was a bubble of laughter and shouts of congratulations as everyone toasted the betrothed couple, touching glasses so that they made crystal chimes. Cassandra, feeling the need to escape, was leaving the salon for the ladies' retiring room when she came face to face with Lady Lydia Lampard, Mark's wife.

Wearing an expression of civil disdain, Lydia smiled thinly. 'Ah, Miss Greenwood. How nice to see you again. We have met, albeit briefly, at Carlow.'

Cassandra met the appraising stare of the proud and haughty woman. Her eyes were expressionless. It was difficult to know what she was thinking. She was attired in watered grey silk and diamonds sparkled coldly at her throat. They suited her, Cassandra thought—in fact, she could not imagine her wearing any other jewel. Mark Lampard and this woman were well matched—both cold and remote. Cassandra could not imagine her glowing with passion. There was something deadly about her, as there is about a snake.

'Yes, I do remember. I must apologise for rushing off. My sister was unwell and I was most eager to get her back to London.'

'Of course. I do understand. Mark and I are in London for the wedding. We are staying with my sister and her husband in Greenwich. You must be delighted with the way things have turned out.'

'I'm sorry? What can you mean?'

'Only that you must be relieved the situation has turned out so well.'

'If you mean the wedding has been arranged to silence the gossips then, yes, I am. But I am also happy for Emma and Edward since they are clearly so much in love. It is a good match.'

'Yes, of course it is,' Lydia murmured, sounding quietly unconvinced and without enthusiasm. 'Please excuse me. My husband is beckoning.'

Relieved when Lydia moved on, Cassandra made her escape. Spending as much time as was possible in the retiring room, when she did return to the salon, William suddenly appeared in front of her. Seeing his fixed expression, she was filled with unease and foreboding.

'A word, if you please, Cassandra.'

'If you don't mind, William, I would like to return to the others,' she told him coldly.

William clamped his hand on her elbow. 'I insist.'

Cassandra beheld a face of such dark menacing rage that she shuddered. 'Let go of my arm.'

'Shut up,' he hissed, maintaining his hold and propelling her inside a room and closing the door. In the oppressive silence as he walked into the middle of the room, Cassandra took note of the judicious set to his jaw. She realised that beneath his bland exterior he was furious. She waited, enduring the icy blast of his gaze. It dawned on her that he was striving to control his anger and she prayed he would gain it.

'Were you deliberately trying to publicly humiliate me tonight?' he demanded at length. 'Come, Cassandra,' he sneered when she merely stared at him, 'don't tell me you are stuck for words. You seemed to have plenty to say to your doting swains when you flirted and hung on to their every word. You are clearly a woman of many pleasures, and it would seem one of them is to try and humble me—you didn't succeed, by the way. I'm too experienced and too thick skinned to be baited by a mere chit of a girl. Why, if you feel compelled to show me you care nothing for me, for my advances, did you need to prove it in such a petty, small-minded way?'

William's reprimand for her behaviour was deserved, but Cassandra had done it with good reason and was not sorry. 'Don't you dare talk to me about being humbled and humiliated,' she uttered irately, slowly walking towards him. 'You seem to believe this is all about you. What did you expect? It was more than you deserved.'

'Really! I disagree.'

Cassandra's mouth went dry when he moved closer. She stepped back. 'Don't you dare touch me. I hate it when you do. I hate you.'

William's dark brows drew together. Reaching out, he

dragged her into his arms and before she knew what he was about his mouth swooped down on to hers. She struggled and tried to pull away, but his arms tightened about her. His lips were hard, the kiss meant to punish—but it had the opposite effect. When his hand closed over her breast and caressed it, teasing the hardening nipple, tingling, pleasurable flames began shooting through her body.

When he felt her begin to respond, William raised his head and looked down at her upturned face and smiled sardonically. 'Now tell me you hate it when I touch you, and perhaps next time you decide to humiliate and embarrass me in public you will reconsider.'

Drowning in shame at her inability to control her own treacherous body, with flaming cheeks Cassandra twisted free as the bewildered terror that had gripped her when he had forced her inside the room evaporated.

'You? Humiliated? Embarrassed? How dare you say that— you despicable hypocrite,' she fired back and had the satisfaction of seeing shock crack his hard, handsome features. 'From the very beginning you set out to degrade me in the most shameful way of all, and yet you accuse *me* of humiliating *you*. Believe me, William Lampard, what happened to you at Almack's tonight was pretty tame considering what you had intended for me. And how dare *you,* the biggest hellion in London, lecture *me* on how to behave when your own behaviour is anything but honourable. You do not deserve to be called a gentleman.'

William cocked a dubious brow, somewhat amazed by the spirit of the woman. He reached out to draw her to him. Furiously she shrugged him off.

'Keep your hands off me. I haven't finished. I'm not too proud to admit that in the beginning I was foolish enough to fall for your charms. It was quite wonderful, the most wonderful and remarkable thing that had ever happened to me, and now I am so ashamed—it was so trite. You're no doubt accustomed to that sort of feminine reaction wherever you go,' she said scathingly. 'I succumbed just like every other unsuspecting woman you take a fancy to—a foolish inclination on my part not supported by anything other than infatuation and my own imagination, because you felt nothing for me at all. That I knew.'

'How? How did you know?'

His shocked expression and the question told Cassandra her mistake, that she had almost revealed her secret, but she was so angry it no longer mattered.

'Because I heard you. I heard you,' she flared, looking him in the eyes, ashamed of the feelings she carried for him in her heart. 'It was at Carlow Park—the morning after you kissed me. Naïve fool that I was, I was so eager to see you I couldn't wait. You were in the library with Sir Charles Grisham. I paused in the doorway, not wishing to interrupt you. I heard every word you said. Do you recall that conversation, my lord?'

Comprehension and a hint of dismay dawned on William's face. 'I do remember,' he murmured. 'How much did you hear?'

'Enough. Enough to learn of your disgusting wager—that if you failed to seduce me before the end of the Season, Charles Grisham would be richer by a horse. A horse, for heaven's sake! Is that all I am worth?'

'Cassandra, I am grieved that you heard that conversation, and please believe me when I say I regret that wager. I give you my word I never intended to hurt you.'

Her eyes were alive with pain and fury. 'Liar!' she cried contemptuously, her chest heaving. 'Your word? Your word means nothing to me.' She was looking at him as if he was obscene.

White faced with guilt and remorse, William tried to placate her. 'It was a temporary madness. It was cruel and thoughtless and I realise you must be deeply hurt.'

'That's correct,' she flared, her eyes blazing with turbulent animosity, 'and there is no excuse. It was my knowledge of what you were doing that kept me ahead of the game. Lord knows how much of a fool I would have made of myself had

I not found out about that sordid wager. What is true of most scoundrels is doubly so of you. You would have ruined me, defiled me without any regard to my feelings and then cast me off as you would a common trull, you—you loathsome, despicable letch. Although I am hardly surprised. You were merely living up to your name.' She turned from him and walked away, as if she couldn't bear to look at him.

'Cassandra—' William began tautly, but she whirled on her heels like a dervish and stalked back to him, her hips swaying provocatively while her eyes flashed.

'What was I, William?' she scoffed sneeringly, jabbing her finger hard into his chest. 'Was I some tender titbit you decided to play with, a simpleton to fill your needs for a night or two? What amusement you must have had playing your sordid little game with me. And how disappointed you must now be feeling, knowing you have lost your wager.'

Nothing moved in William's face, but his eyes darkened. Quietly he asked, 'Will you listen to what I have to say?'

'No. I am not interested. I will never be able to forgive you. But you listen to me, William Lampard,' she said, her chilled contempt meeting him face to face. 'The harm you have done me will stand between us for ever. From now on you keep your distance. Any future contact between us will be impersonal, brief and in public. The wedding means we cannot avoid coming into contact with each other—at such times we will be polite and cordial as protocol dictates. But that is all. Now, if you don't mind, I will return to the others before I am missed and someone comes looking for me. The last thing I want is to be found alone with you, which would no doubt start another scandal.'

With her head high she marched towards the door. As she reached it she turned and glared back at him. 'I don't like being made sport of, but you obviously enjoy causing discomfort in any manner. Someday I sincerely hope you meet someone who will get the better of you.' Stalking out, she slammed the door behind her, leaving him to bear the oppressive silence alone.

Weighted down with unbearable guilt and hating himself with a virulence that almost choked him, William walked over to the hearth. Propping his foot on the fender and resting his arm on the mantelpiece, he stared down into the flames. So that was what all this had been about. In the space of a fraction of a second everything was made clear, presenting the whole sordid picture in every profane detail. Cassandra's revelation answered so many questions—why she had behaved as she had on leaving Carlow Park, why she had told him she wanted no part of him, ever, when he had kissed her at Netherton Hall, when he knew by her response to his kiss that she was lying.

Dear God, he had hurt her very badly. She hated him, and with good reason. And knowing how deeply he had hurt her, the pain William felt was a thousand times worse than any wound he had ever received. But when she had overheard his conversation with Charles at Carlow Park, she must not have stayed long enough to hear him tell Charles the wager was off—and the mood she was in now, she wouldn't believe him if he told her. He was going to have to figure out a way to redeem himself, but it was not going to be easy.

When Cassandra returned to the salon there was no sign of the bitter altercation that had just taken place on her smiling face. William appeared fifteen minutes later. His eyes swept the room, coming to rest briefly on her before he looked away and disappeared into the billiards room.

Cassandra turned and saw Lydia across the room speaking to Aunt Elizabeth. She was also looking at William and Cassandra noted a cold glitter in her eyes—what secrets did those eyes hold? she wondered. She was looking at William as if she hated him.

For the rest of the evening Cassandra stored up a terrible burden of emotion and not until she was back at Monkton

House and in bed did she allow herself to dwell on her confrontation with William, firmly believing he didn't feel any remorse at all for what he had done to her. As she buried her head in the pillows she succumbed to tears.

Her mind had always shied away from delving too deeply into what her feelings were for William, but now she had to ask herself. She did care for him, there was no use denying it merely to keep the fires of resentment burning. Thinking about the times they had been together, she began with their meeting in Green Park. He could have died that day had she not been passing through at the time.

She could not blot from her mind the exquisite sweetness of the times she had been in his arms, the memory of his kisses, of his whispered words of passion that tormented her every day. No matter how hard she tried to think otherwise, nothing had been the same since she had met him. The pleasure, the intensity she had experienced at Carlow Park before she knew about the wager, still vividly etched and clear, were now too painful to contemplate.

Recalling the day he had searched her out at the institute, how he had patiently listened with superior understanding and compassion when she had spoken about the children, she had thought he cared, but it never existed, only in her imagination. She reminded herself that he was a rake and that righteousness was on her side, and she would insulate herself against heartbreak, but, if so, then why did it hurt so much and why was she crying so desperately?

Suddenly Edward and Emma were the darlings of society, London's most talked-about couple—theirs was a heady triumph. The gossips and society columns were full of the forthcoming wedding, and instead of the cruel, ridiculous tittle-tattle that had followed in the wake of their elopement, they suddenly made a fine couple and were clearly very much in love.

Lady Monkton, used to dealing with the pressures of public

life, immersed herself in the extensive wedding preparations that required the efforts of modistes and an army of servants. Harriet, her duties at the institute taking up more of her time as she struggled to keep it open, was more than happy to let her cousin take over. Emma moved into Monkton House where she found herself skilfully guided by Aunt Elizabeth. Visitors were received at the house in staggering numbers and invitation cards piled up on the hall table thick and fast. She was presented to this and that and readily accepted by everyone she met.

Listening intently to what was being said, Cassandra heard the odd speculation about her family—not much money, father a professional man, mother heavily involved with destitute children—but for the most part the comments were complimentary. Emma had youth, beauty, good connections through Lady Monkton and a certain fashionable notoriety.

As Emma was being carried along on the crest of a gigantic wave, and considering she had done quite enough to help her sister become an accepted and popular member of society, Cassandra purposely kept a low profile and kept herself too busy to think of William. He had given Aunt Elizabeth *carte blanche* with the wedding preparations and they saw nothing of him, and Cassandra hoped fervently that this was how it would remain—but she had never felt so wretchedly unhappy.

If she wasn't at the institute, although she refused to attend the levees and soirées she was invited to, or receive suitors following her début at Almack's, she did accompany Aunt Elizabeth and Emma to the theatre and musical evenings. She also went driving in Hyde Park and along Pall Mall and often rode out with Emma and a groom in attendance, now she had conquered her fear of horses and was more confident in her prowess as a horsewoman.

They strolled in London's flower-filled gardens that were dotted all over the city and open to all for a few pennies, and in particular the splendour of Vauxhall, with its rotunda, its lights and groves and whispering lovers. Then there were the shopping expeditions to Covent Garden, Bond Street, the Strand and St James's, which was a predominantly masculine preserve, with streets packed with bachelor lodgings and expensive shops. Its main street was dominated by gentlemen's clubs, such as White's, Brooks's and Boodle's, all out of bounds to ladies of quality.

Lady Monkton would order the driver to take the open carriage slowly past so the bucks and the beaux—foppish young gentlemen, with exquisite clothes and manners so indolent that they seemed half-asleep—seated in the bow windows could ogle her young charges with their quizzing glasses.

The afternoon was warm, the air sultry as they circled the ring in Hyde Park—a rendezvous for fashion and beauty, the preserve of the upper classes. The cavalcade of handsome equipages and men mounted on splendid high-stepping horses with gleaming flanks moved at a leisurely pace. It was one of the ways to see and be seen, to show off new clothes and meet fellow members of the *ton*.

Cassandra and Emma were seated across from Aunt Elizabeth. When the driver stopped the carriage so Aunt Elizabeth could speak to an acquaintance, Cassandra sighed, quite intoxicated by the sight.

'It's quite a turn out, don't you agree, Emma?' she commented, letting her gaze wander aimlessly over the crowd.

'Yes, quite a turn out.' Emma echoed her words with a full heart, seeing little from beneath her pretty parasol beyond the elegant, glittering throng.

Cassandra let her gaze drift over the languidly moving crowd, past a carriage holding three vivacious young women under the stern eye of a chaperon, past a tall man on horseback—her heart gave a leap and missed a beat. He was engrossed in conversation with another gentleman also on horseback and seemingly taking little notice of what was going on around him. In stricken paralysis she stared at him. Everyone else became faceless and anonymous to her. They fell away like shadows. All she was conscious of was William.

He had appeared too suddenly for her to prepare herself, so the heady surge of pleasure on seeing him following her initial shock was clearly evident on her lovely features. Since that night when she had last seen him almost two weeks ago, she had managed to avoid a confrontation with the only man who posed any threat to her control, and already she could feel it crumbling.

He moved with an easy grace, at one with his mount, cutting a dashing swath through the crowd. Cassandra's heart gave a sickening lurch. She could feel his seductive power reach out across the ring to stir her senses, and now he was looking straight at her.

Sensing her sister's disquiet, Emma turned and looked at her. 'Cassy, are you all right?' she asked with concern.

Dragging air into her constricted lungs, Cassandra averted her eyes. She must not allow Emma to see the devastating effect that infuriating man had on her. 'I am quite all right, Emma. I just wish the carriage would move on.'

Unconvinced, Emma glanced in the direction Cassandra had been looking. Seeing Lord Lampard, she believed she had found the cause of her sister's unease. She looked back at her sister, her eyebrows drawn into a frown. 'Cassy, why are you so determined to avoid Lord Lampard?'

'I'm not,' she replied stiffly. 'It's just that I don't care for his company, that's all.'

'So you still haven't changed your opinion of him.'

'No. He's everything I accused him of being on the night of Aunt Elizabeth's ball—the night before you and Edward eloped. He is still a rake and a blackguard and I want nothing to do with him.'

'Rake he may be, but he is the one Edward and I have to thank for being allowed to wed. It is all his doing and I shall be eternally grateful to him. Edward says that at heart he's as honourable a man as you are likely to find. With the wedding looming, sooner or later you'll have to speak to him.'

'Then let it be later.'

Emma looked sceptical. 'When we were in Surrey you spent a good deal of time together. I thought you were beginning to get on better, that you were beginning to warm to him. Did anything happen between you to change that?'

'No.' Cassandra averted her eyes, glad that Aunt Elizabeth was too engrossed in animated conversation to notice their altercation.

Emma's hand tightened on her arm. 'Cassy,' she whispered, 'what did Lord Lampard do? It is clear to me that something must have happened between the two of you, so you might as well tell me.'

'Nothing happened, Emma.'

'It did,' Emma persisted forcefully. 'It's written all over your face.'

Cassandra's face flamed. 'All right, Emma. If you must know he—he kissed me,' she confessed quietly, wondering what her young sister would say if she were to disclose the full facts of that wretched, humiliating wager.

Emma's eyes widened with amazement. 'Kissed you? Goodness! And didn't you like being kissed by him?'

'No—yes—oh, Emma, I don't know. It's just that I don't want to become involved with him. I can't and I shall do my best to avoid him.'

'Well, you won't be able to for much longer because he's seen us and is riding this way. Who's that with him? He looks slightly familiar, but for the life of me I can't think where I've seen him.'

Cassandra glanced at William's companion. 'That's William's cousin Mark Lampard. You met him briefly as we were leaving Carlow Park and you will have seen him at Grosvenor Square two weeks ago.'

'Oh, yes, now I remember. He's terribly serious and his wife was a mite too superior to be nice. Still, I suppose I'd better try and like her since I'm to be family.'

Astride his restive horse, William and his cousin joined the languid promenade of carriages and eventually stopped beside their carriage. Sunlight glittered on the backs of proud, prancing horses; it touched the leaves and lighted on Cassandra's bewitching face. The sight of her after almost two weeks of not seeing her had a devastating effect on William. Never had she looked so radiantly lovely or serene. The truth was that neither time nor distance had blunted the feelings he had for her.

Bitter regret twisted his heart. No matter where he was or what he did, thoughts of her consumed him. Looking into her eyes, he felt as if he were being tortured. His muscles tightened and his whole body ached for her, but it was a hurt he didn't want to be spared.

If William was surprised to see Cassandra in the park, beyond a slight lift to his eyebrows, he made no show of it. She had dressed with special care, deliberating on what gown to wear, as though she was aware that she must look her best. She had chosen a deep pink. Afterwards she had her doubts about the colour, but she had been wrong, for it seemed to reflect in her face, giving it a flush that was extremely flattering. Beneath her small matching hat, her honey-gold hair had been arranged in bright glossy curls. Whatever he had to say, she resolved to appear and speak calmly.

His eyes were cool and expressionless. 'Cassandra. You are well, I hope?'

'Perfectly, thank you,' she replied, her voice toneless, recollections of the last time they had met uppermost in her thoughts. There was a strange silence while she searched her mind for something to add, but he had turned away and entered into conversation with Aunt Elizabeth.

Her acquaintance having moved on, Lady Monkton

focused all her attention on Lord Lampard. 'This is a pleasant surprise, Lord Lampard.'

'You remember my cousin, Baron Mark Lampard. As you know, he's in town with his wife for the wedding.'

'I am delighted to meet you again,' Lady Monkton said pleasantly.

Mark inclined his head. 'Likewise, Lady Monkton. I trust the wedding arrangements are going to plan?'

'They are indeed. We're all impatient for the happy day. Of course you have met my nieces—Cassandra, and Emma, the bride-to-be?'

Mark's cold, humourless eyes skimmed over Cassandra before settling on Emma. 'I have had that pleasure.'

'And how is your grandmother?' Lady Monkton enquired politely.

'She is well, thank you,' William replied. 'You must call on her to discuss wedding plans. She would like that—all of you,' he said, his eyes on Cassandra.

'We would be delighted.'

While William conversed with Aunt Elizabeth, Cassandra studied this strikingly handsome man surreptitiously. People passing by looked openly at him, but he seemed oblivious to them. His long muscular frame was well turned out in a midnight-blue jacket, the colour's starkness being broken only by a waistcoat in light grey satin and a crisp white neckcloth.

It was like coming face to face with a stranger. It unnerved her when those penetrating eyes locked on her and with threatening boldness slowly raked her as if he were stripping her bare. She had forgotten how brilliant they were. It was all she could do to face the unspoken challenge and not flee from the carriage.

While Lady Monkton and Emma continued to banter with Mark, William rode his horse to her side of the carriage. His gaze rested warmly on her face.

'I don't believe I apologised for not escorting you to Almack's, Cassandra.'

'I don't recall whether you did or not,' Cassandra replied coldly, avoiding his gaze. 'Whatever the reason was that delayed you, it must have been of far more interest and importance than escorting some silly débutantes to a ball.'

'It wasn't, but it was important.'

'It has nothing to do with me,' she bit back. 'Go away. I don't want to talk to you.'

'Stop it, Cassandra,' he rebuked in a low voice. 'I want to talk to you without your eyes hurling daggers at me. I desire a few moments of your time, if you can spare them. Kindly have the courtesy to listen to what I have to say. What kept me that night has everything to do with you since apart from myself you are the only one who knows about the attempts on my life.'

Cassandra's eyes flew to his. Deeply anxious for his safety despite everything, her interest was roused and her animosity for the moment forgotten. 'Has anything happened—have they tried again?'

Both happy and touched to see concern for him in her eyes, William's mouth curved in that sensuous smile of his. 'Soothe your fears, my love,' he murmured, 'not since the day I shot that blackguard on the road to Guildford. Mr Jardine, the private investigator I've hired, sent a note wanting to see me urgently that evening. You will understand why I had to speak to him. You may be interested to learn that the man I shot was called Daniel Sharp.'

'How does he know this?'

'The authorities in Guildford found his horse not far from his body. His name was on some correspondence in his saddlebags. Unfortunately, apart from his name we have nothing else to go on, but it's a start.'

'And the name means nothing to you?'

He shook his head. 'Not a thing.'

'Then Mr Jardine is going to have his work cut out.' Aching to tell him to take care—not to ride out alone and to look behind him at all times—at that same moment Emma turned to speak to her, so all she could manage to say was, 'Thank you for telling me.'

Returning to her home in Kensington later that day intending to visit the institute, she was happy to find her mother, who had just returned, waiting to disclose some uplifting news. Harriet told her that there was fresh hope for the institute and it would not have to close after all. Doctor Brookes had called at the institute to tell her that he had had a meeting with a lawyer who was representing a benefactor who wished to remain anonymous for the time being. Apparently he was so impressed by their work at the institute that he had made a considerable donation and would continue to do so on a six-monthly basis. Indeed, it was so generous that they might even be able to look for larger premises and possibly consider opening an orphanage.

Cassandra was overwhelmed with relief. It was like having a huge burden lifted from her shoulders. She was also relieved and happy to see her mother smile again and fresh animation light her eyes—although she thought this had as much to do with her meeting with Dr Brookes as the mysterious benefactor's generous donation. Still, with such a big sponsor, hopefully it would inspire others to donate. Not until she was in the carriage heading for the institute did she begin to wonder as to the identity of the benefactor. He seemed too good to be true—or was he?

He! Suddenly she sat bolt upright. In the space of two seconds blinding realisation dawned. There was only one *he* she could think of who would do something like this. Were there no lengths that man would go to to get her into his bed? Cold fury engulfed her. Of all the treacherous, underhanded tricks… Horrifying clarity had her ordering Clem to change direction and head for Grosvenor Square instead.

She was admitted to the house and told by Siddons—who, recalling another time when this same young lady had stormed into the house without a by your leave, eyed her with wary suspicion—to wait in the salon and he would inform Lord Lampard that she was here. As soon as William saw her pacing irately to and fro, her face like black thunder, he had the distinct impression that he had somehow stirred a volcano.

The sound of the double doors closing brought Cassandra immediately whirling round and she faced him with eyes blazing.

'Cassandra! I am surprised,' he said, coming further into the room with a graceful, half-animal saunter. 'To what do I owe the pleasure of your visit?'

Slowly she moved towards him, planting her small feet firmly in front of him. She faced him squarely, her elbows akimbo. 'This isn't a social call. Far from it. Didn't you hear anything I said to you two weeks ago? Are you deaf as well as stupid? What kind of man are you? What kind of man is it who will go to such lengths as to secure a children's institute in the belief it will lure one of its trustees into his bed?'

If he was surprised that she had found out about his donation, he gave no hint of it. Perching his hip on the edge of the table behind him, crossing his arms over his chest, he studied her impassively. 'I had an idea you would soon work out the identity of the anonymous benefactor.'

'In no time at all. So you don't deny it is you?'

He shrugged, immune to the wrathful expression on her lovely face. 'Since you ask me so pointedly, no, I do not deny it. Come, Cassandra, there's no need to take umbrage. I thought you'd be pleased. You cannot deny I have been helpful.'

'Because you had an ulterior motive—namely seducing me.'

'You make it sound sordid,' William said with an infuriating calm.

'That's because it is. In all the time I have known you, you have not been honest with me. You have used your mercenary qualities to manoeuvre me into your bed. I will not be your plaything. Thank God I found out in time.'

William smiled in the face of her fury, knowing he trod the trembling ground with a fool's boldness. 'I'm trying to reform.'

How she yearned to wipe that look from his face. 'An impossibility for you.' The rising fire of the volcano showed in her eyes. 'I care nothing for your good deeds.' He did not seem surprised or offended. Undaunted, he lifted his brows quizzically, a twist of humour about his beautifully moulded lips.

'I recall you telling me not so long ago that your dream was to open an orphanage. You've got your wish, Cassandra, so stop glaring at me. Are you too proud and stubborn to accept my gesture? I thought there was more at stake than pride and money.'

'You're right,' she snapped. 'The children.'

'Would you like me to withdraw my offer? Is that what you want?'

He was looking at her with the patience of a teacher discussing an illogical subject with a troublesome pupil. His calm made her want to kick his shin. 'Damn you, William Lampard. It's not up to me and you know it. Mama and Dr Brookes hold the purse strings and they're absolutely elated about what you're doing. Besides, how can I deny the children? But I don't like it. I don't like the way you've gone about ingratiating yourself with my family.'

William gazed at the tempestuous beauty standing merely a foot away, her eyes flashing angry sparks, her breasts rising and falling with suppressed fury beneath the grey dress she always wore for her work at the institute, and he felt a tremendous admiration for her honesty and courage in this stand she was taking because she believed he had wronged her. However, he hadn't expected her to react quite so violently to his donation to the institute, or his promise for its future.

Calmly he said, 'I thought you'd be pleased.'

'Pleased? You unspeakable cad,' she flung back. 'I'm pleased the children won't be deprived—of course I am, but I wish the money had come from another source. I find the idea of being indebted to you distinctly distasteful.'

He cocked a sleek black eyebrow. 'Beggars can't be choosers.'

'You're right, they can't.'

'Why does the idea of me funding the institute bring you such anger?'

'Because I know the reason why you're doing it. And don't insult my intelligence by telling me it's for the children, because I will not believe you.'

William studied her angry, rebellious face impassively for a long, silent moment. 'I'm very sorry to hear that,' he said softly, 'because it is true. It's time I did something worthwhile and it is a worthy cause. Besides, I have plenty of money. I can afford it.'

'And what is the price to me? Say what you like, but I know you never do anything without a motive. How long will it be before you demand some form of payment?'

'Damn it, Cassandra,' he cried, unable to repress his annoyance over her argumentative attitude. 'I don't want you to feel obligated to me.'

'I don't. I don't owe you anything and I will take nothing from you.'

Shoving a heavy lock of hair back from his forehead, William sighed heavily. 'You are a stubborn woman, Cassandra Greenwood.'

'You have no idea how stubborn I can be. So far you have only scratched the surface.'

'Are you always so unreasonable?'

'Ha! Because I won't be coerced and cajoled to bed down with you? You are the one who is being unreasonable.'

'That isn't what I want.'

'No? Then the wager was pointless.'

'Then marry me.'

For a moment Cassandra was stunned by his suggestion. She stared at him in astonishment. He was watching her reaction to his offer from beneath lowered lids. 'Marry you? Never.'

He sighed as if forlorn. 'Alas. I am to be tortured more, then. Have you any idea how the merest sight of you is enough to bring me pain?'

His voice had become low and soft in her ears, and Cassandra had to delve deeply into her reserve of will to dispel the slow numbing of her senses. 'What's this? Are you still lamenting the loss of your wager, my lord ? Have you and Sir Charles raised the stakes since we last spoke? Careful, William,' she mocked scathingly, 'he might want another of your horses. At this rate, his stables will be full to bursting with mounts from Carlow Park.'

'But I want to marry you.'

He had to be jesting. He must be—she simply dare not think that he might not be lest it destroy her control. 'I don't want to marry you,' she seethed.

'Does the idea of being a countess not appeal to you?'

Cassandra lifted her chin in scornful resentment. 'I wouldn't marry you if you were offering me the position of Queen of England. Now, no more. Let this business with the institute be enough.' She turned and stalked towards the door.

William's brows drew together. As she had turned from him he had been struck by an astonishing realisation—for despite her magnificent show of spirit and courage, Cassandra was apparently on the brink of tears. 'There—is just one more thing'

She paused. Something in his tone sent a warning shooting along her nerves. Turning, she looked at him warily, waiting for him to speak.

'I've spent some time at Westminster—in the House, recently. You will be relieved to learn that I've succeeded in obtaining some Government funding for your project.'

For the first time since entering the house, Cassandra was rendered speechless. All she could do was stare at him.

'And one more thing,' he said softly. Standing straight, his broad shoulders squared, his jaw set with implacable determination, he emanated the restrained power and unyielding authority Cassandra had always sensed and resented. 'Everything I've done I've done for you. I will stop at nothing to win you. Believe that.'

Unable to find words to answer, drop by precious drop Cassandra felt her confidence drain away. In a blinding streak of suffocating humiliation, she asked herself how she could ever have deluded herself into believing that she could sway him from his purpose. Almost choking on the lump of emotion that had risen in her throat, she went out.

Cassandra leaned her head back and closed her eyes as the carriage bore her away from Grosvenor Square back to Kensington. Feeling much abused and angered, she had decided not to go to the institute after all—she had no heart for it. It was impossible to shut out thoughts of William—when she closed her eyes, the image of his handsome face and blue smiling eyes mocked, challenged and consumed her. Bitter bile rose up in her throat as her thoughts marched in a circle of misery and anger. She would never forgive either William or Charles Grisham that wager, but what could she do? And so she was forced to bear her hurt and shame alone, with no way of avenging herself on either of them. But it was done with and her honour still remained intact.

But she was not content. As much as she forced all her determination to put William from her mind, it had an empty ring. The weakness of it echoed through her brain and the heady memory of his kisses became all the more intoxicating and seemed to ferment in her woman's body.

Over the days that followed, never in her life had Cassandra been so miserable or confused. She could think only of William. It was becoming an obsession. She had never known what obsession was except for the dictionary definition, which could not begin to describe how she felt for him. She hadn't known what it was to think of two things at the same time: to read a book and, while comprehending what was written, to see a darkly handsome face and two flashing blue eyes; to be in a room full of chattering people and at the same time distinctly hear another one. If this was obsession, then it was a miserable condition from which she could see no relief.

Chapter Eleven

The Season was at an end and almost everyone would be leaving town for their country estates. When the day of the wedding finally dawned after weeks of frenetic preparations, a radiant Emma, beneath an enveloping cloud of lace, walked down the aisle to stand beside her beloved Edward to recite their vows. She was accompanied by her bridal attendants with Cassandra as Matron of Honour.

Before going into church, as Cassandra had fussed and straightened her train, Emma whispered, 'You'll be next, Cassy. I just know you will.'

Cassandra had looked at her and smiled wryly, doubtful of that. The only man who continued to occupy her thoughts every waking moment, she had not seen since she had walked out of his house in angry confusion two weeks ago.

And then there he was, standing beside Edward in the church, his head rising above most of the guests assembled, his hands clasped behind his back, his legs a little apart. Her heart gave a joyful leap. His clean-cut profile faced the altar, his powerful shoulders moulded by his dark blue coat. To her at that moment he was pure perfection. Sensing her eyes on him, he turned his head and met her gaze, his deep-set eyes unnervingly intent.

All through the ceremony, Cassandra was conscious of

those eyes on her neck and shoulders and then her face when she turned. She found herself avoiding them because, for all her courage, she found it hard to meet them because of what was in her heart.

The ceremony over, it was a proud moment for Harriet and Elizabeth, dabbing away their tears, as the newly wedded pair walked down the aisle, past the crowded pews and out of the church. The mass of guests in a sea of silks and lace flowed together and, pushing and shoving, twittering and laughing, followed in their wake.

Cassandra's mind was in a strange, feverish state, raging impatiently against all these people who were separating her from William. He had vanished amid the swell and, despite all her efforts, she did not catch a glimpse of him until later at the wedding banquet at Monkton House.

It was a sumptuous feast. William fulfilled his role as best man with his usual careless elegance, engaging in brilliant conversation and seeming to welcome the attentions of the women who fawned and flirted shamelessly with him, much to Cassandra's indignation and dismay as she observed it all from a distance.

Gradually her patience began to fray. Not once did he approach her. It was as if she didn't exist for him. Perhaps now that he had lost the wager, she no longer interested him and the pursuit would be off. Stiffened by pride, she succeeded in being her most dazzling, vivacious self and managed with a painful effort to dominate her disappointment and accept the slap that fate had dealt her.

Their last meeting uppermost in William's mind, until he could speak privately to Cassandra—who seemed either afraid or unwilling to meet his gaze, without being surrounded by strangers—his decision to avoid her became harder to adhere to as the evening drifted on. In her pink satin gown and pink and white roses to match the bride's bouquet twined in her hair, never had she looked more lovely.

After what seemed like an eternity the guests at last rose from the banqueting tables and adjourned to the ballroom, where Edward led his bride of a few hours into the centre of the floor. Others began dancing and Cassandra drifted into the arms of first one partner, then another.

It was while she was taking refreshment in a break from dancing that she sensed William's presence behind her. She even recognised the spicy tang of his cologne. Her throat went dry and a nervous quaking jarred through her as she waited for him to speak to her.

'Dance with me, Cassandra.'

She spun round. He was watching her, white teeth showing in a lazy smile. 'I don't think that would be wise.'

'Nothing you and I have ever done has been wise. Come, all my duty dances are over except one.'

'And that is?'

'To dance with the Matron of Honour—it is the custom at weddings for the best man to dance with the Matron of Honour. Do you intend to refuse me?' he challenged her stunned appraisal. 'Have we been apart so long you do not recognise me, perhaps?'

Cassandra's pride demanded that she show him contempt, but her heart said otherwise.

'I may not be the most popular of your suitors, but I am the most determined, so do not even think of refusing. Come, Cassandra, we've teetered on the edge of scandal once, don't give them more grist to grind by walking away from me. Everyone is watching us.'

Taking her hand, he drew her on to the dance floor and into his embrace. It was a waltz, a swirling, exciting dance that brought couples into close contact as no other—a dance considered to be fast and daring and banned at Almack's. He swung her into rhythm with a sureness of step and she followed with a natural grace.

'I meant what I said, Cassandra.'

'Remind me. I have forgotten.'

'I will not accept your refusal to marry me.'

Leaning back in his arms the better to see his face, she looked at him as if he'd taken leave of his senses. 'Are you telling me you actually meant it, William?'

'I never say anything I don't mean. At some point very soon I will have persuaded you to overlook that damned wager and marry me in spite of it.' The heat of his stare lent the weight of truth to his words. 'My grandmother liked you, by the way. She approves of the match.'

'What?' she gasped. 'Do you mean to tell me that you've discussed me with your grandmother?'

'Of course.'

Cassandra's eyes narrowed in a glare. 'So that's why she directed so much attention to me when we met. How impossibly conceited you are, William Lampard. When I think of what you are guilty of where I am concerned, how can you expect me to marry you? Why, you don't even sound sincere.'

'You are refusing me?' he asked, pretending to sound mortified.

'It's no more than you deserve. Why do you constantly refuse to hear what I say?'

'Because I cannot get you out of my thoughts.' His voice became soft and serious. 'I think of the times we have talked. I remember what it felt like when I held you, how soft your skin and how warm and willing your lips. I remember how you looked that day by the lake with the sun shining on your face. I remember everything, and were we alone I would swiftly prove the ardour you have stirred.'

'William, please stop it.' Blushing under his intimate, predatory gaze, she noticed the increasing interest of the gazes being directed at them. 'People are looking at us.'

'Let them look,' he murmured, his eyes shining softly, hungrily as he gazed down into hers.

'At least try to behave yourself.'

'I am a man and you are a very beautiful and desirable woman. How else should I behave?'

'Like a gentleman would be a start.'

'Ah, Cassandra, my love. Am I really to believe that you care nothing for me at all? How can I believe you when I know you took pleasure in my kisses—and I can pleasure you again. Do not deny yourself, Cassandra.'

His gaze was now direct, challenging, almost insulting, raking her face upturned to his. The bold stare touched a quickness in Cassandra that made her feel as if she were on fire. He was close, much too close, and she was embarrassingly conscious of his hand resting on the small of her back. 'Be quiet, William. Have you no sense of honour?'

His lips twisted in a smile. 'Where you are concerned? At this moment I feel quite dishonourable. Come, Cassandra,' he said, swinging her in a dizzying whirl, 'you want me as much as I want you. Admit it.'

She did want him. She wanted him more than she had ever wanted anything in her life. But she would not admit it. 'It is cruel of you to say such things to me when I cannot retaliate. This is Emma's wedding and I will not spoil it by causing a scene and leave you standing on the dance floor. I will not embarrass you.'

The dance over, he returned her to her place beside Lady Monkton. Defying the stares, he bent and whispered in her ear, 'You cannot have forgotten what it felt like to be in my arms—if you have forgotten, I will remind you, I promise you.'

Some of the guests watched him walk away. A few heads turned to follow him, either because he was an impressive man, or because people were aware that something interesting or maybe scandalous had been going on between these two.

The sun was going down on Monkton House when Cassandra went in search of her mama, realising she hadn't seen her for most of the afternoon. Looking out of the French windows, she saw her on Dr Brookes's arm, strolling on the terrace. Her head was tilted to one side and she was looking up at him with her mouth slightly parted and a look on her face that Cassandra did not know. Why, it was the look of a coquette. Dr Brookes bent his head to her and she laughed at something he said. Cassandra thought what a handsome couple they made, and with a smile she turned away.

The day after the wedding, accompanied by a groom, Cassandra was riding in the park when she saw Sir Charles Grisham galloping across the turf astride a rather splendid dark brown stallion. Impressed more by the horse than by its rider, she reined in her horse and watched him. On seeing her, Charles pulled on the reins and slowed the stallion to a walk, eyeing her with lazy interest.

As he approached, Cassandra quickly weighed the relative merits of letting him know that she knew all about the wager he had made with William. Recalling the humiliation she had suffered since that awful day when she had overheard the two of them at Carlow Park, she decided to be daring rather than cowardly.

Coming to a halt directly in front of her, Sir Charles lifted his arrogant brows and drawled, 'Miss Greenwood! What a pleasant surprise. You have no idea of the effect that simply being near you can have on my poor heart.'

Her smile was cool. 'And I think you must be taking too much sugar in your tea, Sir Charles.'

'Since our last meeting at Almack's I've long been desiring to see you again—but you rejected all my cards asking if I could call on you.'

'As I did all the others. I've decided I don't like being a débutante.'

'Well, I am most put out about it—stricken to the quick, in fact.'

'You'll get over it. I have decided that society is not to my liking.' She regarded him with a bland expression. 'It's a fine horse you're riding. Is it a recent acquisition?'

'Not quite,' he replied, clearly proud of his mount as he patted its glossy neck. 'As a matter of fact, he's been in my possession for several weeks. His name's Monarch—out of the stables at Carlow Park—fastest devil I've ever owned.'

Cassandra's eyes widened in mock-surprise. 'Really! How very interesting.'

His look was sharp and guarded. 'Why so?'

'You will be pleased to know that you will acquire another mount from Lord Lampard's stables shortly.'

He frowned. Clearly he had no idea what she was talking about. 'I'm sorry? This is news to me.'

Cassandra lifted her brows and her smile widened. 'I don't see why it should be if it isn't to me. Lord Lampard has lost the wager, Sir Charles—surely it cannot have slipped your mind.' Her eyes were dancing with laughter as she watched his shock register.

'Well, I'll be damned!' he gasped.

Immediately Cassandra's humour left her. 'And so you should be,' she remarked with no sympathy, 'for trying to make me an object of ridicule.'

'How did you find out about it?'

'I overheard the conversation you had with Lord Lampard when you visited Carlow Park.'

'You were there? You heard?'

She nodded. 'Every damning word.'

Charles cocked a brow imperturbably. 'Not quite all. If you had, you would have heard William renege on the wager— no stomach for it, apparently.'

Cassandra stared at him, a feeling of unease beginning to creep over her. 'What are you saying?'

'He folded, told me he had developed a deep regard for you and he would not dishonour you. But, true to his word, he honoured the wager that same day—Monarch here is proof of that.'

The blood drained out of Cassandra's face and she almost stopped breathing when the implication of what he'd told her rammed home. 'I see,' she said tightly. 'In that case allow me to offer you my belated congratulations. Please excuse me.' Pressing her lips together, she jerked the reins and turned the horse around.

'Miss Greenwood.'

She turned back.

'For what it's worth, I do apologise for the wager.'

'So you should. I do not like being made sport of. Find someone else to play your childish games with next time.'

Her mind was in turmoil as she rode back to Monkton House. What had she done? She felt as if she had lost something very precious, that she had thrown it away, considering it to be useless, and her heart was breaking with the loss of it. But how was she to have known? How could she possibly have known that William had reneged on the wager because he had no wish to dishonour her?

Why hadn't he said anything? Now she saw the truth of it, unobstructed by impractical notions as to his disreputable character or her high belief in human nature. He had been there in the background, understanding her and her desperation to keep the institute from going under, ready to help. He had been there to offer Archie a place in his stables, reading her anxiety and impatience in her eyes when Emma and Edward had eloped and agreeing to let her accompany him to Scotland. He had shown concern for Emma in her illness, been generous when he had put his house at their disposal, had made everything right when the scandal of the elopement had burst on to the social scene, and now this latest—his offer to become a beneficiary in the institute while quietly petitioning Parliament and being granted Government funding.

No man did that for a woman without caring for her. He'd cared for her all along and she hadn't seen it and had been so dreadful to him. Once she thought she had hated him for causes she had thought were justified, but the sting had been taken out of her anger by small degrees and now she regarded him with new respect. The stabilising force of anger had gone, leaving her prey to the softer emotions. Recalling their kiss at Netherton Hall and her angry words afterwards, she realised how much she must have hurt him and he'd been too proud to show it.

Riding a little ahead of the groom, other people on horseback and those strolling through the park gave friendly greetings and she smiled, but did not see them. For when she thought of William, with his handsome face, a trembling came over her and she knew that she loved him. She accepted the truth of it as she would a precious gift, without wonder, without awe, because that was the way of it. She loved everything about him—his smile, his strength, his passion—and she knew he would never let her down.

She didn't know how long she had loved him, but it was true, and if it hadn't been for that wretched wager she'd have realised it long before now. What a complete and utter fool she had been, and how could she go about making amends?

Siddons showed Cassandra into the salon where she was surprised to be greeted by Mark and Lydia. They were seated in plush chairs opposite each other and Lydia was pouring tea on a small table between them.

'I'm sorry,' Cassandra said, feeling a sudden awkwardness. 'I have no wish to disturb you. I hoped William would be at home.'

'I'm afraid you've just missed him,' Mark informed her, standing up and offering her a seat. 'Would you care for some tea?'

Cassandra perched on the edge of a chair, but declined the tea.

'William's accompanying Grandmother back to Carlow,' Mark went on, 'said she'd had enough of the city and wanted to leave early.'

'Oh, I see,' Cassandra replied, careful not to let her disappointment show. 'Will—will he be returning to London?'

'I don't believe so. What with the wedding and everything, matters awaiting his attention at Carlow Park are piling up. Lydia and I stayed here last night, rather than travel all the way to Greenwich. We are to leave for Carlow later, but first we have to go to Greenwich to say farewell to Lydia's sister.' Mark stood up. 'Excuse me a moment. There is a minor matter I wish to discuss with Siddons before we leave.'

'Miss Greenwood,' Lydia remarked when her husband had closed the door. 'I am all amazement. Your visit is most unusual. Is it a habit of yours to call on gentlemen at their homes unchaperoned?'

Cassandra stiffened at the unexpected and unprovoked attack. The tone, lightly contemptuous and at the same time more than a little suspicious, made her hackles rise. A spark of anger momentarily diverted her thoughts from William. She smiled, and in a voice no less disdainful said, 'I do all sorts of things young ladies shouldn't.'

The beautiful brows rose slightly. 'And does your unladylike behaviour not concern Lady Monkton?'

'If anyone should feel any concern for what I do, it is my mother, and she, like me, is open minded about these things.'

'How very odd,' Lydia remarked, reaching for her tea. 'Forgive me, Miss Greenwood, but there is one thing I don't understand. You seem to have developed a peculiar relationship with William. Why, it is almost as if the two of you are...' she gave a low, humourless laugh '...lovers—and there is a rumour that the two of you have been—close—for some time. Can you say there is no foundation in the rumour?'

Cassandra's brows lifted in surprise at her malicious impertinence. 'Whatever the truth of it, I do not choose to answer. That is my business.'

'Of course, but since your sister has succeeded in making a prestigious marriage, in the wake of it perhaps you have aspirations of a similar kind. Are you hoping William will offer for you?'

Cassandra's cheeks burned. How dare she? What she was saying was that Emma was some upstart with pretensions above her station, who had wormed her way into Edward's affections. Her rudeness was not to be endured.

'If William asks me, I shall most certainly accept him if that is what I want. Perhaps you think a connection with me will disgrace him.' There was a flash of something indefinable in Lydia's eyes. For a moment Cassandra couldn't think what it meant and then she recognised it. It was the assessment of one woman for another—from the one who had lost to the one who might triumph.

'I am not ignorant of your condition, and that your connections come through Lady Monkton. Your mother must be feeling extremely relieved this morning to have one of her daughters in a very satisfactory marriage—advantageous for your family, I would think. And consider this. If the scandal of the elopement hadn't come out and William hadn't foolishly intervened, there would have been no wedding.'

Cassandra stared at her as the realisation dawned that this woman might have been responsible for spreading the scandal and causing Emma and her mama such distress. What she felt was beyond expression. Her face became pale with anger.

'Is it possible that you had something to do with that? Were you the one who gossiped and spread the scandal in the hope that my sister and my family would be so shamed that they would be forced to retreat into obscurity?'

Unmoved by any feeling of remorse, Lydia's smile was thin, her eyes hard and brittle. 'One thing you should know about me is that I never gossip. There is always a motive behind what I do. The Lampards are an old and distinguished family—as is my own. To form such a close attachment to a family whose connections and conditions in life are so inferior is not acceptable. Water and oil don't mix, Miss Greenwood, and never will.'

At that moment Mark entered the room, putting an end to their heated discourse, but on observing Cassandra's tense countenance he asked if everything was all right. Forcing a smile to her lips, she told him that she and Lady Lampard had engaged in the most interesting conversation—to reveal the substance of their conversation would only cause unnecessary unpleasantness.

Mark sat down and half-smiled at Cassandra. 'Miss Greenwood, I would like to apologise if anything I said concerning your sister when we met at Carlow Park upset you. Believe me, it was not my intention. I am fond of Edward and that particular escapade made me very angry indeed. However, I realise that in relieving my own feelings I may have wounded yours.'

'I understand. I was angry and upset myself at the time,' Cassandra confessed, thinking that she might have misjudged William's grave cousin and that underneath his seriousness he was really quite agreeable. Perhaps he did not believe in showing emotion, or maybe it was not in him at all. 'My sister can be unpredictable and rather trying at times. Do—you have any siblings?' she asked Lydia pointedly, refusing to appear in any way submissive to this arrogant, dreadful woman.

Lydia stirred her tea and stared into the cup. 'Two, one younger sister and a half-brother, Daniel. We—see each other rarely.'

Cassandra stayed a little while longer, making awkward, polite conversation before making her escape. Still incensed by the conversation she had had with Lydia, it was with a distinct feeling of unease that she recalled the look she had seen on Lydia's face when she had watched William on the night of Almack's—as if she hated him.

She also recalled the conversation she had had with William when they had been travelling to Netherton Hall and she had cautiously asked him if it might be possible that Mark, with much to gain from William's death, could be behind the attempt on his life. William had refused to consider it and now she had spoken to Mark she thought that maybe he was right.

But what of Lydia? And was it a coincidence that her half-brother was called Daniel?

How well did William know the woman who was to have married his brother? Had it been a love match or was she ambitious? How much had Lydia aspired to be Countess of Carlow? When Robert had died she had married Mark. Had she thought William might be killed in the Peninsula, which would have enabled her to realise her desire to be Countess of Carlow?

Cassandra shook her head. Now she was being foolish by letting her mind run along these lines. It was silly and far-fetched to be thinking like this and she must stop it. What an absurd, overactive imagination she had.

But it was too late. The seed had been planted, took root and began to grow, and by the time she reached Monkton House it was a full-grown tree.

Finding her aunt in her sitting room dealing with her correspondence at her writing table, after they had talked and enthused about the wedding and wondered how the newly-weds were settling into their new home, Cassandra casually asked her what she knew about Lydia Lampard.

'As a matter of fact, very little. Her family were gentry and resided in Kent. I know she was to have married William's brother, but when he died in that dreadful riding accident she married Mark instead.'

'Did you ever meet her parents?'

'Yes, several times, though we were never friends. Her mother married twice. I believe her first husband was a soldier—killed in some battle or other abroad.'

Cassandra braced herself. 'Can you remember his name?'

Elizabeth frowned thoughtfully as she forced her mind back over the years. 'Why—now, let me think—although why you should want to know I really don't know.'

Cassandra shrugged. 'No reason really. I'm just curious, that's all. Can you remember, Aunt Elizabeth?' she pressed.

'George, his name was. Yes—that's it, George.'

'George what?'

'Sharp. There, I do remember. He was from Blackheath—and a bit of a blackguard, if my memory serves me right. There was a child—but don't ask me what he was called, because that I don't know.'

Cassandra couldn't believe what her aunt had innocently disclosed. Daniel Sharp was Lydia's half-brother and he had tried to kill William. If Lydia had knowledge of this, then she had to be in on it, too. And, if so, William was still in danger. It was imperative that he knew what she had uncovered.

The following morning, she had a long talk with her mother, in which she gave her a full account of the attempts on William's life and that she, Cassandra, had discovered who was behind it and must now go to Carlow Park to tell him immediately. When her mother had recovered from the shock of it and considered the importance of it, she reluctantly gave her permission for her to go.

'There is something I have to tell you before I leave, Mama,' Cassandra said, clearing her throat, 'something you should know.' Her eyes met her mother's, which were suddenly sharp with questioning regard. Cassandra quailed inside. What would she say? 'Mama—I—I'm going to marry Lord Lampard.'

Harriet's face was incredulous as she stared at her daughter. 'You? You and Lord Lampard?' she exclaimed quietly.

Cassandra nodded. 'I am in love with him—and I—I believe he is in love with me. He—has asked me to be his wife.'

'I see. And what was your answer?'

'I haven't given him one—but I will.'

'Well, what can I say? I knew there was a certain...attraction between the two of you—I'm not blind—and that he seemed to have made quite an impression on you—'

'He is an impressive person, Mama.'

'Yes, so it would seem, but I had no idea it had gone as far as this. Of course he will have to speak to me. But do you know the full import of what you will be taking on? Oh, I am grateful for all he has done for Emma, of course I am, but—I must voice my concern. I know that he's attractive and that he has a way with women—that he is regarded as a—well—you know.'

'A rake, Mama,' Cassandra said, voicing the word that was so difficult for her mother to say.

'Yes. I must say that he has impressed me and I do like him, but his attitude to women is reputed to be quite light-hearted. How can you know he is serious?'

Cassandra smiled. 'Mama, you worry unnecessarily. Truly.'

'It's a mother's right to worry about her daughter. I want you to be as happy and content as Emma. I don't want him to break your heart.'

'He won't, Mama. I know he won't. I do truly love him and would like your blessing.'

Harriet's eyes filled with tears and she hugged Cassandra tightly. 'You have it, Cassandra. Of course you do.' She stood back and looked at her, composed and in control of herself once more. 'Now, you said there have been several attempts on Lord Lampard's life. Are you in any danger?'

'No, Mama, but William will be if I don't warn him.'

Half an hour later Cassandra left with Clem for Hertfordshire.

Two hours into her journey, she tried imagining her meeting with William. Because of her harsh words to him in the past, would he welcome her warmly, or would he be angry and send her back to London? It was a relief when they reached Carlow

Park and the coach pulled to a stop. Climbing down, Clem lowered the steps for her to alight.

Pearson, the butler, recognised her immediately.

'I wish to see Lord Lampard,' Cassandra pronounced when she'd entered the house. 'Unfortunately he is not expecting me. Is he at home?'

'I'm sorry, Miss Greenwood. Lord Lampard is away on estate business, but he is due back shortly. Perhaps you would care for refreshments while you wait.'

'That would be most welcome. Thank you—and would you see that Clem and the horses are taken care of?'

When William failed to return, remembering how lovely the gardens were at Carlow Park, Cassandra left the house to stroll along the paths. It was a lovely day, the air sultry and pleasantly warm, with insects flitting from one flowering bloom to another. The lake beckoned to her in the distance. Deciding to extend her walk, she looked up at the sky where thunderclouds were gathering. They were hours away, she thought.

It was when she reached the lake and had walked some considerable distance along its banks that she paused. There was a sudden stillness in the air. How quiet it was—the quiet before the storm. She had miscalculated. The sky had gone grey and roiling clouds had come from nowhere. A furious wind rose suddenly and whipped up the surface of the lake. Leaves and branches were lashed dangerously about. A chill swept through the air.

She looked up at the frenzied sky just as a bolt of lightning seared the sky, shattering the grey with a silver blue. Hurriedly she began retracing her steps. Heavy raindrops began to pelt her. Battered by the wind, she was soon soaked through. Disturbed by the elements and thinking it was a long way to the house, frantically she sought the shelter of a giant elm, cursing her stupidity for having walked so far.

* * *

William was incredulous and pleasantly surprised when he arrived back at the house and Pearson told him Miss Green-wood was waiting to see him. His pleasure soon turned to frustration when he found the drawing room empty. The glass doors to the terrace were open; surmising she had gone outside, he went to look. The storm chose that moment to break and a clap of thunder shook the earth. Unable to locate her, he scowled as he retreated to the house to avoid a soaking.

Damn! The little fool. His eyes were drawn in the direction of the lake, obliterated now by the rain. Some instinct told him that was where she would be. If so, she would have to find shelter. Anxious for her safety, he hurried to his room. After several minutes he returned, dressed in an oilskin cloak. Rushing out, his long strides carried him quickly through the gardens and down to the lake.

He shouted her name, his words torn asunder by the wind. Lightning flashed repeatedly, followed by rumbling cracks of thunder. And then he saw her, huddled against a tree. She saw him running towards her and seemed glad that he had come.

Taking her hand, he shouted, 'Come with me. We've got to get out of this.'

Another bolt of lightning sizzled and crackled across the sky, followed by thunder. It was as if the very earth was being riven apart. They had no protection from the rain as a heavier torrent of water was unleashed on them, assaulting them from every angle, wetting Cassandra's garments until they became dead weights and hindered her movements. Her skirt caught on something; she turned to look. William tugged at it and ripped it. Then the vague shape of a low structure appeared in the shrubbery. Cassandra recognised it as the little summer-house. Why hadn't she thought of that?

William shoved open the door and thrust Cassandra into the dim interior. The space was small with doors on three sides that could be opened to the weather. Her irresponsible act had put him into a fit of temper. 'You little fool,' he berated angrily. 'You must be mad to venture so far from the house when a storm was threatening—and to shelter under a tree. That's the most dangerous place, don't you know that? What were you trying to do? And look at you. You look like a drowned rabbit.'

Her chin trembling with cold, Cassandra was looking at him in abject misery. 'Y-you don't l-look any b-better yourself,' she bit back indignantly. His anger and her wretched state brought tears to her eyes, which spilled down her cheeks.

When he saw her tears, William's anger immediately evaporated and he murmured gently, 'What's this—tears? Dost the Ice Maiden melt?'

Cassandra stared at him. 'I-is that h-how I appear to you— a-as some hard, c-cold-hearted woman? Is that how you th-think of me? I-it may surprise you to know that I have feelings j-just like any other.'

'I know you do,' he said softly.

She was a sorry sight, soaked to the skin and her hair plastered over her face. Her lemon dress was stuck to her body, moulding to every curve and hollow—the round fullness of her breasts, her tiny waist—and clinging to her long legs. William's gaze went to her mouth, watching as rivulets of water ran down her face and over her parted lips.

Lust hit him with such unexpected force that for a moment he couldn't move. Somehow he managed to say, 'You are cold. Let me warm you. Here.' Removing his cloak, he wrapped it round her. 'We'll be safe enough here until the storm has passed.' Sensing her shaking limbs were about to give way beneath her, he pulled her down on to a wooden bench. Enfolding her quaking form, he drew her against his chest, surprised when she neither resisted nor objected. 'If I thought the storm was going to last, I would light a fire and my pleasure would be to remove your clothes.'

She tilted her head to look up at him. 'Why?'

His eyes gleamed into hers. 'To dry them. What else?'

With the torrential rain drumming on the roof and flailing the earth, Cassandra sighed and nestled against him. The heat of his body was making her warm, so very warm, and she had no intention of escaping the wonderful sensations he was evoking in her. 'What else indeed,' she murmured, wanting this, wanting him—how very empty everything was otherwise.

'Tell me why you are here, Cassandra—what it is you want.'

'The same thing you do.' Lifting her head, she studied him in the dim light. She wanted to feel the broad expanse of his chest pressed to hers, to kiss again those beautifully moulded lips that she knew were the most wonderful lips in the world.

'I have been telling you for long enough that I want you. Do not torture me any more.'

She looked into his eyes and he held her gaze in a wilful, hungry vice of blue. 'I am at your mercy,' she whispered, conscious of a fine trembling throughout her body that had nothing to do with the cold. Raising her arm, she slipped her hand around his nape. Tangling her fingers in his wet hair, she drew his head down to hers.

Deprived of her for so long, the days of loneliness had left William hungry for her. With desire beating fiercely in his veins, he clasped her to him, his arms strong and protective. Smoothing her hair from her face, he placed his mouth on her lips. They were sweet and moist and parted beneath his own. Sliding his tongue between them, his arms tightening possessively around her, he groaned and his long-starved passions flared. Their bodies bent in the ardour of their embrace. The kiss was fierce and stirring, devouring and all consuming. Their mouths slanted across each other with hungry impatience.

One hand caressed her, arousing her, stroking and cupping her breasts, until a warm tide of excitement flooded Cassandra's whole being. Dragging his lips from hers, William trailed kisses along her jaw and down her neck, feeling his wits slipping away bit by bit. He had to stop before all sanity left him. She was naïve, innocent and inexperienced with what it all meant, but he did know and he had to call a halt before he acted on it. It took an extreme exercise of will for him to stop kissing her.

With an audible sigh Cassandra looked at him, her eyes languid beneath lowered lids. 'What is it? Is something wrong?'

'We must stop,' he replied huskily, 'otherwise you are in danger of being seduced by a scoundrel, which is what you have been striving to avoid for weeks.'

'I no longer wish to avoid it. I've decided that I want to be seduced by a scoundrel,' she whispered, placing a featherlight kiss at the side of his mouth that set his pulses racing, 'so do not deny me. Please don't stop now.'

'Not here, Cassandra. This is not the place.'

'You're wrong. This is the very place.'

William's caution was ripped away. His eyes held hers for one long, compelling look, holding all his frustrated longings, his unfulfilled desires, everything that was between them. 'Shameless little fool!' he murmured, wanting nothing more than to drag her down on to the dusty floor and make love to her. It was all he could do to control the urges that swamped him. His mouth swooped down to hers once more as if he could not get enough of their dewy sweetness, parting her lips so their breaths merged and became one.

Lost in that wild and beautiful madness Cassandra undid the buttons of his shirt and slipped her hands underneath, touching the hard muscular chest. Sensing his need and responding to an inner heat, with all the repressions and restraints she had imposed on herself ever since she had known about the wager having disappeared, Cassandra tore her lips from his.

Dragging the cloak from round her shoulders, she spread it on the floor. Kneeling on it, seeing how his hair shone with a soft sheen of dark satin in the dim light, she took his hand and pulled him down beside her, and suddenly they were lying side by side and she felt the hard, manly boldness of him. Their bodies met, feverishly intertwining at last. Clothes were unfastened to accommodate questing hands, and teasing kisses placed on bare flesh. Looking into his eyes, Cassandra saw they were not smiling now—they were intense to such a degree that she experienced a moment of panic, but it was soon gone.

William thought of stripping her bare, but decided against it, for even though his mind reeled and his senses were drugged with the soft scent of her and the feel of her shapely form, he was aware of the discomfort she would feel when she had to put the wet clothes back on. He kissed her throat while his hands tugged at the fabric of her bodice, pulling it until her breasts were exposed. His lips trailed down and kissed their full, soft roundness and the cleft between.

Losing her touch of reality, Cassandra closed her eyes, soft and pliable as he stroked and caressed, feeling her nipples begin to throb and rise up proudly against his mouth. Shifting his position, he lifted her skirts and peeled her stockings down, her legs pale and lustrous, his hand moving up her calf, palms and fingers warm, encircling her knee, then spreading and caressing her aching thighs. A warmth spread in her blood, in her bones, a delectable torture that grew and grew and would soon drown her in a flood of pleasure. With the light slanting on them through the windows, uttering a slight moan of surrender, Cassandra willingly yielded to his need, pressing closer against him, meeting his passion with her own, encouraging him, wrapping her arms tightly around his shoulders as he bathed her senses in extravagant pleasure.

His weight pinioning her, Cassandra clung to him as ivy might cling to a tree, the length of her body pressed against his, which was supple, hard and masculine. Her world careened crazily beneath the savage urgency of his need, and she was swept along on a violent storm of passion. While the storm continued to rage outside, their coming together was wonderful and right, and astonishing that it should be instantly so.

As they moved together to the music of love, tasting the

full joy of their mutual union and surrendering to pure sensation, straining to come closer still, each fulfilling the other in a most sublime act of love, the pleasure became unbearable. Cassandra was lost and went soaring into oblivion until she felt bliss; an ecstasy burst upon them, fusing them together into one being until what they shared drove them on to a shattering climax.

Chapter Twelve

Clasped tightly to him as if he would never let her go, Cassandra felt the thunderous beating of his heart against her naked breasts and heard his ragged breathing in her ear. Tucked securely in the curve of her lover's body, sated and spent, Cassandra slowly began to surface from the splendour of his lovemaking. Raising her head, she gazed at his face, unconscious of the vision she presented with her hair tumbling about her shoulders in loose array. Thinking how unbearably handsome he was, she caressed his lips lightly with her own before letting her head fall back, closing her eyes and letting joy and relief wash over her.

'What are you thinking?' William murmured with a tender smile at her upturned face.

An answering smile touched her lips as he splayed his fingers across her cheek. 'That I've dreamed of this moment.'

Cassandra stared up at him; her magnificent eyes, which had taken on a smoky hue, searched deeply into his, amazement etched on her lovely features, soft now with their loving. Drawing away from her on to his side, resting his head on his hand, he gazed down at her. She lay beside him like an innocent golden goddess. Her passion amazed him. The firm voluptuous body that had lain beneath his had been yielding and welcoming as she gave all her desire, passion and love.

His eyes held hers softly. 'Ravaged and ruined, now you will have to marry me,' he whispered.

Her smile was sublime. Suddenly she felt feminine and absurdly happy. 'I fear you are right. You have taken advantage of me and now I am completely and utterly ruined.'

His lips caressed hers tenderly. 'Are you not regretful, my love—full of guilt?'

Cassandra shook her head, and it was no lie. 'I knew what I was doing and I feel no guilt. All I feel is a sense of rightness in being in your arms. I am content. In fact, I feel quite wonderful. How strange and delightful that making love can make a woman feel that way. What an extraordinary thing.' She looked up at him, a gentle flush spreading over her cheeks. 'Did you feel like that, too?'

'I did,' he murmured, brushing a kiss on her forehead.

'Then how soon before we can repeat it?'

He chuckled low in his throat and smoothed some tendrils of hair from her cheek. 'You are without doubt the most shameless and impulsive creature, but the next time I make love to you will be in bed without the restriction of clothes.' He sighed deeply, his expression suddenly serious. 'You do not know how hard you make it for me to resist you.'

A rosy blush stained her smooth cheeks. 'You do not have to resist me any longer, William.'

'I must—for now, but you cannot guess the depth of torment you have put me through of late, for beneath your taunts I have burned with a consuming desire to possess you. I have never worked so hard to win a woman as I have you. Ever since we met I have sought to gain favour in your eyes.'

'And now you have succeeded admirably, my lord.'

His eyes held hers in an enquiring glance. 'I have, but I am confused by your change of heart, my love. Perhaps you should explain what has brought it about.'

'I thought it was time for me to start being honest with myself about what I feel I want, and I decided that, in spite of everything, I want you, William. I want to be with you always.'

William felt humbled and blessed by her unselfish ardour and his lips curved in a smile. He drew his fingers over the slender column of her neck, a tousled mass of honey-gold curls nestling to one side of her head. 'You really are the most unprincipled young woman, Cassandra Greenwood. You never cease to amaze me. You are also lovely, a temptress, not fully awakened to your powers as yet. Of all the women I have known, none has possessed the fire of spirit, of heart and mind as you.'

'Tell me about the wager you made with Sir Charles, William.'

'Ah—that.'

'Yes, that. I need to know the truth of it.'

'The truth of it may surprise you. I told you I agreed to it in a moment of madness. Within an hour of agreeing to it I decided to renege on it. When Charles came to see me at Carlow Park I told him my decision—and had you eavesdropped a while longer, you would have heard.'

'I know.'

'You do?'

She nodded. 'Charles told me.'

'He did? When?'

'Yesterday, when we met in the park whilst out riding. Why didn't you tell me?'

'Because you were so furious with me I felt my protestations of innocence would fall on deaf ears. I was biding my time until your temper cooled. Is it for this reason that you have come to Carlow Park?'

Cassandra sat up and began adjusting her clothes. 'One of them. There is something else. Yesterday when Charles had told me the truth about the wager, I went to your house to see you. I saw Mark and Lydia instead.' Having fastened her bodice, she looked at William directly. 'William, Lydia is the most dreadful woman I have ever met. And—and you cannot know that she has—had, a half-brother called Daniel Sharp.'

William's jaw hardened. 'As a matter of fact I do, and I cannot believe that the woman who was to have married my brother has been calmly planning my murder. Mr Jardine, who has been staying at the inn in Carlow while he made his enquiries, told me earlier today. Like you, he suspected the person who would benefit most from my death might be behind it. When he delved into Lydia's background it didn't take long to discover that Daniel Sharp was her half-brother.'

'Have you been to see her?'

He shook his head. 'In truth, I wasn't looking forward to facing Mark. I am still convinced he knows nothing about his wife's scheming. How did you find out?'

'She told me she had a half-brother called Daniel. It was Aunt Elizabeth who told me her mother's first husband was called Sharp. She also told me she was responsible for leaking the story about the elopement. Did you know?'

'No, but deep down I always suspected it. Her sister is one of the most notorious gossips of the *ton*. If just a whiff of something scandalous reaches her ears, it's out in the blink of an eye and well embroidered on the way.' Getting up, William took Cassandra's hand and pulled her to her feet. 'Listen, the rain has stopped. We'd best get back before Pearson sends a search party out for us.'

'You're right. At this moment I can think of nothing but the luxury of soaking in a hot tub.'

His eyes raked her bedraggled form from head to toe. 'You look adorable.'

Opening the door, they stepped out into a dripping wet and steamy world, only to find a pistol pointing at them.

'Lydia!' Cassandra gasped, and for a moment the pistol swung in her direction.

'Yes—Lydia. What have we here?' she jeeringly questioned, arrogant in her demeanour, confident with a gun in her hand. 'A love nest, no less. How very sweet.'

William stiffened beside Cassandra, and with a glance she saw the muscles in his cheek had tensed with fury. He stood his ground, his tall frame rigid with anger, cursing the fact that he wasn't carrying a pistol. Cassandra's eyes were wide with horror, and her mind raged on in fear.

'After so many attempts on my life have failed, Lydia, it appears you've decided to finish me off yourself.' Each word had a bite, and William's eyes were deadly. 'Who'd have thought it of my cousin's wife?'

Her smile was icy. 'You never did know me very well, did you, William? You didn't know I had a half-brother.'

'I do now,' he replied in a voice of tightly controlled fury.

'You should. You killed him.'

'He was trying to kill me at the time. The two of you were in this together.'

Lydia raised her head aloofly. 'I do not deny it. We devised the plot together to get rid of you. I should have been Countess of Carlow had Robert not died in that wretched accident. I knew, married to Mark, I still could be if you died in the Peninsula. But you didn't die. You came back to cheat me out of all this.'

'And you have been brooding and seething all this time, and the longer your resentment went on, the more bitter and dangerous you became. You're mad.'

A smile playing about her lips, Lydia advanced on William. 'That's right, I am mad,' she hissed, 'and I have no conscience for what I am about to do. When your bodies are found, no one will have any reason to suspect me.'

Instinctively William's arm curved protectively round Cassandra's waist. 'You intend to kill us both?'

'Why not? It would be suicidal to let her go. She knows too much.'

William was about to tell her that Jardine knew of the relationship between her and Daniel, but too late. The pistol was cocked and raised. With a burst of flame and sound it fired.

'No…' Without thinking, Cassandra flung herself in front of William, pushing him back. Her body jerked as the shot entered her and the impact flung her against the door of the summerhouse, where she crumpled in a heap on the ground.

William fell to his knees beside her, looking at her tranquil face. His world turned to ashes.

As she reloaded the gun, Lydia was distracted when two men suddenly appeared out of the undergrowth. Searching for William and Cassandra, the sound of the shot had drawn Clem and Mr Jardine to the summerhouse. Their expressions were frozen with horror as they looked at Cassandra's inert form and William bending over her.

'Lydia, give me the pistol,' a quiet voice said from behind her.

She whipped round. 'You!' she cried, glaring at Mark. 'Do you have to follow me everywhere I go like a lap dog?'

'When you failed to come back from your ride and the storm broke, I came looking for you. I heard the shot.' Not wishing to provoke her into firing the pistol a second time, he spoke calmly, holding out his hand. 'Give me the pistol, Lydia.'

'Go to hell.'

When she turned and it looked as if she was about to fire at William, Mark grabbed at her hand, trying to wrest the pistol away from her. The weapon arched towards him and he leaped aside. There was a frenzied struggle between the two, who seemed to be locked in some devilish embrace. Hampered by her sodden cloak, Lydia struggled as best she could. Suddenly there was a shot and a cry. Mark staggered back. Lydia, a look of surprise on her face, clawed at her chest where the shot had penetrated. She writhed and then collapsed to the floor. No further sound came from her.

Mark looked down at Lydia in dazed stupefaction, unable to believe what had happened and that his wife was dead.

Raising his head, he stared across at his cousin. 'William—what can I say? I'm sorry. I knew nothing about any of this.'

Mr Jardine put his hand on his back. 'It's not your fault. How did she find out about her brother—that he was dead?'

'A constable came to the house earlier. I confess I was troubled by her reaction to the news. Anyone else would have been grief stricken, but Lydia was furious and immediately left the house.' He went to his cousin. William's face was stricken. Kneeling beside him, he asked, 'How is she?'

'Her pulse is weak.' The blood seeping through her dress from the wound in her right shoulder struck terror in his heart. Her head had fallen back and her eyes were closed. Her face held a deathly pallor. 'Dear merciful God,' he prayed with quiet desperation, having seen countless men die of such wounds in battle, 'don't let it be fatal. Please God.'

'We'll get her to the house.'

William gathered her into his arms and lifted her. He looked at Clem. 'Get Dr Tomlinson, Clem, and for God's sake tell him to hurry.'

The doctor came immediately and worked for two hours to try to save Cassandra. He removed the shot successfully. Fortunately it had missed her heart and lung, but she had lost so much blood it would be a miracle if she recovered.

Clem was dispatched to London to fetch Cassandra's mother, who came with Lady Monkton and a weeping Emma, who was comforted by her husband.

William listened to Dr Tomlinson's prognosis with a feeling of impotent rage—the reason being the doctor's failure to give him hope and his own inability to save Cassandra himself.

Going to sit beside her bed, he refused to move. He sat there, holding her lifeless hand and looking down into her beloved face. She was so beautiful it tore at his heart.

'Dear God, Cassandra,' he found himself saying, driven by anger, desperation and a deep and abiding love, 'don't you dare leave me now we have found each other. If you die, I swear I will follow you and give you no peace. Is that what you want, my love?'

The voice penetrated the void in which Cassandra drifted. She liked being in this nothingness where she was cocooned in darkness, where she was so comfortable and warm and she had no worries, no pain…

'Oh, no, Cassandra,' William said fiercely. 'I will not let you go away. You belong to me. I need you. I cannot live without you. I love you. We belong together. Remember our loving—how exquisite it was? It can be so again.'

The voice was loud in her head. It went on and on without ceasing. It gave her no peace. Why didn't he go away and leave her alone? Didn't he know that she liked it here? She didn't want to leave. There was a sigh.

'What about the children? What will you do about them, Cassandra? They need you, you know that. How can you leave them?'

No, her mind cried.

'Yes,' the voice insisted. 'You cannot desert them now. The children, Cassandra. The orphanage you so desire is yours—or perhaps it wasn't that important to you in the end?'

The voice cruelly mocked. Suddenly the void broke and the darkness became light. Her eyes flickered open to see the source of that voice.

A pair of bright blue eyes looked down at her.

'Hello, sweetheart.'

Cassandra opened her eyes. For a moment she couldn't think where she was. She tried to raise herself and a pain shot through her shoulder. She couldn't think what had happened to her. The walls of the room seemed to close in on her. Her head was spinning. Closing her eyes, she tried to remember what had happened to her, and then it all came flooding back and a terrible feeling of foreboding came to her.

'William!' She uttered his name with a cry of utter despair. She had been shot. Lydia had shot her and she was going to shoot William. She began to whimper. Suddenly someone was bending over her. A gentle hand was placed on her forehead. It was Mama.

'Hush, my dear. Don't fret so.' Her voice was soft and soothing. 'You have been ill.'

'William is dead, Mama. Lydia shot him. I know it.'

'No—no, he's here,' Harriet was quick to reassure her daughter. 'He's been here all along and refused to leave you.'

'H-how long?'

'Three days. You were wounded.'

'I remember…Lydia…'

'You lost a lot of blood, Cassandra, and there was a fever. But you are going to be all right. You'll get better now. But we've all been so worried about you.'

'William?'

And then he was there, his anxiety for her etched deeply into his handsome face. With a quiet smile, her mama left the room as he sat beside her. Taking her hand, he raised it to his lips. The memory of the forceful, often mocking, voice came back to her and she smiled.

'You talked to me,' she murmured, her voice husky.

'All the time, my love.'

'I thought it was a dream.'

'It was no dream, Cassandra.'

'Lydia? What happened?'

His face hardened. 'Lydia is dead. It happened when Mark tried taking the gun from her. But it's over and it's going to be a cloud on our perfect horizon for months ahead, but we won't let it spoil what we have.'

Cassandra drew a deep breath and nodded. 'And Mark?'

'He knew nothing about what she was doing.'

'He must be distraught.'

'He's upset, naturally, but he's also angry that his own

wife could have stooped to murder. They never got on, apparently, and she gave him nothing but trouble. Mark realises she only married him because she saw him as a means of realising her ambition to become Countess of Carlow—which she could only achieve with my demise. But we will speak of this later—when you are more yourself.'

'I am beginning to feel more alive by the minute.'

'Do you remember in your dream that I told you that I love you? Remember that?'

She smiled softly, half-teasing. 'No, so you had better tell me again.'

Threading his fingers through her hair, William framed her face between his hands and gazed at her. 'I love you, Cassandra Greenwood. When you lay injured at my feet and I thought you might die, I wanted to die with you. I love you more than life.'

'How can you love me, when I have beset you at every turn?' Her tone was wondrous, her heart soaring with happiness.

'If I could boast to know the wisdom of love, I would be a rich man. But love you I do.'

'And I love you, William. I have loved you for so long. I wanted to tell you, but so much stood between us and I was so busy waging war on you.'

'So you were my sweet, wonderful, aggressive witch. But no longer, my love.'

His eyes grew languid, sending her senses reeling, and there was a soft union of lips as their mouths clung with a leisurely sweetness that held still every moment in time.

Releasing her lips, he gazed down at her. 'I do believe the fever's gone. Your kiss speaks more of passion than of pain.' His eyes darkened and his expression became serious. 'Marry me, Cassandra.'

'Are you quite certain you want me for your wife?'

'Who else could I ask to be my wife but the one who inspires me with feelings that I have never felt before? For

good or ill, Cassandra, we two are bound together,' he said
with rough sincerity that sent her heart soaring.

The vision of a future stretching endlessly ahead of them
was as golden and fertile as Carlow Court itself. Waves of tremendous happiness spread over her as she prepared to pledge
her heart and soul to her handsome lover. 'I will marry you,
William. I will be proud to marry you.'

Before the end of summer Cassandra and William were
married with none of the pomp of Emma and Edward's
wedding. With family and carefully selected close friends,
theirs was a quiet affair, the ceremony taking place in the
family chapel at Carlow Court. And what rejoicing there was.

Cassandra was happy. There was magic in that wedding, with
her mama looking on with dreams in her eyes—dreams of the
new orphanage—a splendid old house that was being converted
to accommodate fifty children—and dreams of her own future
with Dr Brookes, who had proposed marriage. This came as no
surprise to Cassandra. They were so obviously drawn to each
other and were well suited, since they were widow and widower.

When Cassandra walked slowly down the aisle with her
hand resting on the arm of Dr Brookes, in the candle-lit chapel,
all the radiance in the world was shining from her eyes, which
were drawn irresistibly to the man who was waiting for her.
He was overwhelming in stature, his dark hair smoothly
brushed and gleaming, his midnight-blue coat, dove-grey
trousers hugging his long legs, matching silk waistcoat and
crisp white cravat simple but impeccably cut.

Unable to contain his desire to look upon Cassandra's
gracious form, William turned. The vision of loveliness he
beheld, her face as serene as the Madonna's as she carried a
bouquet of fragrant white lilies, snatched his breath away. As
he viewed her advance, he was convinced she was the most
beautiful of women. She looked, in her bridal finery, as if she
were moulded of light, ethereal and magnificent in her grace.

An awesome pride and wonder almost sent him to his knees. Unbound, vibrant tresses of honey-gold hair fell in a shimmering cascade halfway down her back, and in her wedding gown of ivory silk and lace, the long tight sleeves forming a point over the backs of her hands, he thought she had never looked so exquisite.

Something like terror moved through his heart. Dear Lord, he prayed, make me cherish and protect her all the days of my life, and give her the joy and happiness she deserves. Stepping out, he waited for her in watchful silence.

Cassandra's eyes clung to his, unable to believe that when she left the church she would belong to this handsome, sophisticated, virile man, who was looking at her adoringly, the passion in his eyes compelling and tender. She felt perfectly calm, her mind wiped clean of everything but this, the most important moment of her life. There was a faint smile on William's firm lips, and her heart warmed as if it felt his touch.

When Cassandra reached him he took her hand, his long fingers closing firmly over hers. She responded to his smile, and in that moment of complete accord, her marriage to William seemed right. Together, side by side, they faced the priest to speak their marriage vows.

Emma and Edward exchanged glances as though there was some delightful conspiracy between them—perhaps memories of their own wedding. When William put the ring on Cassandra's finger and they vowed to cherish each other until death do us part, Aunt Elizabeth wept a little—from pure happiness, she assured everyone. And for her mama, happier than Cassandra had ever seen her before, it was her dearest dream come true to see both her daughters so well married.

There was a wedding reception for the guests, when they were congratulated and their future happiness toasted with the finest champagne, and in due course they were alone. It was a day to treasure and remember for ever.

Deprived of loving for so long, the weeks of preparation

for the wedding had implanted them with a desperate need. Cassandra fell into her husband's arms with utter abandonment. He clasped her to him, their bodies bending in the ardour of their embrace. They kissed deeply, pausing only long enough to cast off clothes and fall into the snug softness of their bed. Their coming together was a feverish intertwining at last. The night was long—they loved and slept and loved again until their bodies were sated and content.

In the pale light of dawn, Cassandra glanced at her husband's dark profile and felt the wonderful hardness of his body pressing closely against her own. Turning on to her stomach, she covered his muscled torso with soft, teasing kisses until he opened his eyes and looked down at her shining head. He smiled that crooked, wicked smile that always made her heart flip over.

'What's this, my love? Are you still not satisfied?' He tipped her chin up so that she could gaze into his eyes. 'Have I told you that you are wonderful?'

Her eyes lit with laughter. 'I'm glad my qualities are apparent.' She sighed, resting her cheek on his hair-dusted chest. 'I couldn't sleep. I can't stop thinking of everything that's happened. You have given me everything, William—I never believed I could be so happy. But—there is something we must discuss.'

'What? Now?' he murmured, feeling his ardour stir once more.

'Why not? We're both awake.'

'Very well, Cassandra—what is it that is so important it takes precedence over my making love to you?'

'The orphanage.'

'Ah!'

'The children have become an important part of my life, you know that. When it opens, Mama will oversee the administration, of course, but you won't stop me continuing to do what I can, will you?'

'Would it matter if I did?'

'Of course it would. I want you to agree and approve of everything I do. It's important to me.'

'How could I object? With my money pouring into the venture—and others before too long, I hope—I'm as committed as you are. I know it's the most important thing in the world to you.'

Cassandra didn't reply immediately. Tilting her head, she looked at him for a long moment, caught up by emotions she could not conceal. 'You're wrong about that, William. The orphanage isn't the most important thing in the world to me.'

'Then what is?'

She snuggled against him. 'Do I really have to show you?'

He smiled. Her voice was persuasive and ever so seductive. 'It might be rather interesting,' he said, covering her mouth with his own.

The Correttis

Introducing the Correttis, Sicily's most scandalous family!

On sale 3rd May

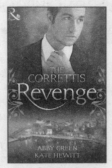

On sale 7th June

On sale 5th July

On sale 2nd August

Mills & Boon® Modern™ invites you to step over the threshold
and enter the Correttis' dark and dazzling world...

Find the collection at
www.millsandboon.co.uk/specialreleases

*Visit us
Online*

0513/MB415

The World of Mills & Boon®

There's a Mills & Boon® series that's perfect for you. We publish ten series and, with new titles every month, you never have to wait long for your favourite to come along.

Blaze®
Scorching hot, sexy reads
4 new stories every month

By Request
Relive the romance with the best of the best
9 new stories every month

Cherish™
Romance to melt the heart every time
12 new stories every month

Desire™
Passionate and dramatic love stories
8 new stories every month